A Sojourner's Life

A Sojourner's Life
The Life of Alexander Maclean

R.D.Dewar

One

The Boy Who Walked Alone

―⚭―

During his years at high school the Boy learned how satisfying solitary walks and the world of his imagination could be.

The Boy's family lived on the edge of the suburbs to the north of the city. In Africa, this did not mean that they were living on the edge of pretty, wooded countryside with rolling fields and picturesque landscapes: this semiurban African countryside was largely uncultivated scrub and *veld* grassland with few trees, and these were mostly wattle, Scots pine and blue-gum, with an occasional indigenous acacia still standing.

But to feed his need for solitude the Boy sometimes walked home from school in the afternoons, first crossing a tiny stream, whose clean-flowing water was channeled between banks that were rich in a pure creamy clay, then walking across a tract of open *veld*, and finally, skirting one of the last remaining commercial market gardens in the area still in operation, he reached the fringes of their suburb. White cumulus clouds ambled slowly across the vast Highveld sky, and the sun, so much warmer than any sun ever known over the British Isles, which is where the Boy's forebears came from, shone down on him from a sky of the most perfect powder blue, and the red dirt and rocky quartzite ground were what he had known for much of his life. The Boy felt a sense of wellbeing, of belonging.

There was almost no animal wildlife left in that region fringing the suburbs, but the birds were plentiful, and sometimes the Boy saw a small creature belonging to the rodent family. Once in a while he would see a snake (only very rarely was it of a venomous species, such as a *rinkhals*, mamba or puff-adder; usually the creatures fell in the category of what the Boy knew as "mole snakes" or "grass snakes"), but such sightings were rare, although the Boy was very light-footed and quiet when he walked. He would see many colourfully marked insects, all larger by far than are seen in northern Europe. They looked as if they had been brightly painted, or equipped with antlers or horns, by their fanciful Maker.

The Boy enjoyed the solitude. It was during these early walks when he was still a school boy that he learned how much he needed sometimes to be alone, far from the sight or sound of his own kind, if he was to sustain happiness.

The Boy's family returned to the Mother City after he had graduated from high school, and he was far, far happier now, living on the Cape Peninsula with its dramatic mountainous topography, the mountain slopes clad in dark pine forests, and never far away the boundless shining sea with its infinite horizons. There was much more wildlife to be seen. Troops of baboons were common, and so too were the small antelopes, civet cats, serval cats, and other creatures the Boy sometimes saw. The sunbirds flitted and hovered in small flocks: they were brightly decorated, tiny shining creatures full of iridescent colour as they sipped nectar from the proteas and other wild flowers on the slopes of the mountains.

During the nineteen-seventies, walking on a weekday, the Boy only very rarely saw any other people in the mountains. He learned to love God the Creator and Sustainer in these mountains. The mountains taught the Boy his first theology.

The Boy knew where the year-round springs were to be found in the mountains, where sundews, small carnivorous plants that grew amidst the mossy beds at these springs, lured tiny insects to their cups and trapped and digested them. The Boy never took water with him, not even during the baking summertime, if he spent a day in the mountains: the Boy took only a collapsible tin mug, with which he drank at these springs; water so pure and refreshing it was a blessing.

Sometimes the Boy would walk the three mile stretch of Long Beach each way, starting at Kommetjie, the small village far down the Peninsula on the cold Atlantic Ocean side. There were then no housing developments; the village was tiny, with a ramshackle hotel where the Boy's uncle took him for his first "legal" beer (the Boy having recently turned eighteen). Walking that clean, wild strand, with its white sand gleaming in the sunshine, and the incoming Atlantic swell crashing in the surf, and he almost always the only human being to be seen, the Boy felt utterly at one with Creation.

The Boy was already, aged only eighteen, learning that to find God, you first had to lose yourself.

In later years, in his thirties, he was to walk – most often alone and without a rifle – in one of Africa's most pristine wilderness regions, far from towns or people. There were then still great herds of elephants and buffalo in that part of Africa; herds of antelope and zebra also; groups of giraffes (who never quite managed to achieve the dignity they so clearly sought); a wealth of bird-life; many small creatures too – and snakes. The man used to walk in open leather sandals, and one day as his right foot was about to come down, he heard a *hsshhh…*" on the ground before him and he leapt backwards off his left foot, and there lay a puff-adder, fat and lazy and with a diamond-back pattern, sunning itself on the sandy path. A puff-adder's venom is cytotoxic. The wound its bite leaves will suffer necrosis, and leave you disfigured for life.

There were hippos grazing ashore if the man got up early enough, before they retreated to the river for the day to seek both safety and the cool of the waters. The man heard leopards coughing close by at night. Once, on his way back to the lodge in the late afternoon, having been out walking alone all day, the man was crouched beneath a stand of jackalberry trees atop a vast termite mound, watching a column of elephants walking by not fifty yards from him, a column which contained mature adults, adolescents and babies. Some of the outlier bulls passed by much closer than fifty yards from the man. The dust raised by the passing elephants hung pale gold in the still air, illuminated seemingly from within by the westering sun. The man felt a frisson of excitement, allied with a suffusing joy. He lost count of their numbers after he had tallied over three hundred of the great beasts. He had very rarely felt so intensely alive. The scents and aromas of the bush were powerful in his nostrils; the sound of the birds calling was a cacophony of noise; the warm air caressed his bare forearms and bare legs; he could taste the aromatic air as he drew it into his lungs.

When the man went walking alone in the bush, all his senses alert, his shadow on the sandy ground a mere pool of shade at his feet, lengthening suddenly towards day's end, he would experience his life as an epiphany, for at such times he was wholly identified with all Creation. He could justly claim (looking back in later life) to have known something of what that first Eden must have felt like for the first man.

Two

The Community

The Boy, whose name was Alexander, or Sandy to his friends and family, had been sickly as a young child (he had suffered badly from asthma and he had come down with many colds and flu), and he had a sensitive, artistic, introspective nature. He learned early in life to escape a reality that seemed at times far from satisfactory, such as incapacitating illness, or misery at school, through reading. This gave him a love of language and a love of books for their own sake: the heft and weight of a well-bound book pleased him; the scent of the ink on the pages of a new book gratified him. The possession and ownership of books was his earliest collector's hobby.

As he reached his teens, Alexander learned that he could also escape the weight of too much consciousness, of too much burdensome awareness, by walking far, fast; by testing his endurance. Alexander sometimes felt that he had much to escape. During his adolescence, he became fearful that he was monstrous: an abomination.

Many years later, Alexander could no longer remember what sort of religious instruction he had received at school, but given that the educational system in that country was officially termed a Christian National Education, and that the mores of the nineteen-fifties prevailed in South African society well into the early nineteen-seventies, the religious instruction classes at school would have been entirely Christian in character – and a stiff-necked, Calvinist Christianity at that. Decades later, Alexander could however remember one lesson during what was termed "Guidance class": the teacher telling the sixteen-year old boys that if they had not yet kissed a girl, there was something wrong with them; that their sexuality was askew.

So Alexander approached late adolescence knowing that he must suppress and hide what he feared he might be, or run the risk of being rejected and outcast. Alexander grew up fearing therefore that he was loathsome and unlovable, and that he – and those such as he feared he may be – were justly the objects of scorn and mockery and derision. So he walked, and read books, and walked harder and further – and read more books. He learned that self-sought solitude is far from being always a lonely condition.

Aged twenty-one, Alexander found himself living in a Christian religious community. By now he was keeping a diary, a habit he was to follow with more or less diligence for most of his life. These diaries, though their bindings were to differ over the decades, were almost always of at least a half page a day, and in them Alexander recorded the events of his day and his feelings, thoughts and observations. His diaries were the means whereby Alexander maintained a lifelong dialogue with his inner self.

He lived then with four other young men in a wing of a very old Cape Dutch house set in twelve acres of oak and pine woods. There was a stream of clear water running through the estate, the water so pure you could safely drink from it, for the stream arose only a few hundred yards higher up the mountainside. There were trout in the stream.

Aside from his studies, Alexander had duties to undertake on the estate: he would fell the dead timber and cut back the encroaching saplings; he used a petrol-driven chainsaw for these tasks. But he did not have to work himself too hard: there was no one overseeing his work; he did each day only what he felt needed doing. There were coloured gardeners tending to the carefully manicured lawns and the trim hedges, and the flowerbeds full of cannas and gladioli, hydrangeas and rose bushes. He enjoyed the work. It meant that he was often alone, and when the sound of the chainsaw was stilled, and he sat quietly for a while, the woods would return to their own tranquility, and many years later the sound of doves cooing could take him back in a flash to the memory of those days.

Sometimes Alexander would sit beneath a tree by a shallows in the stream where it widened into a pool, and the sun shone on the water and made the stones and pebbles beneath the surface dance and coruscate with gold and rich umber. The languid movements of the trout beneath the water, and their sudden fleetness when startled – catching the light like quicksilver – delighted him. He sketched the scene often, and rendered it in water colours with his friend Patrick, a boy his own age who lived not far away in a grand house set on the hillside, with a garden made up of terraces, in one of which was a swimming pool.

The young men lived as a fraternity in the wing they occupied: they cooked for each-other, and kept house together. Those of them who happened to be around at lunchtime would take a picnic lunch to a small lawn beneath the oak trees behind their wing, and eat their lunch *al fresco*, usually with the private secretary to the community's leader, a pretty, prim young woman, keeping them company.

The young men, who were known as the Slaves, were all of them a decent bunch of youngsters, but as with any group, there were one or two for whom Alexander felt a special affinity. One of these was a cheerful, rangy, energetic chap who had been to school in Johannesburg. The other was a mixed race boy, sweet natured and with angelic features and an Old Testament name: he was called Nathaniel.

These young men were not sworn to celibacy, and most of the other chaps were fond of young women. Some of them – Alexander included – would bring a girlfriend to tea (or in the case of the young fellow educated in Johannesburg, two coloured girlfriends one day, twin sisters both, of a high, ripe beauty) with the community's hierarchy and their families and guests on the lawns in front of the big house on a Saturday afternoon, or take their girlfriends with them on hikes up the Mountain. One such well-known ascent commenced only a few hundred yards up the road, through the gates of the Kirstenbosch Botanic Gardens. Alexander had met his girlfriend, Catherine, aboard the mail liner as he was returning from a lengthy visit to Britain earlier that year. He was never to forget her, even though he was finally to lose touch with her in the eighties.

As well as doing some work in the oak and pine woods that made up more than three quarters of the estate, Alexander was in charge of the head of the community's liturgical vestments, ensuring that the correct colours of the day were laid out across the wide counter-top in the vestry to the small private chapel in the big house, ready for Alexander's father in God to don for holy communion: green for ordinary; white for Sundays; red for martyrs; and heavily embroidered gold for certain feast days, such as saints' days, or Easter Sunday and Christmas Day – and a deep, rich, Tyrrhenian purple for Good Friday and for requiems.

Alexander had to dress the altar each morning with the correct colours for the day, and the tabernacle also, in which the consecrated elements of the holy communion were stored. He enjoyed handling the rich cloth: the heavy embroidery – of pure bullion where gold thread was required – gave him much pleasure. When the community's leader stood in the vestry as Alexander helped him don his vestments before holy communion, Alexander felt a gladness of spirit, a happy sense of service, for he admired and respected this man, of whom he was in some awe.

Most days, Alexander had to drive the head of the community to an official function. Most often these were in Cape Town itself (for 1976 was a dramatic year, a watershed in South Africa's history, and the Church was at the forefront of the struggle for racial justice, and the Church's most high-ranking cleric in South Africa would often have to meet with government ministers and officials), but sometimes the drive would be a long one, to some far out-station of a church somewhere in the Winelands or the *Boland,* or once or twice, beyond the mountains themselves. Not infrequently, Alexander had to drive the community's leader to the airport, and then be waiting there with the car to meet him on his return. Alexander was a good driver, and he enjoyed these chauffeuring duties. In the nineteen-seventies the traffic in and around Cape Town was not heavy. Cape Town and the Cape Peninsula then had only a fraction of the population numbers with which they are burdened today. Driving in the city itself was pleasant. It was still a beautiful old city: there was only one high-rise building, located on the Foreshore, where today there is an entire city in itself reaching for the sky, which has shifted Cape Town's centre of gravity much nearer to the docks and the harbour.

After some months had passed Alexander was appointed a lay minister by the head of the community and sent to his own seamstress, a coloured woman, to have a cassock tailor-made for him, with thirty-nine tiny cloth-covered buttons down the front and a wide, generously tasseled sash to wear round the waist. In the old days, he would then have been considered to have been in minor orders.

In his middle age, Alexander was to find that he could still wear that cassock: it fitted him near perfectly. In his forties he had barely gained twenty pounds since his young manhood, though the cassock had become a little tight across his chest and shoulders.

Alexander loved the friend he had made who lived higher up the hillside. This young man, Patrick, had a head of thick golden hair (so much alike to Alexander's own, that they might understandably have been mistaken for brothers) and exceptionally gentle, sensitive features, which were redeemed from outright girlishness by an obstinate jaw-line and a wide, generous mouth. Patrick was a gentle, deeply thoughtful young man, his search for God having taken him for the moment down the road of eastern mysticism. Alexander loved him from the moment he first saw him in the company of one of the Slaves, standing in his bathing trunks by the side of the swimming-pool at the big house, beads of water running down his torso. There was indeed a strong mutual attraction from the start, although the other young man never felt any more than a brotherly affection for Alexander in his turn.

What Alexander realised he felt for Patrick, he had been conditioned to believe, was shameful, and must never on any account be communicated. And for this reason, Alexander kept undeclared his desperate, hopeless love, and for perhaps the first time in his life he became fully conscious of the curse that God had laid upon him. He became aware at that time that he would possibly never come to know the sort of happiness that most men and women experience, a happiness that many of them take for granted. A switch was flicked then inside Alexander's soul, and a slow gathering of despair began to accumulate in his spirit.

Three

Journeys and Voyages

During part of the British summer of 1976, Alexander, aged twenty-one, had lived and worked in Oban, a port town in Argyll, on Scotland's south-west Highland coast. It had been a happy interlude, terminating with his return to South Africa. He had left Oban for London by train one morning towards the end of August. On the evening before his departure, Alexander had been sitting reading in the dormitory room under the eaves that he shared with three other young waiters at the hotel, when he was sent for, and told to put on a clean shirt and a tie. Wondering, he did so, and he went downstairs to the hotel lounge, where he found that a farewell *ceilidh* had been organised in his honour. There were a couple of fiddlers and an accordion player providing the music, and some of the men present were wearing kilts. During the course of the evening Alexander was taught some Highland dances; the dancing and drinking and music continued until late that night, the staff and guests mingling.

For several weeks, the news on the television had been full of bloody scenes of riot and death in South Africa: of *toyi-toying* black mobs performing that deeply disturbing, mindless crowd dance of Africa, before surging forward and receiving blast after blast of buck shot from pump-action shot guns in the hands of the Police. There had been scenes of buildings set afire, and cars overturned and burning, and already, burning alive by necklacing was becoming commonplace. And so the good folk at the hotel in Oban thought that Alexander was the great Hero to be returning to such bloody violence and mayhem. Perhaps some of them felt that this *ceilidh* was in truth more of a wake for Alexander than a joyful celebration.

Alexander was savagely hung-over when the train for London pulled out of Oban the next morning, and he left behind him much good will and many memories of friendship, and a tough Glaswegian lad who had borrowed five Pounds from him some weeks earlier (which in today's money, would be closer to seventy Pounds in buying power), and who had carefully avoided him thereafter until he was safely gone.

That two weeks sea passage home, which Alexander recorded in his diary, remained one of the great experiences of Alexander's life. It was not his first voyage in an ocean liner: as a small child he and his family had taken a British India steamer to England from Mombasa on a long leave, the ship making its way up the Thames to a quayside in the London docks. Alexander was too young to remember much about that voyage, but he could remember much more clearly the family's voyage by Lloyd Triestino liner to South Africa when they left Kenya for ever.

Alexander spent a few days with his aunt in Berkshire, then he took a train to London from Slough early on the morning of the 3rd September, and caught the boat train from Victoria station. The train came to a halt round about eleven in the morning, alongside the passenger terminal on the quayside where the liners docked at Southampton. Alexander had already checked his baggage in at Victoria station: there was no baggage to fetch from the train. It would make its way directly on board ship, and the suitcase and backpack he had marked "Wanted on board", would be sent to his cabin, the remaining suitcase would be stowed in the baggage hold.

The heatwave had broken, but the day was dry. Mounting the gangway, Alexander felt great excitement. He was traveling aboard the RMS Windsor Castle, one of the Union Castle-Safmarine line's two remaining mail liners. Alexander was shown to his cabin in tourist class on E deck, far aft, by a steward in a white coat buttoned up in front. Hearing the thrum of distant machinery and the constant hum of the ventilation system below deck, which made the ship feel as if it were a living thing, a powerful childhood memory was rekindled. He had specified an outer cabin, to make sure that the cabin had a porthole, and the cabin was so near the waterline that the outer bulkhead sloped in at a pronounced angle. There were two good sized berths, one atop the other. Alexander had access to shared lavatories, baths and showers further aft. The baths were slightly saline: there was special soap provided that lathered in the saline water.

Alexander explored the ship whilst they were still moored at the quayside, and because this was their departure day, he was allowed access to first class also. Once on their way, tourist class passengers were forbidden access to first class – though first class could mix with tourist class, if they chose. Some did: tourist class was more fun, and included many more youngsters than first class, which was full of rich, late middle aged and elderly passengers.

Alexander had made his way up to the boat-deck shortly before 1pm, and he was standing not far below the funnel when he was startled by a massive blast of sound just above him. There is nothing like that sound, the deep, prolonged bay of a big ship's steam siren. It makes the air vibrate. Alexander was intensely moved.

The siren boomed again, and Alexander descended quickly to the promenade deck, where passengers were already throwing rolls of paper streamers all the colours of the rainbow across to the quayside, where they were caught and held by people seeing friends and family off. The big hawsers were let slip, and the ship began to move slowly away from the quayside. Passengers and well-wishers called to one another across the widening gap: some people were crying, and folks were waving and shouting their goodbyes, and then the tangled brightly coloured paper streamers from ship to shore began to snap in two, and the ship swung slowly away from the shore and pointed her bows towards the Solent.

The RMS Windsor Castle made her maiden voyage in August 1960. She was not a small ship, being of 37 640 gross tonnage; she was 785 feet long, with a beam of 93 feet. The Windsor Castle had a designed cruising speed of 22.5 knots (about 25.5 miles an hour). She was a twin screw vessel, powered by geared steam turbines: a true steam ship. She carried 191 first class passengers and 591 passengers in tourist class.

The tourist lounge, with panoramic picture windows facing forward, was large enough to seat most of the tourist class passengers. There was a bar at the back of the lounge. They had a library on board also (in which divine service was held on Sundays), veneered in pale wood, with reading tables and writing desks. There was a smoking room beyond the library.

There was a large tourist class dining saloon, with separate tables seating two, four, six and eight diners. Alexander was allocated to a table of eight, and this meant that he very quickly came to know a crowd of young people, and almost everyone at that table had become a friend before the voyage was many days out. He kept up with some of these people for one or two years after docking at Cape Town, and with one of them, Catherine, an English girl, for the next six or seven years.

There was neither a shopping mall nor a casino on board. There were no restaurants. The Windsor Castle was a classic liner, designed in the 1950s, not a cruise ship. There was roulette and *chemin de fer* offered in the tourist lounge in the evenings. There was however a small shop on board, where you could buy an amazing array of goods, including (usefully, as Alexander was to find out) needle and thread, and there was a barber's shop and a ladies' hair salon. The tourist passengers had access to a covered promenade deck on either beam, and there was an open-air swimming-pool aft, with plenty of recreational deck space surrounding it. When, before their departure, Alexander had explored first class, he had been impressed at the amount of wood paneling and fine veneers and gilt decoration in the public rooms. First class passengers had access, for example, to a circular cards room, hung with red silk like a 1950s

Hollywood version of an Arabian sheik's tent, the silken roof supported by a polished brass post in the centre.

While Alexander was changing into a lounge suit for dinner, his Belgian cabin mate appeared. He was a little older than Alexander, short, with a compact build and dark curly hair, and he spoke fractured English, but then, Alexander spoke fractured French, and so they understood one another very well. Alexander wore a dark grey single breasted suit with a light grey check to dinner that first evening out. The only other suit he had with him was black. At the very least, the other young men wore jackets and ties. At dinner, among the people whom Alexander met for the first time at their table, was a very attractive, well spoken, patrician featured English girl about his own age, with honey-blonde hair with a natural wave in it. Catherine was traveling to Cape Town to take up a music teacher's post at a private girls' school. The two of them got on very well from the start, and within a few days, they were spending a lot of their time together.

The food on board was excellent, course after course, *table d'hôte* style. Alexander had a young man's healthy appetite, and he gorged himself on three meals a day, and sometimes he sat down to afternoon tea also, with cakes and sandwiches. The waiters in the tourist class dining room were young white British men: attentive, courteous, even deferential. Alexander was "Sir" to the very young English waiter who served at his table, and Alexander addressed him as "Waiter."

Breakfasts were generous: there were kippers, two kinds of porridge, one of them that South African speciality, "Maltabella" (Which Alexander avoided); there were fried, poached, scrambled and boiled eggs; sausages; fried tomatoes and mushrooms; toast (with jams and marmalades); cold meats; fruit (from the onboard cold rooms); fruit juice, tea and coffee; and always a small vase of flowers, changed every day, the flowers kept fresh in the ship's cold rooms, was present on the table. Luncheon had almost as many choices and courses as dinner. Dinner always included a roast. There was a newly printed menu at each place-setting for every meal, headed and bordered with illustrations of the ship, of South African scenes, and of maritime themes.

In the evenings the gang gathered in the big lounge, or at the bar at the back of the lounge, where the drinks were duty free and very cheap. There was a dance on the first night out, as they were crossing the maw of the Bay of Biscay. The sea was rough and the ship rolled and pitched. Alexander could make out the horizon – as it appeared to ascend beyond the big picture windows forward in the lounge, then slowly descending again – by the lights from the ship which were reflected on the crests of the waves, for the ship was lighted up like a small town. He was not seasick.

Alexander danced with several girls, including Catherine: he danced with un-self conscious pleasure to the insistent rythm of the music as the deck moved beneath him, and it was while performing some rapid footwork in order not to shoot across the deck as the ship described an exceptionally violent motion, that he split his trousers' crotch. He bought needle and thread in the onboard shop the next morning, and he repaired the split seam. He had done no sewing repairs ever before, but the repair held up well for some years thereafter.

As the weather grew steadily warmer the further south they steamed, the youngsters began to gather at the pool in the evenings, rather than in the lounge. Pool parties would last well into the early hours, and they would have stocked up with cans of beer at the duty free bar. Alexander had never drunk so much on a regular basis before.

During the voyage, Alexander chummed up with a chap a year younger than himself. Raymond came from Cape Town. He was a laconic but well-spoken, good looking, tanned lad with dark brown hair. One night they leant over the railings together aft, watching the phosphorescence shimmering in the sea, as they shared a joint. That was Alexander's first experience of marijuana. At the fancy dress party during the voyage, Raymond wore a long wig and a girlfriend's evening dress of dark purple satin. Alexander (who wore his black suit with a black shirt he had borrowed from a shipboard friend and a clergyman's collar he had made of white card) was not the only man present who thought Raymond looked very striking. One of the ship's smart young officers in his evening wear tropical whites was in close conversation with Raymond for some considerable time. Alexander wished he had a smart white dress uniform to wear.

Alexander had not been back home for long before he received a distressing shock: a notice of Raymond's funeral service arrived in the post. The young man had died in a traffic accident. Alexander had not known until then that Raymond had kept his address. He was greatly moved, and he felt for a brief while an intense sorrow. He had not lost a contemporary to death before. The funeral service was held in the Anglican Cathedral in Cape Town; it was very well attended. Raymond came from an old, well known Cape Town family.

It grew warmer each day, then very hot indeed as the ship approached the Equator. King Neptune arrived at the poolside aft when they crossed the Line, accompanied by his motley acolytes, and they subjected a variety of foolish or brave souls to gross humiliations and the application of gooey substances, all of these actions invariably ending in a ducking in the swimming-pool. However, Alexander had crossed the Equator already as a child, and so he stood to one side and merely watched the fun. And then, day by day it began, slowly at first, then faster, to grow cooler again as they entered the cold, foods-rich stream of the Benguela current.

One morning Alexander went up on deck early, and he realised that the ship was moving much faster than usual through the sea, and he saw dense, heavy black smoke pouring from the funnel. He learned that they were making for Walvis Bay (then a South African enclave on the South West African coast), to disembark a crewman with a ruptured appendix. The harbour at Walvis Bay was neither large enough nor deep enough for the big ship, but they halted offshore, and a launch came out to fetch the crewman, who was lowered over the side, tightly bound in a stretcher, and then sped ashore to hospital. Then the ship resumed its course for Cape Town.

Four

Disgraced

The ship arrived off Table Bay at dawn. Alexander was up on deck very early, full of eager anticipation, and he felt a prickling in his eyes as he gazed at the distant silhouette of Table Mountain, and at the sky bursting into flame over the African continent. As they drew closer, Table Mountain loomed ever larger above the old city, and the sun had begun to climb from behind Devils Peak. By the time the ship passed the breakwater, it was broad day, and already Alexander could hear the sound of steam shunting engines at work, clang-bash, woof-woof-woof-woof-woof! Pierre, Alexander's cabin-mate, was with him, leaning on the rail, and he was astonished and delighted to hear the sound of steam locos at work. "The steam engines, they pull the mainline passenger trains in South Africa?" Pierre asked him.

"Yes. The Trans-Karoo express between Cape Town and Johannesburg – Pretoria is still hauled part of the distance by steam," Alexander replied.

It felt as if they were barely moving in the water, but the busy tugboats were doing their job, and the quayside grew ever closer, until, with much shouting in that oh, so familiar, broad accented Afrikaans of the Cape Coloured working class, ropes were flung from shore to ship, and these were whipped around mechanical winches and the heavy mooring hawsers were hauled aboard, to make the ship fast to the quayside. Gangways were wheeled up to the ship's tall sides, and disembarkation hatchways were flung open. Alexander was home, having been away for nine months. The following month he joined the other young men at the religious community.

Alexander left the community in May 1977, disgraced and outcast. This is what had happened: one of the Slaves had entered Alexander's room hurriedly on some errand or other, without first knocking, to find him kissing Nathaniel, the young coloured boy. How had this come about? The angelic-featured Nathaniel had approached Alexander, troubled because he and a friend from his school days felt a powerful attraction for each other. "Will I go to Hell, do you think?" Nathaniel asked Alexander. "The Bible says it is a sin, love like that between two men," he continued.

"Nathaniel, it is not love between two men that the Bible condemns – think of David and Jonathan – but, as the Bible puts it, lying with a man as with a woman. Love is surely never a sin." Alexander looked at Nathaniel's face, unmarked as yet by any of life's cruelties or harshness. It was an open, but right now, troubled young face. Alexander felt a huge tenderness for the young coloured lad in that moment. And more than tenderness, but what Nathaniel did next took Alexander completely by surprise.

Nathaniel leant forward and kissed Alexander on the mouth, who, wonderingly, had returned the kiss – and it was then that another of the Slaves had entered Alexander's room without warning. That young fellow had been shocked at what he imagined he was seeing, which in his imagination was far more than that one almost chaste kiss between Alexander and Nathaniel, and he had reported his semi-fictional observations to the community head's chaplain. Alexander had shortly thereafter been asked to leave the community.

Alexander felt as if the world had turned its face against him. He felt that he would now never come to know happiness. In a single moment his dreams of eventual ordination in the Church had been destroyed. He wished he could have believed there was someone he could have turned to for guidance, or simply for comfort and reassurance. But this was the South Africa of 1977, where such behavior was doubly scandalous, breaking as it did two taboos at the same time: physical affection between two men, and one of those a man of another race. This had been more than even the very liberal Christian community he had been cast out from had been able to tolerate.

Alexander nursed his misery for some months, and then, in September that same year, he flew to London for the second time. From London, he took a National Express overnight coach the five hundred miles to Oban, that port town and islands ferry terminus in Argyll, on Scotland's west coast. The summer tourist season by then was almost over. However, Alexander was not looking to find work, but seeking to escape hurt and pain and heart-ache and loss. Oban was, this time, just the jumping off point for him to reach the outer isles. Remembering the happiness he had known in Oban a year earlier, and almost overwhelmed by present misery, with his plans for the future in ruins, and his longing for his beloved friend Patrick almost more than he could bear, he had returned to Oban. He had no real purpose in being there. Oban and the Isles were better destinations to flee to than many he could think of. Perhaps too the Isles drew Alexander because of his ancestral ties with the region. He had felt it during his first visit to these western lands the year before: a tremendous sense of home-coming and peace.

Caledonian MacBrayne (today operating as CalMac) then as now operated ferry services to the Hebrides, both the inner and the outer isles. The sea voyage from Oban to Castlebay on the southernmost of the main islands of the Outer Hebrides, tiny Barra, was four hours and fifty minutes in duration. Barra is a Catholic island. Gaelic was still spoken on the island. Its story, like that of Kisimul Castle, the castle perched on a rock in the bay that Alexander could see as the ferry drew near to the quayside, is intertwined with the story of the clan MacNeil.

Over the next few days, Alexander hitched his way north up the island chain. From Barra in the south to the island of Lewis in the north, he made use of post buses, a few private cars whose drivers stopped for him, and a couple of fishing boats between islands. Alexander was acutely conscious of his location on the very furthest edge of the Old World: beyond these Western Isles lay the north Atlantic, with nothing in between until you reached North America. Deep within Alexander's racial memory was the understanding that here, he stood at the very edge of the world.

The weather for the most part was excellent; the quality of light, ethereal. Alexander witnessed splendid sunsets across the Atlantic, and magnificent sky and ocean panoramas in which some of his misery was able to dissipate, so vast, so limitless were these vistas. He saw sweeping beaches made of gleaming white shell ground down by the surging Atlantic waters, with the machair grass reaching down to the edge of the beach, and never a person to be seen; he saw moorland, lochans and lochs. Of trees he saw none. Nowhere, until he reached the harbour town of Stornoway, the Hebridean capital on the island of Lewis, did he find any great concentration of humanity, or of the structures humanity builds. Alexander was desperately unhappy, heart-sore and lonely, and these lonely isles on the very outer edge of the old world were the perfect setting for him to lick his emotional wounds. He found a measure of peace as he made his way slowly up the island chain.

Having spent the night in Stornoway, Alexander returned by ferry to the Scottish mainland, once again using the Caledonian MacBrayne service. It was a rough crossing. The weather had changed and a near-gale, rain-laden, was blowing in from the west. The voyage between Stornoway and Ullapool lasted two and a half hours. An island girl with hair the colour of a raven's wing and skin the tone and texture of newly carved ivory and eyes of periwinkle blue, whom Alexander met in the bar aboard the ferry, taught him to drink rum with black-current cordial. Later, he woke as they docked against the quayside at Ullapool, his head resting comfortably against the girl's shoulder. Alexander by now had almost no cash left: the girl gave him five Pounds, which was then a lot of money, to help him on his journey. In years to come, Alexander would sometimes wish that he still belonged to that secret mutual aid society, that free masonry of the young.

Back on the mainland, Alexander made his way without any plan across the breadth of the Highlands to Inverness, on Scotland's east coast, where he spent a night at a bed and breakfast near the Castle. The next morning he stood at the side of the A82 on the town's fringes and hitched a lift with a lorry driver through the Great Glen to Fort William, on Scotland's West Highland coast. Here, with a total of only ten Pounds left in his wallet, Alexander realised his wanderings must soon be terminated, and he made his way to the railway station, hoping for a train to London, from where he could make his way to his aunt in Berkshire. At the station Alexander found the sleeper train for London was due to depart later that afternoon. He killed some hours in the town, then he approached the train manager who was standing on the platform, and paying him five Pounds he made a private arrangement with him for an unofficial *coupé* compartment for the journey, with breakfast in the morning and a hot shower, and so he took the overnight sleeper train for London.

Five

The Cosmopolitan Life – I

In January 1979 Alexander was living in Johannesburg. He applied for a job he saw advertised in the Johannesburg *Star*'s classified section and began working for a tiny private investigation agency with a two room office suite in the high-rise Trust Bank building in Johannesburg's city centre, opposite the Carlton Centre complex. Alexander quickly showed considerable aptitude for the work. In this, his habit of living a lie – of pretending an interest only in the opposite sex – helped him greatly, for so much of his work necessitated the practice of false pretences; of his assuming a false persona. Alexander's boss was a likeable rogue named Manfred, an Austrian in his thirties who had lived in Johannesburg for many years.

Soon after starting work in the city centre, Alexander moved into a bachelor flat in Twist Street, opposite Joubert Park, down the hill from Hillbrow. This flat was a neat, furnished place a few floors above the street, with a balcony overlooking the park, which was full of mature trees and was laid out in colourful flowerbeds and well kept lawns. There was also an open-air giant chessboard with super-sized chess pieces. Middle aged and elderly men from Europe played in front of a scattered audience. Joubert Park was still a safe place for white people to visit in the late nineteen-seventies.

Alexander would often walk to work at the Trust Bank building in the city centre. Some evenings after work he drank beers and smoked Gauloise cigarettes – heavy, harsh Gallic cigarettes – with his boss in the piano bar on the top floor of the Carlton Hotel. Inside, there was a baby grand and a piano man, and later in the evening, a *chanteuse*. The outdoors roof area had a swimming pool, and many big leafy shrubs and small trees growing in large tubs. It was like a garden in the sky, and you could sit and drink beers and look down at the street thirty floors below you. Other evenings Alexander would trek from his flat up the hill to Hillbrow, to sit in the Café Wien, or the Café de Paris, and drink *cappucinos* served by smart black waiters in long white aprons. Exiled central Europeans and old men who had fled the Communists after the War, would gather at these cafés to gossip and play chess and backgammon, and read the foreign newspapers. These newspapers, which were flown in by airmail once a week, were attached to long wooden reading rods tipped with brass ferules, and when you were done with them, you returned them to their racks where they hung, one publication partially obscuring the one below, staggered in a tier. On weekends, Alexander favoured the Café de Paris with its wide first floor balcony, and, shaded from the sun by a large umbrella, he would eat *Sacher Torte*, that most delicious of European *gateaux*, and drink coffee, watching the parade of street life below.

Alexander read very little at this time. Nor did he always keep up his diary very assiduously. He did not belong to a library, and he could not afford to buy new books. But he was so busy with his work, and with evenings drinking with his boss, or spent in the cosmopolitan cafés in Hillbrow, that he had little time to read. He did buy the *Star* every day, the liberal Johannesburg daily. At the cafés he frequented in Hillbrow, he paged through magazines such as *Punch* and *Time*. Sometimes he read one of the English newspapers.

It was at the Café Wien that Alexander met a young crowd one evening. The group appeared to coalesce around a tall, slim young woman with blonde hair and a wide, smiling mouth. She caught Alexander's eye as he looked her way, and leaning across, said to him, "You're a new face. Do you live in the Brow?"

"Yeah – down the hill in Twist Street."

"I'm Alice. Why don't you come join us?"

Alexander shifted his coffee across to their table and sat down. Alice introduced him to the others. There was one other girl, a Rubenesque, dark haired young woman with sleepy eyes and a Jewish look about her, named Jacquie. The members of this group of half a dozen people his own age and younger were soon to become very good friends to Alexander. They all lived in or near Hillbrow, in flats in old art deco apartment blocks, or in complexes that had gone up in the sixties. One of these people was a boy aged eighteen, who had matriculated the year before. He was six years younger than Alexander. Terrance, as Alexander was to learn, was extremely creative. He had a slight build and dark good looks. He had begun his first year film studies at the Teknikon. He lived with a much older sister in her flat in Berea. A rapport quickly developed between him and Alexander. Thereafter Terrance often visited Alexander at his flat in Twist Street, bringing his flute with him, which Alexander enjoyed hearing him play. Often he showed Alexander pencil or ink sketches he was working on.

Terrance asked Alexander to tutor him for his driving test. Alexander tried, but after only one near-disastrous outing together in Alexander's big AMC Rambler, with Terrance at the wheel, Alexander had to decline. The Rambler's steering wheel was heavily geared, in that era before universal power-steering, and it took some getting used to, if you were not to constantly and wildly over-correct when steering the big heavy car. Coupled with the car's power, and the willingness with which it surged forward at the merest touch of the accelerator, this made for a potentially disastrous combination. After several near-misses and only very narrowly avoided collisions, Alexander's nerve cracked, and he said "I think you need to learn on a smaller car."

However, Alexander and Terrance remained close friends throughout that year and friends for many years after. During that first year of friendship the two of them sometimes visited Terrance's family home in the well-heeled suburb of Rivonia. Here, Alexander met Terrance's younger brother, Guy, a kid aged nine years. The first time Alexander met him, the weather was very warm, and the boy was dressed only in shorts and a tee-shirt. He was barefoot. He was very tanned, and his dark hair was rather long. He had very bright green eyes. The boy was enormously gifted artistically. He showed Alexander a project he was working on: it was a fantasy, arboreal world, set in a dried and peeled-bark multi-branched limb from a hardwood tree the kid had seen potential in, and which he had dragged home from some nearby *veld*. This tree-world hosted a complex of tree-houses in miniature, connected by walks and ladders, and peopled with tiny carved wooden figurines. It captivated Alexander, as did the personable, modest little boy himself, who, when he saw that Alexander was genuinely impressed by his work, began to enthuse about it, and tell him about the tree-world he had conceived.

Alexander was to meet the lad several times that year, and again ten years later, by which time he would be nineteen years old.

The group which befriended Alexander at the Café Wien that evening in early 1979 was centred on the figure of Alice, who had a warm, motherly personality. Later that year she moved to Yeoville, an old suburb a couple of miles from Hillbrow, and Alexander, the only member of the group with a car, helped shift her things, including her cat Tigger. Alexander was to spend many evenings gathered with others at Alice's flat, puffing at a joint as it was passed round the circle, chatting, and listening to rock music. "What's up, Sandro," Alice would greet him, for Sandro became his nickname amongst these friends. Evenings with Alice and the others, listening to music tapes, gave Alexander the education in rock music that he had failed to acquire whilst at school. Unlike most of the kids at school, he had never listened to the radio as a teenager.

Hillbrow in the nineteen-seventies and the nineteen-eighties was a compound of all the sin and vice and hopes and life and wonder of that gold mining city, Johannesburg. It was riches and terrible poverty; it was every ethnicity and tongue and creed under the sky, gathered in one crowded district consisting largely of high-rise apartment blocks, some of which were twenty stories high. However, families were raised in Hillbrow. Children grew up there, went to schools nearby, and many Hillbrow residents attended church services on Sunday. Rents were low, even by Alexander's ill-paid standards. It was very easy to rent a flat. There were no character checks, no financial checks; it was then a kinder, simpler age. There were shops and stores and cinemas in the Brow; everything needed to service a vast and disparate community. At Highpoint centre there was a twenty-four hour supermarket, Fontanas (famed for its spit-roasted chickens), with covered car parking below; there were cinemas nearby also; there were pubs, clubs, a public swimming bath, and of course the cafés. If you were merely a timid bourgeois boy up from the suburbs with your chick on a Saturday night, and you wanted to catch a safe thrill, and tell your mates you had been to the movies in Hillbrow, you could park your car below Highpoint, and check out a movie in the movie complex, and you need hardly set foot in the scary night-time streets of Hillbrow at all.

Among Alice's group, clubbing on a Friday or Saturday night was an important way of blowing off steam. Alexander had never danced to contemporary dance music before. He enjoyed it tremendously; he had a good sense of natural rhythm and boundless energy, and – an exhibitionist by inclination – he was not shy on the dance floor. He found club dancing addictive: he lost himself completely in the driving, hypnotic beat of the dance music pounding in his ears, with only occasional breaks for visits to one of the two bars, or to the roof garden for some Mary Jane. He visited one club in particular, Mandys in End Street, many times, with Terrance, Jacquie and others from the group. Mandys had a reputation for sexual ambiguity and frantic dancing on its two dance floors – accompanied by often heavy drinking and the smoking of marijuana. This latter was pursued on the roof garden, which had a number of booths around its perimeter in which you could sit, separated by trellises of jasmine and honeysuckle. Alexander would often dance right through the night, having taken speed at Alice's flat before departing in the late evening for the club ("Obex" weight loss tablets were popular for this purpose), and at dawn, feeling utterly drained but still buzzing, a group of friends would make their way across the jaded city, shivering in the sudden chill, to the towering luxury Carlton Hotel in the city centre for a full breakfast in the hotel restaurant, washed down with flute glasses of Bucks Fizz. It would be late morning before Alexander crashed – quite often at Alice's flat, sometimes at his own place in Twist Street – with the suddenness and totality of a tree being felled.

It was at Mandys that Jacquie first made her interest in Alexander very clear, and nothing loathe to further his experience of living life to the full, Alexander responded in kind. Before long Jacquie and Sandro were known (as the current expression was) as "an item", and it was with Jacquie one night that Alexander eagerly sacrificed his virginity.

It seemed to Alexander, a young man himself, that Hillbrow was a young man's Mecca. Young men from the suburbs and from further afield – from the *dorps* of the *Platteland* – would find their way to Hillbrow in their quest to alleviate the stifling boredom and sameness of their suburban lives, or to escape the narrow confines of their country towns, or to make their fortunes – or just to let off steam on a Friday or Saturday night. For Hillbrow – and Yeoville, one or two miles further east – were full of bars and nightclubs and something still rather new for many: discos. Some of the sturdy Afrikaner country lads, stranded in Hillbrow, penniless, landed up hiring themselves from Johannesburg Station (competing with the heroin addicts) to middle aged homosexuals in the evenings, who cruised the station parking lot in their cars – or these young men hung around the illicit gay bars (for homosexuality was outlawed until 1994 in South Africa), and hoped to be taken home for the night, and given a bath and supper, and in return for the comfort they offered their protectors, they would perhaps be given twenty or thirty Rands also, and then, in the morning, returned to Park Station, or to Hillbrow. Alexander learned early on that Hillbrow had a dark underbelly. There was a lurking spirit of true wickedness that was particularly apparent late at night, if you were n't too drunk or zonked or spaced to notice.

And there were black beggars located up and down the two main streets, Pretoria and Kotze. There was one black beggar who seemed to be seated directly on his legless trunk, on a small wooden platform with castor wheels at each corner, and he propelled himself around with hugely calloused fists. Others occupied disused and closed-up doorways, set back from the pavement, and they would sit there, their stick-thin limbs stuck out in front of them, covered with hideous carbuncles and growths and sores weeping fluids and horror. One or two turned sightless eyes up to a blind heaven, and held out quavering hands. One of these latter often had a small apprentice squatting by his side, to be his eyes. If Alexander gave these unfortunates some loose change as he passed by, it was less from pity than from an atavistic compulsion to avert ill-fortune.

There were black street children also, scores of them, dressed in cast-offs and rags, often barefoot, who swarmed all around you if you parked your car at night, on your way to the movies or a restaurant, and you gave these kids small denominations of silver, and told them there would be more when you returned, if your car was still safe.

And at the far end of Pretoria Street, only a hundred yards from Connections, Johannesburg's best known gay bar, was the Hillbrow Police station, a large fortress-like building of red brick and raw concrete, with its communal police cells for drunks and petty thieves and muggers and drug dealers, and every other worker of night-time vice. Alexander was to spend almost an entire night in one of these stews, a few years later, after he had been pulled over at a Police roadblock on Empire Road while driving, very drunk, and he had been arrested and thrown into the cells. In the cell crowded with white men of every degree, Alexander kept the bold face, and passed round some cigarettes to establish his bona fides. The Police cells were of course then racially segregated.

By the late eighties Alexander had become much more familiar with the dark side. Hillbrow by then seemed to him to be like an aging stage artiste, the paint and powder cracking on her ravaged features, this wicked old woman who still whored herself to youngsters foolish enough to fall for her dubious charms. The district was steeped in corruption by then, a corruption of the spirit, and Alexander was old enough by then – well old enough! – to recognise this, yet still – still! – he could not keep away from this ogling old has-been. It was at this point in time that he was introduced by a friend who managed one of the gay bars, to the Yugoslav Football Club, which was located behind an innocent, narrow entrance in Pretoria Street. If you did not know it was there, you would have passed it by. You turned off the pavement into this entrance, and you walked along a narrow, covered-in, dimly lighted, dog-legged alley, deep in the bowels of the buildings above it. This alley terminated in a heavy steel grill protecting a metal door. You stood so the closed-circuit beady eye could check you out, and you pressed a bell: the buzzer sounded, the locks disengaged, and you were inside.

The Yugoslav Football Club was essentially a cavernous, dimly-lighted, dingy bar, open twenty-four hours a day, every single day of the year. There was a side-room that opened off the main area, where you could drink in a little more privacy if you wished. The club was owned by a young Serbian woman and her mother. Alexander once saw the latter jumping up and down on a man who had offended her. She was wearing pointed heels, and she was a big woman. Off-duty cops drank there, and petty gangsters, and pimps and their girls. Deals went down in that place. It was a sleazy, corrupt environment, and if, by this stage in your life you still found this sort of thing appealing, you were close to sinking forever, beyond trace.

Alexander was the last white tenant left in his block of flats in Yeoville in 1996. By then, he visited Hillbrow only to drink in the early hours at the Yugoslav Football Club, or to visit Connections, which was one of the very last of the old bars in Hillbrow still open for business. The great European cafés, so elegant, so cosmopolitan, so very civilized, had become black shebeens; the streets of Hillbrow, Berea, Bellevue and Yeoville, as Alexander was to find out, were no longer safe for a white man to walk alone, particularly at night.

Six

The Cosmopolitan Life – II

———

When Alexander made his first visit to Britain in 1976 as a young man on an extended working holiday, arriving in southern England in the depths of a cold January wintertime which he found both shocking in its severity and wonderful in its elemental simplicity, delighting in the bright burgeoning spring days of April and May, and sweltering in the hot summer that followed, he was already in love with southern England and with its people, long before he had ever arrived. He loved without question of any qualifications arising in his mind, because he was so certain that everything he saw would please him. And so, for the most part, it did.

When Alexander was just a little child living many thousands of miles away in Africa his mother had read him stories from English children's books, and he had learned to read because he wished to read these stories for himself. He knew all the Beatrix Potter children's stories almost by heart, and the animal characters were old and much loved friends. Aged four, he had run outside one morning to the edge of the forest that bordered the family's back garden, to try to find a red squirrel like Squirrel Nutkin, but instead he found only a troop of little black-faced monkeys in the trees, and one of the naughty little imps peed from a tree twenty feet above him and made Alexander laugh so much he almost wet himself. But he did not find Squirrel Nutkin there.

Alexander was able to quote from A.A. Milne's stories about Christopher Robin and his bear, Winnie the Pooh, and from the poems in *Now We are Six*. He had a clear image in his mind's eye of the Hundred Acre Wood where Owl and Eeyore lived, just as he had a clear image of rolling English countryside from any number of English children's tales written before the War, such as the stories of *Milly Molly Mandy* and her English country cottager's life, by Joyce Lankester Brisley. Before he reached his teens he had read the magical and moving classic, *The Wind in the Willows*, by Kenneth Grahame. As a teenager he had very much enjoyed reading the adventure novels of the English nineteenth century writer G. A. Henty, in which Englishness of a certain class was presented as vastly admirable, and through which the Empire was glorified. Alexander read countless less dated novels set in England. Of course, a Scot via his paternal bloodline, as a teenager Alexander also read the many historical novels written by Nigel Tranter, which were set in Scotland and which taught him so much about the history of the ancestral land he had never known.

But it was the southern England of the inter-war years with which Alexander was most familiar from his reading; the England of his mother's side of the family. By the time he reached adolescence he had already read the *Just William* stories by Richmal Crompton. These stories delighted Alexander and made him laugh. He related to William who prowled the English countryside around his home, seeking adventures and falling into mishaps and mischief, for Alexander too was a great neighbourhood wanderer as a young adolescent, his air rifle in one hand. And in his early teens he galloped through the *Billy Bunter* stories, that Fat Owl of the Remove, and although they were few enough in all conscience, he found sufficient similarities between Greyfriars,

Billy Bunter's minor public school, and his own high school in Africa, to relate to the characters in the series of novels. For a while Alexander had sought to model himself on the languid Lord Mauleverer, whose laconic drawl and monocle in one eye seemed to him to be the very height of aristocratic breeding and disdain.

During Alexander's later adolescence he read every novel by P. G. Wodehouse that he could lay his hands on. Their pre-war upper class Englishness and characters with private means and manservants spoke to him of a culture that represented the peak of urban civilization. Alexander knew that such a culture was long gone, yet these immensely amusing and entertaining stories of idle good breeding exerted a powerful fascination on him.

At high school in Africa Alexander became familiar with Jane Austen's novels, and he had read Anthony Trollope's *Barchester Towers*. As a pubescent he read English comics such as the *Beano* and the *Dandy*, and a little later he was reading *Lion* and *Victor* and *Hotspur*, and he also read the more serious comic publication, *Look and Learn*, which (together with these other comics) arrived by airmail from England every week. In his late teens in Cape Town he bought the English country magazine, *Country Life*, every week, with its page after page of beautiful country houses for sale, and he also read *Punch*, and these magazines held a promise that Alexander had no doubts would be redeemed, if ever he was to visit England. And he was not to be disappointed.

By the time Alexander left home in Cape Town aged twenty, headed the full length of the African continent and across the seas for the British Isles, he had become familiar with an England that, in his mind's eye, consisted only of the glories and wonders of London, that great imperial capital, or of the long-settled countryside: an idealised landscape of lovely rolling hills and cool green woodlands; of quiet, slow-moving rivers whose banks were hung with drooping willows, or fast-flowing, clear streams rising high in the hills; of quaint thatched half-timbered cottages, and noble country houses. And he was to find all these things during that, his first visit since childhood to England.

Early in 1980, when he had grown tired of working as a private eye, and was overwhelmed by the restlessness which periodically overcame him, Alexander left South Africa for London once again. Alexander squandered Time: his life (it appeared to him) stretched out to infinity before him, and he felt no great drive to use his time well.

Alexander was to remember London and the south of England in the seventies and eighties with some affection in later years. London hadn't yet been spoiled for him. The cold, mercenary hand of Thatcherism had barely begun to alter the character of the people of England's south-east, and was yet to make them callous, grasping, greedy and uncaring. Even on this, his third visit to Britain as an adult, Alexander was still finding much that, while no longer quite alien to him, could still seem subtly foreign. Alexander's relations in the countryside, with whom he would often spend weekends, made up their beds using duvets instead of blankets, and the windows were rarely opened in their homes during the five winter months of the year; their houses always seemed over-heated at night. Alexander could not become accustomed to removing his shoes in some of their homes as he stepped indoors. Nor, before his first visit in 1976, had he ever seen anyone washing the dishes in a plastic bowl in the kitchen sink. What was the sink for, he wondered?

Other than the young (who had wonderfully clear, unblemished, porcelain-white, pink cheeked complexions), the English seemed uniformly grey of feature, and they dressed so dowdily. Everyone was bundled up in vast shapeless outer garments. There were many people who Alexander thought at first must be Indians, but whom he was to come to realise over time had Pakistani and Bangladeshi origins. The black and mixed race people he saw may have looked similar to the black and mixed race people he had been familiar with in Africa, but they spoke very differently, and they were far more assertive and confidant. They did not cringe and bob their heads at Alexander. He was standing with his grandmother once, waiting for a bus. When the bus arrived, Alexander stepped unthinking in front of a black man who was waiting ahead of him in the queue. His grandmother grabbed him and pulled him back "You're in England now, Sandy," she whispered.

With the coming of his first English springtime in 1976 Alexander had come to know the wayside plants that members of his family would identify for him as they went walking along country lanes. He delighted in the apple-scented white hawthorn blossom, the mayflower, that grew in all the hedgerows. Alexander learned why people in the cold North yearn for and love the springtime. Decades later, the song of blackbirds in Alexander's garden in springtime would make his heart glad, and trigger happy memories from long ago; memories of a time when he was young, and when everyone he loved was still alive.

Alexander learned how to name some of the trees of the Old World: the horse chestnuts with their fantastic floral displays in late spring; the ancient oak trees, guardians of his North European ancestral soul; the wild cherries in the woodlands with their mass of small white blossoms, and the lovely pink blossomed ornamental cherries in so many of the urban streets; the elegant elm trees (for they had not yet all died and become but a memory in Britain); the noble beech trees, which covered so much of southern England (and some of the Scottish Highland glens also) with a woodland that was cool and green and welcoming in the summer-time. To Alexander the yews in the English country churchyards seemed ancient as Time: twisted, gnarled, glowering; the most ancient of all the trees he might see about him, redolent of a time when they were associated with dark magic and power, before the light of Christ reached the British Isles. Alexander came to recognise hazel, ash and rowan and some of the less considered trees also.

Living in London taught Alexander something about great cities in the North European tradition. Until his first visit to England in 1976, he had never before seen a river as mighty as the Thames, as it flowed through London beneath fabled bridges and past ancient cityscapes. Alexander became acquainted with noble urban vistas; with monuments from an imperial past that seemed to him to shine with a deeper burnish than any artefacts from the present time. He learned to appreciate and value the Royal parks, London's green spaces, of which his favorite was Holland Park, with its lovely Japanese garden, and its orangery; with its precise flowerbeds, and its manicured hedges of box and privet, and its roses which would bloom even into November; with its ancient, thick-stemmed wisteria growing along the arcade, and its dense woodland to the north of the park.

Alexander found London's cosmopolitan culture tremendously stimulating. He often visited Covent Garden, where the old market had recently been cleaned and renovated, and small, quirky retail outlets traded. There was an old fashioned toy shop, and shops selling Victoriana and small antique *bric-à-brac* and collectibles. To reach Covent Garden Alexander would take the Tube to Leicester Square, then cross Charing Cross Road on foot, and St. Martin's Lane likewise, and walk past Rules (the famed game-foods restaurant), and so, crossing the Piazza (where in the summer-time, buskers, street musicians, and mime-artists would perform), he would reach the covered market. There were no coffee shop chains yet to be found in London, but in Covent Garden he could get the only really good coffee he knew of, at a tiny, Italian-owned coffee shop.

During his stay in London from early 1980 through to late 1981, Alexander drank at the Salisbury pub, not far from Trafalgar Square, with its nicotine-stained pressed metal ceilings; its decorative cut glass partitions, the glass beveled and etched with frosted decorations; with its gingerbread-carved woodwork; its massive polished bar-counters; its red plush chairs, its pretty gas lights and *torchères*. If Alexander arrived during the late morning, or at lunchtime, he would drink a pint of Guinness; if he visited in the evening, he would order a single (or sometimes, a double) Irish whiskey, with which to chase his Guinness. He enjoyed the atmosphere of camaraderie and good humour at the Salisbury; the scent of yeasty ales and pipe tobacco and cigarette smoke; the warm, cosy fug when it was cold and wet outside. In the back room, which was completely lined with mirrors (Alexander thought of it as the Narcissus Room), he was befriended by a group of men somewhat older than himself: educated, professional types, or theatre workers, musicians and artists. He enjoyed the conversation. He hardly appreciated that many of these men found him attractive and engaging: someone they looked forward to seeing.

During weekends, when Alexander was not away visiting family in the country, he explored London on foot, walking many miles. He climbed the narrow stairs inside Saint Paul's dome, between the brick-built weight-bearing inner cone and the skin of the outer dome, to the golden gallery just beneath the ball and lantern, with its panoramic views of London stretching away to the horizon, and a great sweep of the River visible, busy with pleasure boats, barges, scows and tug boats. He visited Westminster Abbey and the Tower of London. He explored the Science Museum in Kensington, with its wonderful collection of transport themed displays, which (like the National Gallery, another of his favorite destinations), he was to re-visit many times over many years. He took a riverboat to Greenwich and the Maritime Museum, or upriver to Richmond.

He grew to love London, and to appreciate the subtle differences in character between the series of villages which made up its boroughs: he came to know his way around parts of Camden (where the canal and lock and the houseboats lining the canal became a favorite destination), and much of Westminster also (with its monuments to *imperium* and might, and its magnificent Byzantine-style Catholic cathedral, with its towering campanile). He explored Kensington and Chelsea. There were no skyscrapers yet in London; there was no docklands development; there was no Canary Wharf. Saint Paul's Cathedral still towered above all other structures in the City.

During his 1976 visit, Alexander had learned how to hitchhike, burdened with a big backpack. That summer he had been tremendously excited by his first visit to the Continent, when, with a couple of friends, he had ventured into France and Northern Spain, with a backpack on his back. And later that summer he fell in love with the West Highlands of Scotland, a region to which he would one day, forty years later, return to live.

In London he had learned at last what he had failed properly to learn at school: how to become a social creature; how to chum up with other young people; how to make use of such kindnesses as came his way. He learned that people were often kind to the personable young; he came to see how the young themselves will so often approach their fellows with hearts wide open and spirits filled with amity; how the old will forgive the young trespasses that would go un-forgiven, and fester, in later years.

Alexander learned above all that most people liked him; he even began to suspect that he too was personable and charming: he had never guessed at this before.

Alexander had lost his virginity to Jacquie in 1979, the girl he had first met in the Café Wien, one of Alice's group. Jacquie was visiting him at his flat in Twist Street one evening, when the two began kissing as they sat side by side on the sofa. Alexander had initiated the exchange of intimacies more out of courtesy than through affection or lust, and it seemed quite natural when, after ten minutes of increasingly demonstrative kissing, Jacquie took his hand and led him towards his bed. Despite his fears that he was a monstrous aberration, Alexander had found he enjoyed the experience, and — perhaps because he was thoughtful and creative — he appeared to be good at it: good enough to repeat it again later that night, for Jacquie had indeed stayed the night. It was not until 1981, however, that he had his first same-sex encounter.

Alexander was browsing in a bookshop off Leicester Square, when he noticed a pleasant featured, auburn haired young man his own age observing him discreetly. As Alexander left the shop, this young man approached him and asked, in a Scottish Highlander's accent, for a light. Alexander, who had been smoking since 1979, flicked his Zippo and held it up to the young man's cigarette. The young man cupped Alexander's hand between his own to form a windbreak. Alexander experienced a stirring, a frisson of excitement, at this artfully casual physical contact.

How did a very young man with no experience of such encounters know immediately that this was a sexual proposition? For of this Alexander was certain. The two of them went back to the flat in Kennington, just south of the River, that Alexander then shared with a Church of England curate about four or five years his senior in age. There, the young man he brought home with him, who had wicked, flashing green eyes, wolfed down a plate of sandwiches, and then asked if he could take a bath. In later years, this sequence of events would become recognisable to Alexander: an itinerant young man, straight-looking and straight-acting, half starved, desiring food, a bath, and shelter for a night or two, would offer sex for money.

Alexander was to gain great pleasure and an education both, later that day, and during the night, and the next morning also, from this encounter. The young curate recognized Alexander's guest immediately for what he was, and, laughing, said "I did n't know you went for a bit of rough, Sandy."

Alexander was not familiar with that gay cant term. The young Scot later that next day asked for fifteen Pounds, supposedly to send to a sick mother in Elgin, and Alexander, despite having very little spare cash, gave it to him. Thereafter, the young wanderer left. Considerably the worse off financially, Alexander experienced the onset of shame and self loathing. Yet this encounter had aided him in breaking free – if only temporarily – of the restraints of his upbringing, and in coming to know himself better. On balance, despite his shame, he did not feel materially the loser in this encounter.

Seven

Town and Country

God would not let Alexander go. For the first three decades of his life, Alexander experienced this call primarily as an engagement with the Anglican church, although his paternal ancestry had been Catholic for centuries: the Macleans of Mull, in common with many other Highland and Island clans, had never been turned by the dour Calvinists of the Reformation. However, Alexander Senior's sons had been raised, if anything, as Anglicans, for his own father, Alexander's grandfather, had lapsed from the Catholic faith of his fathers as a young man, although he was later to join the Church of Scotland. Alexander favoured high church Anglican services: he was drawn to the Anglo-Catholic tradition; he thought the liturgy beautiful, and he was attracted to the theatre of the priests in their gorgeous vestments; to the strong, bitter-sweet scent of fuming incense as the acolyte or priest swung the censer back and forth; to the tinkling of the little bell at certain times during the eucharist. Anglican high church services were far more splendid, Alexander was later to find, than most Catholic celebrations of the mass. However, as a boy in 1972, during his final year at school, he was to attend mass at Saint Charles Catholic church in Victory Park, the nearest Catholic church to his home, walking the five miles there and back every Sunday morning, wearing a heavy, hot suit.

When the family returned to Cape Town in 1974, not long before Alexander's nineteenth birthday, he had joined the Anglican congregation of Christ Church in Constantia, in which suburb Alexander's family now lived. Christ Church was a lovely little church built of stone, with a lychgate, and a sparely decorated, simple interior, relying on its use of honest materials (dressed stone, and a roof supported by massive timbers of Cape yellow-wood darkened with age) for its beauty. The floor was of rosy old Cape clay tiles.

Alexander had been christened in an Anglican cathedral in East Africa: Anglicanism was not alien to him, for it had come to him through his mother's side of the family. He was confirmed by the Archbishop at Christ Church in 1974. Alexander's paternal grandfather, who was an elder of the Church of Scotland in Fish Hoek, gave him a fine and weighty Biblical concordance as a confirmation gift. His paternal grandmother had died in February 1974, having at last grown to know her eldest grandson well for the first time, over a stay of two weeks he had spent with his grandparents at their home in Kommetjie, halfway down the Peninsula on the shores of the Atlantic. Her gift to him (and to his brother also) had been a King James version Bible, which Alexander was to cherish all his life. It was to become a well-loved Bible, surviving several intercontinental moves, and more than a few periods of prolonged chaos in Alexander's life. In it, Alexander's handwritten annotations (begun when he lived at the Christian community in Cape Town, during twice-weekly Bible-study sessions), were rendered in handwriting so tiny that in later years he would need a magnifying glass to read them.

The Minister at Christ Church was Canon Michael, and it was he who had called Alexander back from his visit to Britain in 1976, having arranged for him to join the Christian community as a means of assessing whether or not he had a calling to the ministry. It was not in fact the serial horror-story being screened on British television every evening; the scenes of riot and murder in South Africa, which had caused Alexander to leave Oban: his departure had been arranged over a period of some time.

God bothered Alexander mightily. God had bothered Alexander most of his life. God did not bother Roy, his younger brother. Perhaps Alexander did indeed have a calling to the Christian ministry: not the one he had always imagined, as an ordained minister, but a wider, more worldly calling, and many years later, Alexander would strive to practice that calling, in much of what he wrote for the public to read, and in the manner in which he tried to live his life. But Alexander, coming to manhood, was a poor witness to Christ, for he was far too immature, and he was un-tested as yet. He was an even worse witness through his thirties and forties, for at times during those years his life was a mockery of Christian values.

During Alexander's first visit to England, in 1976, he had been a member of an Anglo-Catholic Anglican congregation in Queens Gate, South Kensington. Saint Augustine's had been designed by a well-known Victorian ecclesiastical architect, William Butterfield, and was built of pale yellow brick, darkened by the filth, until quite recently, from London's coal fires, and banded and patterned with red brick and stone. The interior was decorated throughout with polychromatic images composed of painted tiles, illustrating the Stations of the Cross and Biblical scenes, in a high Victorian neo-romantic style, and there was a Lady Chapel with a carved and gilded image of Our Lady in splendor decorated in gold leaf. Saint Augustine's was more gloriously Catholic than many Catholic churches were.

Alexander came to know this church because he lived in a house whose owner was a Church of England curate attached to the church – the first of two curates he was to share a home with in London. Alexander did not like the man very much: he thought him effeminate, and he had a sometimes sharp and cutting tongue in him. But Alexander tolerated him (and the curate, in his favor, put up with a young man who had no sense of shared domestic obligations at all). It was a comfortable and convenient house-share in a good part of London, with a small park directly in front of the house.

The other young housemate was a boy Alexander's own age with a bright, outgoing personality who was originally from Cumbria, but who had been schooled at one of the great public schools in the south. The two young men, the ex-public school boy and the young man from the colonies, got on well together, and they would go out together some evenings, and occasionally during the day also at weekends if Alexander was not away visiting family in the country. They went to the cinema together, and visited pubs in the West End. How the tickets were obtained, Alexander was unable to remember in later years, but he and the Cumbrian lad were able to see Rudolf Nureyev dance in a production of Tchaikowski's "Sleeping Beauty" at the Coliseum in St. Martin's Lane. Alexander was no great fan of ballet, though he had been to a few ballet performances at the Nico Malan theatre in Cape Town, but that splendid theatre, and the magnificent production, starring the world's greatest male ballet dancer, were something to have experienced.

It was during the early eighties that Alexander went to live with the second of the Anglican curates he was to house-share with. This young priest was attached to a church in the south London borough of Kennington, near the border with Vauxhall. At night, Alexander would wake sometimes to hear the reassuring chimes of Big Ben across the River, which was not far away.

Alexander's parents made a trip to England in the summer of 1980, to visit family members in the country, but they did spend some days traveling up to London from Berkshire to see their son. Alexander knew the West End well: he loved London, and he was proud and happy to show off his favourite London sights to his parents. During those few days, Alexander's father bought him a Raleigh bicycle with a Sturmey-Archer three-speed gear box.

Alexander took to cycling all over the West End, and he was able to leave his bike outside any number of destinations, chained to metal railings or perhaps to a drainpipe or a lamp-post. The young curate with whom he shared the big flat near the church in Kennington, once took him to lunch at the Reform Club in the West End, where they were joined by two or three more Church of England clerics. Alexander chose to cycle there. On arrival, Alexander chained his bike to the decorative iron railings fronting the building, and tipped the impressively attired doorman one Pound as he entered.

Sometimes Alexander took his bicycle with him when he went to visit relations in the country, storing it in the guard's van at the rear of the train before it pulled out from Paddington station. On arrival at Kingham, a tiny country station, Alexander would leap from the carriage and run for the guard's van, to retrieve his bike before the train began to pull out again. Then he would spend at least one whole day during his weekend visit cycling the neighbouring countryside. The Cotswolds, with their narrow lanes and hilly country with ever-changing vistas, may have been a challenge for Alexander on the up-hills, but they were scenically very gratifying, and the down-hill runs were fun. There were then few cars in those country lanes in the Cotswolds. Slow-moving tractors hauling slurry tanks in the spring, or haywains in the late summer, were more common.

During 1981 Catherine, the English girl Alexander had met aboard the ship to Cape Town in 1976, contacted him. She had been visiting family in England, and she was in London briefly, *en route* for Australia, and so the two friends arranged to meet. When Alexander saw Catherine he was surprised at how happy it made him to see her again. 1976 and 1977 felt so long ago. Catherine looked unchanged, as attractive as ever, with the same sweet smile. "You have n't changed at all, Sandy!" she exclaimed.

"Nor have you."

They had not much time together. Catherine was flying from Heathrow later that day, so they went to a wine bar in Villiers Street near Charing Cross station and caught up with each other's lives over a couple of glasses of wine in a cellar with a stone vaulted roof, which was located beneath street level, with candles guttering on the tables.

"I spent a couple of years in Sidney," Catherine told him. "But you know that. Perhaps you don't know – I met someone. He's an organist at Sidney Cathedral, and we're getting married."

Alexander felt gladness for his friend, and a small and quickly passing pang of loss also. He leant across the table and took Catherine's hand and kissed her on the cheek. "Congratulations."

Alexander accompanied Catherine by Tube to Paddington station, where she had left her luggage. She was taking the train to Heathrow from here. After he had seen her off, he felt a little lost for some time. It seemed to him that with his friend's departure for Australia, a line had been well and truly drawn under the happiest days of his life, and such times would never again return. Alexander was wrong. He was to know happiness again.

Alexander had two spinster great aunts living in London. These were his maternal grandmother's sisters. One, who still contributed articles for magazines, and was a sociable, gregarious old lady, lived in a tiny cottage near the River in Richmond. Despite Alexander only having visited her three or four times in total between 1976 and late 1981, she had acquired a great fondness for him. The other, older sister, who was more withdrawn and artistic, lived a retiring, private life in a very pleasant flat with a tiny balcony in Saint John's Wood, on the north side of London. Alexander visited her a little more frequently, if only because he found it easier to reach Saint John's Wood than to reach Richmond. Like his grandmother, the old lady had grown up in France. She was a painter, like her father, Alexander's great-grandfather, and she had managed to acquire many more of her father's works than had his grandmother or his mother. Her flat was filled with family oil paintings.

Alexander's maternal grandmother was now living at an old age home for distressed gentlefolk in Wimbledon, opposite the Common. The residents had to have suffered some financial miscalculation or upset, to have gained residency in this very comfortable retirement home, at only a minimal charge. During 1980 through to late 1981, and again in 1988 (when Alexander was once more living in England), he paid his grandmother an occasional visit. He loved her very much. She had managed to hang onto a few of her fine old pieces of furniture and *bric-à-brac*, and some of her father's oil paintings, so her room was full of character and familiar things: it had a large, south facing window, and was flooded with sunshine in the summer. Alexander's grandmother was beginning to suffer from dementia by 1988 (she was over ninety by then), so when they played chess together in her room, over cups of tea and some cake or biscuits the old lady had laid in, Alexander allowed her occasional cheating to go unchallenged.

Once in a while Alexander would hire a car and fetch his grandmother at the home and take her for a drive with some particular destination in mind. She enjoyed long drives; she particularly enjoyed it when the driver got them lost. September 1988 was the last time Alexander took his grandmother on such an outing. He did not know that he would be seeing her only one more time. He took her to Hampton Court Palace, a vast, imposing Tudor residence beside the Thames, built around a number of courtyards in the early 16th century by the mighty Cardinal Wolsey, Henry VIII's Chancellor; a palace given by Wolsey to the King in a fruitless attempt to stave off the King's displeasure with him, a displeasure which culminated in Wolsey's eventual fall from grace in 1529.

Alexander's grandmother was by now very frail, a tiny, shrunken figure not even five feet tall. She clung to her eldest grandchild's arm as they walked beside the River. The sky was grey and overcast, and a cold wind was blowing across the waters of the Thames. They did not walk far before Alexander felt that his grandmother needed to sit down, so he led her to the Tilting Yard, where there was a café where they could sit indoors and drink tea. Alexander was always hungry, so he ordered some cake for himself. By late October of that year, Alexander had returned to South Africa, and his grandmother died just over a year later. She had been alive when Wilbur and Orville Wright made the world's first powered, heavier than air flight in their fragile machine; she had traveled in a Jumbo jet on her last visit to her daughter's family in Africa.

Eight

University, and Growing Up

The young man of those times was still many years away from growing angry and despairing. Too few promises had yet been broken – either by Man, or by God; too few treacheries had yet been experienced; too little pain had yet been suffered; too few battles had yet been terribly lost; too few hopes had yet been betrayed; too few friends had been lost forever; too few people had rejected the love he had offered them. Alexander had not yet suffered enough cruelties, to become despairing . Oh, that young man was still such an innocent!

No wonder that his skin remained, for now, smooth; that his hair remained, for now, thick and shining like bright gold; no wonder that each morning he could still awake to find his energies renewed, his hopes rekindled. The God of broken promises and hopes foresworn whom he would one day come to know, had so far revealed Himself only briefly. He was yet to permit the young man to know the exhaustion of striving to cling to hope when the pursuit of that elusive and fickle blessing has been too many times proven to be a fool's endeavour. A full accession of wisdom was years away yet from Alexander, and so he lived those years in hope.

But if his inner eye had been as wide open as it was eventually to become, then, even as early as the first three months of 1977, Alexander might have been able to apprehend that which his spirit already knew: namely, that he had a doom upon him. Within just a few short months of the start of his friendship with Patrick, who lived in the big house up on the hill, Alexander began to bring a half jack of whiskey back to the Slave quarters twice a week, bought from a liquor outlet on Main Street, and sip at it secretly, privately, alone in his room in the evenings. A wise man would have recognised that Alexander's spirit was sick already with the foretaste of despair. But the young man of 1977 was not old enough to know these things, and he could not recognise them when they had already begun to hint of their presence.

So Alexander sipped and he sipped, in his self imposed solitary state in his room in the evenings, and he felt himself to be guilty of some terrible secret sin (no – the drinking was not in itself that sin: even then, he knew that much), and he withdrew by degrees from engagement with the community, and from that time onwards, even without Nathaniel's intervention, it became inevitable that he would have to go away.

Alexander did not spend all the years between 1977 and 1988 living in England. February 1982 saw him return to university in Johannesburg to continue studying for his undergraduate's degree. Peter, a civil servant, one of Alexander's acquaintances at the Salisbury pub in London, had said to him sometime in 1981 "You have a good brain, but it seems to me that you're wasting it. Go back to university."

Others of Alexander's acquaintances as he sat and drank with them in the evenings, in that room of many mirrors at the back of the pub, agreed with Peter. The curate with whom he shared the comfortable flat within sound of Big Ben had said much the same thing, worried by Alexander's lack of direction. And so, Alexander had written first to his university, and then to his parents, and plans for his return were made.

The university credited Alexander with his first year passes from 1973, the year following his matriculation from high school. With these passes credited to him, Alexander had been granted permission to proceed to his second year studies. In South Africa the academic year followed the calendar year, so in February 1982 Alexander began his second year at university. He was just short of his twenty-seventh birthday.

During his first year studies, nine years earlier, Alexander had still been immature even for his admittedly very young age, and he had remained as solitary an individual as he had been for much of his time at high school. During his first year at university, Alexander had not yet learned how to make friends. By the end of that year Alexander understood, if only subconsciously, that he still needed to do a lot of growing up, and so it was that the years 1974 and 1975 saw him working full time, first as a trainee manager, then (aged only nineteen) as a department manager and buyer for a big retail concern in Cape Town, to save the money he needed to pay for his first visit to Britain since childhood.

He couldn't have made a wiser decision: the nine months he spent in England and Scotland in 1976 (together with his journey through France in an ancient Mercedes-Benz bus, and his stay in Pamplona in Navarre with a couple of friends in July that year) were the catalyst he needed to break free from his shy, solitary ways, and allow another, far more confident, far more sociable side of his personality to develop. The year 1976 remained through all the decades that were to follow as one of the happiest, most thoroughly positive years of Alexander's life.

So Alexander quit London in December 1981, returning to university in Johannesburg in early 1982, and before the first term was over, he had acquired a circle of acquaintances, along with two or three genuine friends. One of these, a Jewish lad his own age, who intended studying law after he graduated, lived not far from Alexander's family home, in an adjacent suburb known as the "gilded ghetto". Filled with wealthy Jewish families living in large houses, there was also a King David high school in the suburb, where the sons and daughters of well-off Jewish parents went to school.

Like about ninety percent of Jewish people in South Africa, Warren's family was originally of Lithuanian extraction. He was not physically prepossessing, but he had a daunting intellectual capacity that Alexander admired. The two had first become aware of each other during Philosophy tutorials, and over coffee and a shared meal in the Students' Union afterwards they found that they shared many of the same intellectual interests. Alexander felt that Warren was altogether more worldly-wise than himself, despite Alexander's years abroad and his travels. Warren was, he thought, better equipped for making a success of his life than he was. Was this perhaps because, as a Jew, Warren had an inbred capacity for accommodating himself to the world as it was, a capacity that Alexander's family, secure in their dominant faith and in their place in western society, had never had to learn? When during the winter month of August Warren invited Alexander down to a small and exclusive country hotel – an expensive and secluded retreat in the Transvaal Drakensberg of the Eastern Transvaal – for the weekend, Alexander was struck by his friend's ease and confidence in an environment of moneyed wellbeing that seemed to him to be rather more adult than his own near play-acting in such surroundings. Alexander intuited that perhaps Warren felt an element of homo-erotic attraction to him: this knowledge caused Alexander no particular discomfort, though he did not reciprocate the sentiment.

Alexander had also formed a friendship with a student ten years his junior. He had first spotted his shining head at a table in the main library, books strewn around him, bent in study of a large open volume. Alexander had stared, and then the owner of that head of shining copper-coloured hair had looked up, and the two had held each other's eye for a long moment. Alexander had immediately recognised that this beautiful young man was going to play a significant role in his life. A short while later, Alexander had bumped into a friend on campus, and the friend was chatting with the owner of that shining head. Alexander stopped and greeted his friend. The young man with the shining hair had smiled at Alexander, and said "I see we have another Bowie fan in our midst."

Alexander was wearing his military surplus greatcoat that day (it was a Highveld winter's day) and on the left lapel of the greatcoat he had pinned a small enamel David Bowie badge.

"Gregory," Alexander's friend had said, "meet Sandy. Sandy – Gregory."

Aged just seventeen, Gregory was a prodigy both of physical beauty and intellectual prowess. A product of an expensive boys' school in Johannesburg, with a comfortable access of family wealth behind him, he was another of those floppy-haired boys with money, brains, beauty, and flawless complexions who were to feature in Alexander's life. Through them, Alexander was able to experience a vicarious joy. Through them, Alexander inevitably came to know an increase of despair.

For one and a half years, Gregory and Alexander were often together, on and off campus. Many mornings, Alexander would give Gregory (who was still too young at first to have applied for a driver's licence) a lift to university in his big American car. They would listen to music tape cassettes on the car's tape player as they drove. One of the compositions to which Gregory introduced Alexander one morning as they drove to university was Allegri's "*Miserere Mei, Domine*" (a setting of Psalm 51, "Have mercy upon me, Oh God, according to thy loving kindness..." probably composed during the 1630s for Pope Urban VIII). This remained throughout his life one of Alexander's favourite compositions, which he was to listen to often, first on tape, then in later years on CD.

Round one o'clock, Gregory and Alexander would join the group of friends (which often included Warren) who met for lunch in the Students' Union. They went to see movies together some evenings; they hung out together many afternoons at a record bar-come-coffee shop which friends of Alexander ran in Yeoville, a part of town that was popular and trendy among the young. Alexander introduced Gregory to his usual running course, a distance of about four miles through a big park and nature conservation area in the northern suburbs, not far from Alexander's family home. Alexander took Gregory hiking in the rugged, wild Magaliesberg, one and a half hours' drive from the city.

Gregory in return introduced Alexander to the gym on campus, and taught him a regime of exercises designed to build up his body. (For, like not a few excessively beautiful boys, Gregory sought to compensate for his prettiness by building up his physique: he had a fine body, many years away yet from that descent to muscle-bound seediness that is the destination of so many body-builders). Alexander worked out twice a week at the gym for the remainder of his years at university. He continued to run also, and he joined the university fencing club.

In 1979, while he had been working for Manfred the private eye, Alexander had fenced at a sporting and country-club, the Wanderers, of which he had become a member, in Johannesburg's northern suburbs. One of the older members had been a South African national fencing champion when he was younger, and he provided Alexander with training, at first in foil, later in sabre. Alexander thoroughly enjoyed these training sessions, together with the friendly bouts with other, more advanced members of the club. The subtlety and cunning, speed and grace of this one-on-one sport appealed to him, as compulsory participation in team-sports at school never had. At university, Alexander further increased his circle of friends from within the university fencing club.

During these years at university, Alexander, who had achieved no sporting renown at school, and whose only exercise then had been tennis, occasional cross-country, and the long walks he took to satisfy his own desire for solitude, became very fit indeed. He was growing year by year into his looks, too: instead of looking like a tall, skinny, awkward boy, he had grown into rather a striking young man – the Thin White Duke of his David Bowie badge, indeed. His physique filled out a little more; his shoulders broadened; his features lost some of their childish smoothness and acquired something of a man's angularity. He knew he looked good. During those years he was very conscious that his appearance worked for him, and this, along with the sense of physical well-being that his fitness gave him, further enhanced his self confidence. He took to walking with a slight swagger. Intellectually more than competent, deriving much pleasure from his course studies, fit and healthy, very much aware of his good looks, rather charming when he set his mind to it, and with an active social life, Alexander acquired a somewhat arrogant outlook.

There were girls too who were now drawn to him. Although he did not have a regular girlfriend during his university years, he enjoyed friendships with several girls in his classes, and one of those friendships became, very briefly, a physical one. Alexander knew however that in this, he was fulfilling an expectation rather than following the desires of his own heart. No girl (or anyone else) truly broke his heart during his student years.

Reading, both fiction and non-fiction, had become – as it had been when he was a child and a teenager – very important to Alexander again. There were the dozens upon dozens of books he read for his course work, as well as non-fiction which covered his own particular interests: shipping, maritime design and engineering, architecture, and the sort of historical and cultural reference works on subjects that were not covered in his history and classics lectures at university (Chinese and Japanese culture and art, as well as Man's pre-history, had begun to interest Alexander especially) and he always had a novel close to hand. Alexander had learned to seek solace in reading as a child, when he was laid up in bed periodically with asthma or illness. Books had mattered very much to him, but for some years he had neglected his reading, and now – even though he lived his life to the full – books mattered once again.

Alexander's friendship with Gregory was not good for him: it hurt him too much. It could not be sustained in the long term. In this, it contrasted markedly with his friendship with Warren. Alexander developed what verged on being an infatuation with Gregory: there could be no happy outcome to such a relationship. One day, with almost no hope of reciprocation, but succumbing to the strain of sustaining what he hoped might still be a secret, he said to Gregory "Perhaps what I'm going to say wont surprise you: I'm in love with you, Gregory."

"I thought you might be," Gregory replied. Perhaps he had been accustomed at school to such declarations coming his way.

However, the not-a-secret being now out in the open, Gregory began to avoid Alexander. By the end of 1983, they no longer met together on campus, or went out together, and Gregory was making very obvious around the campus the fact that he had a girlfriend – really, rather a nice girl, Alexander thought.

During 1984, his honours year, Alexander took to visiting the sports bar at the bottom of campus during the lunch period, where (remembering the Salisbury pub in London, and the Guinness beers he used to drink there) he would drink one or two bottles of Castle milk stout, the nearest equivalent in South Africa to Guinness. In this solitary drinking (for the sports bar was hardly frequented at all during the lunch hour), Alexander was continuing the secretive habit he had fallen into at the Christian community in Cape Town, where he had sipped at whiskey alone in his room in the evenings. This was secretive drinking too: he mentioned it to no one; he invited none of his acquaintances to join him. There were warning signs here that a hardened toper of many years' standing would have recognised.

Additionally, Alexander discovered during that time that he could get a buzz from a certain over the counter painkiller in tablet form, although the medication also made him feel somewhat spaced out. But by the end of his honours year, Alexander was resorting frequently to this horrible medication: he wrote his dissertation while under its influence. Many years later, Alexander was to understand that the young man of those years was not after all as happy as he later remembered him to have been. In growing up, Alexander was experiencing a slow accretion of the anguish and despair that had first whispered of its presence as long ago as early 1977 in Cape Town.

Nine

Going Sailing

God had not ceased to bother Alexander during his years at university. But gratitude, and sometimes joy, though present, were not the foundations of Alexander's relationship with God (sincere gratitude was to come in later years, but he was never fully to comprehend what Christians meant when they spoke about the joy in Christ). It was guilt, remorse, self loathing, and a deep yearning for deliverance from his sexuality, which bound Alexander to God. The tensions Alexander had first begun to feel between what the Christian church taught, and what he felt about himself – the mismatch between the man his Christian faith expected him to be, and the man God had seemingly made him to be – became ever more clearly defined as Alexander grew older. He had no way of resolving these tensions: his sole resort was to crush whom he truly was, and express only what he thought he ought to be. He was storing up an enormous legacy of tension and self-loathing, which would eventually explode into catastrophically self destructive behaviour.

During his time at university, Alexander had been attending mass frequently, though irregularly, at Saint Charles in Victory Park, known locally as the Lemon Squeezer. This was the Catholic church he had first come to know as a seventeen year old while still at school. However, he was unable to go forward to the altar rail during communion, for he had not yet been received into the Catholic faith. It was entirely coincidental that the Roman Catholic university chaplain of that period, a Jesuit priest, was a distant relation, some sort of cousin several times removed, perhaps fifteen to twenty years Alexander's senior. As a teenager, Alexander had met him once or twice at family gatherings, and now he made his acquaintance once again.

In March 1984, during his honours year, after three months' preparation, Alexander was received into the Roman Catholic church. He believed this was a logical move to make, and his sense of history told him that in so doing, he was merely returning to the church that every one of his ancestors had, before the mid sixteenth century, been a member of – and his paternal ancestors much more recently than that.

Alexander had a plan. Long before he was received into the Church, he knew that he wished to become a religious: a member of a religious order in the Catholic church. He had in mind the Franciscans. However, he did not immediately follow up on this goal on obtaining his honours degree in late 1984. He needed to build some credibility as a Catholic first; he needed a record of parish membership behind him.

At about this time, the last of Alexander's spinster great aunts in England died. Alexander had only visited her a few times at her home in Richmond, but the old lady had taken a liking to him. She found his interest in her pre-Great War childhood in France, and in her flapper's life in London, gratifying: she could talk and talk, and Alexander never appeared to grow bored. She had once been a contributor to *The Lady*, that doyenne of magazines for butlers and children's nannies seeking a position, and for ladies of a somewhat conservative outlook looking for advice on domestic economy, on dealing with servants, and on matronly fashion. This old lady left Alexander four thousand five hundred Pounds in her will, a sum which translated at that time as about thirteen thousand five hundred Rands. Alexander had a good idea of what he hoped to do with this windfall: he wished to buy a small sailboat.

Having finished with his university studies, Alexander returned to Cape Town in early 1985, where he arranged to board with his aunt and uncle's family on his grandfather's farm positioned mid-way between Fish Hoek and Kommetjie, half way down the Cape Peninsula. Alexander's grandfather had bought the farm in 1974, after the death of Alexander's grandmother. Alexander regarded the farm as his real home. No matter where his own family was located, the farm, with his grandfather (until his death in January 1987), his aunt and uncle, his two younger girl-cousins, along with various young visiting family friends staying for indefinite periods, was a fixed and beloved star in Alexander's universe.

His grandfather had bought just under one hundred acres of land, most of it gone to scrub, wattle and Port Jackson willow, with some patches of *fynbos*, but there were several acres cultivated with maize, and there was a large kitchen garden. The land was worked by a couple of coloured labourers (who, with their families, lived in shacks behind the farmhouse). Another three acres comprised paddocks bounded by creosoted split rail fencing, with stabling for four horses, a feed and tack room, and a byre for the cow. There was also a big chicken run, fenced in and protected by a close-meshed fence and roof against civet cats and mongooses, with enclosed chicken coops at one end, and there was a smaller covered run with several coops for the half dozen geese. During the day the chickens and geese had free run of the farmyard.

A dairy cow was always kept at the farm. There were half a dozen dogs (sometimes more), and upwards of thirty cats, of whom perhaps a dozen lived in and around the farmhouse itself, the others tending to den in the cow byre and the stables range. When people in the district found an injured or stray cat, they would bring it to Alexander's aunt at the farm. She had a gift for nursing sick animals back to health, and she would never turn away any animal, particularly a cat, in need of help and a home.

The farmhouse, which was set back from the Fish Hoek – Kommetjie road by a distance of about three hundred yards, and was approached via a single-track sandy drive between pines, eucalyptus trees, and ten year old podocarpus (yellowwood) trees, was marked on the government survey maps of the district. The house dated back to the 1850s. It was not very large: it had 3 bedrooms, a lounge, a dining room, a bathroom, and a kitchen with a larder and a pantry – but it also had a deep, covered, full length *stoep* (verandah) along the front of the house, one end of which had been glassed in above the solid waist-high balustrade, creating a small fourth bedroom, which is where Alexander slept. There were also two large wooden cabins in the grounds, where young friends of the family lodged during their sometimes extensive stays.

On the eastern side of the farmhouse, acting as a windbreak against the prevailing south-easterly winds, was a double row of very tall, ancient Scots pines. At night, Alexander could hear the wind soughing in the pine trees, and the muted roar of the Atlantic breakers on Long Beach near Kommetjie.

Alexander had always been happy here. It was impossible to feel lonely at the farm. He was swept up in the family's love, and he was on amiable terms with the young family friends who stayed in the wooden cabins and ate with the family in the evenings. One of these was a lad named Michael – Mike to most – who rode Alexander's aunt's horses like a Red Indian. He rode the way Alexander wished he could ride. His skin was very brown, and he had fine dark eyebrows, and chestnut hair reaching to his shoulders, and he often rode bare-back and barefoot, his long legs dangling straight either side. When he rode, he seemed to become one creature – centaur-like – with the horse. He was in a relationship of a year's standing with Mary, one of Alexander's young cousins. He and Alexander got along very well.

Mike, like Alexander, had a streak of melancholy in him, and like Alexander, he sometimes felt an urgent need to seek solitude. However, these two young men, the one dark, the other fair, and so similar in many ways, would sometimes go out riding together during the morning, when the cousins were away at university in Cape Town, crossing the Fish Hoek – Kommetjie road, then riding through the scrubland beyond, skirting the marshes and quick-sands (the location of which they both knew well), until they reached Long Beach, a three mile long strand of glistening pure white shell sand, on which the great Atlantic rollers crashed after a storm, and which stretched in a long shallow curve from near the tiny village of Kommetjie, all the way to Noordhoek mountain. There was no urban development then anyway near the beach. The two of them would canter and gallop the entire distance along the damp sand at the edge of the water-line, occasional sprays of water being flung up, sparkling and iridescent, by the horses' hooves. They would make a more leisurely return ride, then, if it was summer time and the sun was hot, they would unsaddle their horses and watch with pleasure as the animals flung themselves into the shallows and rolled on their backs, kicking their hooves in the air. Afterwards Mike would smoke a cigarette with Alexander, lying back against the dunes, the saddle-blankets spread in the sun and the horses' reins held in one hand. Back at the farm they would take care to curry-comb the horses thoroughly, to get the salt and sweat out of their coats and skin. These rides helped cement a closeness between the two young men which needed no great amount of conversation to sustain. Alexander was happy then.

Alexander had introduced himself to the priest at Saint John the Evangelist, the Catholic church in Fish Hoek. He began going to the 9.30 morning mass on Sundays. Later, once he had bought a small sailboat and become a member of the False Bay Yacht Club, he would most usually attend the Saturday-for-Sunday mass at 5.30 p.m. on a Saturday afternoon.

His aunt, who knew so many people in and around Fish Hoek (and in Cape Town too), introduced Alexander to an acquaintance of hers, Charles, who was a yachtsman and a member of the False Bay Yacht Club. Alexander met him one early evening at the club bar. The False Bay Yacht Club is located on Simon Town's harbor. There is a lawn in front of the club house, with tables where members and their guests can sit in the sun and bring their own food if they wish. Charles (who was in his forties and lived above Simons Town) and Alexander brought their lager beers out to a table on the lawn. "I know of a Hunter Europa for sale," Charles told Alexander, after the latter had explained to him that he hoped to buy a small sail boat priced at no more than eleven thousand Rands. "If you were to buy it, I would be happy to put you forward for club membership: they're a popular class."

Alexander had been looking at the sailing and yachting magazines during the last few months. He recognised the name. "She's a nineteen-footer, is n't she?" he asked.

"Ja – fin keel, six-foot beam, one and a half thousand pounds displacement. They're a development of a day-sailer, but with the cabin, the Europa has two bunks below, and a fair whack of stowage space."

Where is she moored?" Alexander asked.

"Here," Charles replied, "I think if you bought her, you would be able to keep the mooring."

The two of them walked across to the wooden mooring jetties and Charles pointed the boat out to Alexander. It was a pretty little vessel. They returned to the club house and bought another beer each and sat drinking on the covered deck upstairs and talked about the boat some more. By the time they parted, it was dark, the sky full of stars. Charles had told Alexander he would talk to his fellow member (who was selling the Hunter Europa because he was moving to Johannesburg), and give the man Alexander's aunt's phone number.

Before the end of the week, Alexander had met the man, been for a short sail with him in the Hunter, and bought her for eleven thousand five hundred Rands. She came with an inflatable tender, a four-stroke five horse-power outboard, a full suite of sails (including two genoas and a spinnaker and a spinnaker pole), and charts of False Bay and the Peninsula down to Cape Point and up the Atlantic coast the other side as far as Table Bay and Cape Town. The bunks were equipped with foam mattresses, and there was a chemical potty below. In addition, Alexander found himself the owner of various nautical *bric-à-brac*. Alexander knew he was getting a bargain, especially with the charts thrown in. He gathered that the ex-owner's wife had never enjoyed sailing, and that the man doubted he would ever go sailing again. Charles had spoken to the club secretary, whom Alexander met that weekend, and by the end of February 1985, Alexander had become a member of the False Bay Yacht

Club. His bank account had only a couple of thousand Rands left in it by the time he had paid his membership and mooring fees. He would have to find at least some sort of part-time job.

He went for his first proper sail in the Hunter that Sunday, pretty much crewing for Charles, although it was his own boat (she was named "Synchronicity"). They met at the club at about ten in the morning, although it was almost eleven before they cast off. They sailed up the coast of the Peninsula, half a mile or so offshore, on a broad reach, looking into Fish Hoek bay, then continued the short distance to Kalk Bay. They did not enter the harbour, which was a commercial fishing harbour, but set a new course, this time on a close reach, as far as Seal Island, which they circled (though keeping a very wary distance), to give Alexander a feel of tacking a few times in succession. Then another long, broad reach, and so back to Simons Town, making their mooring by about quarter past four. Throughout the sail, the south-easter blew at between twenty-seven to thirty knots. Whitecaps whipped from the agitated surface of the sea, and periodically, cold spray flew back from the bows and slapped him in the face. Alexander's sleeveless padded top and his shorts were soon wet. But the sun burned bright and hot, and he did not become soaked through. Alexander could hardly imagine when it might be safe to employ the genoa, let alone the spinnaker. He mentioned his concerns to Charles. "During autumn and winter you'll find we have occasional days of perfect weather – sunny, with light winds: that's when we tend to use the jenny most," Charles told him.

Charles had advised Alexander to bring, despite the hot sun, a sleeveless padded jacket (which he borrowed from Hannes, one of the young live-in guests at the farm) and a beanie with him against the wind-chill. Alexander was glad of Charles' advice, as he was also glad of a litre bottle of water he had brought with him. The combination of burning sun (it was high summer in those latitudes), wind, and ocean-glare, had dehydrated him. He felt somewhat burned out, but deeply content, by the time they reached the mooring jetty, and he hugely appreciated the first of two ice-cold lagers on the club house deck, with a stacked plate of ham and cheese sandwiches to fill the emptiness in his middle. "You'll probably want a sailing partner," Charles suggested. "If you introduce yourself to a few of the lads some evening, I expect you'll find someone who would crew for you."

"OK . . ." Alexander replied, but he was not at all sure he would be wanting a sailing partner. None the less, Alexander soon got into the habit of having a few beers at the club bar twice a week, and so he came to meet some other young people. One or two young men sailed only Hobie Cats. Others crewed for other yacht owners. But one of the young men, a cheerful, dark haired young fellow named Roger, told Alexander he could crew for him sometimes if he wanted.

Alexander had already been for a couple of long sails solo before meeting Roger. He found that sailing – like walking, or riding – was an activity that you could pursue alone, without feeling lonely. The fact was, Alexander felt supremely content out on the water in his small boat. Time ceased to have any meaning: there was no sense of its passing. He lived in an extended present that was at times almost sublime, his mind empty of troubling thoughts, the boat requiring subtle handling and coaxing, a living thing, needful of the empathetic bond he felt for her. Sailing a small boat and riding a horse, Alexander thought, called for much the same attributes and condition of mind.

He had copied an idea he had seen on several other small yachts, a length of shock cord doubled round the tiller, and led to either beam and back again via cleats. This would hold the tiller where Alexander set it, and he could go below, to use the chemical potty, or he could handle the sails, without needing to be anxious about not having a hand on the tiller at all times.

Alexander's new friend from the yacht club, Roger, worked three evenings a week at the Brass Bell, a popular pub and restaurant squeezed between the railway and the rocky shoreline at Kalk Bay, not far along the coast from Fish Hoek. He told Alexander that there was a barman's position coming vacant in a week or two. In the early afternoon a day or two later, Alexander visited the Brass Bell, where he spoke with the manager. Aged twenty-one, he had worked behind the bar at the hotel in Oban some evenings, in addition to his usual duties waiting at tables.

As he spoke with the manager, he was only partially conscious of the considerable charm he was exhibiting, a skill he could exercise with hardly any effort when he was trying to win someone's good opinion. Alexander began work Tuesday week, at 6 p.m. He would work four shifts a week, and on this, he calculated, he would be able to give his aunt something towards rent, cover his few outgoings (one of which was the AMC Rambler Hornet, which his parents had kept safe for him when he was living in London), and still put a little money by each month.

Ten

Frances and the Brass Bell

The Brass Bell – or the Bell, as it was popularly known – attracted a young crowd at the bar. After a while, Alexander began to form the usual casual relationships with many of the young clientele (the majority of whom saw him merely as the amiable barman, and, having paid for their drinks, walked away to join their friends at their tables), but with two or three solitary drinkers, he formed slightly less superficial relationships, for they wanted to chat with him. Alexander was good at this: the customers liked him well enough, and some of the older customers would tip him, or offer to buy him a drink. He accepted the tips gratefully, which went into the staff tips jar, however he kept his drinking for the two or three evenings a week he would visit the FBYC bar at Simons Town.

Alexander formed somewhat closer friendships with some of the staff. He did not see much of his sailing friend, Roger, at work, for their shifts did not often coincide, but two nights a week a student at Cape

Town University would work a shift with Alexander at the bar. He got on well with this youngster, who was eight or nine years younger than himself, and was majoring in Romance languages. The kid laughed at Alexander's stumbling French, but it was not mocking laughter, and Alexander grinned back ruefully. "*Parbleu!*" he declared, "*Nom d'une plume!*"

This youngster, Andrew, lived with his parents in Fish Hoek. Alexander invited him to come sailing or riding with him some time, and during the next few months, Andrew crewed for Alexander in Synchronicity three or four times, and joined him on a ride twice. As for Alexander, the old syndrome began to show itself again: he felt himself growing too fond of this personable young man, and he knew there was no prospect of happiness for him down that road.

There was a waitress at the Bell who was very clearly drawn to Alexander. She was older than most of the waiting staff, possibly around Alexander's own age of thirty. She was attractive, fairly slim, with short brown hair and a pleasant smile, and she appeared to have no relationship entanglements. There was, Alexander could see, a shadow of some deep hurt in her eyes. "Where do you live, Sandy?" she asked him one evening as she fetched a bar order.

"On my grandfather's farm, between Fish Hoek and Kommetjie," he replied. "With my aunt's family. What about you, Frances?"

"I've got a cottage at St. James," she answered. "Do you keep horses on your farm?"

"Yeah – my aunt has four horses. Do you ride?"

"When I can," she replied. "I better get these drinks to my table – see ya later."

Alexander had already sailed solo across the wide False Bay to Gordon's Bay and back, but it was only when Andrew was crewing for him one weekend in late March that he tied his boat up at the Gordon's Bay Yacht Club jetty, and (with reciprocal club membership applying) the two of them visited the club's restaurant for lunch. From Simons Town to Gordon's Bay on the far side of False Bay was a close reach sail all the way, the Hunter's best point of sailing, with barely a correction of the sails or the tiller until Gordon's Bay was gained. The return sail was just as easy: a broad reach all the way home again on the opposite tack.

Alexander took pleasure and pride in using the outboard engine as rarely as possible. When docking, he would strive to judge the amount of way the Hunter had left to her as precisely as possible, letting go the sheet of the mainsail, and approaching the jetty under headsail alone, which he would let fly shortly before Synchronicity reached the jetty, so that he could cast on as the boat lost the last of her way. He knew as a simple fact that he had an innate aptitude for sailing: handling the small boat, assessing the prevailing conditions, came naturally to him. It was this instinctive skill which gave him so much pleasure in sailing, and which brought him so much relaxation when he went out in Synchronicity. He offered up thanks to the spirit of his maternal grandfather, who had been a Royal Navy officer before the Great War, for his own love of, and skill with, small boats. The pleasure that sailing brought Alexander meant that he felt complete of himself, rarely feeling the need for company when he was on the water, though he did enjoy Andrew's company, because the youngster's cheerfulness and flashing grin brought Alexander happiness. The two got along together very easily. Alexander had asked Mike at the farm if he would like to come sailing with him, but Mike declined. Horses and firm dry land were Mike's thing, not the horrors and uncertainties of casting yourself on the mercy of the deep in a very small boat.

At work, Alexander rather liked Frances. It would be pleasant to spend some time with her once in a while, he thought. In May, Alexander took Frances riding a couple of times, and some evenings, when neither of them had a shift to work at the Bell, he would take her for drinks at the yacht club, where they would sit outside for a while, but at this time of year the evening air grew chill very quickly, and they soon moved inside. Alexander persuaded himself that a friendship was all that Frances wanted. In this, he was before long to find himself mistaken.

Their rides together, the occasional evenings at the FBYC bar, their interaction at work, brought Frances closer to Alexander. She began inviting him in to her cottage some nights after they had worked a shift together, where she would sometimes snuggle up to him on the couch.

Alexander would then draw her closer to him, sometimes kissing her, because it seemed expected of him, and because he was flattered by her attention. But it would have been kinder had he rejected her overtures from the start. One night in late June, after their shifts at the Bell had ended, and Alexander had given Frances a lift back to her cottage in St. James (her car was not running just then), she said "Why don't you stay the night?"

Alexander was momentarily at a loss. Perhaps on another night he might have been more eager to respond to this invitation, though he doubted that – his Catholic faith was something he was then taking quite seriously, and he had plans beginning to mature in that regard. It did not feel right to him that he engage in what the Church would regard as fornication. As it was, he felt tired that night and wished only to get home and go to bed. He blinked a few times, then replied "Frances, I can't. I don't think it would be a good idea."

Their next few shifts together at the Bell were awkward. Frances could not avoid Alexander: she had to bring him her tables' drinks orders to prepare. But by early the following week, Frances had quit her job at the Bell.

With the onset of the winter rains and gales in July, Alexander stripped Synchronicity's sails and stored them in the bow and stern compartments below. He lifted the outboard engine from the transom and stored it on the cabin sole. He doubled up the mooring cables. He knew that there would be the occasional days of magic weather through the winter when the sun shone, and there was a light wind only. He wished to sail the Hunter on such days if he could. Between July and September he went for a sail four times in such conditions, once alone, twice with Andrew, and once with Roger, the young club member who had first befriended him. On each occasion the sun was shining and there was only a light wind. The sea was calm but for a heavy swell.

The short, wet, cold Cape winter was over by late September. The oak trees turned green again. The club again asked Alexander whether he would n't consider racing in the Hunter Europa class in the coming season. Again, Alexander declined. He had no wish to race. He had little of the competitive urge in his makeup. He felt no need to prove himself in race competitions.

Sometimes Alexander felt an abiding sense of separation from the rest of humanity, except on the farm, where he was gathered up by his family's love, and gratified by Mike's friendship. Away from the farm, the only times he experienced no trace of loneliness were when he went riding, or when he was hiking and climbing in the mountains, and when he went sailing. But at other times, even when amidst a friendly group, such as that at the Club bar, where he knew many people by now, he felt in some essential way removed from the company, as if there was a glass wall between them and him. Sometimes he found himself thinking "Will I feel alone all my life?"

In October 1985 Alexander wrote to the Order of Friars Minor in South Africa, telling them a little about himself, and asking whether they would accept him for next year's postulancy. In November an ordained Franciscan friar, Father Boniface, the Novice Master, visited him at the farm one weekend. He stayed a night, and Alexander gave up his bedroom at the end of the *stoep* to him. He himself dossed down with three or four dogs and half a dozen cats in the sitting room that night. Later that month, Alexander received a letter from the Franciscans, intimating that they would accept him as a postulant in February the following year of 1986. Aged thirty-one, Alexander would be five, even ten years older than most of the other novices.

Alexander spoke to the club secretary about putting Andrew forward for membership of the FBYC. Alexander knew that Andrew would look after and enjoy Synchronicity. By mid-December, Andrew's membership was approved. Alexander paid his friend's membership fees for the following year. In January 1986 he arranged with the club that Andrew would have charge of Synchronicity. Alexander gave him a wad of cash to cover maintenance and other expenses associated with keeping Synchronicity.

In early February 1986, Alexander said goodbye to the priest at Saint John the Evangelist in Fish Hoek. He said goodbye to Andrew too. "Sandy, I can't pretend to understand what you're doing," said Andrew. "But I hope you'll be happy. I'll miss you, my china."

Alexander was touched to see that Andrew's eyes were moist and glistening. On an impulse, he embraced his friend, who hugged him back.

Then, very early one morning, having said goodbye to his grandfather, to Mike, and to his cousins the evening before, and with his aunt standing watching, in her dressing gown, on the *stoep*, Alexander set off in his big car, long before the first lightening of the sky in the east, on what was going to be a very long drive to Ladysmith, in Natal, a few miles outside of which, near a fading community named Besters, the Order of Friars Minor had their novitiate located at that time.

Eleven

The Novitiate

Saint Joseph's was a mission church near Besters, a fast declining hamlet to the north of Ladysmith. The original buildings, about one hundred years old, were of beautifully cut and trimmed stone, with high ceilings and tall windows, and a row of ventilation windows just beneath the ceilings, to allow the trapped heat of the baking summers to escape. The church was an oddity. It had been built by Italian prisoners of war, and its façade was Italian baroque, with a scrolled central gable, pilasters either side, and symmetrical square towers at either corner, the whole plastered and painted white. You could not reach the mission directly from the main north-south highway connecting the Transvaal and Free State with Natal. You had to leave the highway much earlier and proceed along a dirt road, off which, some distance further on, you turned into a long dirt drive which took you to the mission complex. Not far beyond this was the Sand River, fringed with willow trees. Today the N1 tollway roars past only two hundred yards from the mission, but you still have to get onto the old road and then the dirt road, to reach the mission.

Alexander arrived at Saint Joseph's after midnight that night. As Alexander turned the engine off and got out of the car, he was struck by the silence. Father Boniface, the Novice Master, heard Alexander's car pulling up, and came outside to greet him. He was taken to the kitchen, and was offered some sandwiches and a mug of coffee. There was no one else around. Then he was shown to his bare room in a red brick block: it had plastered walls painted pale grey, a simple iron-framed bed with a cotton counterpane on it, a rickety chest of drawers with an old wooden-framed mirror sitting atop it, and a curtain rod spanning one corner of the room at shoulder height, with steel and plastic coat hangers hanging on it. There was a plain wooden desk, a grudgingly padded chair, and above the desk was a crucifix, our Lord gazing down with pity at this bleak environment. The window had a pair of thin cotton print curtains either side. There was a single light bulb suspended from the ceiling, with a metal soup plate shaped shade above it. Below the crucifix was a wooden bookshelf, empty at present but for a Jerusalem Bible and a thick, heavy breviary. Ablution and lavatory facilities were at the end of the corridor.

Alexander met the members of the community, along with the other novices, over breakfast at 8.30 the next morning, having had just a few hours' sleep. Breakfast followed Mass, which was preceded in the church by the offices of Prime (at 7.15 a.m.) and then immediately, Terce. There were four priests: the Father Guardian, a man in his fifties; a very ancient retired priest who had spent most of his life in Goa, whom Alexander took to – he was sweet and gentle, and as Alexander came to know him better, he often went for a short walk with him, and listened to him talk about his life in India; the Novice Master, Father Boniface, who was in his forties; and Father Joseph, a very fluent Zulu speaker, who was much away from the community during the day, visiting out-stations in the Land Rover.

Including Alexander, there were four novices. All were Europeans. Richard, in his mid-twenties, was closest to Alexander in age, and would be going up to the Seminary in Pretoria the following year. The youngest was a boy of eighteen, Ralph, who was also a postulant, having arrived to commence his novitiate just a week earlier, whilst Jeremy, who was a local lad (he had grown up in Ladysmith), was twenty years old, and had completed his postulancy the year before. Alexander was the only novice with a drivers' licence, so Father Boniface would always take him along on weekly groceries shopping trips to Ladysmith, to help load and drive the *bakkie* (pick-up).

After just a couple of weeks, Brother Alexander had settled into the routine of the novitiate. Father Boniface had soon discovered that Alexander had a fine tenor voice, so Alexander was appointed Precentor. He led the three sung offices of the day. There were eight daily offices making up the Liturgy of the Hours, or Divine Office, of which the young men attended six. The first two daily offices, Matins and Lauds, were said privately by the priests. Prime and Terce, which were not sung, preceded the 8 a.m. Mass. The three sung offices were Sext, at noon, which was followed by lunch, then None at 3.45 p.m, and Vespers at 6 p.m. The Angelus was recited immediately after None, and the Angelus bell was rung. This was followed by tea and coffee, with sandwiches. After Vespers there was supper, then an hour's "recreation," when the whole community met in the priests' sitting room. There was general conversation, and sometimes Jeremy played some classical guitar. He played very well, and had a true but reedy voice. Alexander played chess with the old retired priest and with Jeremy. Inasmuch as Alexander had a favourite amongst the novices, it was Jeremy, the local lad aged twenty. Compline, which was spoken, followed recreation, soon after 8 p.m., and after Compline, the novices attended to their ablutions, then retired each to his own room, to read (and in theory, also to pray).

There were two libraries: the main theological library was housed in the same block which housed the novices' rooms. There was also a more general, smaller library containing not only some theological and liturgical volumes, but a collection of general non-fiction and some fiction, in what was designated as the novices' recreation room, a small free-standing structure in the grounds. Alexander, looking for work to do, asked Father Boniface if he could catalogue the contents of the main library. Father

Boniface agreed, and during the ten months he spent at St. Joseph's, Alexander made out individual catalogue cards for every single volume in the main library. Most weekdays, except Saturday, he worked alone in the library after lunch, through to None. After the Angelus was recited in community, Alexander would usually take a walk with one or more of the other novices across the *veld*, to the Sand River, there to sit on its banks beneath the willow trees for a while. One baking hot afternoon, only Alexander and Jeremy walked to the river. On the river bank, Alexander began to declaim to Jeremy, sitting by his side: "By the rivers of Babylon, there we sat down, yea, we wept, when we remembered Zion. We hanged our harps upon the willows in the midst thereof...."

"What Psalm number is that, Sandy?" asked Jeremy.

"Psalm one hundred and thirty-seven, I think. I don't remember who turned it into a popular song. Do you?"

"It was Boney-M," Jeremy replied.

Only on Sundays was the routine broken, for after breakfast, at 9.30 a.m., there was the main Sunday Mass, which many of the local Zulu folk attended. This was celebrated in the Zulu language. Father Joseph, with his fluent Zulu, was usually the celebrant. Each week, one of the novices took it in turn to read the lessons in Zulu. When it was Alexander's turn to do so, he would spend part of the preceding Saturday afternoon reading the lessons aloud, the first few times in the company of a native Zulu speaker – the Zulu cook if she was available, or any one of the local people he had managed to waylay. After a while, it became established that he would meet a Zulu lad aged about sixteen in the novices' recreation room every Saturday afternoon, because Alexander was keen to pursue his studies in Zulu. After some weeks had passed, they began to meet in the open air, in the shade of an acacia tree, where it was cooler. The Zulu boy would correct Alexander's pronunciation, until he was satisfied that Alexander had it right.

This lad was being educated at the mission school run by the friars' sister community of Poor Clares which was located not far from the novitiate. The lad's name was Dumisani: which means, "Praise God." At this, the height of a roasting Natal summer-time, Dumisani often wore just a pair of shorts, and he always went barefoot. He had a fine, spare physique, the colour of old, polished mahogany, and features of remarkable regularity and beauty. They were not at all the typical moon-faced features of the majority of Zulus. In this heat, with temperatures in the lower thirties centigrade (90s fahrenheit), Alexander wore only a hoodless brown Franciscan habit of thin cotton, belted at the waist, over a pair of underpants and a light sleeveless cotton vest. He wore open leather sandals on his bare feet. At his neck, beneath his habit, he wore a small silver crucifix on a chain which his distant cousin, the university chaplain, had given him.

Alexander had found a teach-yourself Zulu book in the library he was working in during weekday afternoons. With this, and Dumisani's help, he was trying to learn some basic Zulu. The boy was bright, and he had an enquiring mind. In return for Dumisani's help with his Zulu, Alexander explained and amplified the English and History that the lad was studying at school. Dumisani would bring his two English and History text books along every Saturday afternoon. Alexander would also find related publications for him from the general library. He found himself looking forward to these Saturday afternoons.

"Saubona, Dumisani," he would greet the lad. "Kunjane?"

"Sekone, Sandy, kunjane?" and Dumisani's features would light up in a grin showing very white teeth.

For all this, Alexander knew that he was missing the camaraderie of the Bell, and of the club bar. He missed the stimulus of the previous year. He missed being a part of the many-facetted lives of the people he had known. By comparison, the priests and novices at the mission were almost childlike in their simplicity and limited experience of life. He missed the joy of a close reach across False Bay in Synchronicity. He missed his friendship with Mike on the farm, and he missed Andrew, with whom he had worked at the Bell and who had so often crewed for him. He missed his freedom. He thought about this, and he concluded that his vocation was not genuine. Sincere it was, but true, it was not. Had it been a genuine vocation, this life at Saint Joseph's should have satisfied him. It did not.

It was July, mid-winter (and the dead grass was sere and brown, and there was a heavy frost some mornings, and the offices of Prime and Terce, followed by the Mass in the un-heated church, were a mild torment to Alexander), before he fully understood that he was yearning after his old life. Even so, he knuckled down and persisted, for his pride's sake as much as for any other reason. He persisted right through the remainder of the year, until, in November, the air warm once again, the green things growing, he went to see Father Boniface and told him he had made a mistake in entering the novitiate. "I don't think I have a vocation, Father," he said. "I want to leave the novitiate."

"I would like it if you would stay longer, Alexander," the Novice Master replied. "We think you may have a true vocation. You have n't given yourself much time to test it."

"I think ten months is long enough. I want to leave, Father."

"Would you not stay on at least a full year?"

"I really do wish to leave, Father."

"Very well. We shall pray for you. When do you wish to go?"

"Tomorrow."

Father Boniface looked pained. "OK – if you come see me in my office just after recreation this evening, I'll return the six hundred Rands you brought with you, and give you your car keys."

Alexander had been keeping his car's battery charged, and checking the engine periodically, taking the car for a drive once a week or so, but Father Boniface kept the car keys. That afternoon Alexander told Jeremy he was leaving the next morning. "Oh Sandy," Jeremy burst out, "I wish you were n't going!"

"I'll miss you, Jeremy."

That evening in Father Boniface's office, Alexander insisted he keep back one hundred Rands of the six hundred Rands that belonged to him, for the mission. "*Pro amore Dei*," he told him.

At 6 o'clock the next morning, Alexander drank a coffee he made in the kitchen. He had very little in his bag. He had arrived with very little ten months earlier, and he had acquired nothing since. He had already said goodbye to the other young men after recreation the night before.

The Father Guardian had not summoned him, nor had the Father Guardian been present in Father Boniface's office the previous evening. A compound of shame and pride prevented Alexander from seeking him out, so he set off without having said good bye to the other priests.

Alexander drove all day, by-passing Durban, then down the Natal South Coast and into Transkei, and by sundown he had still not crossed into the Western Cape. It was dawn before he pulled up at the farm, his ears ringing, and he was feeling de-hydrated and light-headed, but along with several barking dogs his aunt had come out in her dressing gown to greet him. She hugged him, then took him through the silent house, and he felt tears prickle in his eyes as he saw the familiar things. He scratched the dogs behind their ears, and picked his way through the cats. His aunt went back to bed, and he had a large drink of water in the kitchen. Then he made himself a coffee and a sandwich, and took them out onto the *stoep*, where he smoked a cigarette. It felt dry and tasteless in his mouth. When he had drunk his coffee and eaten his sandwich he made his way back inside, used the lavatory, the glass of water having at last re-hydrated him, then he went to bed in his tiny *stoep* extension room.

Twelve

Interregnum

The south-easter was blowing at almost forty knots when Alexander went out in Synchronicity two days later. He had very little sail set, with the mainsail fully reefed and the roller-reefing jib reefed also. He reveled in the sense of liveliness and motion. This was what he had been missing, a long way from the sea, during those baking hot, dry days in Natal. He grinned at Andrew, who grinned back. They exchanged few words when they were out sailing together. But later, over a couple of lagers in the club bar, Alexander caught up with Andrew's doings, and chatted with other members also. He was interested to see that Andrew had acquired a pretty brunette girlfriend during his absence, who arrived soon after they sat down in the bar. "You're Alexander?" the girl said. "You are some sort of a monk, aren't you?"

"I was a friar. Not anymore," Alexander replied.

"It's the celibacy that would get me down," she said, and smiled at Andrew. Andrew caught Alexander's gaze, and his cheeks reddened slightly.

That's OK then, Alexander thought to himself.

On New Year's day, 1st of January 1987, Alexander's grandfather died. He had been hospitalized for just over a week. It had been a subdued Christmas season at the farm. Alexander's father was at the hospital. He had driven down from Johannesburg, where Alexander's family had been living since early 1977. He had taken Alexander's room on the *stoep*. Alexander was sharing one of the wooden cabins with an Afrikaner lad named Hannes, a lieutenant in the South African Navy, who worked at the naval intelligence centre at Silvermine, up in the mountain near Muizenberg. He was an on-off boyfriend of Alexander's cousin, Jenny.

Alexander was not present when his grandfather died. Alexander had not been feeling very well on New Year's day: he had been celebrating New Year's eve at the FBYC bar the evening before. But when the phone-call came in the early afternoon, and his cousin, Mary, brought him the news, he felt suddenly very sober. Alexander was Rory's eldest grandchild, and the eldest son of Rory's only son. The old man had been a somewhat distant figure, both literally and in manner, during much of Alexander's childhood, but Alexander and he had grown to know one another much better during 1985. Rory had mellowed as he had grown older, becoming gentle and thoughtful, and they had often chatted together. About a year earlier, sitting together on the *stoep*, Rory had suddenly, without preamble, said "Sandy, if there's ever anything wrong, something you want to talk about, you can tell me."

There was so much that Alexander would have liked to share with the old man, but he said nothing at all.

Alexander's father was deeply affected by the old man's passing, as was Alexander's aunt. Sharing in their grief was Alexander's uncle by marriage, who had loved the old man, looking up to him and depending on him much as he would have his own father (who lived in Britain).

At the funeral service at the Presbyterian church in Fish Hoek, and during the interment afterwards, at Muizenberg cemetery (where Rory's remains were laid to rest alongside those of his wife, Alexander's grandmother, who had died thirteen years earlier), Alexander felt a deep sorrow rising. He wished he had known his grandfather as well as his cousins had. He wished he had been a better grandson to the old man. He saw his father, always a man whose feelings were close to the surface, with tears running down his face as the coffin was lowered into the ground, and he wished he were a better son to his father. But his feelings for his father were too overlaid with shame and guilt for him to show his father the sympathy and love he felt for him in that moment. Since the age of fourteen, Alexander had been stricken with a sense that – simply by being who he was – he was a source of unhappiness, shame, disappointment and regret to his father, and this had made for a growing distance between him and his father. So he looked away, but he shed some tears of his own.

Alexander had resumed his old job at the Brass Bell in Kalk Bay. Andrew no longer worked there, but they saw one another frequently at the yacht club, and Andrew often went sailing with Alexander. Andrew's girlfriend sometimes joined them. Alexander had made it clear that Andrew was to treat Synchronicity as if the boat were his own. But Andrew always asked him before going out for a sail with his girlfriend. Seeing Andrew with this girl, Alexander felt a return of his old loneliness. He resumed riding with Mike, and they grew closer once again as the year progressed.

Towards the end of that year, Alexander began to feel that old familiar itch to be somewhere else resurface. But now, there was no reason to feel restless, unless it was that his present circumstances were too comfortable, and that he felt stuck in a rut. Alexander had quite a lot of money saved. And there was the yacht, a potentially useful asset – but he felt he could not sell Synchronicity, unless it was to Andrew, for morally, she belonged as much to his friend as to himself.

In November, Alexander bought a one-way ticket to London for the first week of January 1988. In mid December, Alexander asked Charles, the family friend who had helped find him the yacht, and who had put him forward for membership of the FBYC, to keep an eye on Synchronicity, and to let him know via his aunt if any expenses came up that Andrew could not meet. Alexander paid Andrew's club membership fees for 1988. A week before Christmas 1987, Alexander said goodbye again to his aunt and uncle, to his cousins, to Mike, to Andrew, and to some others. He packed his belongings into his AMC Rambler car, and drove to Johannesburg, where his parents' and brothers' homes were. He covered the approximately one-thousand miles in fifteen hours in the big car. As he drove through the Great Karoo, that austere, stark, burning landscape, where the road ran arrow-straight until it disappeared into a heat-shimmer on the horizon, and then continued as dead-straight again to the next horizon after that, he knew that he did not wish to leave Africa. Why then was he set on doing so? Why was he determined to do something that would cause him much hurt? He did not know the answer to those questions.

Alexander had n't seen his mother for almost three years, not since January 1985, although he had seen his father more recently, during the Christmas – New Year period, 1986 – 1987, when his grandfather had died. Alexander had always been close to his mother as a boy, and although there were now long periods spent apart, they corresponded on a weekly basis. Nor had Alexander seen Roy, his younger brother, since January 1985. He was quite close to Roy, who was one and a half years younger than him. He felt a need to see his mother especially, and to see Roy also. It might be some time before he saw them again.

Alexander stayed three weeks at his parents' home. He found he got on with his father rather more easily than in the past, and he began to understand that the distance he had always perceived between the two of them might have been entirely of his own making. Alexander was also glad to be seeing so much of the family cat, Lulu, a Burman who was now almost twenty years old. He had been only just into his adolescence when she had joined the family. He had missed her. He doted on her while he was visiting, storing up memories, for she could n't live for many more years.

His parents owned what in South Africa was called a "townhouse": these consisted of rows of semi-detached bungalows, nicely appointed, with front gardens and (usually) rear courtyards, and were considered quite up-market. His parents' home had two bedrooms, a study, a sitting room and a dining room, two bathrooms with lavatories, and a servant's quarters off the rear courtyard that was accessed via the kitchen door and also via a door off the street behind. There were three rows of eight dwelling units each in the complex, set within their own walled, gated, and security equipped grounds, with a large area made up of lawns beneath well-established trees at the bottom of the mini-estate. In an open space between the trees was a swimming pool for the residents. A stream ran down from the Main Reef ridge, and marked the furthest bounds of the grounds.

Alexander might have been happy those three weeks, but – except when he had been out sailing or riding – he had n't felt truly happy for a long time now, and even simple contentment had been difficult to grasp for long. He had a fair idea that what he was planning to do would end in defeat and failure, if not in outright disaster – yet he felt driven to go ahead with his plans. His imminent departure for England cast a shadow over his days at his parents' home. He found himself becoming very attached again to Lulu. He sensed a foretaste of tragedy ahead.

Alexander landed at Heathrow during the first week of January 1988, at the height of the British winter. Did he yet recognize the pattern he seemed doomed to perpetuate? Up to a point, yes: Alexander wondered sometimes why he was never satisfied, never able to settle down and be content. Did he ever gain a glimpse into the fundamental cause of his restlessness? He experienced times when he believed his sexuality to be akin to the thorn in the flesh with which Saint Paul had been afflicted.* He felt at such times that this set him outside any hopes of attaining lasting happiness. Sometimes, Alexander felt cursed by God, and he would be seized by anguish and despair, and only immediate, desperate prayer would answer. But it would be many years before Alexander understood that he could not hope to keep out-distancing his unhappiness: it would keep pace with him no matter how far he fled.

* 2 Corinthians 12:7-8.

Thirteen

The Old Palace

Sometime in 1980 or 1981, Alexander had befriended a man about ten years his elder, whom he had met quite by chance one afternoon in a pub near Victoria station, and with whom he had fallen into conversation. Over time, Paul, his new friend, had taken him home to his flat near the Catholic cathedral in Westminster, to meet his wife. They had a young son, then aged about four or five years. The friendship had blossomed, and not only because Paul had also been born and grown up in Kenya, and then moved to South Africa. Alexander liked his wife, a plump, pretty Polish woman named Monika, cheerful, motherly, a great provider of tasty meals and tempting snacks. He grew to be fond of the little boy, Peter, also. Alexander had always got on well with children. He was genuinely fond of them, unless they were horribly spoiled and badly misbehaved. Small children (and dogs) generally liked Alexander in turn.

Alexander and Paul would play chess together while talking and sipping at their glasses of whiskey, several games through the course of an evening at Paul's flat. They shared an interest in metaphysics and eastern philosophy. Paul was, for a superficially far from academic man, who had not even matriculated from high school, very well read in these areas. He was a follower of the early 20th century Austrian mystic and philosopher, Rudolf Steiner.

Later in 1981, Paul and his family had moved to a large village named Berkhamsted in Hertfordshire, about one and a quarter hours' drive north-north-west of London, on the A4251 which ran north from the Watford Junction. (Today's A41, bypassing Kings Langley and Berkhamsted, had not yet been built). Alexander, whose British drivers' licence entitled him to drive the quite large removals van that Paul and his family had hired to transport their household goods to their Berkhamsted home, drove for them during this move. Later, Alexander had visited them twice, getting there by train and staying the night each time, enjoying the excellent dinner prepared by Monika, then playing chess, sipping whiskey with Paul, and talking up a storm as the two of them debated various esoteric matters. And after Alexander returned to South Africa, Paul and he had stayed in touch via the post.

Now, in January 1988, Paul had found Alexander a rent-free apartment not far from them at Kings Langley, another large village on the A4251, a few miles closer to London, but still surrounded by pretty countryside. From Heathrow, Alexander made his way via London to Berkhamsted, where he spent a few nights with Paul and Monika, then he moved into the big bedsit on the first floor of a wing of an Edwardian mansion built in the Arts and Crafts style around a medieval core which housed the original hall and solar. The Priory, Kings Langley, which sat atop the valley through which the Grand Union canal ran, had once been a religious house, then a crown property after the dissolution of religious foundations during the Reformation, then the possession of Henry VIII's final (and surviving) wife, Catherine Parr. Several families of school teachers now lived in the old house, which belonged to a Steiner school adjacent to the property. The grounds were extensive, and included several meadows, some woodland, an apple orchard and rows of beehives, as well as a donkey and a nanny goat. The grounds gave onto farm lands on two sides, the Steiner school on the third side, and the village and Langley Hill road on the fourth, from which you walked down a driveway to reach the house itself. Almost opposite the gates to the house, where Langley Hill road turned sharply to the right as it reached the top of the hill, was a pub, the Old Palace, which Alexander was to get to know rather too well.

The bedsit comprised a very large single room, with a kitchen alcove at one end. It was lighted by a continuous range of windows which ran across the front of the room. It shared a front door downstairs with a similar bedsit below (which was currently un-occupied), and was reached via a wide flight of stairs alongside the ground floor parlor-hall, a staircase which gave access not only to Alexander's bedsit, but to a guest bedroom and to the first floor solar, a beautiful space within the original medieval core, poorly lighted by a number of narrow lancet windows set deep within the thick stone walls. This room had a vast open fireplace, the twin of the walk-in fireplace in the parlor-hall below, and a wonderful oak hammerbeam roof. To one side of the fireplace was a narrow, low door, and if you went through it, you could make your way into a range of rooms further along in the Edwardian house, in which a teacher and his family lived. They used their own ground floor entrance at the far end of the house. Off the first floor landing which gave onto Alexander's bedsit and the guest bedroom, behind a door, was a steep and narrow stairway which led to a fine, dry, well-lighted empty attic room above the guest bedroom. Alexander's bathroom and lavatory were on the ground floor, down the wide staircase and along a short corridor. It was an odd arrangement, because the lavatory and bathroom were shared by the guest bedroom and by the ground floor bedsit, and the lavatory itself was also used by the members of the Steiner church congregation which met in the upstairs solar on Sunday mornings. Alexander's walk to the lavatory on a winter's night was a long and a cold one. The medieval core and the adjacent Edwardian additions alongside it, including Alexander's bedsit, had no heating but for the two big open fireplaces.

During his first few months at the Priory, with snow drifts piled high in the narrow lanes surrounding the Priory property well into March, Alexander, who had only a small electric fan-heater to warm his bedsit, would often sleep in front of the fire in the parlor-hall downstairs, an old duvet laid on the wooden floorboards like a futon, two more duvets on top of him. The winter of '87 – '88 was an unusually severe one.

Downstairs, a door gave onto a small, overgrown lawn and a wild wooded area behind the house, the wood comprising old established beech and oak trees, and along its fringes there grew younger trees and saplings and a riot of brambles and nettles. There was much fallen timber, and Alexander foraged this timber, building up a large woodpile in an outhouse a little way along. That winter he kept the fire glowing all night, and he built it up again during the day. The fire was welcomed by the Steiner congregation on Sunday mornings, for they met for tea and coffee and gossip in the parlor-hall after their church service upstairs.

Alexander's bedsit was rent-free, but in return he was expected to keep the solar-come-church and the guest bedroom upstairs clean, as well as the parlor-hall downstairs, and the public spaces – the entrance hall, the wide staircase, the lavatory, and a tiny cubicle off the hall in which were a tea urn, a kettle, a counter-top, a sink, and some crockery and cutlery in the cupboards and drawers. He began by spending two or three hours every Saturday attending to these duties. He was, as time went by, and drinking became an important element of his life, to prove not always very reliable in this obligation.

Once Alexander had started working at Reuters in Fleet Street, London (he began the job in March), he called in daily at the Old Palace on his way home from work in the evenings, usually ordering a meal, his main meal of the day, and he spent a lot of time there on Saturdays and Sundays from late morning onwards, eating his lunch there. The licencee, a man in his thirties, and his wife, soon came to value Alexander's custom: one way or another, he spent a lot of money at the pub each week. The publican and his wife had a son in his early teens, a quiet, thoughtful boy who went to a local state school. As was invariably the case with children, this boy too got on well with Alexander, who enthralled him with stories of Africa.

Soon after moving into the Priory, Alexander visited the Old Palace for the first time on a Saturday early afternoon, to find only half a dozen customers there, all men. "Good afternoon," Alexander sang out, in his then rather upper class English accent, in which was not a hint of South Africa (the upper class accent being a left-over of Alexander's first two stays in London, when he had mixed with men who had been to good private – or "public" – schools). Two or three of the men in the saloon bar responded in a similar accent. One, Robin, was quick to introduce himself to Alexander, shaking his hand. He was quick also, in fairly short order, to interrogate Alexander, clearly trying to place him within the English social structure. "Do you live locally?"

"I live across the road, at the Priory."

"Oh – you're on the staff at the Steiner school?"

"No," Alexander smiled. "What about you? Are you local?"

"I live just around the corner," Robin replied. "May I ask – are you working locally?"

"I'm starting work in March," Alexander replied, "at Reuters in Fleet Street. What about you, Robin? What sort of work do you do?"

"I'm a wine importer," Robin replied. "What sort of work will you be doing for Reuters?"

"Researching and writing about conditions for regional investment in particular industries in sub-Saharan Africa," Alexander replied.

"What experience do you have to have to get a job like that, Sandy?" Robin asked him.

"None, in my case. They offered me the job because I have an honours degree from a South African university, and because my boss believes – so he told me – that humanities graduates have the right skills and temperament to undertake research, analysis and evaluation." Alexander was drinking a Guinness. He took a draught from it, then asked "Where did you go to school, Robin?"

"Harrow. What about you?"

"I went to school in South Africa."

Robin smiled. "You don't sound South African."

Alexander laughed. "A lot depends on where you lived in South Africa, and where you went to school – what sort of accent you acquired. I spent quite a while living in Cape Town."

Over time, Alexander came to realise that Robin did very little wine importing, but lived largely off his wife's earnings. She was a solicitor in Hemel Hempstead, the big town not very far away. Robin was almost always to be found at the Old Palace when Alexander called in there. The two men grew to know one another better, but Alexander felt a certain measure of reserve in ever sharing too much about himself with Robin. There was something slightly off kilter about friend Robin. However, he made an amusing drinking companion.

Alexander met other local people at the Old Palace. One of these became a good friend. Max dropped in most early evenings and weekend afternoons, with his two Alsatian dogs. He was in his early fifties. He had been born in Germany just before the War. He had a nice house a couple of hundred yards away, and he was married to a somewhat overbearing woman (as was Robin too, for that matter); in Max's case, to a staff nurse working at the hospital in Hemel Hemsptead. They had a son in his very early twenties, a regular drinker at the Old Palace, through whom Alexander came to know a young crowd, younger than himself by ten years or so for the most part: local lads and some girls; and with one exception they were friendly and open, accepting him at face value. The exception was a young man with saturnine, scornful good looks, who made it clear he did not like Alexander. Sometimes he greeted Alexander in a mock posh accent. Too bad, Alexander thought: his accent was not an affectation, even if the assumptions it gave rise to (that he was English, and public school educated) were not in his case true.

Through that long winter, Alexander drank every day. He drank not just a couple of glasses of Guinness, either: early on he took to drinking rum and black current cordial, perhaps four tots of rum an evening at the Old Palace. He soon discovered that he could consume large quantities of alcohol without becoming noticeably drunk. Instead he felt happier in his own skin; better able to live with himself; less aware of a glass wall between himself and the rest of the world of mankind. Alcohol seemed to deliver Alexander for a while from the curse of intense self awareness. Working in London, he had fallen happily into the remnants of Fleet Street's hard-drinking culture, left over from a time when all the big dailies were published in Fleet Street, and the street had been full of hard-drinking journalists and hacks. At lunchtime he would have one or two beers at the White Swan, or at Cogers, both built within the Reuters building, on the ground floor. The entrance to the White Swan faced St. Bride's, whilst Cogers was accessed via Salisbury Square round the back of the building. After work, he would walk to Covent Garden at least twice a week, to drink in the small upstairs bar in a pub in Maiden Lane. Today these premises house a restaurant, but back then it went by another name. The first floor bar was a gay hangout, very theatre, with a personable young barman serving behind the counter. There were big comfortable leather-upholstered chairs in the upstairs bar, and stacks of newspapers and periodicals on a table, and framed theatre posters on the wall. There was a small coal fire in the elegant fireplace. The room, which was lighted by two big sash windows through which you could see the young waiters at Rules across the road getting dressed and undressed above the restaurant as they began and ended their shifts, rarely held more than a dozen customers. It had a clubbish atmosphere. All the regulars knew each other.

Here, Alexander would down two or three glasses of Guinness and as many whiskey chasers before even making his way to Euston station by Underground, where he caught the train to Kings Langley. His alcohol intake every day that winter was considerable. He rapidly became first psychologically, then over time, physically addicted to liquor. He preferred never to have to be fully sober, if he could avoid it, for when he began to sober up, he felt the stirrings of mild withdrawals commencing, and if he waited too many hours before having a stiff drink, these mild withdrawals became acutely uncomfortable.

This then is what happened to Alexander during those first few months of 1988. He became a practicing, rather than merely latent, alcoholic. His destiny had caught up with him at last.

Edwin Lutyens, the acclaimed architect who had designed the government buildings in New Delhi, and the Union Buildings in Pretoria, South Africa, as well as many other public projects and grand private residences scattered across the old Empire, had designed the Reuters building at number 85 Fleet Street in 1935. Reuters had moved into it in

1939, just before the outbreak of the Second World War. Above the main entrance was a large recessed roundel set in the stonework, in which was a bronze figure of "Fame", a winged figure seated astride a globe, blowing a trumpet. The *Daily Telegraph*, one of Britain's leading national dailies, was located just down the street, in a fine building named Peterborough Court. It had not yet made the move to Canary Warf (and the much later move to Victoria, near Buckingham Palace). The *Daily Mail*, the *Express* titles, and some other publications, were still located in Fleet Street. But Fleet Street had been dying ever since Rupert Murdoch had vacated his papers' premises in Fleet Street and moved the *Times* and the *Sunday Times* to Wapping in 1986 (and in so doing, broken the printers' unions). None the less, Fleet Street retained its tawdry, dynamic and boozy mystique, and it still meant something to say you worked in Fleet Street.

Each weekday morning, Alexander caught the train for Euston, London, at Kings Langley. At Euston he got on the south-bound Northern Line, and six stops later, he changed at Embankment onto the District or Circle lines east-bound, one stop to Temple, or two stops to Blackfriars, from either of which he would walk for about ten minutes to the Reuters offices in Fleet Street. He spent three hours a day in total on his commuting to and from work. He had, as a consequence, little time to cook in his kitchenette, generally eating instead at the Old Palace. He struggled to find time to do his laundry, usually leaving it for the weekend. But aged only thirty-three, he was at the peak of his physical stamina, and it would be many years before his drinking affected either his stamina or his surprisingly good health. He did not even catch a cold that winter.

Alexander, with Max's help and advice, bought himself a *mobilette*, a two-stroke, 49cc pedal-scooter with automatic transmission. To start the motor, you pedaled the machine a short distance before the engine fired and took over. Alexander's machine did not have the tiny, wobbly wheels of many mopeds, but the relatively large wheels of the true Continental *mobilette*, which made for a safer, more stable, more comfortable ride. Behind the single saddle was a closed, lidded box for carrying your shopping and whatever. The scooter's top speed was about twenty-five miles an hour with the wind behind it. It was painted scarlet. Alexander loved this machine and kept it protected when not in use by a plasticized canvas tailor-made cover. On weekends, with the coming of springtime, he would ride for many miles down the narrow country lanes and into the Chiltern Hills, exploring the countryside. He was now able to ride to Paul and Monika at their Berkhamsted home. He also used the scooter to visit a German family a few miles away who had befriended him. Alexander had met them via Paul and Monika. This family lived in a large, sprawling, contemporary ranch-style house up a narrow country lane. There were two little boys, aged ten and twelve, their boxer dog, their cat, and various rabbits and hamsters. Their father was managing director of the British subsidiary of a German engineering firm. The mother took Pilates classes, and socialized with other well-off parents of children at the Steiner school to which Paul and Monika (who were poor, and got by with help from social security), also sent their son, Peter.

The ten year old German boy was named Friederich, and was known as Freddy, and his older brother was Wilhelm, or Bill. They spoke English with a native middle class English accent, for they had lived in England since they were toddlers. Both had hair the colour of flax, and both were already tanned by the sunshine of late spring. They were skinny, very active little boys. Freddy was county squash champion for his age group. He was the more open of the two boys, and with his bright smile and dancing eyes he quickly became Alexander's favourite. Bill was more reserved: Alexander sometimes felt that Bill did not altogether approve of him. Freddy and Alexander played chess together sometimes. Freddy always beat Alexander. The brothers enjoyed riding Alexander's scooter up and down their long driveway. Sometimes Alexander was invited to dinner with the family, and after dinner he would read to Freddy, who sat on the sofa alongside Alexander, his legs folded beneath him, shoved up hard against him, completely engrossed in the story. Alexander enjoyed being an honorary uncle to the lads.

Almost until the end of his stay at the Priory in Kings Langley, Alexander never lacked for company and friendship. Once again he was reading very little for pleasure. He was not a member of a library. There was no bookshop nearby. He bought a newspaper each morning, but it was only over the weekends that he read the papers thoroughly. He read little because he felt no great desire to escape his reality: he was content.

Thrice that summer Alexander rode his *mobilette* into Hemel Hempstead and padlocked it to the cycle rack at the bus station, where he caught a bus into Oxford. He loved exploring Oxford, with its medieval, narrow lanes and ancient buildings; its many churches and church steeples; its dozens of belfries which on the hour and the quarter hours would set up a great and varied chiming across the city. He walked all the way around Christ Church Meadow: down Christ Church Meadow Walk alongside the River Cherwell, along the left bank of the Thames (here known as the Isis) and past the moored houseboats of the University college rowing clubs, up Poplar Walk and back along Broad Walk towards the Botanic Gardens. And Alexander, who had read so much about student life at Oxford when he lived thousands of miles away in South Africa, hired a punt on each of these three visits and taught himself to handle a punt very capably along the Cherwell river. Alexander was to return many times to Oxford in years to come, though no longer alone on those later occasions.

Alexander was content then, that summer of 1988. Yet, despite his contentment, his drinking increased. At work, Alexander would arrive with a double whiskey already under his belt. He was good at his job, which was researching and writing both industry-specific and general commercial and investment overviews commissioned by clients looking to do business or invest in Africa. Whilst he worked through the course of the morning, he forgot about the need for a drink until about midday, but he waited until lunchtime at one o'clock before going downstairs and outside and into the White Swan (his favourite of the two pubs located within the Reuters building's ground floor), where he drank one or two Guinnesses and a whiskey chaser. He found the later afternoons in the office would begin to drag, and his focus would begin to waver by four o'clock, when he felt a growing need for a drink. He held out until five o'clock, when he had a quick double whiskey in the White Swan downstairs, before making his way either to Euston station, or to the upstairs bar in Maiden Lane. If he chose to go straight on home after work, he would always stop at the Old Palace and drink at least two rum and cordials. Only if he was late getting back home from London would he go straight up to his bedsit, and later he would have a generous whisky or two. He kept a bottle of whiskey in his bedsit.

It became difficult by the end of summer to keep secret his dependence on alcohol, for there was always a hint of the sweet stench of liquor about him. His faculties were not generally impaired: he did not behave as if he were intoxicated, but the tube of toothpaste he had taken to keeping in his pocket, from which he would periodically squeeze a hefty dollop into his mouth and work it around his palate, only partially disguised the stink of liquor. Inevitably, people round the top village became aware that he was a heavy drinker, and as the old house and the Steiner school dominated the top village, this awareness was gossiped about and took wings and flew. Neither Paul and Monika, nor his German friends, proved as welcoming as before. But Alexander's suspicions that there was more behind their growing distance than his drinking were confirmed one Saturday afternoon in mid September, as he was helping Monika and another woman set up chairs in the hall-parlour in preparation for some or other Steiner talk that evening. He overheard Monika (who was perhaps fifteen feet away) say to the other Steiner mother working with her "I think if I ever learned that someone I knew had been molesting my son, I would kill him."

For a moment Alexander was n't sure he had heard Monika correctly. He felt shocked, suddenly short of breath. He had always possessed a powerful intuition, and he knew that he was meant to hear what Monika had said to her companion. He realised in that instant that she had learned or guessed that he was a homosexual, and that she was expressing a common prejudice against homosexuals; a prejudice that was groundless ninety-nine times out of a hundred.

And Alexander knew then that his friendship with Paul and Monika (and with Freddy's and Bill's family also) was now over. He felt a profound distress. He found himself (as he had once before, in Cape Town in 1977) the helpless victim of an alienation forced upon him by his sexual orientation. He walked through the room and did not look at the two women, but went upstairs to his apartment and poured himself a large whiskey from the bottle he kept there.

At work not long after this incident, Alexander's line manager asked him to step into his office one day. "I do not want to stick my nose into your private business, Sandy," he began (and Alexander knew immediately what the topic of this talk was going to be about), "But I suspect you may be struggling a little with your drinking."

"Do I not do my work well?" Alexander responded. "Are you dissatisfied with my work?"

"No..." the man replied, "Your work is fine. But there is talk..."

"I assure you, I do not have a problem I'm not on top of," Alexander responded. But he knew that he was no longer in control of his drinking. Recently, he had taken to keeping a half-jack of whiskey in his brief case, and he had resorted to having a quick slug at his desk mid-morning and mid-afternoon.

Alexander was very bright and drink had not dulled his intuition. By October that year he knew his time was fast running out – both at the Priory, and at Reuters. He went to see his line manager. "Barry, if I offer you my resignation, would you give me a decent reference? My work is good – you've said so yourself."

The manager looked thoughtful, then nodded. "I'll do that, if you hand in your resignation by the end of the day, effective immediately."

So Alexander walked away from the Reuters building later that afternoon of Tuesday 11th October, unemployed. His final paycheck would be posted to him within a few days, as would his reference. Alexander needed a drink. He began walking to Maiden Lane.

Fourteen

Paris

Alexander entered into that state of mind that distress and a sense that his options had run out always induced in him: an acute state of unreality, and he chose this moment to visit an acquaintance of his who lived in Paris. Late October was still sunny and warm this year. He hoped the weather was much the same in Paris. He had met Raymond at the Salisbury pub during summer. They had continued to bump into each other over a period of several weeks. Raymond, a little younger than Alexander, had been working in London during June and July, a member of the stage team of a French theatrical production. He had invited Alexander to spend a weekend with him at his flat in the 11th *Arrondissement*, near the *Père Lachaise* cemetery. Alexander rang him, using the pay-phone outside the Old Palace. Having arranged that he would be arriving in Paris during the night of Friday 14th, Alexander hired a car from the National Car Hire branch on the A4251, using the first credit card he had ever possessed. He collected the Ford Mondeo at 8 a.m. on Friday. Its headlamps had been fitted with yellow Perspex covers which re-directed the main beams slightly to the right. French cars then had yellow headlights. He reached Dover in the early afternoon, and, although he had been sipping from a half-jack of whiskey on the long drive down, he navigated the complex lanes system without mishap, was waved through immigration control, and rolled onto the ferry at about 3 p.m. It was only many years later that he came to realise how tough and resourceful he must have been, undertaking such a journey half inebriated: crossing the Channel by ferry for the first time, then driving on the right hand side of the road (another first) from Calais to Paris (most of the journey via fast-moving, toll-paying motorway, a journey of almost four hours), and finally, navigating the strange streets and fierce traffic of Paris on a Friday night, and, without having once got lost, he was able to locate Raymond's apartment block and park the car.

Alexander's first and only Channel crossings so far had been in an old Mercedes bus with a friend from Cape Town and his Australian chum in early July 1976, via a giant hovercraft. On that occasion they had been making for Pamplona, for the festival of *San Fermin*: the running of the bulls festival that attracted young backpackers and campers from across Europe and beyond. Alexander, who was passionately fond of boats and ships, enjoyed the ferry crossing. He spent the first part of the one and a half hour crossing on deck. Eventually the wind grew too cold, and he made his way to the lounge and bought a coffee. When the public address system warned drivers to return to their vehicles for the disembarkation, he returned to his hire car.

The route to Paris, via first the A26, then, near Arras, joining the A1, took Alexander almost four hours to complete, including a stop at a motorway halt to use the lavatory and buy a coffee. There were several toll-booths along the way. Alexander had changed one hundred Pounds for Francs before leaving England. It grew dark as Alexander neared Paris. He was approaching Paris from the north. At the junction with the *Boulevard Périphérique* he turned left, and followed the *Périphérique* around Paris to the east until he reached the turn off to *Cours de Vincennes* leading into Paris. At the huge multiple junction traffic roundabout of the

Place de la Nation, where Alexander wished to turn right into the *Avenue Philippe-Auguste*, his somewhat addled and exhausted wits deserted him momentarily, and instead of turning right into the roundabout, following the traffic flow anti-clockwise, he turned left, and proceeded half way round the circle against the oncoming traffic. Cars swerved, the finger was given, epithets were hurled at him (*"Espèce d'un cochon!"* and *"Sale Anglais!"* were just two of these), and it was with great relief that he swung left into *Avenue Philippe-Auguste*, making sure to get into the right-hand lane. Raymond's flat was near the *Père Lachaise* cemetery. It was not far now.

After a welcome coffee, Raymond and Alexander drank some of the wine he had brought. There was only a large double bed in Raymond's tiny flat, which the two men had to share. Alexander, exhausted by the day's stressful journey and the large amount of liquor he had been drinking through the day, fell asleep almost as soon as he lay down. In the morning, over coffee and warm croissants with *confiture*, Raymond, who was an easy-going, always elegantly dressed, rather thin young man, asked Alexander what he would like to see in Paris. "I don't know Paris at all," Alexander replied. "I would like to visit *Notre Dame*. Oh – and the Jim Morrison tomb in *Père Lachaise*. But I'm in your hands."

"You are in my hands?" Raymond responded with a naughty grin. "*Quel merveilleux*! OK – we will visit *Père Lachaise* for Jim Morrison, and *Notre Dame* this morning, and perhaps walk in *Le Marais*. *Le Marais* is a preserved *quartier*, with old merchant houses of the 17th and 18th centuries, and many *cafés* and bars of atmosphere."

"I shall enjoy that, I'm sure."

The sun was not shining. It was in fact rather cool, and drizzling. However, Alexander had brought with him his long Aquascutum tweed overcoat, very stylish without padded shoulders (which he had bought at the Aquascutum shop in Regent Street for three hundred Pounds earlier that year), dark woolen trousers with a pleated waist and turn-ups, the barely worn bespoke brown leather Lobbs shoes he had been given by his great-uncle in the Cotswolds, whose narrow Maclean feet were identical in shape and size to those of his great-nephew, and a dark brown fedora hat that he had bought at a shop in Sloane Street. Alexander had acquired several cravats, and he wore one now. He felt he was adequately dressed for the weather, and during the weekend he came to feel at least as elegant as the stylish young Frenchmen like Raymond whom he was to see so often in Paris.

Alexander had never heard of Jim Morrison until he began his education in rock music at Alice's flats in Hillbrow and Yeoville (so bereft was Alexander's adolescence of the usual interests of his peers), and when he had first heard "Riders on the Storm", and "The End", he had been carried away by enthusiasm. Later, he had watched Francis Ford Coppola's movie "*Apocalypse Now*", with Jim Morrison's atmospheric and doom-laden track "The End" as a visual-oral image he did not think he would ever forget. Alexander had of course read Joseph Conrad's "*Heart of Darkness*" (the novel which inspired the movie "*Apocalypse Now*"), while he was still at school. That Jim Morrison was both a beautiful and a tragic figure, only twenty-eight years old when he died in 1971, added to his appeal for Alexander.

But Jim Morrison's tomb came as a terrible shock to Alexander. It was rather small and insignificant, to be sure, though the bust of Jim Morrison's head was well done, but it was thoroughly defaced with graffiti and a garish amateur paint job. With the candles stuck in their own wax, and the empty wine bottles with flowers in them arranged at its base, Alexander thought the tomb looked like a Voodoo shrine. None the less, he said a prayer for the repose of Jim Morrison's soul, and was glad not to linger. "Let us hope *Notre Dame* is not also spoiled," he remarked.

On later visits to Paris, Alexander was often to re-visit *Notre-Dame de Paris*, which had not disappointed him on this, his first visit. They had coffees, salads and a *croque-monsieur* each at a *café* in *Le Marais*. By then, the drizzle was coming down quite heavily, and it was mid-afternoon, so they returned to Raymond's flat. In the evening they walked less than a hundred yards to a *brasserie* where Alexander ate a simple and very good supper of green beans fried in oil with buttered potatoes, accompanying a couple of grilled trout, followed by a cheese platter (as Alexander tried to avoid eating cows' cheese, and he had already ate more than he should at lunchtime, he had asked the waiter to point out the *fromage de chèvre*). They shared a carafe of house white during the meal, followed by an excellent coffee. In bed, Raymond wished to engage in erotic play, and Alexander acceded with only minimal reluctance. It seemed, after all, expected of him. The full measure of self-loathing, a compound of revulsion and guilt at that and many other similar encounters with many other young men over time, was to come in later years.

On Sunday morning Alexander and Raymond visited *Les Halles*, a vast underground modern retail development located where the old fresh produce market of Paris had once stood. Here, Raymond took him into a sex-shop, and Alexander felt suddenly very weary: weary of Raymond's conventional, uninspired homo-eroticism, and weary of his own weakness, as he glanced through a gay pornographic magazine, sickened at the attraction some of the photos held out for him. He knew he was letting himself down, denying his better nature, in engaging in this sort of activity.

From there, they walked to the *Centre Pompidou*, and Alexander, now feeling ready to find fault with the rest of the excursion, was struck by how ugly the building looked, with its angular exoskeleton on display. The sun came out, and they had an unmemorable light lunch sitting outside the *Café Beaubourg*, opposite the *Centre Pompidou*. During the afternoon, Raymond and Alexander walked around *Montmartre*, having taken the *Funiculaire* to ascend the hill. They entered *Sacré Coeur*, and walked around the basilica, then went back outside and stood on the terrace and gazed across Paris laid out below, with the distant landmarks of *Notre Dame*, *la Tour Eiffel*, and the dome of *l'Église du Dôme* clearly visible. That afternoon's exploration of *Montmartre* and yesterday morning's visit to *Notre Dame* had certainly been the highlights of Alexander's visit to Paris. But Alexander was to enjoy some far happier visits to Paris in later years.

Alexander reached Kings Langley again at 3 a.m. on Monday morning. He remembered he had no job to go to, and he began to understand that his drinking had become a real problem. He decided (as he sat in his chill bedsit with the fan heater blowing, in that big old house, feeling cold and worn out in those still early hours, with his head aching from the long journey and the whiskey he had consumed during it) to go home to South Africa.

Alexander, who had visited his grandmother – his mother's mother – at her old age home in Wimbledon three times already that year, and had only quite recently taken her on an outing to Hampton Court, made one more visit to the old lady before he left England again. She was now in her nineties, and her mind was wandering a little. Over a lengthy game of chess, and several cups of tea and some rather stale biscuits which the old lady had obviously been saving for some time, they chatted about long ago. Alexander did not think he would be seeing his grandmother ever again. Alexander loved his grandmother, but for most of his life, she had been, literally, a distant figure. During his Kenya childhood, his maternal grandparents had lived several hundred miles away, on the Kenya coast, and then, after Alexander's family emigrated to South Africa, those few hundred miles became several thousand miles. Alexander had been back in South Africa for over a year when, in November 1989, his last surviving grandparent died. Alexander shed some tears at the news of her passing. With none of his grandparents now left alive, Alexander felt his childhood slipping just a little further beyond recall. He was glad he had seen so much of his grandmother, having made the effort to visit her fairly often. He felt he need not be reproached by his conscience in this regard.

Fifteen

Fame and Fortune

Alexander took an evening flight to Johannesburg on Thursday 20th October. It was early summer in South Africa. He felt a tremendous sense of deliverance, the shedding of what had recently become a heavy burden of loneliness, exile and anxiety, as he landed at Jan Smuts airport in Johannesburg on Friday morning. He had drunk no alcohol during the twelve hour flight, nor during the couple of hours of check-in and waiting at Heathrow. This was the longest period he had gone without a drink since springtime that year. His father and mother were waiting at Jan Smuts airport to meet him. At home, he was delighted to see the old family cat, Lulu, still alive. She was aged twenty-one now. Alexander's mother was clearly happy he was back. Of his father's views, Alexander was less certain. It had been a long time since Alexander had felt easy with his father. This saddened him. He remembered how he had loved his father when he was a little boy. The time would come when Alexander would wish that he had been more generous with his love, but by then, Alexander would have to live with the remorse and regret he felt, unable to make good the hurt he had caused over many years of having distanced himself from his father.

Alexander's brother, Roy, was living not far from their parents' home. Alexander, at the age of thirty-three, was now living with his parents again: this shamed him. But he vowed to himself that he would change this as soon as he could. It was his mother who, about a week after his return, suggested that he approach a TV casting agency for roles in television commercials. Alexander looked through the Yellow Pages, and decided on a casting agency located in the old Johannesburg suburb of Rosebank. The agency was much taken by him, assuring him that the cameras would love him. Within less than half an hour after his arrival at the casting agency, they had lined up an audition for him for the following morning. By noon the next day, he had landed a starring role in a TV commercial which was to be shot the following week. Alexander was to star in three more TV commercials, two of them for the original client, by the end of January 1989.

Alexander earned two thousand Rands for his first shoot. At the time, two thousand Rands bought about five hundred Pounds in Britain – but its buying power in South Africa, where the cost of living was so much lower than that in Britain, was far greater. With his fee Alexander bought a second-hand Audi, the latest but one luxury model with the two litre, five cylinder electronic ignition, fuel injection engine, with automatic transmission and an air-conditioner. He bought the car at a substantial discount below the list price, via the good offices of a cousin who worked for BP in Johannesburg, and who was able to pass on one of the BP time-expired company fleet Audis to him for only one thousand eight hundred Rands. Alexander was delighted with this car. The big old AMC Rambler, which had always been registered in Alexander's father's name, had at last been sold by his parents during his absence in England. A car was essential in South Africa, far more so than in England.

By the end of that year, Alexander was able to put down six months' rent for a very comfortable, partially furnished flat in Bellevue, with a wonderfully ancient cast iron white enameled mains gas cooker in the kitchen and a rather more contemporary washing machine. Bellevue is an old suburb located between Hillbrow and Yeoville, consisting of single-story houses dating back to the late 1920s, and low-rise, often art-deco, apartment blocks of the 1930s. The lease was to run from January 8th, 1989.

By late January 1989, Alexander had acquired a limited and brief fame. He was sometimes recognised in shopping malls and stared at, and once a group of giggling teenage girls approached him, and one of the girls asked him for his autograph. "OK," he said. "What's your name?"

"Charmaine".

He wrote in the small note book she handed to him, with the ballpoint pen she provided, "*To Charmaine, with love from Sandy, the Château Liberté Wine Man,*" with a couple of Xs after these words.

Far more than his grandmother's death, although he had loved her very much, it was the old cat, Lulu's death, at the age of twenty-one, that knocked Alexander off his feet. She had become very frail and thin and unsteady on her legs, and had clearly been suffering from pain through December of 1988, and one day during the first week in January, with Alexander and his mother the only family members at home, he could not bear to think of the darling old puss suffering any longer. "Mum, we've got to call the vet to have her put to sleep. It's not fair on her. She's helpless: she relies on us to do the right thing for her".

His mother began to cry. Alexander put his arm round her and hugged her, then made for the phone. Lulu was put to sleep at home in Alexander's arms. He was weeping silently as this was done. Afterwards, he went into the garden and dug a hole of about three and a half feet in depth, and wrapped the pathetic old body in her favourite blanket, and as his mother stood watching, weeping, he laid her in the grave and covered her up.

Mother and son then sat and wept together for a while. "Let's go for a walk," his mother said. "I cant stay in the house right now".

"That's a good idea".

They drove to the Botanic Gardens above Emmarentia Dam, a few miles from home, and here they walked for over an hour, plump white cumulus clouds progressing slowly across a vast Highveld sky. The birds were calling and the wind blew gently in the trees. They spoke very little to one-another.

Alexander grieved, and periodically wept, for Lulu for a week. He was supposed to be moving into his flat in Bellevue, but he put it off. His left chest hurt painfully all the time. He had never in his life known such sustained misery, and he was literally heart-sore. For all his thirty-three years of age, Alexander became just a little boy again in that time, but a little boy who knows that there is nothing anyone, not even his parents, can do to help him. He had begun to drink again after his first few weeks back in South Africa, keeping a bottle of whiskey in the servant's room across the back courtyard, which he had kitted out as a study: he kept some of his books there, and he had an oscillating fan, a typewriter, a radio, a desk and a chair. His mother no longer wanted a resident black domestic servant, so the room was Alexander's to use. His drinking had not become out of hand, but the day he and his mother had Lulu put to sleep, he ceased to drink. This, he felt, was to honour the old cat's memory. A week after Lulu's death, he told his parents he was going to drive down to the farm. "I need a complete change of scene. I'm doing myself no good here right now."

He left the next day at one in the morning. He had already passed Bloemfontein by breakfast-time, but he did not stop. Soon after crossing the Orange River into the Cape, he reached Colesberg, at the start of the semi-arid Karoo, where the widely-spaced sheep ranches incorporated scores of thousands of hectares in extent. It was now late morning. Here he stopped for petrol and he used the lavatory. He also bought a late breakfast at the service stop. He drove through the Karoo in the heat of the day, using the air-conditioner periodically. The road ran dead straight for mile after mile, never quite reaching the far horizon which shimmered under the burning sun. If the road altered direction, the alteration was fractional, and another almost infinitely long dead-straight stretch commenced. In the early afternoon he passed Beaufort West, and later, Touws River, having at last traversed the stark Karoo, after which the road began to run between ranges of low mountains, and his spirits rose as he ate up the miles at a steady one hundred and twenty kilometres an hour (seventy-five miles an hour). He drove through the lovely Hex River Valley, with its vineyards and jagged mountain peaks, and at the top of Du Toit's Kloof Pass he stopped again, peed behind some scrub growth, and gazed across to the distant profile of Table Mountain. A troop of baboons barked at him, and kept an eye on him from a distance, the babies cavorting and leaping and mock-fighting with each other.

He did not drive through Cape Town, but swung round to the south of the city proper, and onto De Waal's Drive below the University, and then he joined the Blue Route, which ended just before Muizenberg, from where he began the ascent to Silvermine. From the top of Silvermine nature reserve, and all the way down the far side, the Atlantic ocean kept coming into view, sparkling and glinting under the sun, with a heavy bank of low dark cloud on the far distant southern horizon. At the bottom of the pass he swung left onto the old Kommetjie Road, and shortly thereafter, turned right off the road and made his way along the tarred suburban road that had replaced the sandy driveway to the farm.

He had known to expect changes: following his grandfather's death, the land was being sold off by his aunt as suburban plots (although two or three of those plots belonged to his father), and where once there had been a long dirt driveway between pines and blue gums and yellowwood trees, there were now houses being built. The old farmhouse was unchanged, and the stables were still standing, but there was only one paddock left, and the opportunities to ride out across the *veld* were fast being gobbled up by the suburban development on what had once been his grandfather's land, and over which he and Mike had so often rode in the past. None the less, there was still a feel of "home" about the place, and it seemed to Alexander that all the old familiar furniture and paintings and *bric-á-brac* that had belonged to his grandparents gave him a greeting. Alexander's aunt too made him feel very welcome.

The next day, he and Mike (who was still living on what remained of the property, in one of the wooden chalets), rode out, making their way initially between houses in varying stages of completion, before they crossed the Kommetjie road and were then able to urge their mounts to a canter. At Long Beach the tide was in, and the two of them set their mounts to a noisy splashing canter and were soon thoroughly soaked. Mike whooped with joy and Alexander grinned at him.

During the ten days that followed, Alexander went sailing in Synchronicity with Andrew. Andrew had graduated at the end of 1988, and had started work with an academic publishing house in Cape Town. "If you ever decide to sell Synchronicity," he said, as they reached across the Bay, "would you give me first refusal?"

"Ja – I'd do that, Andy," Alexander replied, "But I don't know what my plans are yet."

The visit had been a good idea. In this environment, associated only with happiness and warmth and love, the grief Alexander had been experiencing at his parents' home following Lulu's death, loosened its grip, and he determined that when he returned to Johannesburg he would find a proper job. Then he would sell his yacht to Andrew. He felt that that era was past now. He had achieved one of his modest dreams, owning and sailing a small yacht on the ocean, and he had lived again as a Capetonian. He felt intuitively that a new door was about to open for him. When it did, he must be ready to step through it.

There was something Providential about the way he saw an eighth-page advertisement in the Johannesburg daily, the *Star* for a business researcher wanted for a company in Orange Grove, when he returned to Johannesburg. The company's offices were not at all far from Alexander's flat in Bellevue. Alexander knew the job was his: there would be few applicants, he thought, who could match his recent experience working for Reuters in London. He was right: the interviews went very well indeed. He was interviewed first by the research director, then by the managing director, who was also the company's biggest shareholder. Alexander had a niggling fear that if the company contacted Reuters, something damaging might be said about his drinking, but the excellent, factual Reuters reference he was able to show them, on a Reuters letter-head, proved to be sufficient. That, and the way he presented himself – positive, self-assured, well-spoken – impressed both men. In those days, Alexander was still full of self confidence. The starting salary was modest, whilst not being poor: he was told that after three months, his salary would be reviewed. He began work in February. By then he had settled into his flat and found some items of good second-hand furniture to complement the furniture with which the flat was already provided. Alexander also renewed his contacts with Alice in Yeoville (the neighbouring suburb to the east of Bellevue), and with other old friends.

The apartment block in which Alexander's flat was located was three stories high. It had been built in the Johannesburg Art Deco style which predominated in the district. He had an entrance hall, which was large enough to use as a study. There was a big sitting room, and an equally large bedroom, and at the end of the short corridor were the kitchen, and the bathroom with a lavatory. A back door opened off the kitchen, giving onto a service stairway. On the flat roof of the block were located servants' quarters, which were occupied by black domestic staff. He arranged with one of these people to clean his flat once a week, and to do his laundry and ironing.

The floors of the flat were of solid wooden parquet laid in a herringbone pattern. There was an original built-in electric triple element heater unit located against one wall of the sitting room, with bookshelves situated either side of it, and a mantelpiece above. The light fittings and the light switches on the walls were also original art deco fixtures from the 1930s. Running the length of the front of the sitting room and the bedroom, was a verandah. The flat was on the ground floor, but it was almost six feet up from the street level outside. Beneath the apartment block was a partially naturally lighted basement parking garage with spaces for nine cars: Alexander's rent included one of these parking bays. The street entrance to the parking basement was protected by a sliding steel grill which was kept locked. The parking basement was accessed from within the apartment block by a stairway to one side of the lift. The rent Alexander paid for all this was far from burdensome. Tens of thousands of people of all ages lived similarly in Hillbrow, Berea, Bellevue, and Yeoville between the 1960s and the early 1990s. It was a civilised, rent-friendly era which was to seem but a dream in future years. By 1989 the infamous Group

Areas Act, the bedrock of Apartheid, was already being openly flouted in the district. It was to be repealed the following year. One of Alexander's neighbours was a young Asian man.

Alexander rang Andrew in Cape Town, and asked if he still wished to buy Synchronicity.

"Yes, I do. What would you ask for her?"

"I paid eleven thousand five hundred. You can have her for ten thousand five hundred, Andy. Have you got that sort of cash?"

"No – but I can get hold of it."

"OK – she's yours then. I'll ask Charles to handle the sale, shall I?"

"Thanks, Sandy. I love that boat."

"I know you do, and that you'll take good care of her."

One of Alexander's old friends from Alice's gang, Terrance, was now in his late twenties. He had graduated from film school, then undergone his military service in the army. As a college graduate, he had been commissioned a second lieutenant. He and Alexander had kept up a correspondence during that period, and Terrance had illustrated his letters with often amusing, sometimes poignant pencil sketches of army life during the bloody and savage war in Angola. But Alexander had not seen Terrance since 1984.

After he moved into his flat in Bellevue, Alexander quickly rebuilt a social life centering on Alice's group (the core of which still contained many of the same members Alexander had first come to know ten years earlier). Now Alexander met Terrance again at a party thrown by Alice's boyfriend, and Alexander had been both moved and surprised at the warmth and affection of Terrance's greeting. Terrance and his long-term girlfriend were living in a big house in Bezuidenhout Valley, one of Johannesburg's old-established eastern suburbs, along with Guy, his nineteen year old younger brother – whose artwork as a little boy had made such an impression on Alexander ten years earlier.

In April, invited to Terrance's birthday party in Bez Valley, Alexander had seen Guy, his younger brother, for the first time since 1979. He was rendered momentarily speechless at the sight of the tall, broad shouldered, long limbed young man he was re-introduced to. Guy aged nineteen, with dark hair and green eyes, was strikingly good looking. There was nothing soft or stylishly androgynous about his appearance: the planes and angles of his face and the profile of his arched nose were strongly defined, with a masculine determination about them. After he had recovered his wits, Alexander set himself to making a favourable impression on Guy, employing all his not inconsiderable charm to do so. It was via his sincere admiration of Guy's artwork that Alexander was able to create an immediate rapport with the young man. Guy took Alexander upstairs to his studio, a large, brightly lighted room on the top floor of the house. Guy's latest work was a larger than life-size owl: an assemblage of peeled wood and real feathers, with carved wood talons and a carved warthog tusk to mimic a cruel beak, all these items gleaned and foraged from the wilderness around Terrance's and Guy's family game lodge in the Lowveld. The owl was stooping upon its prey, wings outstretched, talons flexed, ready to seize its victim. It was a wonderfully dynamic, somewhat sinister art-piece, and Alexander was profuse in his praise for it; praise so sincere that he made an immediate offer to buy it, an offer that Guy accepted. Guy sold it to Alexander for four hundred Rands. Alexander was happy to pay the price. But he would pay much more than that in emotional currency over the next few years.

Alexander had been struck helpless by a *coup d'amour*. He arranged to meet Guy, who was fifteen years his junior, the following weekend in the garden of a popular and trendy bar in Yeoville. They met again one evening soon thereafter. In later years, Alexander could not remember what they talked about when the two of them were together; what, apart from a shared interest in art, and of love for Guy, they might have found in common. By late May, Alexander had told Guy that he loved him. (Love? It may have been more accurate to state that Alexander was in the grip of a powerful infatuation). The beautiful young man was neither shocked nor dismayed, and at their next meeting less than a week later in the garden of the same trendy bar in Rocky Street in Yeoville, the cool night air scented by jasmine, marijuana and tobacco, Guy had said "Those feelings you told me about, Sandy: I think I feel the same about you."

Inwardly astonished, Alexander responded "What are we going to do about this?"

Guy's head was lowered, and in the light cast by the electric light bulb close by, Alexander could see that a long lock of Guy's dark hair hung across his cheek, and his curling lashes were lowered over downcast eyes. "Uhh . . . let's just see how it goes for now."

Alexander, alone in his flat later that night, wondered at Fate. Guy was almost an archetype for the sort of masculine beauty and grace he had often admired and yearned to embrace. It felt to Alexander that he had waited half his life to find Guy. He was thirty-four years old, and at last, someone with whom he thought he was in love, loved him in return.

Sixteen

Things Fall Apart

Throughout that southern hemisphere winter of 1989, and into the following spring, Alexander and Guy spent much of their free time together. They went to movies together; they ate at the curry house in Hillbrow, and drank together at clubs in Rocky Street. They went picnicking in The Wilds, those rocky, ridge-top public gardens planted up with indigenous shrubs, trees and flowers, which were not very far from Bellevue. Often, Guy would ring ahead to say he was on his way to Alexander's flat, and they would spend the evening at home, content in each other's company. After a month or two had passed, Guy spent his first full night at Alexander's flat, and the relationship became one of shared physical intimacies. Thereafter, Alexander became greedy for the young man's perfect body and beautiful face. At the time Alexander felt completely free of the guilt and self loathing he associated with homosexual intimacies (does being in love with your partner free you of guilt, he wondered?) but in the deepest recesses of his heart, Alexander did not believe he was worthy of being loved. He did not believe that such a tainted love as that which he felt for Guy deserved to endure. He began to drink again. He drank in terror of his inevitable eviction from the Garden. At first, it was just drinks with Guy at pubs and clubs, or a couple of drinks at his flat of an evening when Guy was visiting. But by the arrival of spring in September, Alexander was on his way to heavy drinking again.

Alexander was doing well at his work, which he enjoyed. He had been awarded a salary increase after his first three months on the job, and a further increase after six months had passed came his way. Alexander was earning quite a lot of money now. Alexander had always declined the offer of a whiskey or a lager when, at the finish of work on a Friday, many of the staff (including the managing director), met together downstairs for a couple of drinks. He would drink only a Coke or a coffee with the others. But from September onwards he began to join his colleagues in a beer or two, and after a while, he was putting back a couple of whiskeys after work on a Friday.

There were periods, sometimes up to a week's duration, when Alexander's fears lessened, and his drinking diminished accordingly. Such times often coincided with the two of them driving down to Guy's family game lodge in the Transvaal Lowveld. It was situated in a private game reserve contiguous with the Kruger National Park, between the two of which no game fence existed. Alexander discovered a deep love for the bushveld (a love that had perhaps been birthed during childhood family safaris to Masai Mara in East Africa), and he delighted in driving through the mopani woodland in Guy's family's battered old Mark I open-top Land Rover, or heading out on foot into the bush with Guy, both of them wearing tee-shirts and sarongs (what Alexander thought of as a "*kikoy*", the Kenyan word for a wrap-around piece of "*mericani*" cotton cloth). They both wore leather sandals on their feet. Perhaps incongruously, Alexander always wore a wide-brimmed bush hat also, and he had bought himself a good bush knife which he wore in its sheath attached to the leather belt that held up his *kikoy*. Guy too wore a bush knife. He regarded such outings as scavenging trips, to see what he could find for incorporating into future art works. They both felt confident in the bushveld, and neither ever gave any thought to the absence of a rifle between them, although they were often not far from elephants, sometimes quite close to a herd of buffalos, and once, from a distance of about two-hundred yards, they chanced upon a pride of lions resting up in the shade of an acacia from the heat of the day. The two men glanced at one another, and Guy raised his chin and jerked it fractionally towards his left shoulder, and they walked slowly backwards until they merged into the mopani and bush willow once again. Guy had a very young man's belief in his immortality. Alexander was by now the supreme existentialist and fatalist. He did not believe it was his destiny to be killed by a wild animal.

These visits to the game lodge never lasted longer than Friday night through Saturday and most of Sunday: Alexander had work to go to on Monday morning; Guy had art school at the Teknikon to attend. Alexander would *braai* over a wood fire each evening: *boerewors* with potato salad; mutton chops with *stywepap* and a tomato sauce; or cleaned and trimmed chicken breasts in a sauce of chopped fresh tomatoes, tomato puree, onions and garlic, the whole tightly wrapped in tinfoil and secured between the two sides of a double wire grill rack and placed over the coals. For desert there was icecream they had brought with them, kept cold (along with the beers and the milk) in the fridge which ran off a cylinder of gas.

In later years, Alexander was to remember those visits as simple, happy times. In the bushveld Alexander was able to leave behind the anxiety and sense of incompleteness which were so often present in his life in the city. Freed from the urban crowds and the noise, the traffic and the pollution, Alexander was able to live in the moment. He left behind too the voracious physical passion he felt for Guy in the city, and, eschewing the narrow single beds indoors, they slept chastely at night in their separate sleeping bags, side by side on the insect-screen protected *stoep*.

Guy tolerated Alexander's drinking, even, up to a point, finding his drink-fuelled antics amusing. For Alexander could be witty, articulate and entertaining when he drank. One Friday evening, Alexander had been to Yeoville alone (Guy had been visiting his family for the evening), and he had been drinking whiskeys until after midnight at a bar way down Rocky Street. At one in the morning, when the bar closed, Alexander found he had no idea where he had left his car. He had to walk back to his flat in Bellevue, and in the morning, feeling frail and ill, he rang Guy and asked him to find his car for him. Guy had to walk across from his flatshare in Berea to fetch Alexander's car keys, then continue on foot to Yeoville, and begin his search. It was late morning before he returned with the car. "Why do you have to drink so much?" he asked Alexander, looking at him with his emerald green eyes.

"Because I'm afraid."

"Afraid of what?"

"Of losing you one day."

"You shouldn't have to need me that much," Guy responded.

They drove down to the game farm again that weekend, and Alexander forgot to be afraid, and he drank far less than he did in Johannesburg, and both men were happy and content. On the Saturday and Sunday mornings, Alexander taught a yellowbilled hornbill to come eat chunks of wholewheat bread from his hand, whilst Guy slept in.

By November, with summer having set in, and Guy's affections seemingly undiminished, Alexander's fears for the future had lessened somewhat. He drank less; he had more energy. Sometimes he organised a hike to one of the kloofs in the Magaliesberg, away beyond the northwest of the city, with Alice, her boyfriend, and one or two others, and Guy would be there also. They would all travel in Alexander's car. Although most of the others had cars of their own now, the Audi was bigger and more comfortable than the other cars. These Magaliesberg kloofs, on the north slopes of the range, were wondrous places where their own microclimates and ecosystems prevailed. They bore no relation to the generally rather treeless and spare Highveld plateau. In the kloofs, in the bottom of which flowed rapid streams of clear water broken by series of mini waterfalls, and in which were deep rock-girt plunge pools you could leap into from high above, and in which you could bathe, an almost sub-tropical ecology could be found. The sides of the kloofs were heavily overgrown with lianas and hanging ferns; the dense forest cover was home to troops of vervet monkeys, little black-faced imps who would creep up behind you as you sat and ate, and steal your food. There were leopards also in these kloofs – that was well attested, for periodically, one of these cats would slink down from the hills where they ran into Pretoria's northwestern suburbs, and stalk the suburban streets at night. Alice would bring some marijuana with her. It did not seem to have done her harm, all the years she had been smoking grass. To Alexander, she seemed to be just the same friendly and affectionate person he had first grown to know ten years earlier. She was at that time Alexander's oldest friend.

When Alexander was happy, liquor hardly affected him, except to raise his spirits to almost manic levels of good humour and playfulness. He could then be genuinely entertaining and very good company. No doubt this was why Guy put up with his drinking for one and a half years. Alcohol did not make Alexander angry, or dour, or mean-tempered, or violent. When Alexander was drunk, he hardly showed any physical signs of his inebriation, and he became amiable and affectionate and high-spirited. So he continued through 1990, and his work did not suffer. He was given another salary raise in February 1990. He was putting money away in a savings account, and he also had a sizable amount left of the ten thousand five hundred Rands which Andrew had paid him for the yacht. That he felt financially secure, that he enjoyed work for which he was properly rewarded, and that Guy continued to love him, helped keep his drinking under control. Only occasionally did he go on a two day binge, though he routinely drank every day, topping up at lunch time, then drinking a fair quantity in the evenings, and starting the day with hair of the dog. He tried not to allow the alcohol level in his bloodstream to reach zero: he began to experience acute discomfort, unease and anxiety if he did.

One afternoon in March, Alexander had arranged to meet Guy at the Johannesburg Art Gallery at Joubert Park. Alexander was early. He parked his car in the underground parking garage near the gallery, then he entered the park. Killing time, he walked across the park, which was crowded with black people, many headed for the Wanderers taxi rank in Klein Street, when he was suddenly confronted by two black men directly in front of him, blocking his way. One of them held a knife low down in his hand, inches away from Alexander's abdomen. Alexander backed away, only to come up against a third black man directly behind him, and when Alexander looked over his shoulder, he saw that he also had a knife in his hand. Alexander said "You want my money? You can have it."

"Give me your wallet!" ordered one of the men. Alexander did so. Inside it were his credit and cash cards, and about fifty Rands in cash.

"Now your coat," one of the men told him. "Take it off!"

Alexander shrugged out of his off-white cotton summer jacket, which one of the men grabbed. The three of them then disappeared: they did not run, they simply melted into the throng of black people, some of whom had stood watching the show.

Alexander turned and walked towards the art gallery. There on the steps, Guy was waiting. "Guy – we've got to go home. I've just been mugged."

"Are you OK, Sandy?"

"Ja – I'm OK. But they got my jacket – and my wallet and cards. I've got to ring my bank and cancel them."

"Where's your car, Sandy?"

"In the parking garage. Luckily, my keys were in my trouser pocket. And my silver cigarette case."

"Are you OK to drive?"

"I'm OK, Guy."

Alexander felt strangely unmoved by the entire episode, as if it had happened to someone else. He had felt rather the same way when he had witnessed the *Guardia Civil* opening fire on the crowd of Basque separatist protestors in northern Spain in 1976; and afterwards, when he had seen one of the *Civiles* lean down and fire a bullet each into the heads of two of the injured, as they lay on the cobble-stones of the plaza, Alexander had continued to feel as if the scene was being witnessed by someone else, someone he in turn was observing.

When Alexander got back to his flat in Bellevue with Guy, he was neither shocked nor trembling. He poured himself a scotch, then went to ring his bank. He took a deep gulp of the scotch, and suddenly spewed it up again. His hand began to shake. He had to replace the handset.

"I'm going to make you some tea with plenty of sugar, Sandy. I think you're in shock."

Alexander and Guy sat drinking their tea, then Alexander tried ringing the bank again. A recorded message gave him an out of hours number to ring: the branch had closed for the day. "Shit!" Alexander said.

He rang the next number, and after some waiting, he was explaining the situation to somebody the other end.

Later, Guy had commented "Sandy, you are . . . I don't know . . . you are amazing. I don't think I would be as calm as you."

Alexander blinked and looked out the window. "Things happen. That's all."

During the long Easter weekend in 1990, Alexander, his brother, Guy, Alice and her boyfriend piled into the Audi and drove across the Free State to Qua Qua homeland. They followed the dirt road for many miles, climbing gradually, until they had reached Witsieshoek, over eight thousand feet above sea level, at that time a small, unassuming holiday camp in the northern Drakensberg, where they parked the car. They shouldered their backpacks and set off up the slope, heading for the chain ladder which would allow them to ascend the precipitous cliff face, until they had attained an altitude of ten thousand feet, only one thousand feet below the peak of *Mont-Aux-Sources*. They continued hiking along the lip of the Amphitheatre, until they reached the nascent Tugela River, at this point just a shy stream, but which fell from the edge of the escarpment in a spectacular drop of more than three thousand feet. Here they made camp, pitching two two-man tents, and a pup tent for Alexander's brother. Roy, along with Alice's tough boyfriend, Roman, disappeared on day-long hikes the next two days, returning in the evening, but Alexander, Guy and Alice were happy to sit near the edge of the drop, with only occasional chat between them, as they gazed across the limitless miles of Africa far below, to a horizon which faded into infinity. They saw *lammergeiers*, bearded vultures, far below them, the huge birds riding the updrafts in great wheeling circles.

In late October of 1990, Alexander and Guy were invited to a mutual friend's party. There, Alexander saw Guy dancing with a very pretty girl, and although Guy had danced with several partners already that night, Alexander immediately felt his stomach turn sickeningly. There was an obvious mutual fascination between the two which caused Alexander, always highly intuitive, to feel deeply troubled.

In November, Guy began to find reasons to turn aside from Alexander's attempts at intimacy, and in late December one morning he declared, without any attempt to soften the blow, "I don't love you anymore, Sandy."

Alexander felt the blood drain from his face. "It's Renata, is n't it?"

"Yes."

Alexander, his voice very faint, said "I don't think I can bear to lose you, Guy."

Guy stared at him from green eyes from which all expression had been wiped clean.

Within a few days, Guy had moved into Renata's flat. She was, of course, the girl Alexander had seen Guy dancing with at the party in October. Alexander now hit the bottle savagely, determined to numb his pain. He did not turn up for work for three days, nor did he phone in to the office. He drank until he passed out. When he came to, he began to drink some more. He did not eat. He did not wash. For three days he lived and slept in the same clothes. For two nights running, he knocked on Alice's door late at night, late enough to wake her from sleep each time. He embarrassed her by weeping at her doorstep when she opened the door to him. Each time, she let him inside her flat. It was obvious to her that he was very drunk.

On the fourth day, Alexander turned up at work. It was only a few days short of Christmas. He was far from sober. Although he had made some effort at cleaning himself up, he stank of liquor and sweat. He had cut himself badly whilst shaving, and he had bled profusely into his shirt collar afterwards. "You had better go home," his boss said to him. "I'll get Marge to follow in her car, to make sure you get there safely."

Marge, a young woman who undertook basic research, followed Alexander back to his flat, which was not far, in her car. She was concerned for Alexander, and she asked him when he had last had something to eat.

"I don't know," he replied. "I cant remember."

"I think I should ring someone. What's your parents' number?" Marge asked him.

Alexander's father called for him the next morning. "I've booked you into a clinic in Boksburg", he told him. "Surely you must see that you need help."

Alexander was beyond arguing. He grabbed a few items haphazardly, stuffing them into a sports bag, hiding a bottle of whiskey amongst them, and got into his father's car.

The bottle of whiskey was found and confiscated immediately upon his arrival at the clinic. Alexander was technically sober within five days. He went through what he felt was Hell to get there. Sober he may then have been, but he was a long way from being well. He stayed a full fortnight at the clinic, through a bleak Christmas and a New Year that seemed to offer him little in the way of hope. His employment-linked medical insurance footed the bill. He returned to work in early January 1991, but within a few days he was drinking again, and just as savagely as he had been drinking before he had entered the clinic. After four days of this he was fired with immediate effect. He would be paid an extra month's salary in lieu of notice. Alexander wished he could commit suicide, but he lacked the courage, or sufficient will. Instead, after several days had passed, during which he had made a great nuisance of himself late at night to his friends in Yeoville, Alexander re-entered the clinic. This time, he would have to pay the clinic's fees out of his own pocket.

Alexander remained sober after leaving the clinic a second time, but it was a desperate, anguished sobriety, sustained by willpower alone. He felt a burden of grief and loss so overwhelming that he did not wish to live. He wept silently at odd moments. He neglected his personal hygiene and his appearance. His parents had not allowed him to return to his flat, but had made him move into a spare bedroom at their home. After a week of this, Alexander pulled himself together sufficiently to take stock of his financial position. He still had quite a lot of money put away, despite the clinic's fees. His parents did not put up much of an argument when he told them that he was returning to England.

Seventeen

A Move To Malta

In London in February 1991, Alexander put up in a shabby rooming house, one of dozens upon dozens of so-called "hotels" near Paddington station. It was mid-winter: London was very cold, with a lowering, grey sky and incessant icy rain. Before even the onset of that first early nightfall, Alexander knew he had made a terrible mistake in returning to England. He would have turned tail and caught the next flight back to Johannesburg, except that his pride prevented him from doing so. Alone in that cold, bleak and ugly room his first evening in London, it appeared to Alexander that his life so far had been nothing but a terrible failure. He could not rid himself of the fear that he had at last achieved the destiny that had always been awaiting him: that of a defeated, solitary exile in a cold, dark, foreign city, without even the means to end his life when it became more than he could endure. Those first few evenings, he dared not go out. He knew that if he did, he would find a pub, and if he began to drink again, he wouldn't stop drinking – and this, this squalid place, was not the environment to descend into alcoholic helplessness. So he stayed in his dingy room those first few evenings, the noise of the traffic his only companion; his yearning for Guy so intense, it made him groan.

Checking the "Bedsits for Rent" columns in the Evening Standard, within a few days Alexander found himself a bedsit in Queens Park, north London. As bedsits went, it was not a bad place, and it looked onto the park, but compared with the lovely old flat he had rented in Bellevue, Johannesburg, it was squalor incarnate. He shared a lavatory and a coin-operated shower on the landing with adjacent bedsits. Some of his neighbours were of indeterminate ethnic origin. Of the European fellow-residents he came to know well enough to greet on the stairs that late winter (and even, one or two of them, to know their first names), none was British. They were Italian, Irish, and eastern European: fellow exiles all of them.

Alexander rarely thought about God anymore. He had almost lost his faith. If God was still bothering him, he could not hear Him. But as the winter days gradually lengthened, and there appeared the occasional weak ray of sunshine, his faith in himself, in his ability to make something of his life right now, came slowly back to life, even if its flame was weak and flickering.

"I have to go somewhere warm and bright, somewhere the sun is shining," he told himself.

Perhaps the spirit of his maternal grandfather spoke to Alexander from the hereafter, for he thought suddenly of Malta, that tiny island archipelago in the Mediterranean where, according to his grandfather's memoirs, his grandfather, as a very young Royal Navy officer with the Mediterranean fleet before the Great War, had had such a happy, jolly time. There were daffodils in London's Royal parks, and every day the sun was stronger, and Alexander felt himself begin to live again, and he was motivated sufficiently to buy a one-way air ticket to Malta in late March of 1991.

Coming in to land at Malta airport, as the aircraft banked and slowly descended in a wide circle over the sea, Alexander could see through the window much of the main island, which is only seventeen miles long by nine miles wide. Malta's total land area is a mere one hundred and twenty-two square miles in extent. The population is just under four hundred and fifty thousand people. Malta is therefore a densely populated, tiny country. Its highest point is only just over eight hundred feet above sea level. The airport is a neat, modern building, small and manageable. Alexander passed through immigration and customs very quickly. He noted that his passport had been stamped with a three month visa only, for Malta was not yet a member of the European Union.

Alexander had booked a room in a hostel in one of the back streets of Sliema, which is a district found across Marsamxett harbor from Valletta, the walled capital city. Leaving the airport, it appeared that within minutes the taxi was driving through heavily built-up streets, a commercial district interspersed with small industrial concerns. Many of the buildings were run down and neglected, which, in that bright sunshine, was not as depressing as it would have been in Britain. The sun shone strongly, though it was only late March. Alexander felt too warm in his pullover and coat: it had been about eight degrees centigrade at Heathrow; it felt like about seventeen – or more – in Malta. He checked in at the hostel, in *Triq San Piju V*, at about four o'clock. He had a backpack and a suitcase with him, as well as a large carrybag. Everything he was likely to need within the first few weeks was packed in his backpack and suitcase. Alexander had left a big metal trunk of books and other possessions with one of his ex work colleagues from Reuters, with whom he had formed a friendship.

Out for a walk after he had been offered, and accepted, a coffee by the young man on duty at the desk, Alexander followed the hill down towards the Sliema waterfront. He passed a small supermarket on the way, which he noted: he would buy a better quality jar of instant coffee than the coffee he had been given at the hostel, to keep close by him. He needed cigarettes also. The view across Marsamxett harbor, an extensive natural inlet, was stupendous; surely, one of the world's great settings: Valletta, the colour of pale honey – with its immensely high fortified city walls, its domes, steeples, turrets, and roofs of every shape and description – was dazzling under the bright sun. The light scintillated on the water. Alexander was wearing a pair of sunglasses he had not worn since leaving

South Africa. Almost all the buildings he had seen so far in Malta were built of pale yellow limestone. He had observed a new structure being erected: the stone was so pale when newly cut, it was almost white. He noticed a large sign calling his attention to the Valletta ferry, running every half hour. In the middle of Marsamxett harbor he could see further extensive ancient fortifications, on what appeared to be an island: he was to learn that this was Manoel Island. There was a row of buses straight out of the 1950s lining the promenade, in the dominant island bus company colours of yellow and orange. There were also a couple of tiny, one-horse open carriages with frilled canopies for hire, which Alexander was to learn were called "*karozzin*". The pavement was lined with shops, bars, and hotels. There were a few big yachts and some large luxury motor boats moored just offshore. Alexander felt almost happy. "I'm going to find a way of staying here," he told himself.

Alexander quite enjoyed the hostel. Living there was very much a public affair, and he lacked the opportunity in which to remember his grief for what he had lost. He shared a room with three other men, all younger than himself. They were from Australia, Canada and Germany. The hostel provided cereals and fried and boiled eggs with toast and marmalade for breakfast: other meals you were expected to see to yourself. The next morning, Alexander, exploring the neighbourhood, found the Hole in the Wall pub at the corner of High Street and *Ghar il-Lembi*, not very far from the hostel. Inside he ordered his first drink – a beer – since leaving the Johannesburg clinic a second time, in January. The ceiling was very high, lost in shadow; the walls were covered in rock and music posters and etchings, and there was a tiny gallery above the room at one end, with a drums set arranged in it. Alexander was to listen to a variety of musical ensembles performing from that gallery as time went by. The barman on duty was young, with long blonde hair gathered in a pony tail. His accent was northern English. Alexander was to treat the Hole in the Wall as his local during the course of the one and a half years he was to remain in Malta.

There were several restaurants scattered amongst these narrow streets of Sliema. Alexander had meals in one or two, soon learning that *fenek* (rabbit) was a Maltese national dish. It was prepared in a number of ways, and all of them were delicious. It was only some years later, on a return visit to Malta, that Alexander suddenly awoke to the fact that these were not happy wild rabbits he was eating, but sad rabbits reared in cages, and he ceased eating *fenek* thereafter. The selection of seafoods on offer was, naturally (with the furthest you could get from the sea in Malta being only four and a half miles), very good. Alexander often ordered swordfish steaks with a substantial salad, and a half carafe of house white. Alexander was now drinking again, but because he was no longer desperately unhappy (his grief and sense of loss having become much less acute under the influence of the bright sunshine and the sparkling ocean), he did not return to the shockingly high levels he had sustained in Johannesburg. He totally avoided spirits.

It was inside the Hole in the Wall that he saw a card pinned on the community notice board, advertising a room to let just down the street in *Ghar il-Lembi*. He went to look at it. It was a reasonably large first floor room, with a tiny kitchenette, and a shower and lavatory cubicle. The full-length windows opened onto a minute balcony with wrought iron railings. There were wooden shutters which could be closed across the windows against the sun and heat. Malta grew very warm indeed during the long summertime. There was a double bed, a wardrobe, a table, an armchair, and two upright chairs. There was also a small coffee table and a bedside unit. The curtains, of patterned cotton print, were lined. The walls were plain plaster painted a pale yellow. The room was accessed via a narrow stairway which opened directly onto the street below. Alexander liked the room. The rent was far less than he had been paying for his miserable bedsit in Queens Park. He took the room there and then, putting down two months' rent in advance.

An acquaintance Alexander made early on at the Hole in the Wall, an Edinburgh Scotsman in his early thirties named Robbie, taught English at a language school. When Alexander told him about his background as a business researcher for Reuters and for the company in Johannesburg, Robbie said "The school needs someone to teach business English. I imagine you have a university degree?"

"Yes – an honours degree."

"Why don't you come talk to the school's owner? We're in Saint Julian's. The Global School of English."

"I would n't have thought the Maltese people needed tuition in English," Alexander remarked.

"They don't. We teach English to visiting foreign students." Robbie called to the barman. "Heh, Phil, can you lend me a pen and a wee scrap of paper please."

Robbie wrote down the owner's name – Anton Baldacchino – and the school's address. Saint Julian's was the next district along the coast from Sliema.

The next morning, Alexander caught a bus on Tower Road – *Triq It-Torri* – (what Alexander thought of as the "Promenade", for it ran beside the sea, and a wide paved promenade ran alongside it between the road and the shoreline) for Saint Julian's. The road the school was situated on, *Triq Il-Kbira*, ran parallel with the *Triq Gorg Borg Olivier*, which is what the *Triq It-Torri* became after a while. Alexander got off the bus at Balluta Bay, far too soon he was to realise, and he began walking until he reached the junction where the *Triq Il-Kbira* led off. Anton Baldacchino was a middle-aged Maltese man, with fading and thinning copper-coloured hair combed backwards from a high forehead. Alexander had noticed that quite a few Maltese people had hair that rufous colour, perhaps some genetic legacy from the Norman adventurers who had seized Malta in the 12th century. Alexander took to him: he had an easy manner and a pleasant smile.

"Robbie tells me you have a university degree and some business experience, eh?"

"That's right, Mr. Baldacchino. I have a bachelor of honours from the University of the Witwatersrand, one of South Africa's foremost universities. I did business and economics research for Reuters in London, and for another company in Johannesburg."

"But you do not sound South African, I think?"

Alexander grinned. "I know. I was born in Kenya. I'm a British citizen. I've spent a lot of my time in London. I never picked up a South African accent."

"There is a standard teaching textbook we use in our business English tuition. You will need to buy a copy at Meli's book shop in Valletta. Here – I'll write the textbook's name down."

Alexander realised the job was being offered to him. "I've not talked about the salary," he thought to himself. "Mr. Baldacchino, what would my hours be, and how much would I be earning?"

"Please call me Anton," the man smiled at him. "I will pay you nine Maltese Lira an hour. You would work six hours a day. The school is closed during November, December and January. You may find you only work mornings, or perhaps three or four days a week, for a month either side of that."

Alexander struggled to keep a grip on what Anton Baldacchino was saying. "May I scribble some quick calculations, Anton?" he asked.

His would-be boss pushed a piece of paper towards him. Alexander used his own ballpoint pen and did the arithmetic. Nine Maltese Lira was the equivalent of about eleven and a half Pounds. He worked out that he should be able to cover his rent, with adequate pocket money left over each month. As to the winter months, he'd get by if he was careful to put something by during the rest of the year.

"My passport is stamped for only three months," he told Anton Baldacchino. "How do I obtain permission to stay beyond that time, and the right to work?"

"That should not be a problem for a British citizen. I can help you with that."

"OK," Alexander smiled at the man. "I'd like to work for you."

Anton held out his hand. "The job is yours. There's some paperwork we must complete."

Alexander shook Anton's hand.

Alexander was impressed by Meli Book Shop, in Old Bakery Street, Valletta. It had a very wide range of books, both fiction and non-fiction. Alexander had always enjoyed book shops. He found the standard business English teaching text he was after. He read it from start to finish over the next few evenings. He was to start work at the language school the following Monday. He had already learned that his self confidence had n't taken as severe a beating as he had thought: he was sure he would be good at his work. He was soon to discover that he was indeed good at his work: during the week that followed, he quickly became familiar with the teaching method, and he found that he enjoyed teaching the largely Chinese and other Asian students business English. At quarter past four every afternoon, he caught the bus back to Sliema with Robbie, his work colleague, and invariably they would meet again later that evening at the Hole in the Wall pub, just up the road from Alexander's room.

Robbie was short, with a slight, wiry build. He had dark hair and a narrow face. He spoke with an educated Edinburgh accent, rather pleasing to Alexander's ear. He was single, and after a while, Alexander guessed that he was probably homosexual. Then, sometime in June, Robbie came home with Alexander after they had spent a couple of hours drinking at the Hole in the Wall, and later that evening, physical intimacies developed. Thereafter these were periodically repeated, either at Alexander's room, or at Robbie's two-room flat in *Triq Il-Karmnu*, not far from the pub. Robbie had (Alexander thought) a beautiful body. He was not a big man. He was spare and lean, but with a fine musculature. His shoulders were broad in proportion to a slim waist and narrow hips. He had a narrow head and sensitive, intelligent features which Alexander found very attractive. Alexander obtained much pleasure from the occasions of intimacy they shared together.

Once in a while, Alexander was stricken by a sense of sinfulness in his relationship with Robbie. Then he visited the *Stella Maris* parish church near his room, and spent a long time on his knees in front of the shrine to Our Lady. But even as he prayed for her intercession with her Son, he knew he could not claim forgiveness, for he had no intention – yet – of foregoing the pleasure he derived from his physical intimacies with Robbie. At such times, Alexander felt a dangerous inclination to commence drinking spirits again, but he knew that he dared not drink anything but beer – and perhaps, sometimes, a glass of wine. Alexander's alcoholism was not in abeyance: it was merely under a somewhat fragile control.

Neither Robbie nor Alexander was exactly in love with the other: over time Alexander's fondness for Robbie grew into genuine affection, but theirs was a relationship bereft of any great depth of emotional input. Alexander did not mind this. He was very afraid now of allowing his emotions to become entangled in any relationship. Occasionally, Alexander became aware that his life itself had little real depth to it, but these moments did not last. He had his work; the sun almost always shone; the proximity of the ocean soothed his spirits; the honey-coloured buildings gave him pleasure, as did the old city of Valletta, with its high-baroque architecture, magnificent churches and cathedral, and plazas in which to sit in the open air beneath a large sunshade and drink *Kinnie*, coffee, or a lager.

Just a little way up from the Sliema ferry landing on the Valletta side of Marsamxett harbour was a bar and restaurant, the Cockney Bar – or Cockney's, as it was more familiarly known. This rapidly became one of Alexander's favourite venues, as he sat at a table on the terrace across the narrow road from the bar with a coffee in front of him, or a *Kinnie* (a deliciously refreshing, bittersweet Maltese-made carbonated soft drink with a bitter orange and wormwood and herbs base, served very cold), or a cold lager, the glass bedewed with moisture, and sometimes he would order an excellent seafood lunch accompanied by a massive and substantial salad. From the terrace Alexander could gaze across Marsamxett harbour towards Manoel Island with its massive fortifications, the fort as perfect as an architectural model. He could watch small craft entering and leaving the harbour: yachts, cabin cruisers and working boats. On the further shore Sliema's hotels, apartments and higgledy-piggledy roofscape formed a pleasing backdrop, every surface and angle thrown into high definition by the bright Mediterranean sunshine.

The Cockney's interior consisted of two adjacent rooms, hollowed out of the base of the fortifications that comprised Valletta's 16th century defensive walls. There was a serving counter in the main room, and there were four or five small tables, each with four chairs, located in each room. Inside, late middle aged and elderly men sat and drank their coffees if it was still morning, or their beers if it was later in the day. Over time,

Alexander came to be fairly well-known here, and some of these men would engage him in conversation. Many of them had at some time lived in London. Some had been in the British merchant marine, while a few had served in the Royal Navy. "*Hello. Kif int?*" Alexander would greet one or two of them, as he entered the room.

"*Jien tajjeb grazzi,*" they would reply. "*U int?*"

From the Cockney Bar it was rather a steep climb, via a number of narrow streets with high 19th century tenements towering over them, the tenements decorated with broad but shallow boxed in balconies overhanging the street. Alexander knew that these closed balconies, whose louvred shutters you could open, were a cultural residue of the Arab occupation of the island – as well as being a sensible answer to the extreme heat of summer. Alexander was making his way up the slope once when he saw a boy on a delivery bicycle stop beneath one such box balcony on the second floor, whistle piercingly a few times, and a shutter was thrown back and a woman's head and shoulders appeared, and she began to lower a basket down to the street on the end of a rope. Inside the basket was a small fluffy white dog. When the basket reached the ground, the dog jumped out and began to sniff about, then do its business, and the grocer's boy placed a package in the basket, which was hauled up to the balcony. As Alexander continued to watch, he saw the now empty basket being lowered once again, and as it reached the bottom, the small dog jumped into it, and was hauled up again to the balcony. Alexander laughed with unfeigned pleasure, then continued up the slope to *Triq Republika* (Republic Street), the central thoroughfare which runs through Valletta along the spine of the peninsula on which the city is built, and along which many noteworthy baroque buildings are located: the Grand Master's Palace (which is today Malta's parliament house), the National Library, and set a little back, Saint John's Co-Cathedral, being the most prominent of these structures.

Alexander gained a huge amount of pleasure from walking this, and other streets, in Valletta on the weekends, when he had two days of leisure to himself. He usually walked alone, only very rarely meeting up with Robbie. He felt very much more at home in this largely 17th and 18th century city, with its 19th century additions, than he had ever felt in London, which (despite several lengthy stays), still retained an alien air about it for Alexander. In Valletta the people were for the most part rather swarthy, and they shouted cheerfully when they conversed with one another, and the tourists mixed with the natives as they paraded the *Triq Republika*, or sat drinking coffee in the square opposite Café Cordina, under the ever stronger Mediterranean sun. Alexander realised he did not possess the soul of a Briton.

The Café Cordina, in the centre of Valletta, was one of Alexander's favourite coffee stops. From March onwards it was much frequented by tourists, but local people continued to meet there also. The interior had a magnificent barrel-vaulted, painted ceiling, in the classical baroque style. If you ascended an elegant curving staircase, you reached a long mezzanine room directly beneath the further end of the barrel-vaulted ceiling, set with tables and chairs. On the ground floor at the rear of the café, beyond the curving staircase, also beneath a painted, but in this case, flat ceiling, was a large room with small tables and chairs arranged along the sides, with mirrors set in the walls, between beautifully painted murals of pre-pubescent, semi-naked boys in classical poses. In the invariably fine, sunny weather that prevailed from early April onwards, Alexander sat outside in Republic Square, at one of the tables beneath a large brightly coloured umbrella, in front of the elegantly housed National Library. If Alexander had been asked to define the reasons for the pleasure he felt as he sat outdoors in Valletta, drinking coffee, or *Kinnie*, or a lager, he would have replied "Observing people, sitting in the sunshine, and admiring the architecture."

Another favoured halt, particularly if he wished to drink a lager, was the Kantina Café, adjacent to the classical baroque main entrance façade of Saint John's Co-Cathedral. This café-bar was a basement room, reached via a rather steep flight of stairs. But Alexander always sat outside in front of the café, at a table beneath one of the *ficus* trees, to be served by a waitress as he observed the passing show.

Sometimes Alexander would visit Saint Paul's Shipwreck church, not far from the Cathedral, with its relics of Saint Paul: a section of the stone column on which the saint was beheaded in Rome, and a bone from the Saint's right wrist. The interior of the church was particularly rich and splendid, with not an inch of the walls left un-decorated: glowing, patterned marble panels of many different tones and colours clad the walls and columns; the huge, deeply embossed altar front of the high altar, along with the altar fronts in the side chapels, was of gleaming silver, as was the altar rail, padded with red velvet, below the high altar. Alexander was to join a couple of tours of the impressive 17th century *Casa Rocca Piccola* palace, still a family home, in Republic Street during his stay in Malta. On his second visit to the palace, the Marquis himself, a short, slightly overweight, middle aged gentleman with an English public school accent, wearing a shabby pullover and baggy slacks, who looked like everybody's favourite uncle, was the group's tour guide. Alexander approached him afterwards and thanked him. "That was a most enjoyable tour, sir," he said. "I gained a real feel of the house as a genuine family home."

"Thank you," the Marquis replied. "We are proud of our home."

"Actually, this is my second visit," Alexander said.

"We'll give you a free ticket for your third," the Marquis replied. "Tell them I said so."

Alexander laughed. "OK. I'll do that, thanks. Goodbye Sir".

At Fort St. Elmo at the tip of the peninsula, early during his stay in Malta, Alexander went to watch the *In Guardia* parade, where men wearing 17th century military dress, with steel breastplates and backplates, and steel morion helmets, marched and wheeled to the beat of a drum, and fired their (blank charged) arquebuses, amidst much noise and clouds of black smoke, at the culmination of the display. Also at Fort St. Elmo, which had repelled numerous bloody attacks by Turkish forces during the Great Siege of 1565, were situated the National War Museum's two locations, one just outside the fort, and one within the fort complex, which Alexander visited several times during his stay in Malta.

As time went by, after Alexander had struck up a friendship with a local man, Filippu Dingli, he was to be shown much more of Valletta (and also of the island, for Filippu had a car). Professor Filippu Dingli was a native of Malta. He was the professor of political history at the University of Malta, at its main campus in Msida (which, although located on the far side of Malta's only motorway, was not far as the crow flies from Sliema). Alexander had met him round about lunchtime one Saturday, at the Hole in the Wall, where Alexander was drinking a lager. The late middle aged man with short grizzled hair and a long, humorous face, had sat down at a table next to Alexander's, greeting him with a slight smile and a "Good afternoon".

Alexander had a book in front of him on the table, a history of the Order of St. John of Jerusalem – the Knights of Malta, as they were to become better known. "Are you interested in Maltese history?" asked the man.

"Yes – I'm interested in the history of the Mediterranean and the Levant in general," Alexander replied.

"The story of the Knights is a fascinating one," the man continued. "Their influence on European history was profound – in light of the part they played in keeping the western Mediterranean open to European shipping. In fact, Malta's influence on European history was out of all proportion to her size." The man leant across, his right hand extended. "Filippu Dingli," he introduced himself.

"I'm Sandy Maclean," Alexander replied, shaking hands.

The two men chatted for a while, before Filippu Dingli had to leave. A week or so later, they met again, by chance, at the same bar. A friendship began to develop between them, with Filippu offering to drive Alexander the coming weekend to the *San Anton* (Presidential) Gardens at Attard. Filippu was at least fifteen years older than Alexander. He lived in Sliema. His manner was easy going and he was soft spoken, although he could enthuse about history: he would speak knowledgeably about any aspect of the history of the Mediterranean. The friendship between the university professor and the exile who did not feel like an exile at all, continued to grow, and it was to last until Alexander finally returned to South Africa in September 1992. It was to endure beyond that even, for Alexander stayed in touch with Filippu, and met up with him twice on holidays spent in Malta during the early 2000s.

As a passenger in Filippu's small car, Alexander became more familiar with the two islands. Most cars were small in Malta, because the roads were generally narrow and winding, and the traffic was heavy, and as challenging as the traffic in Rome, in whose drivers the Maltese appeared to have found much inspiration. With Filippu, Alexander visited the picturesque fishing village of Marsaxlokk in the south-east of the island, being driven past many acres of vineyards to get there. He was delighted by the many colourfully painted, high-prowed *dghajsas*, with their Osiris eyes painted at the bows, and there were a few of the bigger *luzzijiet* also moored in the harbour. Under the Mediterranean sun, colours were brighter, more intense, and the surface of the sea sparkled and danced in the sunshine.

One Saturday afternoon, Filippu asked Alexander whether he had a bathing costume. "Bring it – and a towel – if you do," he said. "We're going to the beach."

They took Route 1 north, following the somewhat heavily built-up north-east coast, and then headed across the island to Ramla beach in the west. As they crossed the island, Alexander was struck by the tiny, irregularly shaped, emerald green, artesian-watered patchwork fields separated by drystone walls. Situated in Golden Bay, the good sized beach was made of fine golden sand. It was by now August, and the temperature stood at thirty-one degrees centigrade (88F). The water looked very inviting. There were no waves at all, only the gentlest lapping of water against the beach. Alexander was wearing his bathing trunks beneath his slacks, and he stripped off there and then, on the beach. He then understood that what he had thought were rather odd, very colourful baggy shorts Filippu was wearing, was his bathing costume. Alexander had n't gone swimming in the sea since 1977, in Cape Town. He knew he was very pale, the tan he had acquired during 1989 with Guy, on repeated visits to the Lowveld, having faded. As he waded into the sea, then flung himself full length into the water, memories of childhood visits to the beach came rushing back. He shook them off as he rose from the water, tossing his head. Filippu, who was standing in the water up to his waist, was staring at him, but his gaze was unfocused, as if he was thinking of something or someone else.

Filippu had brought a small wicker picnic hamper, with sandwiches and some gateaux and a thermos of black coffee, some sachets of sugar, a couple of teaspoons, and two china mugs. There were also several bottles of the refreshing *Kinnie* drink that Alexander had acquired such a taste for, kept cold in a cold bag. "This is super, Filippu," Alexander told his friend. "Very thoughtful of you."

Alexander lighted a cigarette. For years, he had carried his cigarettes in a very old, monogrammed silver cigarette case that had belonged to his great-grandfather, who had had the same initials as Alexander. Alexander had been using a brass Zippo lighter since 1979: one of Alice's gang had given it to him. He lay back on his towel, and gazed at the cloudless blue sky through his sun-glasses.

"I used to bring my children here when they were young," Filippu said.

"I did n't know you had kids."

"They are grown up now."

Alexander wondered where Filippu's wife was. His friend had never before spoken about having any family.

"Are they boys, girls – ?"

"A boy, the eldest, and a girl. I don't see them very often. When my wife and I separated, well – the children see more of her than they do of me."

Alexander was silent. He did not know what to say, so he said nothing. He felt too relaxed after his dip in the water to worry too much about Filippu and his family concerns.

"Would you prefer a coffee, or a *Kinnie*?" asked Filippu.

"I'll have a coffee for now, maybe a *Kinnie* later, Filippu. Thanks."

Filippu stirred sugar into the mug of black coffee, and passed it to Alexander. Filippu, like Alexander, took his coffee black, with sugar.

Alexander drew on his cigarette and sipped at his coffee. He knew that right this moment, he was happy.

Eighteen

Maltese Excursions

The melancholia which had stalked Alexander as a teenager and a young man was apt to return with little warning, but experience had taught him that living as full a life as possible, whilst also seeking some time to be alone with himself, helped keep it at bay.

Alexander had little time now to pander to this melancholic streak: he worked five days a week till four o'clock in the afternoon. He spent at least four evenings a week at the Hole in the Wall (without, so far, returning to the savage drinking of the past, perhaps because he was, for the present, reasonably content with his life). Alexander knew a number of regulars at this pub, including Robbie. Filippu dropped in quite often. Some evenings, when Alexander was feeling troubled, or he needed to walk off a black dog mood, he might head down the street from his room to the nearby Tower Road – *Triq It-Torri* – the busy road fronting the broad shore-side promenade, which had, in places, narrow gardens between the promenade and the sea. This was a popular location among Sliema residents for strolling in the evenings (and walking the dog, and jogging, also), with the small trees lit up by hundreds of silver fairy lights, and the sea just alongside, and the soft evening air a relief after the heat of the day. Sometimes Alexander would walk to Saint Julian's Tower, and on round the headland alongside the gardens into Saint Julian's Bay.

At other times, Alexander would walk down the hill to Sliema waterfront, which was lined with shops, bars, cafés, small hotels and small apartment blocks. From here at night, the view of Valletta across Marsamxett harbor – the massive, fortified city walls glowing pale gold in the floodlights, the floodlighted steeples and domes behind the city walls stark against the night sky – was splendid, truly one of the great urban vistas of the world.

Then Alexander felt content with his own company, but the pavement was always crowded, so he usually crossed the dual carriageway to the Sliema promenade, where there were fewer people walking, and the sound of the sea lapping just below him was soothing and reassuring, and just off-shore he could see a few scattered lights from the yachts at their moorings, or from the night-fishers headed out to sea in their small boats. It was almost impossible for someone without a car to find a location on the island where he could be truly alone: the island was too small and too crowded for that, but Alexander had learned at school how to be alone in a crowd.

Sometimes, during the day, Alexander would make his way along the *Triq Ix-Xatt* which followed the Sliema shore of Marsamxett harbor, walking as far as the bridge to Manoel Island, which he would then cross, and keep walking until he had reached the Manoel Island Yacht Marina, where he could gaze at the rows of yachts tied up at the jetties. It was, by the time he had returned to the Sliema waterfront, a long walk, so he often stopped at a bar for a lager, or at a café for a coffee, before heading up the hill for home again. By then Alexander had walked off the unquiet restlessness which sometimes overcame him if he was alone over the weekend.

One Saturday afternoon Filippu drove Alexander to Mdina, the ancient inland capital of Malta, perched on the edge of an escarpment with wide views across the green fields to the north and east, with the Mediterranean visible in the distance. Mdina too had been heavily re-fortified by the Knights after the Great Siege of 1565. You approached the city from the south, to find that it was protected by a wide, deep, dry moat. You entered the city across a narrow road bridge, and went through a magnificent neo-classical gateway. Mdina's streets were a maze of narrow, dog-legging, twisting ways and alleys, but in front of the superb baroque cathedral, with its symmetrical façade and twin belfries, was a plaza. Across this tiny city, if you made your way to the northeastern walls where the ground dropped steeply to the fields far below, was the *Palazzo de Piro* restaurant, built atop and alongside the walls. Your view as you sat and drank coffee, or a beer, or ate your excellent meal, was magnificent. "This is a wonderful location, Filippu," said Alexander.

"I thought you would enjoy it." Filippu took a deep draught of his lager. "Tell me, do you have any political views?"

Alexander put his coffee cup down, and placed the cake fork on the side of the plate. "I don't think I have any political views to speak of. I'm broadly conservative, I suppose. Why do you ask?"

I have some friends in a political movement that I wondered might interest you," Filippu replied. "A Maltese nationalist movement."

"That's anti-immigration, yeah?"

"We're opposed to Islamic immigration, yes. We suffered for centuries, struggling against Islamic rule and subsequent attempts by Muslims to re-conquer these islands," Filippu replied. "And now we are witnessing their return."

"Filippu, I really don't think I have thought about it much."

Which was not true: Alexander had sometimes felt some concern at the intensity of Islamic immigration to Britain, but not sufficiently so as to exercise his mind much, and certainly his concerns were not so far advanced that he wished to get involved in the British nationalist, anti-immigration movement. He hoped that Filippu would drop the subject. In fact, Filippu did not raise it again on that occasion; instead, he asked Alexander whether he would like some more coffee and cake.

Alexander smiled. "This gateau is very good. I'll have a second slice with some more coffee, thanks."

Filippu ordered another coffee and slice of cake for Alexander, and another beer for himself.

In November, Filippu and Alexander visited the megalithic *Hagar Qim* temple complex high above the cliff-side on Malta's south-western coast. This collection of structures now open to the sky was built of massive blocks of limestone, and dated back to the 4th millennium BC. The sky was overcast. It was, for Malta, cold, and Filippu wore a padded, quilted coat. Alexander wore corduroy trousers and his old tweed jacket and a tweed cap. The location was very much a rural one, reached via a series of very narrow lanes passing between drystone walls demarcating the tiny, bright green, irregularly shaped fields. As Alexander considered the temples' vast age – they were more than five thousand years old – and the labour that must have gone into cutting, shaping and transporting the huge stone blocks, the work directed perhaps by a single mind, he was awe-struck. How, in the 3 000s BC had there been a large enough labour force on this tiny island, expendable in terms of being withdrawn from food production and animal husbandry, to embark on such a vast, long term project? And who were the kings, or priest-kings, or what was the priestly hierarchy, what was the culture, what the religious organisation, that had levied so much power over that population as to be able to gather, organise and motivate it for a construction process that lasted generations, if you included the other temple sites across Malta and Gozo islands?

There was a cold wind blowing, and Alexander now saw that Filippu was turning blue beneath his tan. They were both rather relieved once they had got back in the car and the heater could be turned on. Once Filippu was able to talk again, he said, as he drove "Those are the oldest standing man-made structures in the World: older than the pyramids."

"I am awe-struck, Filippu. Viewing that site raises so many questions in my mind, questions to which we will never know the answers. I cannot begin to visualize the society that prevailed when they were built."

"You do know that at that time, Malta was very well wooded?"

Alexander reached for his cigarette case. "What an ancient species we are," he remarked.

"That is true – yet we are the youngest of all the animal species," Filippu replied.

Neither of the men wished very much to do any more walking or sight-seeing in the open that day. Filippu drove back to Sliema, and by mutual accord, they repaired to the Hole in the Wall for a snack and a drink.

By December there were sudden, violent storms sweeping in across the islands from the sea. Alexander was astonished at the height of the waves breaking on the promenade alongside *Triq It-Torri*: some of the waves broke thirty feet high and swept across the promenade and into the road. The winter weather brought rain and cold, too: nothing like the sort of cold Alexander was used to in Britain, but it had the Maltese people wrapping themselves up as if they were traveling to the Arctic. During January and February 1992, the coldest months, the temperature fell as low as nine degrees centigrade, and never rose higher than sixteen degrees centigrade. Alexander had no work to go out to from early November through to the end of January. He stayed in bed later than usual in the mornings, but he always got outside later in the day. He enjoyed the walk along *Triq It-Torri* promenade: there was an elemental appeal for Alexander in the stormy sea. Often, the Sliema – Valletta ferry service was not running, because of high winds across Marsamxett harbour. Then, if Alexander wished to reach Valletta he would have to take the long bus ride round the head of the sound, in one of Malta's 1950s buses, with its driver's station kitted out in religious iconography, tassels and gewgaws. He was not fond of traveling by bus in Malta. The seats were tiny, and too close together for his six feet and one and a half inches in height.

Robbie and he over-nighted at each other's flats quite often. During those winter months, Alexander felt his attachment to the Scotsman growing: there were times when he wondered whether he was in love with him – then he remembered what he had felt for Patrick in Cape Town, and for Guy in Johannesburg, and he knew that if he was in love, it was in a lower key. Alexander saw little of Filippu during those winter months.

In February one late Saturday afternoon, Alexander and Robbie were returning from Valletta. The ferry was running, and as they were docking at Sliema, a squall of ice hit them. Alexander and Robbie ran across the road and took shelter in the café opposite, from where, in amazement, they watched the street turn white with hailstones. Afterwards, as they walked up the hill to their homes, the break between street and pavement kerbside was hardly discernible, so deep had been the ice-fall. It felt cold even to these two men accustomed to winters in Britain. They went to Robbie's flat, because he had a bath. Robbie ran a hot bath, and they shared it, to get warm again. When, later, they visited the Hole in the Wall, there were almost no Maltese customers there: the Maltese, faced by what seemed to them to be Polar temperatures, were staying at home that evening.

Spring comes early and sweet in the Mediterranean. The skies were more and more frequently a wonderful, pure blue, in which fleecy clouds paraded one after the other. The sunrises seen from Tower Road promenade were magnificent: some mornings, when Alexander woke very early, he would pull on a pair of tracksuit pants and put on his trainers and grab a coat, then walk down the street to Tower Road and stand on the promenade and gaze at the sunrise. There were a strata of colours from crimson through molten gold to lemon yellow to salmon pink, burdened by a heavy range of lowering clouds the colour of bruised plums, hanging beneath a sky still showing the lingering night. The days warmed rapidly: by late March, there were days when the temperature reached twenty-one centigrade. The trees were suddenly covered in a lacework of bright fresh new green. Alexander began going to work in a light woolen jacket, bare-headed, rather than in his heavier tweed jacket and cap. There were still days of consecutive rainfall, but these periods rarely lasted longer than three days, before the sun burst through and drove away the dark clouds, and the warm dry weather began to dominate. By April, Alexander was wearing light chinos and a linen jacket – though many of the locals were still wearing heavy coats. The air was scented with snatches of perfume, as a zephyr wafted the scent of some flowering tree or shrub to Alexander, and he would stop and inhale, but it was rare that he could target the scent's source. In springtime you forgot that, come summer, during days when there was not a breath of wind from the sea, it would be the diesel and petrol exhaust fumes from the heavy traffic that you would smell, the metallic odours trapped beneath the high pressure system that prevailed in July, August and September.

Alexander wrote to his mother once every seven to ten days. Her letters were regular weekly communications. His father, who was essentially an open, affectionate man, always sent his love, but Alexander knew his own love in return was an arid thing, though once in a while, usually late at night, he sat and remembered how much he had loved his father when he had been a small boy, what a loving Dad his father had been, and Alexander felt tears come to his eyes for the loss of that innocence and happiness and security. In condemning himself for what he was, he had condemned to imprisonment the love he had felt for his father. On the rare occasions he wrote to his father, it was almost always late at night, when his defences were down, and his heart felt tender, and he wished with all his soul that he had never had to grow up, and that he could have remained a child. Those late nights when he felt unmanned by nostalgia and sentiment, were dangerous times for Alexander: then, he sometimes experienced a powerful longing for a large whiskey. But he stuck doggedly to drinking nothing more than beers and the occasional glass or two of wine.

His mother sent Alexander photographs of the tiny black cat, Sooty, whom he had given to his parents in mid 1989, to try to fill a little of the gap that Lulu's death had left. Sooty had belonged to Terrance and his girlfriend, but they were then moving to a smaller house in Orange Grove, and they were keen to find homes for their two cats. Alexander went to fetch both the cats, and brought them home to his parents, only to find that no sooner had they been introduced to their new home, than the tabby became very aggressive towards the little black cat. It was decided that one of them would have to be returned, and they kept Sooty, because she was the more vulnerable and defenceless of the two. Loved, cherished and cosseted, like all the Maclean family cats, Sooty developed a great deal of character. Alexander had grown very fond of her during visits he made to his parents once a week. One day, he would say to himself, I shall have cats of my own.

But would such a day ever come? Alexander was making no provision for his old age. He had acquired no property. In his moments of honesty with himself, he knew that his insecure and peripatetic lifestyle, whilst possibly suited to someone still in their twenties, was unsuited to a man aged thirty-seven. But he could not see that there was anything he could now do about this situation. However, Alexander's bank balance was growing: he spent little on himself, outside of drinks and the occasional evening meal at the Hole in the Wall, and the coffees, beers, *Kinnies*, and very occasional lunches he bought in Valletta during the weekends. His growing bank balance provided him with some sense of achievement and a comforting feeling of security.

Nineteen

A Summertime Liason

In May, Filippu invited Alexander to a reception at the old University buildings in Valletta itself. It was something to do with a visiting academic of some international repute. "I thought you might like to meet some more Maltese people," Filippu said to Alexander.

"I'ld like to come. Thanks for the invitation."

Sunset in Malta in May was at 8.20 p.m, and the reception was set for 7 p.m, so Alexander, wearing one of his London suits, crossed Marsamxett harbour with the sun quite low in the western sky. The cityscape across the water was particularly lovely, the pale limestone fortifications and walls glowing with soft golden light. The reception was held in a large, elegant room in the old University buildings. The floor was of glossy, polished, patterned parquet. The walls were lined with mirrors that reached almost from the floor to the ceiling, in heavy gilt frames set between the shuttered windows. The plasterwork moulding of the cornice and frieze was picked out in gilt. There was a string quartet from the music department at one end of the room, and a bar at the other. Waiters with glasses of wine on trays also circulated. Filippu introduced Alexander to a number of academics. One, a professor of classical languages, was an extremely elegant, beautifully dressed and coiffed woman of about thirty-five. Her patrician features, which struck Alexander as very lovely, were cleverly made up: so cleverly, that you were not sure whether she was wearing any makeup up at all. She spoke an excellent, educated English, and after chatting to her for a while, Alexander learned that she had been to Wycombe Abbey, a private girls' school in Buckinghamshire in England. He also learned, on further enquiry, that she had been to university at Oxford.

With little initially in common other than a mutual pleasure in the other's clearly enunciated, somewhat upper class spoken English (when Alexander felt himself to be on display, or on less than totally familiar terms with the person he was speaking to, he slipped unconsciously into the accent and speech patterns he had acquired during his early stays in London), and with considerable common ground in the books they had loved during childhood (and later, as Alexander was to learn, a mutual delight in each other's looks), Alexander none the less found himself strongly drawn to the woman. He had not felt such a powerful attraction, with such distinctly erotic undertones, for a woman for many years. Alexander had always been attracted by smartly turned out, intelligent women with a restrained femininity. His first girlfriend, Catherine, had possessed just such qualities. Furthermore, Alexander had always felt very relaxed around evidence of wealth, and the woman's style – her hair, her understated, expensive jewelry, her costly outfit – bespoke greater wealth than was customary in an academic. Marija Caruana was clearly very bright indeed, but she had a sense of humour also: within a short while, she and Alexander were sharing anecdotes about some of the types of British tourists who visited the island.

"The English couple," Alexander recounted, "whose table I had to share at the Café Cordina, said to me: 'But Valletta has such a seedy air.'" Alexander blew the smoke from his cigarette to one side. Marija Caruana was also smoking; in her case, she favoured long, slim, pink, red, green, yellow or purple Sobranie Cocktails. "Of course," Alexander continued, "it is precisely that genuine, lived-in atmosphere that is one of the things I enjoy about Valletta."

"Yes, in England, wherever you go in the countryside, it looks like a picture on a chocolate box".

Alexander laughed. "That's exactly what I said to them. I said 'If you like chocolate box pretty, then you should have stayed in England. Malta is authentic and alive.'"

Alexander was introduced to a further two or three academics by Marija, with whom they both chatted for a while, but it was with each other that they spent most of their time. Alexander saw Filippu watching him, and when he met Filippu's eye, his friend smiled at him. Alexander had been at the reception for perhaps one and a half hours when Marija told him she had to leave now. "My son will be waiting for me."

"You have a son? How old is he?"

"He's fourteen. He's my family now. I separated from my husband some years ago."

"Would you like me to walk you to your car, Marija?"

"Thank you, yes please. I must just say goodnight to Filippu"

Alexander too wished Filippu a good night, shaking his hand. Then he and Marija made their way into the open air. Alexander felt the evening air as a welcome, refreshing tonic after the crowded warmth of the reception.

As they walked through the soft velvety Valletta evening, through streets in which people enjoying themselves thronged, Marija asked Alexander where he lived. When he answered, "Sliema," she responded "I live in Saint Julian's. I can give you a lift, if you like."

"That would be nice. I struggle to fit in the seats in the buses."

Marija laughed, and stopped and turned, and looked him up and down, as if assessing him. "I can imagine!"

When Marija dropped Alexander off at his flat in *Għar il-Lembi*, she reached into her tiny handbag and withdrew a card. "Here are my telephone numbers. Please give me a ring sometime."

Alexander felt a wave of happiness. "I shall do that, Marija. I've enjoyed meeting you. Thanks for the lift. Good night."

"Good night Sandy," Marija said, offering him her hand, which he shook.

Alone in his room, Alexander stood in abstracted thought. "I'm right, are n't I?" he thought. "She likes me a great deal. And I think she's very fine indeed. But what if she wants more from me than I can give her?"

He made himself a coffee, and took it out onto the tiny balcony, where he sat on one of the two little round-bottomed wrought iron chairs he had there, and he listened to the rumble and rush of traffic from Tower Road not far away, and he could see a wide track of moonlight reflected on the surface of the sea beyond the promenade. "Perhaps," he considered, "this is something I should do . . . after all, how often does this sort of thing happen to me?"

He lighted a cigarette and sipped his coffee.

One and a half weeks later, Alexander rang Marija's home number on the Saturday. A teenage boy's voice answered the phone. Alexander asked to speak with his mother.

"Marija?"

"Sandy! How nice to hear from you. How are you?"

"I'm fine, Marija. Are you well?"

After chatting for a minute or two, Alexander said "I would like to invite you to a show at the Manoel theatre. They're staging Ravel's *Daphnis et Chloé*. I thought we could have supper afterwards."

"That would be lovely."

"I don't know Valletta's restaurants, Marija. You can choose."

"We'll go to *Rubino's*. It's just around the corner from the Manoel, Sandy. It is one of Valletta's oldest restaurants, serving Maltese dishes".

"I would enjoy that, Marija. They have tickets for *Daphnis et Chloé* available still for this Friday and the following Monday nights. What evening would suit you?"

"Friday would be perfect, Sandy."

"Good. I have your address here on your card. Shall I call for you at seven?"

Later, Alexander rang Filippu, and asked him if he knew of a reputable taxi company. "I'm taking Marija to the Manoel, and supper afterwards."

"That's good!" Filippu declared. "I hoped you would get to know someone at that reception."

"Yes, and I appreciate your having introduced me to Marija, Filippu."

The following Friday, Alexander had booked a taxi to fetch him – Filippu had been able to advise him which taxi company to contact – and then proceed to Saint Julian's, where Marija lived. Alexander was wearing the only suit he had with him in Malta, a dark grey single breasted suit with fairly narrow lapels and trousers, one of two good suits he had bought in London when he was working at Reuters. The apartment block, which was only three stories high, but which had a fine view across Saint Julian's Bay, looked expensive, with a doorman on duty and a marbled foyer. Alexander kissed Marija on the cheek in her hallway, which had a pink and blue patterned silk rug from Iran on the polished parquet floor, and some original framed oils hanging on the veneered wood walls, and he offered her the tiny corsage he had bought after work: a single yellow orchid with a small spray of leaves.

"This is beautiful, Sandy," Marija told him. "Bernard!" she called. "Bring me a pin, will you."

Her son, who was tall for his age, dark and slim, appeared, and Marija introduced him to Alexander. His manner towards Alexander was not warm. Corsage pinned to her gown – Marija was wearing a full-length evening gown of what looked to Alexander like raw silk the colour of old ivory, which suited her dark hair and dark eyes – Marija was ready to leave; another plus in her favour: Alexander did not like to be kept waiting. She shouted goodbye to her son, who had disappeared again, grabbed a tiny gold lamé handbag, and a fine black Maltese lace wrap which she wore off her shoulders and gathered in her arms, and they took the lift down together.

It was almost quarter to eight by the time they reached the Manoel theatre. Alexander realised that the foyer had been extended into a grand neighbouring building. Marija told him this was the *Palazzo Bonici*. Alexander had not been to the Manoel before, and when they had been shown to their box in the third tier, he looked around him with some curiosity. He had always had a keen interest in architecture and interiors. Though not very large – the theatre seated about three-hundred and fifty people – it was finely proportioned and superbly decorated. The three tiers of boxes were arranged in an oval all the way around the auditorium, broken only by the stage and the proscenium, and their wooden structure was entirely covered in gold leaf. The oval ceiling was painted in a pale blue *trompe-l'oeil* effect, resembling a cupola. A massive chandelier hung from the centre of it.

Maurice Ravel's *Daphnis et Chloé*, first performed in 1912, was a one act ballet in three parts, or scenes. There was no interval. At just less than an hour long, the lack of an interval was no great hardship. Alexander thought the music was passionate and lush. He was no great fan of dance, but he often appreciated the music to which ballets were set. Marija appeared to be enjoying it.

They reached *Rubino's* restaurant shortly before nine-thirty. *Rubino's* had opened in 1906, and Alexander wondered whether his grandfather, as a junior officer in the Royal Navy's Mediterranean fleet, based in Malta before the First World War, had known it. The restaurant was in Old Bakery Street, only a short walk from the Manoel theatre. It had a modest façade. The restaurant was busy, but Alexander had booked a table five days earlier. Marija clearly knew some of the other diners, for she greeted several couples with a wave and a smile, and stopped to chat briefly with a couple who had been talking together in Italian.

"I think a red wine might be a good idea," Alexander remarked, when, shortly after they were seated, a waiter asked him what they would like to drink. "We can order a half of white with the desserts. Unless you would prefer something else, Marija – a soft drink, perhaps?"

"A red wine would be good. Have you tried one of our local Maltese wines?"

"Perhaps as a house wine served in a carafe. But I would n't have known what I was drinking. Why don't you choose a local wine for us, Marija?"

When the bottle of red wine arrived, and Alexander sipped at the taster the waiter poured into his glass, he thought it was more than passable. He nodded. "That'll be OK," he told the man.

Marija advised Alexander to begin with the *Aljotta* – the fish soup. Alexander was happy to take her advice. Marija ordered *Gambli homor* – red Mediterranean prawns – for her fish course. Alexander played safe and ordered the sea bass *Involtini*, with pine nuts and mint. Their conversation during the fish course revolved largely around Alexander's tales of growing up in Kenya and South Africa. Marija seemed genuinely interested. Her father owned a small fleet of Mediterranean freighters: the sort of small cargo ships that Alexander often saw off-shore. He could afford to send her to the élite Wycombe Abbey girls' school in England

Alexander had always enjoyed slow-cooked lamb shank, so he ordered the *Haruf brazzato* for his main course; Marija ordered pork fillets marinated in honey and thyme. Their conversation moved on to travel: places they had visited, sights they had seen. Alexander was able to make Marija laugh as he recounted some of his more amusing African experiences: like his father, Alexander could always tell a good story.

Neither had drunk more than two glasses of the red wine by the time they came to placing their orders for dessert. "Shall I get a half bottle of white with this?" Alexander asked Marija.

"That would be a fine idea," she responded.

Again, Alexander allowed Marija to make the actual choice of wine. Marija ordered her dessert – a gelato of layered ice cream – at the same time. Alexander asked for the *Imqaret* – dates wrapped in pastry, deep-friend, and served with honey and vanilla ice cream.

"Eating like you have tonight, I wonder how you stay so slim?" Marija asked, smiling at Alexander.

Alexander smiled back at her. "I've always been like that, Marija: I can eat as much as I want; I never gain any weight."

"Lucky you, Sandy."

They were still drinking their coffees, Alexander with a cigarette in his hand, when he signaled to the waiter to bring the bill. He had a horror of waiting at the end of a meal for the bill to be brought to him. He took the bill from the waiter, and glanced at it. The total was as steep as he had anticipated.

"Sandy, we must go halves on the cost of the meal," Marija said.

"Oh no! Thank you Marija – but no: this is my treat."

"Next time then, it will be mine," Marija responded.

Alexander had paid off the taxi at the theatre. The night was warm. There was no wind. The streets of Valletta were still fairly busy at a quarter to eleven. Marija was happy to walk along Republic Street towards the Triton Fountains, where there was a taxi rank. Alexander, who could never entirely divorce himself from a sense of life's theatre, was struck by the cliché of this evening: here he was, a tall, slim, blonde-headed fairly good-looking man, with a beautiful, expensively dressed and very elegant thirty-something brunette by his side, strolling through the night-time streets in an exotic city after an evening at the ballet. He smiled to himself.

He was walking on Marija's right. She took his arm in hers. Alexander, emboldened by the wine he had drunk and by the staginess of the evening, reached his free arm across and squeezed her hand momentarily. "I am so glad I'm here with you in Valletta, Marija," he declared suddenly, "rather than slouching along a wet pavement, alone, in London."

"Oh – Sandy!" Marija laughed, and turned her head and smiled at him. "I'm in perfect agreement with you."

"I may be British, but I wasn't really made for Britain. My temperament isn't right for Britain. If I hadn't been born in Africa, I would hope to have been born a Maltese. I envy you, Marija."

"I love these islands," Marija replied. "It's where I wish to be – most of the time."

By July, Alexander and Marija were meeting for lunch on Saturdays almost every week. They usually had lunch at the Cockney Bar. Marija would park her car near Alexander's room in *Ghar il-Lembi*, and together they would walk down the hill to the Sliema promenade and take the ferry across Marsamxett harbor to Valletta. Sitting at the terrace in front of Cockney's under a large colourful umbrella, looking across Marsamxett harbour towards Sliema, Alexander felt a sense of well-being and a sociable ease he hadn't felt for a long time, perhaps not since his days sailing out of Simons Town. Conservative by temperament, Alexander almost always ordered either the *fenek* (rabbit), or swordfish steaks. The latter came with a vast mixed salad, which was a meal in itself. Alexander still had a very healthy, young man's appetite. He had always enjoyed his food tremendously, ever since the age of fourteen. However, his trousers still had a thirty inch waist. Because Marija liked a glass or two of wine with her meal, Alexander shared the carafe of house wine with her, rather than ordering a *Kinnie* or a lager, as he would have done had he been alone.

Each of them was very relaxed in the other's company. Sometimes they sat for five minutes at a time – or longer – without needing to exchange a word. Marija did not seem to mind Alexander's staring at her, his mouth curled in an admiring half smile. Once, Marija turned her head and their eyes met, and for some reason Alexander did not understand, they both laughed, but easily, without embarrassment. Other times, they would share memories of London. Sometimes Marija would talk about the Maltese nationalist movement. Like Alexander's friend Filippu, she leant towards Maltese right wing nationalist politics.

Alexander did not visit Marija at her apartment in Saint Julians: rather, after a couple of suppers together at *Ta' Kolina* restaurant, which specialised in Maltese cuisine and which was located on Tower Road in Sliema, a destination they could easily walk to from Alexander's flat, Marija sometimes came upstairs for coffee afterwards at Alexander's room, and they would sit together on his tiny balcony, where the air was a little cooler than it was indoors.

One night during the third week of July, after a supper together at *Ta' Kolina*, Alexander, moved by the cool beauty of Marija's profile and by the romance of the Mediterranean summer night, took her hand across the tiny table on his balcony and leant towards her. Marija turned her head towards him. Other than chaste kisses on the cheek, he had not kissed her before. Now, with the fairy lights twinkling on the trees along the promenade visible in the gap at the bottom of the street, and the dark sea beyond that, and the yellow or white riding lights of ships that had anchored for the night shining some distance offshore, Alexander cupped her cheek in his left hand and kissed her on the mouth, and Marija responded with a willingness which did not surprise him. He had known intuitively that she would reciprocate his interest. They both stood, Alexander holding Marija's hand, but it was she who led the way to his bed.

It was hardly necessary for Alexander to act a part: he had long wished to make love to Marija. There was a complexity of emotions at play in him, of which narcissism was not the least significant. The idea of his making love to such a desirable woman appealed strongly to him. They helped one another undress, somewhat clumsy in their haste, and Alexander felt a powerful stirring when he saw her naked breasts, which were full and firm, with dark aureoles. Alexander mastered his haste and drew the tips of the fingers of one hand gently across Marija's lips and then he followed the contours of her jaw and so down to one shoulder and then to her breasts, and as his fingers traveled slowly across the nipple of one breast, Marija sighed and said simply "Yes."

But Marija, a mother with a teenage son waiting for her at home, did not spend the night with Alexander. Nor would she ever do so. After they had made love together – hungrily the first time, more gently not long after – she spent some time in the bathroom, then Alexander walked her down the street to her car, and she drove home to her son. Later that first night, Alexander worried that he might have killed the friendship; he wondered whether he would see Marija again. He need not have worried: within less than a week, this coming together at Alexander's room after a supper together, was repeated. And again after that. Alexander found himself betraying Robbie with little heart-searching or internal moral debate.

And then, with the August sun blazing down, and the temperature during the still, windless days rising well above thirty degrees centigrade, Marija went away on holiday with Bernard, her son. Alexander was unable to get an answer when he rang Filippu's number, so he presumed that Filippu was also away on holiday. But, the summer being the language school's busiest period, Robbie was to hand. Perhaps this betrayal of Robbie's trust and friendship did not come as easily to Alexander as he had at first thought it did, for his conscience troubled him when he was with Robbie, and he experienced a strong urge to tell him what he had done with Marija. He did not tell Robbie, however: it was easier to let his conscience fight its own battles. "You don't seem quite yourself these days," Robbie said to Alexander one evening at the Hole in the Wall.

"It's the weather, I think. I find the heat a bit of a burden, Robbie."

Alexander and Robbie saw less of each other that August than was usual between them, and he was intimate with Robbie on only two occasions that month – and each time, he had had a lot to drink. When the question of whether he was being unfaithful to Marija in turn on these two occasions entered Alexander's mind, he reasoned that he had a relationship with Robbie, but was merely enjoying a liason with Marija. Having had few friends at school to learn about loyalty from, and never having been a team-player, Alexander had not come to understand the concept of loyalty to others very well.

Twenty

Gozo

Towards the end of August, Filippu rang the language school and left a message for Alexander: he was back from Italy, where he had spent his holidays, and would Sandy be at the Hole in the Wall tomorrow evening? Alexander met him there. He was glad to see his friend again. So it seemed was Filippu pleased to see him, too. "Sandy! My friend! *Llni ma narak! Kif int?*"

Alexander grinned. "*Jien tajjeb grazzi, Filippu. U int?*"

Filippu was full of his travels in Italy, visiting sites associated with the classical writers and poets. He enlarged at some length on the Italian contribution to Maltese culture and to the Maltese language. Then he began to talk about the ancient history of the archipelago itself. "Have you been to Gozo?" he asked.

Alexander had not. He had wondered about joining a guided coach tour, but he had never got around to it.

"Then let's go this Sunday. We'll take the car across on the ferry."

"OK Filippu. That sounds like fun."

"We should leave early. I'll fetch you at your flat at eight-thirty, OK?"

Alexander had taken to wearing a pair of old shorts on the weekends, during this the hottest time of the year. They were baggy khaki cotton, reaching to his knees. He wore his old pair of leather sandals also, and a tee shirt. He was fast re-acquiring his tan. When Filippu collected him the following Sunday morning, the sky was, as usual, a cloudless blue. The temperature was already in the mid-twenties centigrade. Alexander wore a Panama hat he had bought years earlier in London, and a pair of sunglasses. Filippu was dressed in crumpled chinos, open sandals, a short sleeved shirt, and a floppy cotton hat. He had a camera with him.

They followed Route 1 up the north-east coast, the country becoming less densely urbanised after they had left Saint Julian's behind them, although many freestanding villas, the most attractive of which were built of the local limestone, were evident in various stages of completion and occupation throughout their journey. The countryside was very dry, and Alexander was glad of the sunglasses he wore: the rocky landscape glared almost white under the strong light. Prickly pear plants grew along the roadside, and behind drystone walls were bright green, tiny fields, not one of them the same size or shape as the next. For much of the journey, they could see the sea not very far away to their right. Along the coast, spaced every few miles, were 17th century watchtowers built of honeyed limestone. They were usually of three stories, and the entrance was on the first floor, originally via a ladder which could be drawn up. They had been part of Malta's defence against Barbary pirates and slave raiders. Equipped with balefire beacons on the roofs, they could signal – smoke by day, flame by night – to the larger, more widely spaced towers, mini-fortresses, which had housed the cavalry garrisons which could ride out against raiders.

Bugibba, on Saint Paul's Bay, was heavily urbanised, with, further along the coast, another concentrated settlement at Mellieha Bay, where there was a long, narrow, sandy beach. Not much further along, Alexander saw a great square castle-like fortress, the colour of old, dried blood, situated on a high eminence. "What is that place, Filippu?" he asked.

"*It-Torri L-Aħmar* – the Red Tower. It was built in the mid-seventeenth century. It is empty now. Perhaps we can look at it on the way back."

It was almost eleven o'clock by the time they reached the ferry terminus at Cirkewwa, at the extreme northernmost tip of the island. There was a ferry alongside the quay, with its gaping bow entrance standing open. Once Filippu had paid their passage and parked the car within the bowels of the vessel, they went above, to an open deck where many of the passengers had gathered. They stayed there as the ferry pulled out. Then Filippu said "I would like a coffee. How about you?"

Filippu showed Alexander the way to the lounge, which had a cafeteria at one end. They bought a coffee each, and took them to a table up against the full-length windows at the forward end of the lounge. From the equally large side windows, Alexander could see they were passing the tiny, apparently barren island of Comino, with its watchtower at the near end, which Filippu told him was the *Santa Marija* tower. "The island has a permanent population of three people," Filippu told Alexander.

As Alexander gazed at the view, the ferry's twin on the return crossing passed them by: Alexander was intrigued to realise for the first time that the ferries were like the Pushme-Pullyou, that is, they were identical at either end, with twin bridges forward and aft: they could go forward or astern without turning around. He grinned at a sudden recollection: an Italian armoured car from the Second World War which had duplicate driving stations at either end, which had been one of his favorite displays at the Johannesburg War Museum near the Zoo. Filippu had his camera pointed through the glass at the passing sister vessel. Then he turned and took a photo of the grinning Alexander. Alexander's grin had stayed on his face through an access of happiness: he was always happy aboard a boat or a ship. They were drawing closer to Gozo. "We had better get back to the car," Filippu said. They went below.

They docked at the port of Mgarr, drove the car into the bright light of day, and began to ascend the fairly steep roadway running diagonally up the hillside. Once on the island's central plateau, Alexander observed that Gozo was far more rural than the main island: the same small, irregularly shaped, bright green pocket-handkerchief fields hedged around with drystone walls dominated the landscape, but there was less evidence of urbanisation. They drove slowly through the island's small centrally located capital, Victoria, also known as *Rabat*, with its medieval Citadel rising above the town itself, in which 17th, 18th and 19th century architecture dominated. "Sometimes I have lunch at one of the restaurants here," Filippu remarked, "but usually I prefer to have lunch at Xlendi Bay – that's what we'll do today."

As they drove leisurely through the countryside, passing the occasional tourist bus, or one of the island's 1950s-bodied buses (which here on Gozo were painted grey, with a white roof, and a narrow maroon stripe running just below the windows), Alexander could see a vast, pale honey coloured limestone church in the distance: it dominated the entire landscape. "What is that church?" he asked.

"It's the National Sanctuary of the Virgin of *Ta 'Pinu*, built in the 1920s with funds collected on the island. It is actually a basilica. There has been a sanctuary to the Virgin here for many centuries. Pope John Paul II celebrated mass here two years ago."

Alexander wondered whether contemporary Maltese people were as pious as he imagined they were. He turned his head "Filippu – how religious are Maltese people today? I mean, are they all practicing Catholics?"

"Most of us would term ourselves Catholic," Filippu replied, "though many of the younger people are not regular mass-goers. The Catholic faith and the Maltese national identity are so intertwined, that it is hard to be a good Maltese without being at least officially a Catholic also."

Alexander tried to remember the last time he had attended mass. It would have been about four years ago, when he had sometimes attended the late morning Catholic Sunday mass celebrated in the Church of England church at Kings Langley. Alexander considered himself a Catholic still: he said his prayers on an irregular basis, particularly when he was hurting inside. He would sometimes recite the *Ave Maria*. But he felt no need at present to attend mass.

Filippu drove right across the island, towards Dwejra Bay, on the island's north-west coast. The car park was full of small tour buses, one or two larger coaches, and a number of the 1950s-styled Gozo buses. They left the car and began walking across bare rock. "Do you see them?" asked Filippu.

"The . . . what are they called . . . trilobites?"

"No – they're ammonites," Filippu corrected him.

In the rock at their feet, in great numbers, were large spiral-shelled fossils. But as the famed limestone arch drew into view, Alexander forgot about them. The archway, a natural limestone phenomenon, was huge. It reached out across the blue water: a reasonably large boat could have been driven beneath it. Alexander could see some people, tiny from this distance, on top of the archway. Filippu allowed Alexander to draw ahead of him somewhat. "Would you please turn around, Sandy?" he called.

Alexander turned, smiling, and Filippu clicked the camera's shutter, capturing Alexander framed by the archway beyond him. "We'll go for lunch now," Filippu told Alexander, when they had got back into the car.

The drive took them through Victoria a second time, and lasted almost an hour. There was no direct route between Dwejra Bay and Xlendi Bay. The island roads were narrow and winding. But as they descended a rocky defile, Alexander could see the blue sea sparkling ahead of them, and suddenly they debauched into a small village with a row of tall multi-storied buildings ahead of them. There was a big car park in front of these buildings, which Alexander realised were hotels, and they left the car there and walked round the side and so to a terrace which ran the length of the pebbly beach fronting the hotels. On the terrace there were tables and chairs beneath large umbrellas against the sun, most of them occupied with holiday makers and visitors. In front of them was a low stone balustrade, and below that the narrow beach. The view opened out in front of Alexander: a lovely, almost landlocked azure bay lay between rocky headlands reaching far out on either side, with one of the ubiquitous 17th century watchtowers high above the sea at the furthest extent of the left-hand headland, which was heavily built up for some considerable distance. There were small motor boats and yachts anchored or moored in the bay. It was a wonderfully peaceful scene. They found a table in front of the largest of the multi-story hotel buildings – the St. Patrick's Hotel.

After he had sat down, Alexander removed his Panama and mopped his face with a handkerchief, then lighted a cigarette. Filippu did not smoke. A waiter approached them, and Filippu ordered a half carafe of house white. Alexander asked for a *Kinnie*. He felt a touch dehydrated, and it was very warm.

Filippu ordered a sea bass; Alexander a pasta dish with a salad, much as he often ate at the Cockney Bar above the ferry quay at Valletta. "I would like to holiday here some day," Alexander told Filippu.

"My wife and I spent our honeymoon here," Filippu responded. "Back when we were still in love."

"But you return here?" Alexander asked.

"Oh yes – it holds happy memories. That we are now separated does not spoil those happy memories."

The two friends lingered so long over their lunch, which had been followed by a lager for Alexander after his *Kinnie*, and over their coffees afterwards, that it was near three-thirty before they were ready to leave. They had to drive through Victoria a third time to reach Mgarr, then they took the five o'clock ferry crossing back to Malta, and perhaps they both felt rather tired after the long day and the journey, so they drove on by without taking the side road that led up to the Red Fort. The sun was very low in the sky by the time they reached Sliema. Filippu dropped Alexander off, and drove straight on to his own flat. Alexander watched the eastern sky darkening from the corner of his tiny balcony as he drank a coffee. Alexander did not know it, but his time in Malta was fast winding down, and he would not be sitting on his balcony as the evening drew in many more times.

Marija returned from holiday in early September. Alexander met her one evening at *Ta'Kolina's* in Tower Road. It quickly became apparent to Alexander that Marija had decided to treat the three occasions she had slept with him as a summer fling. She was speaking of an old family friend she had met up with again, a man living in Italy whom she had known well when they were teenagers together, and their fathers were business partners and friends. When she took a photograph from her handbag and showed it to Alexander, he saw a photo of a good-looking, rich looking man somewhere in his late thirties or early forties. Alexander easily understood the message Marija was sending him: their affair was over. After dinner, they went their separate ways.

Thoughtful and introspective, Alexander was prone to self analysis. He recognised that he had felt slightly soiled by the nature of his narcissistic relationship with Marija: there was no love present, and although there was much liking, there was not much respect for her on his part. He felt that a woman prepared to sleep with him was prepared to sleep with other men, and almost certainly had – and would do so again. Alexander was old fashioned enough to view such a woman with something less than complete respect. And he was honest enough with himself to view his own exploitation of Marija's passing interest in him as morally demeaning. Now that the affair was over, Alexander felt relief more than any other emotion. There had been a degree of play-acting on his part in his relationship with Marija, and he had found it quite tiring. And now he need deceive and betray Robbie no longer.

Alexander was never to see Marija again.

A week or two into September 1992, Alexander received one of the familiar blue South African airmail letters from his mother. He had picked it up downstairs as he returned from work. He read the letter on his balcony, while he drank a coffee. That there was something wrong, some unhappy news, took a minute or two to filter through to his conscious mind. Alexander's mother wrote that his father had been diagnosed with an advanced brain tumor. He read that his father had perhaps no more than two months at most left to live – less than that now: the letter had taken over a week to reach him.

Alexander left his coffee on the small wrought iron table, went inside to his bed, and knelt against it. He prayed for healing for his father. He prayed for forgiveness. He recited an *Ave Maria* also, and he prayed God's blessings on his mother. It had been some time since he had prayed so lengthy and heartfelt a prayer. When he had finished praying, he went to the table and took his fountain pen and wrote to his parents. He told them that he would be returning to South Africa within a couple of weeks, if he could arrange it. (He thought it quite probable that he would be there before his letter arrived). He kept stamps in one of the drawers in the kitchenette. He addressed an airmail-weight envelope and fixed the stamps to it, and then he posted it on his way to the Hole in the Wall. There, he drank his first whiskey since 1988. Alexander stayed in the pub for almost two hours, having drunk two lagers after that single whiskey. There was a guitar and mandolin duo performing in the pub that night, singing Maltese folk songs. As the music soothed Alexander's jagged emotions, he became aware that he had been homesick for Africa for some time; homesick for a wider land, where you could escape from the crush of people. Alexander knew that it was not only the news the letter from his mother contained that was urging him to return to South Africa. Yet he feared that old self destructive compulsion that had often harried him into actions he would later regret. Yes, he thought: I need to see my father while I still can – but I do not have to quit Malta, or Robbie, or my job.

"I love this island. I don't want to leave Malta," he said aloud, as he walked the short distance back to his room that evening. By the time he got home at nine o'clock he had decided that he was probably making a mistake he would come to regret in leaving Malta for good – and that he was going to do so anyway.

Twenty-One

A Funeral & A Bush Camp

———

Alexander landed at Jan Smuts international airport, Johannesburg, early on the morning of Thursday the 1st October 1992. As the plane began its long descent Alexander felt a joyfulness rising in his spirit. He knew there was not much waiting for him; he knew that he was arriving amidst a tragedy unfolding – but it was happiness that suffused his soul. He had left South Africa twenty months earlier. It was early summer in South Africa. Roy, his brother, was at the airport to meet him. They drove to Roy's house in Honeydew. Despite his exhaustion – he had merely cat-napped during the night-long flight from Heathrow, unable to find a position in which his long frame could be comfortable – Alexander experienced that gladness of heart he always felt when he returned to South Africa after a long absence, that sense of home-coming. The grasslands surrounding Johannesburg were greening up, the rains having arrived in late September. But after Malta, it did not feel overly warm. "How is Dad?" Alexander asked.

"He's become a very old man," his brother replied. He turned his head, and there was a stricken look to his face. "He's very gaunt. You must prepare yourself, Sandy."

They continued driving in silence for a while. Then Roy said "He has extreme mood swings. Sometimes he's very angry, and vocal with it. It's the tumor, what it does to his brain. Sometimes he wont speak at all."

Alexander had designed Roy's house in Honeydew. He had yearned to become an architect since his early adolescence, but his matric maths pass had not been good enough to get onto the university architectural course. The house was in the Cape Dutch style, with a symmetrical façade. Alexander had taken care to get the proportions right. The details were also correct: there were simple partially stepped gables at either end of the house – the house was too small to carry off curlicues to the gables – and a smaller gable above the kitchen wing at the back, matched by a gable in the centre of the front façade. One of the end gables incorporated a centrally located chimney for the fireplace in the sitting room; the others each had a louvred vent set in the gable, to let the hot summer air escape from the roof. There were four tall windows in the front façade, two either side of the centrally-positioned front door. Above the front door, and extending several feet to either side of it, was a wooden trellis on four vertical squared, varnished timber posts, with jasmine already creeping half way up the posts. Beneath the trellis there was red brick paving. It was a tiny house, incorporating just a sitting room-dining room, a kitchen, a narrow entrance hall, two bedrooms, and a bathroom and lavatory, all arranged on a classic T plan, with the kitchen forming the footing of the T. There was an open fireplace in the sitting room, with a mantelpiece of old, weathered railway-sleeper teak. There was a serving hatch between the kitchen and the dining area. The kitchen was large enough to contain a table with four chairs, where Roy (and now, for a time, Alexander) would usually eat.

It was the first house to be built in this new development, near the crest of a rocky slope. It had views of the distant Magaliesberg to the north-west. It contained a cat called Smokie, whom Alexander sometimes referred to as "The Bandit." Smokie was a very beautiful long-haired grey

Persian cat with a white bib and white paws. Roy was as fond of cats as Alexander was. Alexander picked the cat up and gave her a cuddle when he went inside. During the coming four weeks, Smokie was to be Alexander's main daytime companion. Alexander had sold his car prior to departing South Africa for England and then Malta; the house was several miles from the nearest shops or liquor store. Almost no one called. Roy was away at work during the day. Alexander quickly became soul-crushingly bored and lonely. He missed Malta very much. He remembered Robbie.

Saying goodbye to Robbie had been hard. "Robbie, I'm going to miss you very much," Alexander told him.

"We had a good time together," Robbie was holding one of Alexander's hands, "but nothing's for ever, Sandy. Life moves on."

However, the sun shone down every day at Roy's house in Honeydew, and Alexander would lie stretched out on a towel on the lawn, wearing only a pair of shorts, and work on his tan. Sometimes his mother would drive over during the morning, and fetch him. His parents' home was only five miles away. Alexander's father, a year short of reaching retirement, was at home full-time now.

On Alexander's first evening back in South Africa, when Roy returned from work at about half past five, and after they had ate a supper of grilled chicken breasts which Roy had cooked, they went to see their parents together. It was as well that Roy had warned his older brother about their father's appearance: he was gaunt to the point of emaciation, and his features were parchment white. His hair, which had been a thick faded red, was now very sparse, and he wore his old Kenya bush hat all the time, indoors and out. Alexander Senior moved slowly, painfully. He rarely raised his eyes to look directly at whoever was talking to him, as if to do so took him too much effort. What he appeared to want was to sit and doze in his armchair. He did not get up when Alexander greeted him. He did however smile, and return his eldest son's handshake. "I'm glad you're home, Sandy."

"I'm glad too, Dad. I'm so sorry you're not well."

"Yes. There's nothing to be done about that."

Alexander's mother managed to look younger than her sixty-two years, but her features were a touch drawn, and during the course of that evening, she disappeared several times, and Alexander thought she was probably crying. "Oh my God," Alexander thought. "This is all so horrible."

It was to get worse. Later that evening, Alexander's mother said to her husband, "I think you should get ready for bed, Darling, don't you?"

Alexander's father snarled and swung on his wife. "I'm sick of being told what to do, God dammit! I've got both my sons together for the first time in a long time, and I don't want to go to bed yet. Leave me alone, will you!"

Then his face sagged, and he said "I'm sorry, Sweetheart. I did n't mean to be like that."

Roy caught his brother's eye and gave a single tiny shake of his head.

On their way back to Roy's home later that evening, Alexander said "I don't think I can bear this for very long. It's as if all our lives are on pause."

Less than a week later, their father was taken to hospital. Both brothers visited him there every evening for the duration of his ten-day stay, picking their mother up on their way to the hospital. Towards the end of his stay, Alexander's father was heavily sedated with morphine against the pain. When he was awake, he had moments of mental clarity. During one such moment, Alexander said "I'm sorry I was n't a better son, Dad. I'm sorry I was n't grateful enough. I do love you."

His father looked at him, his eyes a little unfocused. Then he said "Sandy. You just make sure that Mum is going to be OK."

"I'll look after her, Dad," Alexander replied. "Both of us – Roy and I – we'll make sure Mum is OK."

"That's good," his father said, and closed his eyes.

Roy got a phone call at work from their mother during the late afternoon of the 16th October. Their father was fading fast, the hospital had told her. Would they pick her up as soon as possible, and take her there?

Roy left work immediately, collected Alexander at home, then the two brothers fetched their mother and drove to the hospital. Alexander could see that Roy was on the verge of tears. They went upstairs to their father's private room. They had spoken to the doctor first. Alexander senior died soon after eleven o'clock that night. His wife and her two sons were by his bedside. Their father was only sixty-four.

It was almost one in the morning before the three of them left the hospital. Alexander drove Roy's car. Roy was in no state to do so. Alexander was dealing with the situation in the same way he had dealt with pain and hurt since his earliest childhood: he walled it off, and functioned around it, beyond its perimeter.

Alexander, by default, assumed responsibility for arranging the funeral and settling his father's affairs. He rang his aunt in Cape Town, and his relations in Britain. He rang his father's workplace. He notified family friends. He phoned the lawyers who held the original of his father's will. Decades earlier, his father had appointed his bank as his executors, and Alexander had to notify his father's current bank branch also. Margaret, his aunt, suggested that her brother's remains be interred at Muizenberg cemetery, on the Cape Peninsula, where his own father, mother and sister, Mary, had been buried. Alexander spoke to his mother and brother, and they agreed with him that Margaret's suggestion was a good one. The two brothers, with their mother, flew to Cape Town on Wednesday 21st October, which happened to be Roy's birthday. It was quite overlooked this year. Alexander had made arrangements with the funeral directors for his father's remains to be flown to Cape Town, where the funeral would be handled by a local associated concern. His aunt shed some tears when Alexander embraced her, but not many: she had always been a strong, self controlled woman, little given to emotional outbursts. Her sister in law was accommodated in Alexander's grandfather's old bedroom; Alexander had his old glassed-in room at the end of the *stoep* again, whilst Roy shared with Hannes, who was still boarding with the family, staying in one of the two wooden chalets. The new double story house that Margaret was having built would not be completed for some months yet. Mike too was still living with the family, now cohabiting with Alexander's youngest cousin, Mary (named after her aunt), in the larger of the two wooden chalets.

The minister from the Church of Scotland congregation of which Alexander's grandfather had been an elder, conducted the burial service two days later, on Friday the 23rd. It was a simple service, and it did not take long. Alexander and Roy flanked their mother. The two brothers were both wearing suits. As the coffin was lowered into the ground, Alexander recalled the previous two occasions he had stood in this cemetery, burying family members: in February 1974, his grandmother had been buried here; then, in January 1987, they had buried his grandfather next to her. He did not remember being present at the funeral of his aunt Mary when he was fourteen years old. He was stricken by a sudden desperate sadness and he felt his eyes grow moist. He saw tears on his aunt's face also. She had lost both her siblings now: her sister, Mary, and now her brother also. After the funeral, which three of Alexander's father's work colleagues had flown down from Johannesburg to attend, but was otherwise attended only by the immediate family and old Cape Town family friends (along with the two lodgers, Mike and Hannes, who had been fond of Alexander's father), the funeral party returned to the farm. On Sunday, the two brothers and their mother flew back to Johannesburg. Alexander had barely wept since his father had died, although he felt as if a terribly important part of himself was now missing. He had no idea what he was to do next with his life.

November arrived. It was growing very warm, but with almost daily short, heavy afternoon rain showers, the humidity could not build up, and so the heat was manageable. Alexander wore shorts and a tee-shirt during the day, and went barefoot at Roy's house. He was now very tanned. One evening Alexander was paging through a recent copy of *Getaway* magazine in Roy's sitting room, when he noticed an advertisement for a course which trained field guides. It promised SATOUR accreditation for those who passed the course, which was conducted on a private game reserve adjacent to the Kruger National Park.

Getaway was a South African outdoors publication. Many of the adverts in the back pages of the magazine were for luxury private game lodges in the Transvaal Lowveld, and for adventure holidays. Alexander remembered with happiness the visits he and Guy had made to Guy's family game lodge in the private game reserve near Hoedspruit. Reading the field guide training course advertisement a second time, an idea began to take hold of Alexander. With his savings, he could easily afford to pay for the course. He was certain that, with his love of the bushveld, he would enjoy it very much. It would lead to his being able to earn a living, much of it in the bushveld, showing off the fauna and flora to visitors from abroad. He thought he would be good at that sort of work. He was, in time, to be proven correct. The next morning he rang the Hoedspruit phone number provided, and spoke to the course director, a chap named Will Armstrong, who was an ex-Selous Scout. Alexander booked himself a place on the January 1993 course.

Alexander thought it was time he bought a good second hand car. He would need it to reach the private game reserve bordering the Kruger park. He had a fairly good idea of what he wanted: a six cylinder car, perhaps five years old at the most. He read the used car ads in the *Star*, the Johannesburg daily, for several days, and bought the first car he and his brother Roy went to look at. Roy was a gifted mechanic, and he knew a lot about cars: after taking it for a long test drive, and looking for a long time under the bonnet and beneath the car, he said "I think it's a safe buy, Sandy. The price is good, and the mileage is fairly low for its year. It might save us a lot of trouble if you were to buy it."

"I like it," Alexander replied. "We'll buy it."

The car was a four year old Ford Granada, with a 3-litre six cylinder engine and an automatic transmission. The sale was a private one: the owner showed the two brothers a complete service history in the log book that came with the car. It had about 20 000 kilometres on the clock. Alexander's father had owned a couple of Granadas in the early 1980s: it was the sort of big, powerful, comfortable car that Alexander and his brother understood and related to.

Alexander had given up drinking altogether since his return to South Africa. His father's death had distressed him, but he had not felt the least wish to drink over it. That Christmas and New Year were very subdued affairs in the Maclean family. The two brothers spent Christmas day at their mother's home. Small gifts were exchanged. Neither of them celebrated New Year's Eve, but instead they stayed in at Roy's house, and they were in bed before midnight.

At odd moments during the day Alexander found himself stricken with grief over his father's death. He would never be able to make good all the hurt he had caused him now. And if this grief were n't enough, Alexander found himself grieving for the life he had left behind in Malta. He wondered whether he would ever again know the sort of happiness and fulfillment that he had experienced on the island. He was almost thirty-eight years old now: he feared that perhaps Robbie would prove to have been the last lover he was ever to know. He tortured himself sometimes with vivid recollections of physical intimacies with Robbie – and before that, with Guy. Then he would make a conscious effort to look forward, and to anticipate his forthcoming adventures as a field guide. But sometimes he struggled not to feel overwhelmed by a sense of failure and loss on many fronts. During the first week of January 1993, he began to wish he dared to have a drink. He knew however that in his present frame of mind, to do so would be very dangerous. He hoped he would forget that temptation once his training course began on the 11th January.

Alexander knew the way to Hoedspruit very well, of course, from visits with Guy to the game lodge. Guy's family lodge and the tented training camp that the course instructor, Will, had established, were both to be found along the same long dirt road, reaching many miles into the Klaserie bloc, which shared an open border with the Kruger National Park. Will's camp was situated about as deep into the game country as you could get, short of crossing into the Kruger Park itself. To reach Hoedspruit, Alexander set off in his big Ford along the N4 to the east of Johannesburg, leaving the motorway to turn off for Belfast, then making for Lydenburg. This was a region that had been settled by the earliest Boer trekkers. Alexander cut through the living rock of the Transvaal Drakensberg escarpment via the J.G. Strydom tunnel. Here, as he exited the tunnel, he pulled over at the side of the road where the curio stalls stood, and gazed at the hills, covered in bush and acacia woodland, receding into a distant blue haze. Then back on the road, which continued descending, and at last Alexander had his first clear view of the Lowveld proper, lying far below: bushveld reaching away to a horizon so distant and so obscured by heat-haze, it hardly existed. Far below, as the road began to level out and Alexander knew he was now in the Lowveld, the air was very much warmer, and it had a quality about it that Alexander could only think of as "bushveld." It was a quality he associated with happiness and adventure, and the association probably originated as far back as his earliest childhood years in Kenya.

At Hoedspruit he bought a carton of cigarettes, two six-packs of Coca-Cola cans, and a jar of good instant coffee. He did not buy any beers. He turned right out of Hoedspruit, and after about five miles, he turned left off the tarred road for the dirt road that led towards Klaserie, after passing the Hoedspruit Air Force base on the left. The first time he had visited this district, with Guy, it had been night-time, with a full moon, when he had driven down this road, and on the way to the game lodge they had come across a pride of lions resting on the road, their hides silver in the moonlight, soaking up the day's heat trapped in the sandy surface. Alexander had had to drive very slowly towards them, and they had moved off the road only with reluctance. Later, they had seen three elephants, silvery-grey, alongside the road. But now it was noon, and the road was pale under the powerful summer sun. Alexander felt as replete as a cat in the warmth, and he drove slowly with the window wound down.

There was a hand-painted signboard directing him off the road along a narrow sandy track which twisted and bumped through the mopani bush. There were many scattered big trees also: leadwood, camel thorn, umbrella thorn and jackalberry were the most common. The track dipped as it crossed a sandy dry watercourse. Alexander drove very slowly, so as not to touch down. The camp was situated in a cleared area beyond the watercourse. There was a large khaki canvas tent to one side, and through the mopani bush, he could see some smaller two-man tents. The centre of the clearing was left free except for a huge cast iron tripod pot, beneath which were the makings of a fire. There was also a place for a camp-fire, demarcated by round stones from the watercourse, with a number of folding canvas chairs half circling it. There were some young men already seated on the chairs, holding beers in their hands. They all wore varieties of bush outfits, similar in the main to Alexander's khaki shorts and short sleeved khaki shirt. Some wore cotton bush hats on their heads. Most wore hiking boots: Alexander wore only his old leather sandals. The most vocal of these young men had a fine English public school accent. He was noticeably good looking: tall, slim, with broad shoulders and a narrow, expressive, rather arrogant face. His dark hair was cut short. He had an excellent tan. He came forward almost immediately to introduce himself to Alexander as Ralph Nuffield-Hawke. He pronounced his Christian name as "*Rafe.*"

Alexander dumped his old backpack on the sandy ground, and declined the beer that another youngster offered him. A tough looking man with a seamed, lived in, leathery face, probably six or seven years older than Alexander, welcomed him to a week in the bush. This was Will, the course instructor and organizer. He was the only other man there who was wearing a pair of sandals on his feet. "You'll bunk with Ralph," he told Alexander; " that tent over there," and he pointed at one of the small tents partly hidden by *wag-n-bietjie* thorn and mopani scrub. Alexander's accent, of course, was not dissimilar to Ralph's: the base note was Kenya colony, a considerably more refined accent than the South African one, and the oral impact of living and socializing with public school-educated men during his early years in London had not faded yet. Perhaps Will, hearing his accent, had assumed he must have much in common with the self-assured and somewhat loquacious Ralph. No matter the reason, Alexander, who loved to have beautiful people around him, was delighted at this happy circumstance.

After a cold lunch (Will having decided not to wait any longer for the two men yet to arrive), their course instructor, a heavy calibre rifle slung over one shoulder, led the young men into the bush. Instruction began immediately, with animal tracks being pointed out and explained, and their attention being drawn to useful plants. It was almost sun-down by the time they returned to camp, and they had seen a variety of game. Back in camp, instruction continued, this time in the preparation and cooking of *boskos* – bush meals – at the open fire. Alexander began to realise that Will was possessed of seemingly limitless energy, and that there was to be no down-time during this week in the bushveld.

Will was a rough diamond: physically tough, with little polish, hard on slackers, and quick to use the sharp edge of his tongue against anyone who challenged his authority, or against anyone who seemed to him to be willfully stupid, but he was tremendously knowledgeable about the bush, about wildlife and natural history in general – and more. The schedule he set was exhausting. Instruction was constant. If one of the young men angered Will, he yelled "Give me ten!" and the offender had to fling himself to the ground and do ten press-ups, fast. Ralph was a frequent offender for talking out of turn: he appeared unable to learn that his clever off-the-cuff comments delivered in a lazy public school drawl irritated Will hugely – or, knowing, he was nonetheless unable to resist indulging in them. Alexander was targeted once or twice for what Will perceived to be a lack of enthusiasm during lessons in setting animal traps. Trapping small animals for food fell under the broad category of lessons in bush survival tactics, which Alexander found extremely interesting in a general way.

An afternoon was set aside on a rudimentary shooting range in a clearing in the bush, where rocks brushed with white paint had been set up at various measured distances in a line approaching the shooter, to represent the surging bounds of a charging lion. Will carried a Brno 458, a real "elephant gun," which took only four fat rounds (plus one ready chambered). Alexander had used a rifle before, but nothing as big at this one. He knew enough to hug the stock in tight against his shoulder, but one of the youngsters failed to do so, and was thrown flat on his back by the kick when he fired the weapon the first time. Will laughed. "Man!" he exclaimed, "You'll have a colourful bruise there tomorrow!" He turned to the others. "Let that be a lesson to you all," he said. "Steve is lion-bait now."

Alexander, who, unlike many of his school-fellows, had not had to undergo military service on leaving school (this because he had informed the authorities that he did not intend relinquishing his British citizenship, and the South African military did not then want *uitlanders* serving in the SADF), enjoyed this rough, vital, masculine environment. They were a good bunch of blokes. Alexander was still quite fit, and though very lean, he had good muscle tone, even though he had not worked out at the gym since his university days. He had a deep tan. He felt thoroughly at home in the bush, and the heat did not get him down, dressed as he was in baggy cotton shorts, a loose shirt, a bush hat, and open sandals. Will's camp had twin showers set up behind a reed screen on the fringes of the camp. Above each shower was a galvanized open-topped metal container with a shower-rose set in its base, and if you wanted a hot shower at the end of the day, you took a bucket (or two) to the Mandela microwave (as the big cast-iron cooking pot over the open fire was named), and filled them with hot water, carrying them back to the showers, lowered one of the galvanized buckets on its pulley, and emptied your buckets of hot water into it. You showered in company with the showers' second occupant, who, one evening, was his tent-mate, Ralph, whose body, Alexander had already noted with an appreciative eye, was perfectly sculpted, and it was clear that when he tanned, he wore only the briefest of briefs.

There were also twin long-drops located on the edge of the camp, again, screened by woven reed and grass matting. Will had a resident black camp servant recruited locally, who kept the camp clean and tidy, and guarded it during the day when the rest of them were out walking in the bush. He ate with the young men in the evenings, and would accept a beer from Will, but he would fairly soon take himself off to sit outside his tent.

In their tent, Alexander and Ralph had a paraffin lamp. They doused it as soon as they were ready to lie down, which was never any later than ten-thirty p.m., after the tough day they had spent out walking. Each kept a torch by the side of his camp-bed. Their conversation, as they quickly got ready for the night, consisted of little more than a few laconic, but amiable, asides to each other. Sometimes, as they got ready to bed down, they might hear a hunting lion's roars somewhere in the distance, which the ear felt as a subtle vibration of the air, as much as a noise. Both men would glance at each other then, though neither ever commented on the sometimes disturbingly close proximity of the roars, which once or twice were less than half a kilometer from the camp. Ralph had a very young man's confidence in his survival, and Alexander was a firm believer in Fate. He did not think it was his destiny to be killed by a lion – or to suffer harm from any animal. Anyway, how likely was it, he asked himself, that a lion would come wondering into a camp where there were so many concentrated man-scents? Judging from his breathing, Ralph fell asleep almost immediately every night, and Alexander in those days was sleeping well again, rarely waking for eight hours unless he had to pee, which he would do only a few feet from the tent during the night, being careful however to slip his sandals onto his feet against crawling creatures that bit or stung in the dark. He had a particular horror of scorpions, and sitting around the camp fire in the evening, they often saw these horrible creatures, attracted perhaps by the warmth and light from the fire. Alexander feared them more than he did snakes, which he knew would usually get out of your way if you were n't walking too fast. One night, as he and Ralph got undressed, he realized that he was more than content: he was happy. Happiness was uncommon enough for him that it could still take him by surprise.

Alexander turned the wick of the lantern down, dousing the flame, and lay down on his camp-bed. "G'night Ralph," he said.

"G'night Sandy," the younger man replied.

Alexander fell quickly asleep to the sounds of the bushveld at night.

When the week was up, on Saturday 16th January, the youngsters went home for two weeks. In Ralph's case, this was to Windhoek in Namibia, where he worked for a big bush tours and eco-resort outfit based in Windhoek, called *Bwana Mkubwa*. Will had set them a great deal of studying to do, covering wildlife and natural history, ecology, environmentalism and conservation, geology, climate, firearms protocols, and vehicle maintenance. Some of this was already familiar to Alexander. They also had to prepare a talk to the others, covering any aspect of any of these subjects. Alexander, with his interest in history, researched the history of the Kruger National Park, and drafted the text of a talk on the subject. They were to meet again at the camp on Monday the 1st of February, for another week in the bush. On Tuesday morning the 2nd of February, the returning men would write an exam based on the subjects they had studied at home. On that same afternoon, each was to deliver his talk to the rest of the group. Will would grade them on their exam results, and their talks, and, at the end of that week, he would also grade them on their manner and general behaviour during their time spent in the bush. Based on his having scored an acceptable outcome for these grades, each young man could apply for official recognition by SATOUR as a field guide. SATOUR was the South African parastatal tourism authority. They would thereafter be authorized by SATOUR to conduct not only bush tours anywhere in South Africa, but all and any other tours for which they felt competent.

On the night of Friday 15th, Alexander asked Ralph "How will you get to Jan Smuts for your return flight to Windhoek, Ralph? I can give you a lift to the airport if you want."

"Will says he'll give me a lift to Nelspruit airport, Sandy. I can get a connection for Jan Smuts there."

"I'll be passing by Jan Smuts tomorrow, Ralph. Are you sure you don't want a lift?"

Ralph grinned. "OK. That would save me a lot of hassle. Thanks."

The next morning, having said their temporary goodbyes to the others, Alexander and Ralph got into the car together. Alexander felt it had been far longer than just under a week since he had last sat behind the wheel. He had only shaved twice during that period, and showered only three times. He was already looking forward to returning on the 1st of February.

At Jan Smuts Airport, Alexander dropped Ralph off. "Be seeing you in a couple of weeks, Ralph," Alexander said.

"Yah. Stay cool, Sandy."

Twenty-Two

Kwando River Lodge

It was an ebullient group of young men who gathered from noon onwards at the camp in the bushveld on the 1st of February. Only two of the original group were missing. Nobody asked Will why this was so, and Will did not elucidate. Alexander greeted Ralph warmly, and Ralph clapped him on the shoulder as he shook his hand. "Hullo, old man, so you made it!"

"Old man?" Alexander wondered. Well, yes: he would be thirty-eight years old in another three weeks' time. To a twenty year old, a thirty-eight year old must have seemed an old man. Alexander did not look anywhere near thirty-eight years old: he could easily have passed for ten years younger. Nor did he feel thirty-eight years old. He felt young. Most of his class mates at school would have teenage children by now, and lucrative careers, and big houses.

As before, they had a cold lunch when everyone had gathered, then went for a walk, returning by sundown. They got downwind of, then followed a small family group of elephants as they browsed their way through the bush, pausing to pull down young trees to get at the tender leaves near the tops, and tearing down branches from bigger trees. Once, Will made the entire group stand still quietly, and they could hear the rumblings of the herd at the very lowest periphery of their hearing as they communicated with one another. Will reminded them that they were not hearing the elephants' digestive rumblings: the animals were talking to each other as they moved slowly through the *mopaniveld*. They came across a dozen white rhinos also. Will walked his group slowly through the herd, and the rhinos grazed on as placidly as cattle in a field. "I would n't try that anywhere near black rhinos," he said afterwards.

Alexander reveled in walking so close to these big, and potentially very dangerous, animals. So certain he was that Fate had a very different end planned for him, that he felt not the least anxiety. Instead, he felt an almost mad joyfulness, akin to (but far more intense than) the way he had felt when sailing Synchronicity on False Bay, or riding at a gallop with Mike on Long Beach.

Alexander learned more about his English chum, Ralph, that evening as they sat round the fire. Ralph's father was a London financier, well able to afford having sent his son to Eton. Ralph was an only child. He did not talk about a mother at all. Alexander did not pry. Ralph shared a house in Windhoek with a number of young men who worked for *Bwana Mkubwa*. He had a girlfriend. Alexander was to meet her later that year: a very lovely local girl of German settler descent who worked in the tour company's offices in Windhoek. Ralph intended starting his own eco-tour operation one day. Alexander thought "And you will, too: you are one of life's Golden Boys. You'll always get whatever you want."

He felt no jealousy, just a touch of envy, and he wondered what it felt like to be blessed by Fortune. Alexander did not understand that to many observers, he too appeared to be blessed by Fortune.

Those final five days in the bushveld would have been a time of unalloyed delight for Alexander, had not memories of visits to Guy's family's bushveld lodge intruded two or three times. But he shrugged them off, these memories, and enjoyed the present time. Saturday 6th February arrived, it seemed to him, far too soon. The youngsters said goodbye to each-other, and to Will. Will would be posting their certificates to those who had passed. Alexander had no fears on that count. Moved by a sudden prescience, Alexander said to Ralph when he dropped him off again at Jan Smuts airport on the way back to Johannesburg "We'll be seeing each other again before long, you know."

"I'd like that," Ralph replied.

As the Lowveld receded behind him in his rear-view mirrors, Ralph sitting next to him in the car, Alexander felt a creeping *tristesse*: the Highveld plateau, with its corn fields, coal mines and power stations, seemed dull and drear by comparison with the colour and life and warmth of the bushveld left far behind and below him. In his pocket he had a talisman: one of the big rounds from Will's Brno 458 rifle. He felt a mildly superstitious conviction that this heavy slug of lead in its brass cartridge case would call him back to the bushveld. He was very tanned, and he felt fit and healthy. He had not touched alcohol since October the year before, in Malta. The following week he wrote both to SATOUR, requesting his official accreditation as a field guide, along with his badge and ID card, and to *Bwana Mkubwa*, the tour operator based in Windhoek that Ralph worked for. He was to learn later that it had been Ralph's recommendation that had ensured that within four weeks of his writing to *Bwana Mkubwa*, the company had offered him a job as resident naturalist and guide at their lodge on the Kwando River in the East Caprivi. Alexander's badge and ID card had not yet arrived from SATOUR when he received this job offer. He hoped they would reach him before he had to set off for Namibia.

Bwana Mkubwa operated a private game lodge situated on the banks of the Kwando River, in a vast game district in the eastern Caprivi. Alexander left Johannesburg by road in the early hours of Sunday 14th March 1993, driving all day, and arriving in Windhoek in the early evening. He spent the night as a house-guest of *Bwana Mkubwa*'s operations manager, Graham, a big, friendly white Namibian in his thirties. The two men drank whiskey together while Graham's girlfriend prepared dinner. Alexander thought he could chance a couple of whiskeys after such a long period of abstinence.

The next morning, Alexander met *Bwana Mkubwa's* owner and managing director, John, a short, slightly built man also in his thirties, who had a cast in one eye. Alexander did not take to him: or rather, he felt that John had not taken to him. Perhaps it was just his way, he thought, but he struck Alexander as distant and unfriendly. Graham then showed Alexander where he would be living when he was in Windhoek: at an old suburban house in a rather parched garden which a number of *Bwana Mkubwa* tour guides shared when they were not away on tour. Here, Alexander was delighted to find Ralph, who was staying in Windhoek between tours. "Sandy! Welcome to the Lost City!" Ralph declared. "You were right: we meet again." Alexander grinned with pleasure and shook Ralph's hand warmly. "I see you're driving the Ford," Ralph continued. "Has anyone warned you about Sammy's cavalcade?"

"No – what's that?"

"Uncle Sam likes to drive around Windhoek in a stretched Merc limo, with a couple of troop carriers in front and behind, and Police outriders on big bikes in front: you know he's coming when you hear the sirens, and you get off the road immediately. Get two wheels up onto the pavement. If you don't, you're in deep shit." Ralph laughed. "You're not in Kansas now."

That evening, Ralph took Alexander to Joe's Beerhouse in Eros, a well-known restaurant-bar with a bush-shack ambience. Alexander ate a large springbok steak for supper. They sat with other guests at one of a number of tables beneath a reed-thatched canopy fringing an open-air *lapa*, with a wood-fire burning in a huge metal brazier in the centre. Alexander nursed a Windhoek lager, and then another one. The bush ambience, the warm night air, the beers, the aroma of roasting meats, and Ralph's company all combined to induce in Alexander a warm sense of well-being. They took their time over supper, but round about nine o' clock, they climbed into Ralph's Land Rover Defender (a *Bwana Mkubwa* company car he seemed to have unlimited use of), and returned to the house in the suburbs, where Alexander had a bedroom to himself.

The next morning, Tuesday 16th March, Alexander said goodbye to Ralph and set off in his car for the game lodge in the East Caprivi.

From Windhoek he headed north along the B1, through Otjiwarongo, and at Otavi he took the B8, stopping at Grootfontein for a Coke and a pee at the garage toilets. Past Grootfontein, he headed north-east for Rundu on the Kunene River border with Angola. He recalled that his friend Terrance had crossed the Kunene into Angola with the SADF during the Angolan campaign. At Dlvundu he entered the West Caprivi, and followed the B8 until he crossed an invisible line drawn on the map and entered the East Caprivi. Some distance further on he crossed the Kwando River, and just beyond the river, at Kongola, he turned right onto the dirt C49, heading south, with the Kwando on his right. It was only mid-afternoon. Alexander knew he had found his way into an earlier time when he overtook a black tribesman with a pair of oxen yoked to a large forked branch, the forked ends trailing in the dirt, across which was a wooden frame, piled high with sacks of meal: this was how the man transported his goods, not yet having moved up to the wheel. At about four o'clock Alexander saw the signboard for Kwando River Lodge and turned down the narrow, sandy track.

The terrain – river, swamp and pale sandy soil – sheltered a wide variety of plants and trees. Alexander was to see *phoenix reclinata*, or wild date palms growing in profusion along the banks of the river, with their bunches of date fruits dangling from the crown of the tree; there were large stands of fever trees, *acacia xanthophloea*, with a greenish-yellow tinge to their bark, growing on low-lying terrain at seasonal swampy areas (and where they grew, fever – that is, malaria – was endemic); and there were many deep-rooted camel thorns, *acacia erioloba*, the darkest of all the acacias, with their very noticeable seed pods. The umbrella thorn, *acacia tortilis*, that most noble and iconic of the acacias, was ubiquitous, as was the baobab tree, *adansonia digitata*, with its upside-down appearance, and its multiplicity of uses – including (at Katima Mulilo, the nearest shopping town, close to one hundred miles away, which Alexander was to visit with the lodge manager on weekly supplies trips) a lavatory outhouse carved out of the living tree during the second world war, and still to be seen. Jackalberry trees, the *diospyros mespiliformis*, a large, noble, generously-sized tree, with an excellent hard wood (they were sometimes known as the African ebony tree) were scattered across the landscape, and Alexander was to see stands of several jackalberry trees growing atop the giant termite mounds that dotted the terrain. Leadwood, the *combretum imberbe*, another hardwood tree, was also common. This tree provided a much sought-after firewood, and a camp-fire that is meant to burn all night should be made up of leadwood timber, for the wood burns very slowly, with an intense heat. Mopane, *colophospermum mopane*, favouring light, sandy soil, formed a major part of the woodland, along with *combretum*, in which was found russet bushwillow, or *combretum hereroense*, with its beautiful, autumnal-tinted leaves. Mopane and combretum were the most common ground covers in the terrain. Egyptian papyrus grew densely along the banks of the river. Each of these many species had its uses to man and beast both. Almost all the acacia species bore highly nutritious seed pods of varying sizes and shapes.

The bird life was superb: there were paradise flycatchers with their long pennant-like tails; there were a number of kingfisher species along the river – the lovely little malachite kingfisher, the impressive giant kingfisher, the black and white pied kingfisher, and the delightful dwarf kingfisher. Pygmy geese, so cute and comical, were also found on the water. There were white fronted bee eaters and carmine bee eaters nesting in communities of small holes in the earthen cliff-faces at the bends of the river. These brightly decorated birds were a spectacular sight when you drew up quietly in one of the boats, then clapped your hands loudly, or revved the engine, and they flew *en masse* from their nesting holes, a palette of colour in motion. There were herons of every description, including the Goliath heron; there were African jacanas, such dainty lily-trotters, on their extraordinarily long-toed feet; there were hornbills, both grey hornbills and yellow-billed hornbills, who made such a drama of coming in to a landing in the trees; there were splendid lilac breasted rollers, with their acrobatic flight. The grey louries – the "go away bird" made a call like grizzling babies in the bush. There were coucals, which, though not members of the *corvus* family, made Alexander think of brightly coloured crows, for they were quick and clever. They were easy to tame. The list of avian species ran into scores upon scores.

Of the animal life, the huge herds of elephants were the most spectacular: Alexander, out walking in the bush one day when there were no guests staying at the lodge, sat at the foot of a pair of jackalberry trees, his knees drawn up beneath his chin, alone in the bush but for the animals and birds around him, and he watched a column of elephants passing by, and he lost count after three hundred animals. There were great herds of buffalo also, and Alexander could walk past them, not so very far away, and they would raise their heavy-bossed heads and stare incuriously at him, just like cattle. He knew to avoid the lone buffalo bulls, or the small groups of two or three bulls together. There were leopards at night (he often heard them coughing outside as dawn was approaching, and he was waking up in his *rondavel*, knowing that he would shortly have to walk through the mopani and bushwillow to the main lodge building, to light the stove and prepare tea and coffee and rusks for his guests before setting off on a dawn game drive). Lions forded the river sometimes from the Botswana side, and the river itself was home to many hippos, who came ashore at night to graze, and whom Alexander had to evade before dawn every day, when he left his *rondavel*.

Alexander drove old Land Rovers. The Series III was his favourite, though sometimes he drove a forward control, ex-army Land Rover. The nearest town – Katima Mulilo, on the Zambezi River – was almost 100 miles away, along a road that was dirt for part of the way, and the nearest commercial airstrip was located at Katima Mulilo. The lodge had its own small dirt runway a quarter miles away, where light aircraft landed, bringing in guests. Alexander was to get to know some of the bush pilots, and once one of them allowed him to sit in the co-pilot's seat and take the plane up from the dirt strip, and head west along the Caprivi strip for fifteen minutes, before circling and returning for a landing which the pilot himself then took charge of.

Alexander's guests were usually wealthy, educated, middle aged couples from England, Europe, and North America. He took them on a dawn drive every morning, the lodge manager's old army service Lee-Enfield .303 rifle in its rubber-padded brackets across the top of the dashboard, the dawn being announced by a splendid, technicoloured sky which seemed to be catching fire by stages. In the afternoon, round about four o'clock, he took his guests on a river cruise in one of the boats, arriving back at the lodge two hours later as the sun was falling to the horizon, the sky turning scarlet and gold. Well into the tropics as they were, the sun fell almost vertically towards the horizon, and it fell so fast: one moment it was still daylight; the next, it was night. There was no dusk at all. As the sun was tumbling towards the rim of the earth, flooding the sky with bands of colour from fiery crimson to molten gold, through salmon pink to lemon yellow, there would be a frantic shrieking and gobbling, cawing, hooting, and calling, from birds and animals, and then a brief stillness before the night sounds began.

When Alexander was out with guests on an afternoon river cruise in the ski-boat (which was a fast, light planing boat), and he saw a hippo pod ahead, he would move the gear lever until they were holding stationary against the current, and then wait for seven to eight minutes, by which time each hippo in the pod had surfaced at least once, to breathe. Once he had fixed an image of their disposition in his mind's eye, Alexander would warn his guests to have their camcorders and cameras ready, and then he would ram the throttle forward, and get the boat up on the step, and speed through the pod. Then Alexander would spin the boat round beyond the pod, and the hippos would be roaring in his wake, their great gapes wide, their huge peg-like tusks visible. Alexander called this "hippo slalom".

Sometimes the screw (or screws, on the big twin-engined double-decker barge he sometimes went out on if there were many guests) would be fouled by river weed, and Alexander would have to remove his shirt and go over the side, and use the saw-toothed edge of his bush knife to hack away the weeds, coming up every now and then to gasp for air. There were crocodiles in this stretch of the Kwando, but not many. But only twenty kilometres downstream, at another lodge, a young game ranger, celebrating his twenty-first birthday, went for a night swim in the Kwando, and disappeared. His remains were found a few days later, lodged between the roots of a tree on the river bank, just beneath the water: he had been seized and partially eaten by a crocodile.

Alexander looked after an English guest once, Jim Harper, a chap in his late fifties, who was visiting in company with a much younger woman. He and Alexander walked out into the bush one morning after the dawn drive. Alexander did not have the .303 rifle with him. His only weapons were his bush knife and a short, broad-bladed Zulu stabbing spear he favoured when he was out walking alone. He had found it in one of the outhouses at the lodge, and he had put a new edge to the blade using a file. The Englishman wanted to get up close to buffalo, and Alexander was fairly certain that he knew where he could find an old bull, an *mzee*, and his two *askaris*, the younger bulls who kept him company. He found their spoor after a couple of miles' walking, and the two men followed the spoor, and after a while, having come across some very fresh dung, Alexander tested the air: there was the hint of a wind, and he left the spoor, to get well downwind of the buffalos, and the two men swung out in a wide arc.

Alexander found his guest his buffalos; three of them. Alexander saw a massive termite mound some distance ahead, and he guessed that the animals were close by the other side of it, and – still downwind of the animals' presumed location – he and his guest crept closer, and leopard-crawled up to the crest of the termite mound. The three animals were there, only yards away from the men, below the termite mound. There was a massive old bull, with a heavy boss and a spread of double-curved horns that spanned three and a half feet in breadth, standing so near that Alexander could see the fat purple ticks gathered in the folds of skin at his throat and behind his ears. Ranged watchfully alongside him were his two younger companions. Alexander and the Englishman lay silently, flat on their bellies just below the crest of the termite mound, peering over the top, and gazed with wonder at those magnificent beasts. Alexander had not allowed his guest to bring his camera – the click of the shutter would have spooked the buffalos, and possibly put the two men into a danger they could not have escaped. So Alexander and the older man simply gazed at the three buffalos, admiring, hardly breathing.

On the way back to the lodge, Jim Harper, charged up with excitement, could not keep quiet. The experience had filled him with wonder. "I've often been out shooting – game birds and deer too – but Sandy, I have never felt such a thrill as I felt lying flat on top of that termite mound with those brutes just yards from us." A while later, Jim Harper continued "And all we brought to that amazing experience were our wits, not a rifle between us!"

"I was excited too, Jim," Alexander responded. "It's something very few men will have experienced – being that close to three buffalo bulls, un-armed, in the open, and coming away unscathed."

(Some years later, when he was once again living in England, Alexander spent the night and the following morning at Jim Harper's home on his one-thousand acre mixed farm outside Newbury in England. Jim was by then alone, and dying of cancer, but as they sat and sipped at scotch whiskey together that evening, a fire burning in the grate, their reminiscences about Africa brought the Englishman obvious pleasure).

During Alexander's time at the lodge, two young men arrived independently of one-another on extended visits. They were not the usual sort of guests: they were spending time at Kwando River Lodge as part of their gap years, having finished school the year before. Their parents had some sort of pull with the directors back in Windhoek: they were there just for fun. The first of the young men to arrive was a Frenchman, Jean. "*Bienvenue, Jean*," Alexander greeted him, as he stepped from the small aircraft at the lodge's dirt strip.

The boy slept in the spare bed in Alexander's own *rondavel*. He was a pleasant youth in every way, inoffensive, keen to participate in Alexander's work. He followed Alexander around, and Alexander tried to teach him some of what he knew, so that he had something to take away with him when he left. "*Le plus important chose se souvenir dans le bois de l'Afrique, Jean, c'est à bien courir – oui?.*"

Jean laughed. Alexander enjoyed his company, but the young Frenchman stayed for only four or five weeks. "*Au revoir mon ami. Sois sage!*" Alexander called, as the young man climbed into another small aircraft, headed for Windhoek, at the end of his stay.

The second youthful visitor was a charming, rather well bred young Englishman, who reminded Alexander very much of Ralph. Giles was a tall, sturdy good looking boy, and, aged only eighteen, he exerted that particular charm special to boys who know that they are popular and well liked, but who seem just a little embarrassed at the knowledge. Giles' connections must have been of another rank to the young French lad's, for he was given his own *rondavel*. He could not get out of bed early, and he missed almost all Alexander's dawn game drives. He was far less assiduous than the French boy had been in his attention to trying to learn from Alexander, but his charm was such that Alexander found it difficult to be irritated by him.

When he first arrived, Giles had an English pallor, but he had dark brown hair and brown eyes, and during his first week at the lodge he tanned quickly. He also got horribly bitten by mosquitoes, despite Alexander's efforts to persuade him to do as he did, and shower and change soon after sundown, getting dressed in a long sleeved shirt and slacks, with shoes and socks. Alexander undertook this ritual every evening, and then for good measure he rubbed citronella onto the back of his neck, on his wrists, and on his ankles. He was never bitten by mosquitoes. At night, everyone slept under mosquito nets. The black staff however were always going down with malarial attacks, and they were very ill each time, laid up in bed, and sad as sick dogs. Alexander was lucky: despite taking nothing against malaria (on the grounds that long term anti-malarial medication is harmful; it can cause liver-damage), either there in the Caprivi, or in the Transvaal Lowveld, he never went down with malaria.

Giles enjoyed joining Alexander on the river cruises in the afternoon. Then he was in his element, lazing elegantly in the sunshine in the boat's stern, and entertaining the guests. They were attacked by a hippo once, when they were out in the small ski-boat. Giles was lounging aft; there were perhaps three or four guests in the boat also. Alexander had taken the boat close to the reeds by the river's banks, to watch a dainty lily-trotter (jacana), and suddenly, there was a great bellowing and a thrashing of water, and a hippo broke from the reeds and began to surge through the water towards them, her jaws agape. Alexander guessed they had accidentally come too close to a cow whose calves were hidden in the reeds, and she had taken fright at their proximity. With each porpoiselike surge through the water, she covered about five feet, two-thirds of her full length. Alexander was thrilled; he felt a spirit of wicked mischief seize hold of him (but there was some calculation also; he knew that it was for experiences such as this that their guests visited the game reserve): he held the boat stationary, watching, and at the last possible moment, by which time two of his guests were yelling, he rammed the gear lever into reverse and spun the wheel; the boat turned sharply aside from the hippo cow, almost on its axis, and then Alexander shoved the lever hard forward and opened the throttle, and they sped away from the animal. Giles' face had gone white beneath his tan. Later he told Alexander "I've never been so scared in all my life."

Giles went to Sandhurst in September that year. He was commissioned the following year, and he went on to serve with the British contingent of the UN peace-keeping forces in Bosnia. Giles joined a cavalry regiment: they used Warrior armored fighting vehicles.

One day, when there were no guests staying at the lodge, Alexander took Giles out walking in the bush. Alexander had no rifle with him: the lodge manager would not permit him to use it except on duty. Some miles from the lodge, the two men began to come across a great deal of evidence of fresh buffalo sign: the imprints of many hooves, and fresh dung also. The terrain was sparsely covered by *combretum* (bush willow), and large growths of *wag-n-bietjie* thorn, along with other shrubs and the occasional acacia, and Alexander said "Giles – give the bushes and thorns a wide berth as we pass them: there could be a buff or two behind any one of them."

Giles grinned. "Stop trying to scare me," he responded.

They were approaching one of these large thorn bushes, and the two men split up, one walking either side of the bush, and there was a sudden, shocking commotion and a snorting beast with a grey-brown hide covered in sparse bristles, with ivories either side of its head, burst forth from behind the bush. Giles and Alexander both yelled and they took off fast in opposite directions, before coming to their senses: the creature was not after all a buffalo, but only a startled warthog. The two men spent the next few minutes laughing uncontrollably at one-another. "You should have seen yourself!" Giles exclaimed, when he could talk again.

"You should have seen *yourself!*" Alexander responded, still laughing.

Lest Alexander begin to think he had found a Paradise on earth here in the East Caprivi, he had to contend with the deeply unpleasant lodge manager and his even more unpleasant common law wife. On a visit to Windhoek for a few days off, after some months at the lodge, Alexander had been told by Ralph that Gary Vorster, the lodge manager, had not wanted a white resident game guide sent to him. "He sees you as a spy for head office."

Alexander thought there was more to it than that: it was a matter of jarring personalities. Gary's social skills with the guests showed up as sparse when compared with Alexander's easy, confident, articulate interaction with these foreign visitors. Gary was a physically powerful, brooding man of very few words. Alexander sometimes thought that Gary had taken against him the moment he had climbed out of his car: Alexander was very slim, and compared to Gary's hulking build, he appeared willowy, frail and physically inadequate. Whatever the reason, Gary Vorster did not like his new resident naturalist – and he never would.

By June, Alexander was becoming ever more infatuated with Giles. The boy represented much that Alexander wished he himself might have been. Thus, when Giles and Jill, the Canadian girl who worked in the main lodge, began to flirt with one another, Alexander knew jealousy and misery. He himself did not entertain erotic feelings for Jill. She was on the plump side, with bright yellow hair and a high complexion, and only mediocre intellectual faculties. It was Giles he wanted. The thought that Jill might be gaining access to that beautiful young man, began to unhinge Alexander. One evening after dinner, Alexander was reading by paraffin lantern in his *rondavel*. He heard Giles' voice not far away. Giles' *rondavel* was the next structure along the staff lines, about forty feet away. Alexander doused his lantern and crept to the window that gave onto that side. He saw Giles meet Jill outside his *rondavel*, and he watched the two of them enter the hut. The pair showed up well through the un-curtained window against the light of Giles' paraffin lantern. The blind was not lowered. Alexander knew that he was invisible. He could no longer hear them speaking, but he watched as Giles embraced and kissed Jill. Alexander felt his face burn with rage and jealousy as he saw Jill remove Giles' shirt. Then the couple disappeared from sight, presumably making for the bed.

It was following this unhappy observation that Alexander began to drink much more heavily. Up to that time, he had drunk a glass of wine with his meal at dinner-time, and perhaps a couple of lagers afterwards in the lounge, marking them against his staff tab. He had not thus far wished to drink in order to get drunk. That changed now. He began to drink every evening in order to get drunk, and short of stealing the liquor, which Alexander would not contemplate, he could not hide the amount he had begun to drink, for he entered his drinks on his tab, to be deducted from his monthly salary. Gary Vorster knew how much Alexander was drinking, and this was to give him a stick with which to beat Alexander.

Had he not enjoyed his work so much, Alexander might quickly have descended into highly destructive drinking. It was his work which saved him from this: he took a great pleasure in it. He learned to treat Gary Vorster as he would an unpleasant weather phenomenon: as something to live around, and try to ignore. He knew that when the guests enthused over dinner in the evening about the sights Alexander had shown them that day, and the adventures they had enjoyed, it made Gary grind his teeth. And of course, Alexander spent much of his day in Giles' company, and Giles was a light-hearted, cheerful, uncomplicated young man, singing snatches of pop songs and whistling happily. However, in July the youngster returned to England. He would be entering Sandhurst, the British military academy, in September. As Giles was about to climb into the tiny single engined aircraft in which he was to return to Windhoek, he said to Alexander "You gave me a good time, Sandy. Even if you scared the hell out of me sometimes!"

"You take care!" Alexander said, shaking his hand.

"Yah – and you take it easy."

Watching the aircraft as it climbed and circled in the sky and set a course for the west, Alexander felt very alone. But there would be guests whose company he would enjoy during the remaining months he was to spend at Kwando River Lodge. He continued to keep his drinking just barely in check. By the end of the day he was too weary to stay up late, drinking. For the same reason, he read little. There was a collection of popular novels in a bookcase in the lounge for the guests to borrow, along with volumes on natural history. It was one of these that Alexander preferred to have by his bed in his *rondavel*. He was usually too tired to read more than a few pages in the evening.

One day, when the lodge was devoid of guests, Alexander set off walking, alone and un-armed but for his bush knife and his *assegaai*, or stabbing spear. By the time he sat down beneath a camel thorn acacia to eat the sandwiches Jill had prepared for him, he was about five kilometres from the lodge. He had seen several family groups of elephants, and a large buffalo herd not far away, along with large herds of zebra and impala. Walking in this terrain was not difficult. Although there were only occasional four-wheel drive double tracked trails through the bush, the bush itself was not heavily overgrown. Alexander could set a course through the bush and follow it without major deviations. After his snack, Alexander began to head back to the lodge. It was then that he saw what looked like the spoor of many big dogs in the sandy soil. It did not seem to Alexander to be hyena spoor. He began to track the spoor, which was easy enough, and after only ten minutes he came to an open clearing, in which a drinking hole, a big pool of muddy water with a pair of knob-billed ducks swimming in it, was still to be found in this dry season. On the far side of the water he saw a pack of wild dogs.

Alexander was thrilled. He stood still – he knew he would have been spotted, but the dogs were one-hundred yards or more away, with the water between them and him, and they would not be feeling threatened. Alexander had n't seen any wild dogs in the region before. He knew from something that Gary had said at dinner one evening that there were thought to be no wild dogs left in the region. These Cape Hunting Dogs, *Lycaon Pictus*, were smaller than hyenas, not unlike long-legged, heavy-muzzled domestic dogs from afar, except that they had huge, rounded ears. Their hides were individually dappled, blotched, spotted and brindled with tan, dark brown, and patches of white. They were indeed "painted wolves", as their Latin name indicated. Alexander stood and gazed at them for fifteen minutes or more. The pack was resting. Several of the dogs were lying down in the shade of an umbrella thorn acacia. There were pups with them, playing and gamboling and mock fighting with each other. Alexander heard a constant chorus of squeaks, whines, and squeals from the little creatures. Watching the pack, Alexander felt supremely happy.

When Alexander returned to the lodge and mentioned his sighting to Gary, the normally taciturn man became almost enthused. He told Alexander that it had been thought that wild dogs were effectively extinct in the East Caprivi, shot out during the civil war. "You must enter what you saw in the record of significant game sightings I keep in my office, and when I call Windhoek tomorrow on the radio telephone, I'll ask head office to report the sighting to the conservation department at the ministry of the environment. It's the sort of report that will please them." The big, unfriendly man regarded Alexander thoughtfully for a moment. "I would like to have been able to see them."

Once in a while, when he had a day free, instead of heading out for a day's walking in the bush, Alexander drove his Ford Granada to Katima Mulilo, because a car standing idle too long becomes a sick car. He seized the opportunity then to buy a dozen bottles of cheap scotch whiskey, which he would store in the car's locked boot. From this store he would ensure that he always had a bottle of whiskey hidden in his *rondavel*. He knew enough about black domestic staff to realise that his stash was probably no secret from the staff who cleaned his room every day, but he hoped that they saw no reason to talk about it to Gary Vorster or to his common law wife, especially as he tipped the cleaning staff quite generously every month. By September, Alexander was beginning his day with a hefty slug of whiskey before he brushed his teeth, and sometimes, after lunch, he would go to his *rondavel* and take another slug.

It was during the evenings, after dinner, that Alexander drank openly. He would often begin with a single scotch, before moving on to a couple of lagers, and he would chat with the people at the bar at one end of the big lounge beneath its high thatched roof, some of whom were local people, such as the young Englishman who was carrying out a game survey for the WWF. He did not stay at the lodge: he lived alone in a house with a corrugated iron roof down a track leading off the main road to Kutima Mulilo. His work meant that he was often found within the lodge concession area. He sometimes visited the lodge at lunchtime, joining the others in a meal, and he enjoyed drinking at the lounge bar several evenings a week.

Alexander got nearly drunk very quickly, because he was tired and ready to go to bed by nine o'clock, and he sometimes became expansive and loquacious, and it was then obvious to many that he had drunk too much. Rationally, Alexander knew that he could not hope to hide a drinking habit in such a small community.

One early December morning, just after breakfast, Gary Vorster said to him "You're drinking too much. You have got to cut down. You're giving the lodge a bad name."

Alexander felt his face grow hot with shame and embarrassment. He did not know what to say, so he turned aside and walked away. He knew his drinking had now become a problem, and that Gary would use it to hurt him if he could. Later that morning, having brooded on the problem, Alexander found Gary Vorster again, and said "I want to talk to Graham at head office in Windhoek. I've worked here long enough. I want to leave. I'm sure this will please you, Gary. I need to use the radio-telephone."

"Tell me what you want to say to them. I'll tell them."

"No. I'm leaving either way. It will look better if I talk with Graham first, because if I don't, then when I see Graham I'll have to tell him that you wouldn't allow me to talk to him."

So Gary Vorster permitted Alexander to call Windhoek on the radio-telephone link. Alexander knew that Gary would be standing listening just beyond the door to the office. There was nothing he could do about that. Graham, the *Bwana Mkubwa* operations manager in Windhoek, at whose home Alexander had spent his first night in Namibia, asked him why he wanted to leave the lodge.

"I've got a problem. I cannot fix that problem if I stay here," Alexander told him.

"Very well. We'll find you something to do here. When are you leaving Kwando River Lodge?"

"Tomorrow morning, Graham. I should reach Windhoek by nightfall."

Alexander knew that Gary Vorster would be on the radio to either Graham or to John, the MD, that afternoon, bad-mouthing him.

There was no one at the lodge itself that Alexander felt obliged to say goodbye to. He had never grown close to Jill. But that afternoon, Alexander visited the black staff lines and sought out the black Headman, and gave him seventy Rands to distribute among the staff. The sum was worth a lot more out here than it would have been in Windhoek. The next morning, at seven o'clock, the Headman was the only person waiting outside Alexander's *rondavel* to see him leave. Alexander drove between the gateposts of Kwando River Lodge for the last time.

Twenty-Three

Namibia

Windhoek was a small, schizophrenic city. Depending on your business, and whom you mixed with, it was either an entirely white city (excepting only the servants in your home), or almost entirely black. The President, that ex-freedom fighter (or for many, that ex-terrorist), Sam Nujoma, lived in Windhoek, when he was not holidaying at his seaside house, built as a summer residence for the colonial-era German governor, in Swakopmund. For the next few days, Alexander's Windhoek was a white man's city. He socialised with Ralph and one of the other young guides, who were in town at the time, and in the evening they went out eating and drinking together. Ralph's presence brought him both pleasure and pain. Alexander found that he had transferred his infatuation for Giles straight back onto Ralph, who was after all its progenitor. It was an infatuation utterly without hope of any satisfaction, and Alexander's drinking increased drastically. But Ralph appeared to be blind to Alexander's longing and desire for him, and he took pains to include Alexander in his social life over the next few days.

Before Alexander's drink problem became unavoidably evident to everyone at *Bwana Mkubwa*, he spent nine days touring Namibia in a sturdy, diesel-engined four-wheel drive Toyota Hilux pick-up, a black guide his only companion. The journey was a rare and wonderful interlude for Alexander, for all that he drank fairly heavily throughout it. The Toyota was loaded with two large collapsible internally framed bell-tents, several jerry-cans of diesel fuel, a couple of large cans of motor oil, some big plastic containers of water, a carton of water purifiers, two big Cadac pressurised gas cylinders (for the powerful gas lanterns Alexander took with him), and several cold boxes packed with perishables in ice: fresh vegetables, cold drinks, and strings of sausages and cuts of meat (for *braaing* or barbequeing). There were two boxes of tinned foods and general groceries supplies, and stacks of corded firewood for the camp fires. Alexander and the black guide each had his own kit bag as well, with changes of clothing and personal items. Inside Alexander's kitbag were three bottles of whiskey.

The two men set off north from Windhoek in the early morning of Monday 13th December, with only two weeks left of 1993, and drove straight past Okahandja, then through Otjiwaarongo and up to Tsumeb, where they had lunch at an eatery by the roadside. By the late afternoon they had reached the Etosha National Park, a vast game reserve in the north of Namibia, well served with good roads and tracks. At the heart of Etosha is the Etosha Pan, a large body of water that expands and contracts with the seasons, but never goes dry, and is vital to the region's ecology. Alexander made camp that night at a clean, orderly camp site with an ablutions block, where he could shower and shave with hot water in the morning. The terrain was mixed *combretum* and scrub, with the occasional acacia and boabab tree. Accustomed to the ecology of the Lowveld in South Africa, and more recently, to that of the eastern Caprivi, Alexander was struck at the difference in the country's appearance: it was not nearly as lush, nor the cover as dense, as was found in either of those regions.

Alexander's black companion was surly and silent, and no help at the campsite. Alexander, who had little experience of black people other than as servants or labourers, was not bothered by his silences, and he enjoyed barbequing the *boerewors* (spicy, traditional southern African country sausages made of beef), the beef steaks, and the mutton chops or the chicken breasts, over the fire. Alexander drank more or less openly from his bottle of scotch in the evenings. He could no longer go an entire day without liquor: had he tried, he should have begun to feel very edgy, and he would have got the shakes, and have been unable to drive. Alexander's black guide was coming along for one reason only: it was not for companionship, but to show him the route. The plan was that Alexander would take over the camping tours that embraced the route they were following. It was a plan Alexander knew was stillborn, for it required that he be strong, fit and sober. He had no idea how he was to sober up. He dared not think of the future. He lived entirely in the moment.

They left Etosha by one of its westernmost exits, and drove a short haul to Sesfontein, a tiny settlement where they made camp again in the afternoon, on sandy soil beneath some camel thorn acacias. The next morning they crossed the Namib desert. Here in the north the sandy surface was stony: stark, sear, barren. At one point, Alexander stopped the car and turned the engine off. Sitting for a while, he could hear the metal of the engine clicking from the heat. He left his black guide sitting in the car and he walked away for a hundred yards, then listened: he could hear nothing. There was total and complete silence. He thought, I have never listened to total silence before. This was one of the world's most barren deserts, and certainly its oldest, yet tiny creatures, beetles and arthropods, survived in it, and certain large animals, such as oryx antelope and the famed desert elephants, had adapted to survive this harsh terrain and climate, though of any such, the two men saw no sign as they crossed the desert that day. They did however see a *welwitschia*, an extraordinarily ugly desert plant, sometimes known as a living fossil, which grew two large, gnarled and twisted leaves reaching several yards in length.

They reached the Atlantic coast, near Cape Cross, in the afternoon, and Alexander's black guide showed him the way to the Cape fur seal rookery there. Alexander could smell and hear the seals long before he saw them. There are Bushman rock paintings far inland across the desert, showing seals – among other creatures. The smell close up was almost overpowering, like being in a cod-liver oil factory. Alexander was glad to see the ocean. The sight of the Atlantic breakers was a welcome change after the inland bushveld he had been accustomed to for so long. The coastal road was good: it was two lanes wide, with a firm, smooth surface made of a compound of a cream coloured, gypsum-like substance that was smoothed out every night with the settling of the sea mist, and was smooth and hard again soon after sunrise the next day. There was absolutely nothing to be seen, mile after mile, but the ocean to Alexander's right, and sand to his left.

Later that same day they reached Swakopmund, a remarkable late 19th century/early 20th century German resort town built on the Atlantic shore. Swakop, as the locals call it, is a fairy tale town, it is so improbable, and Alexander gazed with pleasure at the incongruity of a small German town of a hundred years ago, transplanted to the edge of the desert on the one hand, and the edge of the ocean on the other. Many of the buildings are two stories tall, many-gabled, north German in style, with the occasional turret or crenellation, and even the odd Bavarian style half timbered structure.

They entered the town through a gap in the great desert barricade of heaped up sandbags which reached above ten feet high. Once past this restraining barrier, they were driving through a neat, clean, orderly little town, with streets laid out in a grid pattern, and on the Atlantic edge of the town there was a narrow strip of park with a green lawn and palm trees, and flower beds bright with cannas and zinnias and agapanthus, which fronted a bathing beach.

Alexander's black guide had family living here, so he and Alexander split up for the next two days, but Alexander had an address to visit: a third or fourth generation German-Namibian family, who lived on the edge of town, and who were to put him up during his brief stay. These were kind, hospitable people, a husband and wife in their forties. Alexander's host took him walking around Swakopmund in the late afternoon, showing him the town, and his wife prepared a very good supper at their home. The next day Alexander drove into town alone, and he found a hotel bar across the road from the beach and the park, where he could sit outside at a table beneath an umbrella, and he drank lagers, ice cold.

Here, Alexander met by chance a couple of young girls from Germany, whom he had last seen a month or two earlier at the lodge on the Kwando River, where they had stayed a few nights. The three had lunch together, and agreed to meet later that evening at the hotel bar. Alexander enjoyed having pretty feminine company at the bar that evening, and during supper. They were both attractive girls in their twenties, not the usual run of guests to have been found at the lodge on the Kwando, for they were neither as old, nor (Alexander supposed), nearly as rich as the guests he had usually looked after. Margit, with dark brown hair and a deep tan, was the more outgoing of the two. She made Alexander feel appreciated and attractive. She laughed a lot, and touched his bare forearm often as she talked. Her English, though mildly accented, was good. Her friend, Katarina, a honey-blonde with a warm golden tan, was quieter, and her English was more halting. She had a charming, shy smile. Katarina drank little, but Margit kept pace with Alexander, who was downing cold lagers. Alexander learned that they would be in Windhoek within a short while. He obtained a Windhoek phone number from Margit.

Before Alexander departed Swakopmund he bought more supplies, including cigarettes, whiskey, and cords of firewood, and he packed the icebox with fresh ice and cuts of meat, and had one of the part-empty Cadac gas cylinders exchanged for a full one at the Cadac gas depot in town. His silent black traveling companion reappeared early the second morning, and they resumed their journey, still headed south along the coast. They drove through the South African enclave of Walvis Bay (off which the RMS Windsor Castle liner had halted while a sick crewman had been lowered over the side, during Alexander's voyage home from Britain in September 1976). They passed a lagoon that was pink with flamingos, the first flamingos Alexander had seen since leaving Kenya, then headed inland across the Namib Naukluft National Park, a region of semi desert with the occasional oasis. At one point Alexander crossed a stream of clear water at the bottom of a tree-shaded kloof.

They camped at Sossusvlei that night, a salt and clay pan surrounded by high red sand dunes, which changed hue with the going down of the sun. Alexander climbed to the knife-edge crest of one of the dunes, hundreds of feet high. They were utterly bereft of life, like the planet Mars, but beautiful, in a stark, off-world fashion. The two men had pitched camp amongst some stunted acacias. There was a standpipe and a water trough for water drawn from deep underground by an adjacent wind pump.

In the Maltahohe district of the Namib the next morning, Alexander's guide directed him off the main road onto a sandy, pebbly track which ran dead straight across the scrub for many miles. After a while, in the far distance, against a backdrop of iron-dark hills, Alexander saw an extraordinary sight: a fortress built of red stone. It grew larger and larger as they neared it. It appeared to be two stories high, with a third story in the central watch-tower. This was *Schlöss Duwisib*, built in the early 20th century by a Captain Hans Heinrich von Wolf, who had bought eight farms in the area. After the Nama war, he settled in South West Africa to breed horses for the army. What a remarkable place the *schlöss* was, thought Alexander, with its twenty-two rooms, many with fine, heavy, Teutonic furnishings and heavy gilt framed oil paintings – ancestral portraits and landscapes – hanging on the walls. The fortress was built around a courtyard in which was a well fed by a year-round spring, with two large acacias growing in the courtyard, and inside the *schlöss* was a great hall with a minstrel gallery and a huge fireplace, and the walls were hung with weapons – swords, spears and axes. There was a genuine dungeon below the hall, and there were crenellated battlements. This was a true, defensive fortress, for the region had only recently been pacified by Germany, when the *schlöss* was built.

There was just one Nama keeper in evidence when Alexander visited, and he allowed Alexander to wander round the castle unaccompanied, at his leisure. Alexander's black guide, disinterested, dozed in the shade of one of the big trees in the courtyard. They were the only visitors. The Nama keeper told Alexander that sometimes many days would pass without anyone at all visiting the *schlöss*.

Von Wolf died in 1916, at the battle of the Somme, having rejoined the Imperial German army, and his American wife, who had made her way to England via South America when the Great War began, never returned to claim the castle. Desert horses still roam the district.

The two men made camp that evening at the Helmeringhausen Hotel campsite, Alexander's guide still as uncommunicative and unhelpful as before. He was willing enough, however, to eat the food Alexander prepared each evening. Alexander sat drinking coffee laced with whiskey that evening after supper. After a while it began to rain. This so startled the black guide that he declared "Hau! This rain is very unusual." Alexander fell asleep to the sound of rain on the tent canvas.

The next morning, Alexander's guide directed Alexander onto the C14 running south. At Goageb Alexander left the tarred road for a dirt road, and after many miles continuing south, they swung east, towards the Fish River Canyon. They came across a watercourse in spate. "I have never seen water here," the black guide said.

"I'm going to engage the four-wheel drive," Alexander told him. He got out of the car and turned each front hub, until the four-wheel drive was engaged. Then he set the car's nose for the watercourse. The water came up and over the door sills, but no further. In low gear, Alexander kept a steady pressure on the accelerator. In his rear-view mirror he saw a Volkswagen Kombi campervan commence to follow in his path. As he had anticipated, the campervan came to a halt in mid-stream, the engine air intake flooded. Alexander backed slowly up, no great distance, and he opened his door. Water surged inside across the floor of the cab. He was wearing shorts and leather sandals. He climbed down into the floodwaters, holding onto the side of the Toyota pick-up. He found the coiled rope he was looking for, and attached one end to his vehicle, the other to the front of the Volkswagen camper. The water was buffeting him in surges, but accustomed to having to go overboard in the Kwando River, to clear weeds from the boat's props, he was unconcerned. Then he climbed back into the cab, and set off very slowly in first gear, until the slack of the rope was taken up. Thus he dragged the Volkswagen campervan clear of the flood water and left it dripping on the far side of the stream. The young foreigner and his girlfriend, who were the campervan's only passengers, rooted around inside the vehicle and then came towards Alexander, the man with a bottle of wine in his hand. "Here," he said. "Please take this. We are very grateful to you."

Alexander smiled and took the proffered bottle of wine. "Have a safe journey now," he said.

It was early afternoon when he and his guide reached the mighty Fish River Canyon. Both men got out of the car and followed the path towards the edge of the canyon. There, they stood staring at the vast visa. The canyon swung round here in a huge loop. The weathered canyon face consisted of rock strata of red-brown and tan. Far, far below, the Fish River was broad as it flowed in flood. Alexander sat down close to the edge of the drop and lighted a cigarette. After a while, his guide also sat down. Neither man spoke a word. They stayed there for about half an hour, then walked back to the Toyota pick-up. It was late afternoon when they reached the Alte Kalkofen campsite at Goageb.

Alexander and his guide did not have to hurry the following morning. They had an easy run ahead of them that day to a campsite at Hardap Dam, on the B1 main road north to Windhoek. On the way they stopped at Keetmanshoop, a small town laid out in a number of grid patterns. The railway to Windhoek from the Western Cape ran through the town. Here they ate an early lunch. During the afternoon, Alexander was not much impressed by the terrain they were driving through: there was little that was scenically noteworthy in it, and the road was quite busy. They were traveling the main road linking the Western Cape, via Springbok, with Windhoek. They arrived at the Hardap Dam campsite at about four o'clock, to find Margit and Katarina had pitched their tent just yards away. This was to be the last night on the road for all four of them before reaching Windhoek. That evening, while the black guide kept to himself, Alexander sat with the two German girls and told tall, but not entirely untruthful, tales, and got quite drunk. He had by now reached a point in the cycle of this prolonged bout of drinking where mania dominated, and he no longer felt anything but overwhelming self-confidence, and the conviction that (somehow!) all would be well. In this assumption, Alexander was of course very much mistaken.

The next day, having arranged to meet up with Margit and Katarina again in Windhoek, Alexander and his guide pulled into *Bwana Mkubwa's* yard. It was the 21st of December: they had been traveling for nine days. Caught up in his manic phase, Alexander gave little thought to the impression his far from sober appearance was having on either Graham, the operations manager, or on John, the managing director, and he unpacked the Toyota feeling quite blithe. But that evening, alone in the house the young tour guides shared – for the others were all away on tours – it began to dawn on Alexander that his Namibian interlude was fast approaching its end. Shame and humiliation began to overtake him. How was he to explain to his brother, Roy, or to his mother, that he had failed ... again?

Alexander went through to his bedroom. He was tired, and ready to pass out from drink and from the reaction to nine days' of driving. As he sat on the edge of his bed, a thought came to him: he would n't now be seeing Margit or Katarina again. He lay back on the bed in his bush shirt and short trousers, kicked his sandals off his feet, and passed out.

Early in the morning of the 22nd of December, Alexander came to, and in the kitchen he found someone's tin of instant coffee and some sugar. He drank two glasses of water also, brushed his teeth, stripped, stood under the shower for a while, then managed to find some clean underwear. All this was achieved by eight o' clock. He quickly packed his kitbag again, and his suitcase, checked that he still had cash in his wallet, and took his bags out to his car, which was parked in the front garden where he had left it ten days ago. He slammed the front door to the house behind him, and he left the keys in the plant pot nearby, hidden under some cacti. He would stop at the petrol station, check his car's water, oil and tyre pressure, and refuel it. By nine-fifteen that morning he was leaving Windhoek behind him, the road south, and home, beckoning. He had a new bottle of scotch, bought two stores along from the petrol station, lying on the passenger seat alongside him, but just for now, he was relatively sober. He had closed his mind to the full implications of what he was doing. It was better not to think at all.

Alexander did not plan on driving back to Johannesburg. He felt ashamed, beaten and broken. He kept driving south, headed for Cape

Town and the farm. It was the one place left in the world that he associated with nothing but happiness. Alexander drove all through the day, stopping only thrice. At Keetmanshoop he stopped for some coffee and something to eat, and he needed to use the lavatory; at Springbok, he stopped again, to refuel his car and to drink some more coffee and use the lavatory again. It was dark when he stopped a third time, at Piketberg, for another coffee. Then he drove on, into the night.

He skirted Cape Town and drove over the top of Silvermine. The only lights visible were far below. The dark sky was strewn with stars. He reached the Fish Hoek – Kommetjie road around midnight, and was momentarily confused by the changed appearance of the approaches to the farm, for he had forgotten that there was now no trace of the long dirt track that had led between pines and yellowwood trees. He had in fact entirely forgotten that what had once been his grandfather's land was now a residential suburb, built over with houses except for a few empty plots here and there (two or three of which had belonged to his father, and presumably belonged now to his mother). He pulled up at last in a wide graveled turning space between the old farmhouse and the new double story house where his aunt and uncle now lived. It was about fifteen minutes past midnight.

Dogs were barking, and Alexander sat in his car, ready to go straight to sleep, but his aunt appeared after a little while, and he wound down the window. "Sandy! What are you doing here? Never mind – you can tell me in the morning."

"Can I sleep on the couch in the sitting room until morning, Margaret?" Alexander asked his aunt.

"Yes. Come in."

Alexander followed his aunt inside via the kitchen. "Help yourself to coffee if you want. I'll get you a pillow and a blanket for the sofa. Oh, Sandy, you don't look well at all."

Alexander's aunt disappeared, to reappear within a few minutes with a pillow and a blanket. Alexander bent to kiss her cheek. "Thank you Margaret. Good night. I'm sorry I got you up."

"I'll see you in the morning," she replied, and left Alexander with the two dogs.

Alexander stretched out on the sofa, which was broad and long. He was profoundly disturbed by the conjunction of a sense of home-coming with an interior setting that was new to him, for this house had still been in a state of incompletion when he and his family had visited for his father's funeral. But he was still asleep within minutes of laying his head on the pillow.

Alexander's aunt could not get a clear account from him the next morning. Alexander felt too ashamed to confess that he had drunk himself into a corner, and then run away. However, she was not unfamiliar with alcoholism, and she recognised immediately that Alexander was, or had been, drinking very heavily. "You can stay here for as long as you like – on one condition, Sandy: you do not bring liquor into my home."

Alexander agreed, but he knew he would break his word.

And break it he did. There was not much left in the bottle of whiskey he had had with him on the drive south from Windhoek, and later that day he walked to the new Sun Valley shopping complex that had sprung up since he had last lived on the farm, and went inside a bottle store there, and he bought two half jacks of scotch. He bought half jacks because they were easier to hide on his person than a single full-sized bottle. He left one of the half jacks in his car, and the other he sneaked into the bedroom his aunt had given him upstairs, which was not difficult, because Margaret was not in when he returned from his walk to the Sun Valley liquor store, and his uncle, who appeared to be entering premature senility – this perhaps a product of a lifetime of on-off alcohol abuse – was sitting dozing in front of the TV with the sound on.

But Alexander was not entirely lost to consideration for others. On his second morning at the farm, he drove to Fish Hoek. He entered the Standard Bank branch there, and transferred the reasonably healthy credit balance in his Windhoek account, into which his salary had been paid while he had been working for *Bwana Mkubwa*, to the Fish Hoek branch, from which he then withdrew a sum. He bought his aunt a large, lavishly illustrated coffee table book on Cape domestic interiors; his uncle a carton of Peter Stuyvesant cigarettes; and for his two cousins (both of whom still lived on the farm: Jennifer with her husband and two small children, in what had been the original farm house; the younger, Mary, in one of the large wooden chalets, with Mike) he bought a bottle of decent Cape white wine each. It was the day before Christmas.

Alexander still had additional funds available to him in his original South African bank account. The cost of his training as a field guide, and of the purchase of the Ford Granada, had not exhausted them. However, a sense of his own catastrophic failure haunted Alexander, a failure he seemed to be doomed to repeat over and over, no matter the circumstances in which he found himself. As a consequence, he sought to anesthetize his feelings, and the best way he knew to do this was through drink. And so he continued drinking. Between Christmas and New Year, this became very clear to his aunt. His behaviour became noticeably erratic: his mania was returning. "You've broken your promise to me," his aunt said to him shortly before New Year. "You're drinking every day. And Sandy, this cannot continue."

Alexander, who had a disconcerting trick of maintaining very intent direct eye contact with his interlocutor when he had reason to feel guilt or shame, stared hard at Margaret. This seemed to make her angry. "What are your plans? What are you going to do next?"

"I don't know," Alexander replied.

"If I ask you again not to bring liquor into the house – will you stick to your promise?"

"Oh yes," Alexander said, staring fixedly into his aunt's eyes. "I'm sorry." And even as he spoke, he knew he was lying to her. What he did not yet understand – and was not to understand until some way into his recovery from alcoholism, which lay some years ahead – was that a steady intake of large quantities of alcohol over an extended period was the trigger for the madness that all alcoholics are born with. Alexander, who had always in any case had a gift for living in the moment, refused, when inebriated, to acknowledge that there might be a long term future he should be striving to achieve. In truth, he did not now believe he had a future. He was intelligent enough to know that at the rate of abuse to which he was subjecting his body and soul, he would likely die sooner than later. And this thought hardly distressed him.

Some of these moments he was now living were indeed very pleasant. The high summer weather of the Cape Peninsula was excellent: the days were full of sunshine, warm and dry, and the prevailing south-easter kept it from growing too warm. Often, Alexander drove to Fish Hoek beach, wearing just shorts, a tee-shirt and sandals, and, having removed his tee-shirt, he sat on a bench on the catwalk in the sunshine, with the waves breaking against the rocks just below him. He worked on his tan, staring out across the blue, sparkling waters of Fish Hoek Bay. There were public lavatories to hand when he needed them, and he could get coffee at the beach café. He would pass most mornings in this fashion. Back at what he still thought of as the farm (and to be sure, there were still chickens and geese on the property, and a large paddock remained, with adjoining stables, where his aunt and his married cousin Jenny still kept a horse each), his family largely shunned him. His two cousins were distant and polite when they saw him. His aunt had nothing anymore to say to him. It was only in memory of his father, the brother she had loved, that she had not yet told Alexander to leave. Only Mike, who had been Alexander's friend in previous years, was still friendly and open towards him. Alexander knew very well that his presence was resented now by the family. However, the prospect of facing up to the reality of his situation appalled him, and he took pains via drink to ensure that he did not face it.

Fish Hoek had always, by local statute, been a dry town, but in the spirit of the new commercialism that was now engulfing South Africa, that ordinance had been swept aside, and one night in early January of 1994, Alexander had gone drinking until late at the new O' Hagan's pub in Fish Hoek. By the time he got back to the farm it was after midnight. His aunt and uncle were long asleep in bed. Alexander was extremely drunk, yet (as always) he was physically capable, and he able to drive back safely to the farm. He had a companion with him: a young man with neat, regular features, short brown hair, and a skinny physique. "We must keep our voices down," Alexander told him as they went upstairs. "My aunt and uncle live here."

"But wont they want to know who I am, what I'm doing here?" the young man asked Alexander. One of the dogs had followed them upstairs. Margaret and her husband had their bedroom downstairs.

"Let's not worry about that," Alexander replied. He drew his companion towards him as the two sat down on his bed. After perhaps fifteen minutes had passed, there was a knock on the bedroom door.

"Sandy. Who's there with you?" asked Margaret from the other side of the closed door.

"No one," Alexander responded.

"I know there's someone with you. I'm coming inside."

Alexander's aunt opened the door and looked inside the room, where she could make out the forms of Alexander and another man, both of them apparently near-naked. For a moment there was silence, then Margaret said in a very level tone "Alexander. Get this person out of my house," and turned and left them.

"I'm sorry," Alexander said to his companion. "I don't know what I was thinking. I'll take you back to Fish Hoek."

There was no traffic on the road to Fish Hoek. Neither Alexander nor the young man had anything they wished to say, until, as they reached the town, Alexander asked his passenger where he wanted to be dropped off. "Outside O' Hagans will do fine," the young man replied. "You've humiliated me. I hope I dont see you again."

"I don't think you will. I think my stay here is over," Alexander said quietly to himself. His erstwhile companion was walking down the pavement in the dark.

In the morning, once Alexander had got out of bed, Margaret said to him "I do not want you staying here any longer. Go back to Johannesburg. Your behaviour last night disgusts me."

Alexander was feeling contrite and ashamed and embarrassed. "I'm so sorry, Margaret. I'm sorry for the mess I'm in. I'm sorry I've abused your kindness."

"You've abused more than my kindness," his aunt replied. "You've abused my love, and your Father's memory. I don't want to see you again."

Feeling hung over and shaky, Alexander packed his backpack, suitcase and kitbag. He left without seeing anyone. He left without giving any of the animals a hug. He had enjoyed the cats, one of whom was an especially sweet old darling, who had often slept on his bed with him. He was consumed with misery, shame, remorse and self loathing. He wished his father's revolver was to hand, rather than at his mother's home in Johannesburg. He would have found it easy to blow his brains out right now. He was desperately weary of his own sexuality, of his drinking, of his failures, and of his loneliness. He was stricken by remorse at what he had done to his aunt. He felt an overwhelming sense of loss. He was also in desperate need of a drink. Just before reaching the Fish Hoek main road, he pulled over and found the half jack of whiskey he had left in the car, and drank quickly from it. After a short while, the trembling eased, and he felt a little less as if he was about to die. It was half past nine by the time he reached Fish Hoek, where he parked near a café in town and he bought a coffee and a croissant. After drinking two cups of black coffee loaded with sugar, and eating half the croissant, he felt a little better. "I need to check myself into a clinic," he thought. "I cannot endure living this way any longer."

Alexander only got as far as Beaufort West, at the start of the Great Karoo, before he knew he could drive no further that day. He checked in at the Wagon Wheel Motel, which he remembered from childhood, and lay down in his clothes on the bed and slept. It was after dark when he awoke. For a minute he did not know where he was, and when he remembered, it took him another minute to find a light switch. He checked his watch: it was half past nine. All he had had to eat all day was half a croissant. The restaurant would be closed now. He foresaw a long night ahead of him, with only the remains of his half jack of whiskey to keep him going.

The next morning, having driven into Beaufort West to find a bottle store, where he bought a carton of Peter Stuyvesant and a bottle of scotch, he returned to the motel and ate a breakfast of sorts in the restaurant. Then he settled his bill and hit the road again. It was late afternoon before he reached Johannesburg. He had driven more than a thousand miles since leaving the farm. He drove straight to the clinic in Boksburg, where he had stayed a year earlier, and they allowed him to check in immediately.

Alexander knew that he was in for hell. It was not just that the physical withdrawals were very bad, worse each time, but that they were accompanied by a devastating despair, shame and remorse. The first three to five days were the worst. Although he was given lithium, one of the standard drugs administered during severe alcohol withdrawals, and he was encouraged to drink huge quantities of sugared water, he still suffered several minor fits, which terrified him, and he had the shakes all the time, along with sudden convulsive movements of his limbs and head, a clenching up of his chest and difficulties in drawing a full breath. He suffered from periods of extreme anxiety accompanied by sudden intense panics, and he was subject to constant profuse sweating. The despair and remorse lasted for much longer than three to five days, but these too decreased in intensity over time. His first three days and nights were spent in the acute treatment ward, where he and two others were watched round the clock, then he was moved into a general ward. Within a week he had formed friendships with two or three other patients, one of whom was a solemn, softly spoken, fragile youngster of about eighteen, with a beautiful face, who was coming off a drugs dependency, and towards whom Alexander felt very protective.

By the end of his two week stay, Alexander was suffering no physical cravings at all, but he often experienced a sense of acute anguish, along with an intense remorse. He could not cease dwelling on how he had abused his aunt's trust and love and care, and he feared she would now never wish to see him again. In addition, he often thought about his father, and he suffered a deep sense of regret at his failure to have loved his father as he had deserved. As a consequence, Alexander became prayerful once again, saying his prayers on his knees before he went to bed, and again when he got up in the morning. He was determined, simply by staying sober, to try to make up for the hurt he had caused others.

On the morning of Friday 28th January, 1994, Alexander left the clinic, completely sober, but whether he was recovered, only time would tell. He drove to his brother's home in Honeydew. Roy was out at work, but he was expecting him. Roy had hidden the spare front door keys beneath a particular shrub in the flowerbed that fringed the driveway. Alexander let himself in and de-activated the electronic alarm system by keying in the code his brother had given him, then he picked up Smokie the Persian cat and hugged her to his breast, rocking her gently in his arms. He could not remember the last time he had cried properly (although he had shed some tears at his father's funeral), but now at last, holding Smokie's warm, soft, furry body in his arms, Alexander began to cry.

Twenty-Four

The Cadres

There was still one old friend from Alice's gang whom Alexander thought might even now remember him fondly: Graham had remained single when everyone else had, one way or another, paired off with someone else. Alexander remembered him as a somewhat laconic young man his own age, who, when he did speak, could display a dry wit, and who had sometimes shown a somewhat mocking fondness for Alexander. Graham and he had sometimes hung out together in Hillbrow, and once or twice they had visited a gay bar together. Graham, however, was no more camp than was Alexander. In early February, alone all day but for Smokie the cat at Roy's house in Honeydew, Alexander had rung Graham one early evening. Astonishingly, the phone number Alexander had in his old address book still reached him. "So you're still in the land of the living, Sandro. That's good," Graham said at the other end of the phone. "What have you been up to?"

"Quite a lot, but nothing right now. What about you?"

"I'm still working at Exclusive Books – at the Hyde Park store", Graham replied. "The Hillbrow branch closed last year."

"That's so sad," Alexander responded. "I've not been anywhere near Hillbrow since 1990."

"I'm having a party on Friday night," Graham continued. "People from the block of flats, mostly. Alice and some of the others will be there. Would you like to come?"

"I'd like that. Do you still live at the same place?"

"I do," Graham replied. "Ground floor, number one."

"What time should I be there?" Alexander asked.

"Eight will be OK."

"I'll see you Friday evening then. And – thanks."

It had been more than three years since Alexander had last visited Yeoville. From what he could see beneath the streetlights and the brightly lighted neon signs outside the clubs and pubs and restaurants in Rocky Street, Yeoville appeared to be unchanged, but then Alexander realized how many black faces he was seeing on the street – a consequence of the abolition of the notorious Group Areas Act in June 1991. It was nearly four years since Alexander had last seen Alice and some others of the old gang who were at Graham's party. There was a certain coldness in their greetings; only Graham was happy to see him. "Sandro!" he exclaimed. "A blast from the past! Come and get a drink."

There was dance music playing in the sitting room, and the carpet had been rolled up, revealing the bare, waxed floorboards. In the hall there was an array of drinks and canapés set out. In response to Alexander's assertion that he did not drink, but he would have a soft drink, Graham gave Alexander a cold can of Coke, and asked what he had been doing. Despite his manner, it was clear that he was impressed by Alexander's adventures in Malta and Namibia. "Many of us thought you were finished, the last time we saw you. You were pitiful!"

"I seem to be at a loose end right now, and I don't know what I'll be doing next."

"I expect you'll continue to astonish us – *nê?*"

Alexander, sober, felt not the least wish to dance, so he found a chair in the hallway, and sat and drank his Coca-Cola and smoked a cigarette. He already regretted having come. He was afraid he might see Guy again. Guy did not in fact appear, but when Terrance, Guy's older brother and once Alexander's friend, entered the hallway for a beer, he did not greet Alexander. Alexander remained silent in his turn. He knew he had made a mistake in coming here. You could not re-kindle a fire from nothing but cold ash and clinkers. He decided to leave. However, at that moment a black man appeared from the sitting room, a can of beer in his hand, and sat on the chair next to Alexander. "Good evening," he said to Alexander, who replied "Hullo."

The black man, who looked to be in his late forties, and who was wearing a rather baggy suit, continued "It is too noisy for me in there. And they are dancing."

Alexander smiled. "I used to dance. I don't think I do anymore. Do you live nearby?"

"I am one of Graham's neighbours in these flats. My name is Lindisizwe. It means, 'waiting for a country.' When I was named, we had no country."

"I'm Sandy." The two men shook hands.

When the Apartheid laws had been repealed a little under two years earlier, Alexander had been living in Malta. He had barely been aware of that momentous occasion in South Africa's history. However, he did know that South Africa's first multi-racial elections were to be held in April – in just two months' time. It was generally thought that the ANC would win the elections comfortably.

Lindisizwe asked Alexander what work he did.

"Until recently I was working as a game ranger in the Caprivi Strip in Namibia," Alexander replied. "Before that, I was teaching English in Malta. What business are you in, Lindisizwe?"

"I own a supermarket in Mayfair," the man replied. Mayfair was an inner city Johannesburg suburb. "I also have business interests in the Eastern Cape – in Transkei."

After a short silence, Lindisizwe turned to Alexander again, and said "So you are not doing anything now? As a game ranger, what sort of work did you do?"

"I worked at a luxury game lodge in a big wildlife concession. It was my task to show the guests the regional wildlife and natural history."

"So you know about looking after residential guests?"

"I would n't say that. But yes, I know a little about how a game lodge is run."

"I have shares in a hotel in Ezibeleni, at Queenstown," Lindisizwe said. "It was mismanaged. We are trying to get it back on its feet again. We need a manager. Would you be interested in talking about this?"

So that's it, Alexander thought. I thought there must be a purpose to his questions. "I'm not sure . . ."

"We can meet again, and talk about it, I think?" the man asked.

"OK. When?"

"Are you free tomorrow, at lunch? We can meet at the steak house in Rocky Street. It is just round the corner from here."

"Yes, I know it. I could do that. What time?"

"Let us meet at one o' clock."

"Right-O." Alexander had already had enough of the very loud music from the sitting room, and he felt awkward and unwanted here. "I have to leave now. I'll see you tomorrow at one." He stood up. "Cheerio," he said, and extended his hand.

Lindisizwe stood, and shook Alexander's hand. "Tomorrow then. I think what I have to say will interest you, Sandy."

Alexander smiled, found his jacket on the bed in the bedroom, and, unwilling to brave the sitting room to find Graham, left the flat directly and walked to his car, which was parked not far down the street, and he began the long drive through Johannesburg's night-time suburbs for his brother's home in Honeydew, on the farthest fringes of the far side of the metropolis.

Lindisizwe's English was clearly his second language. Although he had a good grasp of the idiom, his accent was typically that of a black South African. But Alexander appreciated what an achievement it was for a black man educated in rural apartheid South Africa, his English teacher another black person to whom English was also a foreign language, to speak comprehensible English at all – yet millions of blacks in South Africa did so, and many spoke Afrikaans also. Lindisizwe wore his rumpled suit with only haphazard care: unlike so many black South Africans he was not a sharp dresser, and this for Alexander was a point in Lindisizwe's favour. Alexander thought that he was probably honest. He was also punctual, arriving at the steak house in Rocky Street the next day only a few minutes after one o' clock. As always, Alexander was hungry. He ordered a steak, well done, with chips and salad and a couple of bread rolls. So too did Lindisizwe, who added a lager to his order. Alexander stuck to Coke.

As Alexander tackled his steak, Lindisizwe explained that they needed someone who would find a way of re-activating the hotel's lines of credit, re-stock the bar, motivate the staff, and turn the hotel into a profitable enterprise once again.

"Does the hotel have substantial debts?" Alexander asked.

"The liquor wholesaler is owed money. So is Eskom: the electricity has been cut off. If you can get the bar running again, you can generate enough money to pay the Eskom bill."

"I don't know that I can do these things," Alexander responded. "But if I try, how much would you be paying me?"

"You may not be paid a salary for the first month or two. It depends on getting the bar running again. But if you can do that, and you stay on as manager, the directors will pay you a salary of four thousand Rands a month, and you will be living and eating at the hotel for free."

"I need to think about this for a few days. Can you give me your phone number, Lindisizwe?"

The man reached into his jacket and withdrew a wallet, from which he extracted a business card which he gave to Alexander. It read "Lindisizwe Dlamini – Lucky Choice Supermarket, Mayfair." A Mayfair, Johannesburg address followed. There was also a Queenstown, Eastern Cape address. There were three phone numbers, two of which were Johannesburg numbers, and one of which was, presumably, a Queenstown phone number. "Please give me your phone number, Sandy," Lindisizwe said. Alexander gave him Roy's home number. "Can I phone you in two days' time?" the man asked Alexander.

"OK. Or I'll ring you."

The two men began to pay more attention to their food, and when they had finished their meal, each ordered a coffee. They chatted about Alexander's experiences overseas. Lindisizwe seemed to regard London as something akin to a promised land. When they had finished their coffees and split the bill between them, Alexander stood, and shaking hands with Lindisizwe, he took his leave of the black man. "We'll be in touch soon. *Sala kakuhle!*"

"*Hamba kakuhle,*" Lindisizwe replied.

Alexander told Lindisizwe, who phoned him at his brother's number three days later, that he would give the job a go. Despite all his setbacks, Alexander still believed that he could accomplish almost anything he set his mind to. For a boy who had had very few friends at school, and in whom self confidence had been markedly lacking; a solitary boy who had rarely actively sought the company of others, partly for fear of rejection and partly due to an inclination for his own company, Alexander had found within a year of leaving school that he had a surprising store of belief in himself.

Roy serviced his car for him at home. Roy, an engineer, was good with cars. Alexander was still sober. He said goodbye to his mother and her cat, hugged Smokie, his brother's cat, and at eight o' clock that morning he set off across Johannesburg for Lindisizwe's flat in Yeoville. Lindisizwe would be coming with him. It was ten o' clock before Alexander continued his journey, the black man in the passenger seat next to him, and within a very short while, using the elevated dual carriageway, he had crossed the city and taken the turning for the N1 south for Bloemfontein. Queenstown lay four-hundred and seventy miles ahead. The motorway as far as Bloemfontein was familiar to Alexander, for it was the same route you took for Cape Town. Outside Bloemfontein, the two men stopped for fuel, a pee, and some coffee with something to eat, and then set off on the N6 south for East London. There was not very much traffic on the road. It was an easy drive. The day was warm and sunny. Alexander reached Queenstown in the Eastern Cape at half past six in the evening. This was Lindisizwe's home town. His family home was here. Alexander was to spend the night there, and Lindisizwe would show him the hotel the next morning.

In the lounge, where the only pictures on the walls were framed prints of what looked to Alexander like chocolate box reproductions of Alpine and rural English scenes, the over-stuffed furniture was decorated with much faux gilt. There was a vast TV set at one end of the room, and a hi-fi set with massive speakers in one corner. Lindisizwe offered Alexander a beer. Alexander declined. "I'd prefer a coffee, please."

There was a bewildering number of people at Lindisizwe's house that evening. Alexander was not sure which of the two large women he met was his associate's wife: perhaps both of them. But from Alexander's conversation with Lindisizwe over lunch at the steak house in Yeoville a week earlier, Alexander had gathered there was also a wife of some degree in Lindisizwe's Yeoville flat. There were children ranging in age from a baby still being breast-fed, to two young women in their late teens, one of whom was nursing the baby. It was clear to Alexander that he was being shown off, for there appeared to be friends and neighbours present also, though as they spoke almost exclusively in Xhosa, he could not be sure who exactly they were. He suspected that at least two men, who appeared about half an hour after Lindisizwe had made some phone calls, were business associates of Lindisizwe, perhaps even investors in the hotel.

Alexander felt close to being overwhelmed by the alien atmosphere. He felt infinitely more out of his depth than he had ever felt in Malta. And perhaps Alexander's reaction was not unusual for a white man who had grown up in South Africa during the apartheid era. Indeed, what was unusual was that he, a white man of his generation and background, was now a houseguest in a black man's family home.

At about eight o' clock a meal was served. They ate at table in the dining room, with the people for whom there was no space at the table being served their food on trays in the sitting room. The two women served lamb chops, with vegetables and what Alexander knew as *"styve pap"*, a stiff, stodgy maize meal preparation. Alexander, at that stage of his life, could still eat almost anything. He was hungry, and he did the meal justice. He noticed that the others at table made liberal use of the spicy condiment, *Aromat*, sprinkled heavily on their lamb chops. He could not remember using *Aromat* before: it was not something he had grown up with, but he was to use it with eagerness at every meal at the hotel during the three weeks to come.

Feeling desperately tired, Alexander sat through a gabble of talk in Xhosa for an hour after the meal was finished, once the gathering had returned to the lounge. It was half past ten before one of the two women showed Alexander to a bedroom, where a bed with fresh linen had been made up. From the things on a dressing table, he gathered this was usually one of the girls' rooms. As he brushed his teeth in the bathroom down the corridor, he wondered what he was doing here, so far from everything familiar. He wished at that moment that he had never agreed to this scheme. He wished he was at home with Roy and Smokie. Alexander felt desperately alone and isolated. He wondered too how much longer he was going to remain sober, because he felt a nagging desire for a very strong drink. Before he got into bed, he did something he had not done since leaving the clinic in Boksburg: he knelt and said his prayers. He woke only once during the quiet night, to use the lavatory down the corridor, and he was asleep again very soon thereafter.

The hotel was a modern, single story brick building situated in Ezibeleni, the black township outside Queenstown. Ezibeleni had a population of about twenty thousand people. The hotel had been built to cater to local black travelers and businessmen. There was a small staff remaining, to whom Alexander was introduced by Lindisizwe. Then Lindisizwe left Alexander at the hotel, the only white man in the entire township. Alexander explained to the staff as best he could, in a mix mostly of English with some *Fanagalo* and Zulu he had picked up over the years (Zulu, which Alexander had been trying to learn at the mission in Natal, was similar in many respects to Xhosa) that he could not pay them for a while (or himself, for that matter), but that they could continue to live and eat there for free. During the course of the next two weeks Alexander, using the phone (which was still working), and driving into Queenstown frequently, managed to re-stock the hotel's bar with a basic stock of Coca-Cola, a few bottles of scotch, and several creates of Lion and Castle lagers.

His greatest coup was in obtaining credit from Eskom, the state monopoly electricity supplier, who turned the power back on. Water could now be heated other than in containers on top of the gas range; electric heaters could be used during the sometimes surprisingly cool evenings. There were customers again in the bar in the evenings, and during the day also over the following two weekends. A scattering of guests began to return to the hotel.

Then, in very early March, Alexander had a visitor, a young black man, who, he was to learn later, had spent the last few years training at an ANC bush-camp in Zambia, and had just recently returned to South Africa with some of his *cadres*, in anticipation of the almost certain ANC win in the forthcoming general election.

"We do not want you here, white man," the young man told him. "This is our place. You leave now." Alexander had never before seen such naked malice in a black man's eyes. There had been no malice in the eyes of the black men who had held him up at knifepoint in Joubert Park four years previously, only mercilessness and cold intent.

Alexander took no action, other than to phone Lindisizwe and tell him what had transpired. Lindisizwe, by his long silence, followed by a poor attempt over the phone at reassuring him, did not make him feel very secure, but Alexander continued with his work at the hotel. He was trying to improve the standard of service at the hotel, which meant training the staff in various functions, and although he had no experience of book-keeping, he was trying to keep simple books as well.

Rather late one evening, Alexander was sitting with the Xhosa night-watchman in the foyer, in front of the oil heater which was turned low against the slight chill. The foyer was lighted by only one low wattage wall light. The old man's grizzled hair and seamed and lined features placed him somewhere in his sixties, but he could have been as young as Alexander, or as old as seventy. After a certain point, black people seem to stop aging. Alexander liked him. He had that gentle, patient forbearance that Alexander associated with some older black men. He had a little English, and Alexander had been chatting to him about the old fellow's herd-boy childhood.

Neither man had spoken for a while and Alexander's thoughts were far away, with memories of Guy, when there was a shockingly loud burst of gunfire from outside, and the big glass doors shattered. Alexander and the night watchman, both of whom were uninjured, leapt to their feet and fled, bent double, for the dark kitchens at the far end of the unlighted corridor, and now Alexander could hear shouting behind him. Using the phone extension in the kitchens, for there was just enough light coming through the windows for Alexander to read the dial on the phone, he rang the Ezibeleni Police station, which was located less than a mile away. The gunmen (Alexander had no idea how many there were) were now inside the hotel, but none had yet entered the kitchens, where he and the night watchman were keeping low, quiet as mice in the near-darkness. The armed Police arrived within less than five minutes. Indeed, they would have heard the gunfire from the Police station. There had been no overnight guests staying that night, nor were there any customers still drinking at the bar, and the staff in their quarters out back had wisely remained there while the gunmen had rampaged through the lounge and bar, firing off occasional short bursts of gunfire.

With the arrival of the Police and the flight of all but one gunman (whom the Police rapidly disarmed and handcuffed) through the emergency exit at the back of the bar which opened onto a narrow service lane, Alexander, who had now begun to feel a slight physical reaction to his fright, went to the bar and poured himself a whiskey. He downed it in one gulp, then poured another, and sat drinking it more slowly, puffing on a cigarette, whilst two of the black policemen questioned him about the incident. The arrested gunman had been taken outside. As he passed Alexander, under close restraint by a pair of armed policemen, Alexander recognised him as the young man who had visited and warned him that he was not wanted in Ezibeleni. Alexander told the Police about the visit he had had from the young black man a few days earlier. Later that night, Alexander slept in a different bedroom, and the next morning he rang Lindisizwe and told him he was quitting the job with immediate effect.

This was the third time in his life that Alexander had been in very close proximity to gunfire. In 1976, during his camping visit to Navarra in northern Spain, a twenty-one year old Alexander had been one among a large, excited and emotionally charged crowd in the town plaza when the

Guardia Civil had opened fire on the gathering. Within a few minutes the plaza was empty, but for several bodies lying on the ground. Alexander had ducked sharply into a side alley, but he had then poked his head round the corner and had watched with something akin to total disbelief as a *Civil* draw his sidearm and shot two of the people lying on the ground in the head. Yet then, as now, Alexander had felt a certain detachment from the scene. He had not felt the sort of shock he imagined was proper on such an occasion. Later that night in the crowded campsite outside the city where he and his two companions had pitched their small tent, the sound of gunfire close to hand had drawn Alexander from the tent in its wake, and in the star-lit night he could just manage to make out the forms of four or five people running up the rocky hillside on the far side of the river, with half a dozen *Guardia Civil* lined up on this side of the riverbank, firing at them.

Lindisizwe tried, over the phone, to persuade Alexander not to leave. But Alexander was adamant: the job was not worth his life. Later that morning one of the investors in the hotel, the son of a local tribal chief, called on Alexander. He was a fine looking man of considerable height and girth, and he advised Alexander that he was arranging for an armed Police guard at the hotel. Alexander however had had enough. His earnings so far had been zero: he felt he owed Lindisizwe and his associates nothing. He did however ring Lindisizwe again, to tell him where the books for the hotel were kept, and to remind him that the hotel would have to settle the Eskom bill within a very few days, and make a further arrangement with the liquor supplier.

It took Alexander little time to pack. He drove away in his car at about midday. He had one of the bottles of whiskey from the bar with him in the car. Its purchase had been the last entry he had written up in the bar's sales records. It was just after eight-thirty in the evening by the time he reached his brother's home outside Johannesburg.

Twenty-Five

Debauchery

There now began a period in Alexander's life of mounting disorder and alcoholic excesses. He lost all sense of any direction to his life. Alexander remembered, however, to vote in the elections of the 27th April which were to be won by the ANC, and were to signal, for many, the final collapse of the entire Apartheid regime, with Nelson Mandela becoming President. Alexander and his brother feared black majority rule, having seen what had happened in Zimbabwe: they were both products of their colonial past; in their view, widespread corruption, gross mismanagement and the eventual exclusion of whites from society would result from majority rule, so they both voted for the Afrikaner-dominated Nationalist Party.

Still based at Roy's home outside Johannesburg (Alexander could no longer afford to rent a place of his own), he was soon feeding a diazepam habit. Soon after returning to Johannesburg, Alexander had begun suffering vivid nightmares in which he experienced, over and over, scenes of violence in which he was the intended victim. At times during the day he would experience an extreme agitation of mind, accompanied by a mounting sense of panic. He grew to dread and fear sudden loud noises. The sound of people shouting, or of running feet, made his pulse race and his breath catch in his throat. He told his general practitioner about these symptoms. His doctor, without offering a diagnosis (at the time Alexander had never heard of post-traumatic stress disorder) had prescribed diazepam (valium). Alexander had quickly become dependent on a dosage of ten milligrams in every twenty-four hours, and although his day time mental agitation diminished, the nightmares continued. He soon noticed that he felt extremely anxious and disturbed if he forgot to take his five milligram dose of diazepam in the morning, or again in the late evening. In addition to the diazepam, Alexander had done as so many people suffering from some or other mental disturbance did: he self-medicated, using alcohol. If he drank enough during the day and evening, he could sleep without nightmares. With alcohol he could get through the day also, without being rendered almost dysfunctional by fear and anxiety. Alexander became rapidly re-addicted to alcohol, returning to the same levels he had been sustaining before his stay at the clinic.

Anesthetized by alcohol, Alexander was able to visit Cape Town twice in 1994. He traveled there and back by rail each time, with his first journey being made in late June. He explained these trips to Roy by selling them as attempts to find work as a tour guide in Cape Town, but Alexander knew that he was drinking far too much to do anything of the sort. He was by now living entirely in the moment: he had become the ultimate existentialist.

Alexander made both journeys on the Trans Karoo Express, traveling in a two-berth *coupé* each time, which he had to himself on each journey, and which he could still afford to pay for from his own resources. Traveling by train exerted a huge appeal for Alexander. He loved the ponderous solidity of the rolling stock and the cunning of the coaches' interior design. The sound of the wheels clacking across the joins in the rails (for the track was not yet welded) was a lullaby as comforting to Alexander as a mother's loving voice is to a small child. It seemed to Alexander a very civilised way of making the nine hundred and ninety mile journey between Johannesburg and Cape Town. The train had an air-conditioned lounge car with a bar, where Alexander spent much of his time during the journey. There was also an air-conditioned dining car, where he was served dinner on the first day out, and breakfast the next morning, these meals inclusive in his fare. The cuisine on South African Railways was excellent. Alexander had brought a dark jacket and a couple of ties with him: most men still wore a tie and jacket in the South African Railways dining cars at dinner time.

Not only were the mainline trains provided with excellent dining facilities, but the individual compartments in the corridor coaches were cleverly and conveniently designed. Most were four berth compartments, with the two upper berths folding away during the day, and the two lower berths becoming very comfortable sofa-seats. At night, the two upper berths would be lowered from the bulkhead and would serve as bunk-beds, the sofa seats serving as lower berths. The hire of clean, crisply starched and ironed bedding – sheets and pillows, along with blankets – was optional, but most first and second class travelers would ensure that their berths were made up into beds for the night. Each compartment (whether four-berth, or a two-berth *coupé*), had a small table projecting from beneath the window, and the table surface could be raised and folded out of the way, to reveal a basin beneath it, supplied with running cold water. There was room for luggage in each compartment above the doorway, a wide inset shelf above what was the connecting corridor outside, and space below the lower bunks also. Each coach had a lavatory cubicle at either end, and both second and first class had a shower at one end of the coach, with hot and cold running water, and there were basins in the two lavatory cubicles, also with hot and cold water on tap, and a mirror, for shaving. The compartment windows themselves (along with the windows in the corridors) were provided with a canvas blind, a riot screen of metal slats which could be wound up from the bottom of the window sill, and the glass window itself, which you could raise and lower fully. Due to the relatively narrow gauge – it was just three and a half feet wide – the trains traveled slowly, and journeys were lengthy and your comforts mattered.

On the way to Cape Town Alexander crossed the arid Karoo through the course of the night. During the daytime the Karoo could become a baking hot furnace. In the early morning, while it was still dark, the train reached Touws River, an important railway junction, and having made the journey before, Alexander felt his spirits rise soon after Touws River: breakfast would shortly be served, and he knew that the scenery was going to become more and more striking. At breakfast the tables were set with clean, starched linen, and the cutlery was of heavy silver plate. The crockery was of china and there was a clean folded and ironed napkin at each place setting. The waiters, mostly young Afrikaner lads, were smartly turned out, polite and attentive. During breakfast the train wound its way slowly through the startlingly dramatic Hex River valley, which sheltered vineyards in the valley bottom, and was bounded by soaring mountain peaks, which in late June were already snow-capped, the snow a gleaming white in the early morning sunshine. The rail-track wound and twisted for many miles and began its descent of the mighty escarpment, doubling and redoubling on itself, passing through several tunnels cut in the living rock, until at last it reached the coastal plain, and the train halted at the first big town, Paarl. Between Paarl and Cape Town, the track was level, with long straight stretches, and the train would pick up speed again as it crossed the Cape Flats, reaching Cape Town station later that morning.

Steady, round the clock drinking had robbed Alexander of his moral restraints. During the first of these two journeys by train, there had been a knock on his *coupé* door at about ten-thirty that night. He had been drinking fairly steadily since dinner, but in his usual fashion, Alexander hardly felt, or showed, any physical effects. When he slid the door back, he found the young waiter who had served him dinner that evening, dressed in jeans and a leather jacket, standing outside the door. "Come in," Alexander had said.

There was nothing effeminate about the boy, unless a certain fineness of features is considered effeminate. The lad, who was perhaps nineteen or twenty, had short, ash-blonde hair. The skin of his torso, as Alexander was to discover, was creamy white, smooth and flawless as silk. He stayed until shortly before midnight.

During both visits to Cape Town that year Alexander stayed at the same old residential hotel in Long Street, a street which descended from the lower slopes of Table Mountain, reaching as far as the old docks. The street, which had been much frequented by visiting seamen for several hundred years, and had been lined with establishments catering to their needs, still retained a somewhat *louche* character. Long Street still carried the remnants of easy-going disrespectability and nocturnal liveliness. Early to mid-nineteenth century architecture, much of it in the Cape vernacular style, dominated. The residential hotel Alexander stayed in on each visit was an early nineteenth century building, with tall shuttered windows, and a wide first floor verandah with wrought iron railings, which ran along the street frontage and around the corner. The more sought after bedrooms, of which Alexander had one, opened directly onto the verandah. Alexander could sit out there and listen to the street sounds, or watch the parade of street life below.

During his first visit, Alexander came to know one of the hotel's permanent residents in particular, a Cape Town girl in her late twenties with a slim build, short brown hair, and *gamine* features. Sustained drinking stimulated Alexander's libido, and not only in respect of his own gender. Alexander knew from the start of their acquaintance that they would in time engage in intimacies, and he was not surprised when this came about. But the young woman had moved on by the time of Alexander's second visit to Cape Town in November; instead, he picked up a young man one night at the Whistle Stop at the top of Long Street, a bar where he spent the afternoons and evenings drinking and playing pool. They returned to Alexander's hotel bedroom, and the youth spent the night, sharing Alexander's single bed. These loveless, entirely carnal encounters (in which, at best, there might exist a momentary tenderness on Alexander's part) were to add to the sum of Alexander's self loathing in later years.

In November, during Alexander's return trip after his second visit to Cape Town, the express had been hauled by a steam locomotive. This was by then fairly unusual. Alexander had woken briefly twice during the night, and each time he had heard the rapid beat of the locomotive's pistons up front – and once, he heard the long double wail of the engine's whistle, a sound both lost and defiant as it reached out far into the dark night across a boundless land. This latter sound had moved Alexander as a child, on journeys by train between Nairobi and Mombasa, and it moved him now. In that moment at least, Alexander shed the depraved, cracked gloss of adulthood, and reverted for a short while to the innocence of a childhood that seemed so far away now. There was the potential still for redemption alive in Alexander's spirit.

As Christmas of 1994 approached, Alexander experienced an urgent need to reclaim his moral and spiritual integrity. He could not endure the prospect of another stay at the clinic, so he began, each day, to drink a little less than the day before. This meant that although for over a week Alexander felt a constant yearning for more alcohol than he was permitting himself, a constant low key edginess, he spared himself the horrendous withdrawals that accompanied ceasing to drink overnight. He told his brother and his mother what he was doing. "Oh, Sandy," his mother said to him, "If only you could stop drinking. It's clear to us that you dare not drink. I will be so relieved if you can stop."

"I think I shall manage, Mum," Alexander replied. "This time."

Within a fortnight – by the end of the first week of January 1995 – Alexander was dry, and he no longer craved alcohol. His brother and his mother were happy and relieved. "This year," Alexander told them, "I'm going to do something with my life. Perhaps I'll begin working as a field guide." He looked down at the floor. "And I'm sorry."

Alexander's report from Will at the end of his training as a field guide had been extremely positive. He possessed the full SATOUR accreditation, and he could work as a guide anywhere in South Africa. He approached a wildlife tours operation based in Johannesburg's northern suburbs, which was advertising for additional field guides. He made no mention of his time in Namibia, and he hoped that they would not have heard of him before. Perhaps they had not, for they signed him on as a field guide for a variety of different wildlife tours, ranging from short two and three nighters to tours lasting nine or ten days. The tours this outfit offered to its foreign clients were expensive, but destinations were usually select private game reserves with luxurious lodges and accommodation and *cordon bleu* cuisine. The number of guests in a party was kept very low. Often, Alexander found himself driving and guiding for just one (usually middle-aged) couple only. Sometimes he might be guiding for a small family group. Alexander drove an E-class Mercedes or a BMW 7 series saloon, and on the rare occasions he was in charge of a group of more than two clients, he would drive a top of the range Volkswagen bus with the powerful five-cylinder Audi engine and plush upholstery and air-conditioning.

On one level, Alexander found this work easy. It called for the practice of skills which he could exercise with little effort. Which is not to say that the work could not sometimes be demanding: he would be on duty round the clock during a tour, sometimes having to deal with a guest's most trivial needs outside of normal working hours. ("Sandy, I need some batteries for my radio" – this at nine-thirty on a Sunday evening many miles from the nearest store). He would be driving long distances between Johannesburg and the tour stops; he would have to consider his guests' lavatory needs and rest stops along the way. On the cheaper tours they would be headed for one or two of the camps in the Kruger National Park, where they would stay in pleasant, thatched *rondavels*, and eat their meals at the excellent camp restaurants; and on the more expensive tours their destination would be one or more of the internationally renowned private game reserves along the western fringes of the Kruger Park; game reserves such as Londolozi, Mala Mala, Manyeleti and Sabi Sands, which offered superb accommodation, highly attractive *ambiances* and excellent cuisine. On the way to the Transvaal Lowveld, Alexander would talk about the country they were driving through and the sights he was showing them, located on sites which might include natural wonders such as the Blyde River Canyon, or features of the region's history, such as the charming and beautifully restored Victorian gold mining town, Pilgrims Rest, whose structures of corrugated iron (houses, shops, a functioning hotel where Alexander's guests would have lunch) had been preserved, many of them furnished with antique Victoriana, as if time had stood still.

Although Alexander would accompany his guests in the open vehicle on the morning game tours in the private game reserves they might be staying at, he would do so almost as a guest himself, for the game reserve's own resident ranger would be in charge. But Alexander knew this work of course, having himself been the resident ranger at the Kwando River Lodge in the Caprivi. At these private game reserves, Alexander would almost always be accommodated in the same luxurious conditions his guests were. He would eat with them, enjoying the same magnificent bush cuisine. Often, he felt he was being paid for going on wonderful game tour vacations.

Alexander did not enjoy it when his employers put him in charge of a French speaking party. His French was not up to it: he struggled terribly, and he spent the entire tour in a state of advanced stress. But the company he worked for had a higher opinion of his spoken French than was merited, and was glad to avoid paying the high rates a fully bilingual French speaking field guide would have demanded. It was during one such French speaking tour in late 1995 that Alexander had his first drink since January that year: a couple of beers.

Once in a while, Alexander would conduct a tour lasting nine or ten days, starting at Johannesburg (often, as with many of his tours, meeting the guests off their international flight as it landed at Jan Smuts airport), then taking in three or four nights at different camps in the Kruger National Park, or visiting some of the adjacent private game reserves, then driving through the small land-locked bushveld kingdom of Swaziland, over-nighting near Mbabane, the capital, in a five star hotel, then exiting Swaziland the next day so as to enter South Africa in Maputoland, in the far north of Zululand, and taking in two days and nights at Hluhluwe-Mfolozi game reserve, famed for its elephants and rhinos. Then, arriving in the afternoon, they would over-night at one of the choice private game reserves in the region, with a dawn drive the next morning. Heading south the next day, they would visit Lake Saint Lucia wetland park, the largest estuarine lagoon in South Africa.

Here they would have lunch, and take a boat tour of the lake, from which some of the lagoon's rich birdlife and its hippo population might be viewed. They would overnight nearby. Just to the north of Durban, Alexander would show his guests around the reptile park (which he could remember visiting with his family as a child), before they checked in at one of the five star hotels on the Durban Esplanade. The next day Alexander's guests might have an opportunity to explore Durban on foot with him, before being driven to the airport. Alexander might spend another night at the hotel, alone, before driving back to Johannesburg the following day, or, having said goodbye to his guests at the airport, he would return the car he was driving to the local branch of the nationwide car hire agency from which the car had been hired in Johannesburg and catch a flight himself for Johannesburg that same afternoon. Alexander enjoyed these long tours. He would get to know his guests very well, and only once did guests prove difficult to deal with. If he was staying a night alone in Durban, he enjoyed his late afternoon and early evening walks along the Durban Esplanade, watching the Zulu rickshaw boys in their fantastic head-dresses as they leapt into the air, reveling in the soft balmy air, and always ordering a curry dinner at a nearby restaurant. Durban, with its large population with origins in the Indian sub-continent, was justly famous for its curries.

Alexander proved to be generally popular with his guests. He was knowledgeable about the countryside through which he drove them, its history and the sights along the way, and he shared his knowledge with enthusiasm. He knew his wildlife and birdlife, and he knew his flora also, and he was able to share a wealth of detail about the birds and animals they saw, and the trees and shrubs he pointed out to them. During meals shared together, where Alexander could advise on which of the Cape wines to order, he was able to engage in wide-ranging conversation: he was well spoken and well-read, with a smattering of several European languages. His years spent living abroad meant that he was free of the parochialism that afflicted many of the (typically) younger South African field guides. Alexander collected generous tips (often in hard foreign currency) at the end of almost all the tours, and often his guests would give him their contact details as they were saying goodbye, so that he could look them up should he ever be visiting their home countries.

In December 1995, high summer in South Africa, Alexander rented a flat in Yeoville. It was a fourth floor flat in a nineteen-sixties built apartment block, with jacaranda trees growing in the street below, and only local traffic passing by. There was the usual fairly large entrance hall, with a kitchen in which was a 1960s gas cooker, a great, solid piece of engineering, only marginally more modern than the 1930s gas cooker Alexander had used in his Bellevue flat. Alexander liked cooking on gas: he felt you had much more direct and immediate control of the heat settings. The bathroom with a lavatory was a nice sized room, and the sitting room-dining room was very big, as was the single bedroom. Both of these rooms fronted the flat, and opened onto a full length, deep covered verandah. Alexander parked his car in covered parking below the flats, access to which, both from inside the block and from the street, required keys to the locks. The flat came unfurnished, but Alexander had picked up a second hand lounge suite and other items of furniture at good prices from a used furniture dealer in Braamfontein. The shop had delivered for him. Alexander still had some pieces of furniture dating back to his previous stay in the district – in Bellevue – in 1989 and 1990, which had been stored all this time at his brother's house in Honeydew, and he brought them with him. One of these was the old metal framed single bed he had used right through his childhood since his family had first arrived in South Africa from Kenya.

Alexander was by now the only remaining white resident in this block of flats. Yeoville had become a very black suburb since Apartheid's collapse. Alexander did not feel that his white skin was unwelcome in the apartment block. His black neighbours were no more rowdy or ill behaved than his white neighbours in Bellevue had been five years earlier. When Alexander walked the two blocks down to Rocky Street and then up or down Rocky Street, he would sometimes be the only white face within a hundred yards. This did not bother him if it was daytime, but at night, he would usually take the car if he was visiting the pub.

Alexander still had Alice's phone number for her flat in Hunter Street, and he rang her one evening and arranged to visit her the following evening. He had not seen her since Graham's party in February 1994, and then only to exchange a few words with her. When he knocked on her door, bearing a large bunch of chrysanthemums and carnations, he was nervous of the reception he would get. But Alice offered her cheek to be kissed, and sat him down on the couch alongside her, having moved a cat out of the way. Yet things were n't right: Alexander felt a distance between the two of them. He tried hard to rekindle something of the old friendship, but his drunken antics some years earlier had created a gulf between them which it was clear would not now be bridged. He left after only an hour with Alice, and he was unhappy. She had been such a good friend, the focus of Alexander's social life years earlier. As Alexander walked downstairs and got into his car, he thought to himself "I have no friends left anymore." How could this have happened?

Most of the pubs and clubs in Rocky Street that Alexander remembered from the old days were gone. But far down at the east end of Rocky Street, Caravans, the gay pub he remembered from years gone by, was still open. Alexander would relax here in the afternoons or evenings between tours. There was a small garden with tables and chairs beneath large colourful umbrellas where he could sit outside in good weather. He soon grew to know most of the regulars, and there were some he enjoyed sitting chatting with over a drink. There were only two full-time barmen, and both were straight young white men, whom Alexander found it easy to chat with as he drank his beers. Alexander drank only lager beers. Because he was neither extremely unhappy, nor facing financial problems at the time, Alexander did not find it difficult to avoid spirits. He knew by now that without any doubt, spirits were the beginning of a slippery slope for him.

Sometimes Alexander would visit Hillbrow, to drink at Connections, or at the Yugoslav Football Club. He would park his car beneath Highpoint. When he walked the couple of hundred yards to Connections, near the far end of Pretoria Street, he would be one of very few white faces in the street. Twice, he picked up women at the Yugoslav Football Club. In both cases, he did so by the simple and direct means of suggesting that the woman come home with him. On both occasions, the women were in their thirties, and not unattractive. One was an English speaking South African. The other was European, but from what part of Europe, Alexander did not learn. He experienced what even at the time he knew to be a morally repugnant boost to his ego at the ease with which he was able to persuade these women, both of whom had been drinking, to return home with him for the night. In each case, the sex was – for a casual pickup – adequate, and repeated more than once during the course of the night. Alexander suppressed the self disgust he felt at the time. It was to surface only some years later, allied with a profound sense of shame: to have taken advantage of a woman in drink was a disgusting and immoral thing.

At Connections Alexander sometimes found a good looking young man who was eager to come home with him. But on two or three occasions he picked up a rent boy and took him back to his flat for the night. These youths, in their late teens or early twenties, always wanted a bath and something to eat. And money. They wanted money, and Alexander would not quibble at anything up to fifty Rands for the night. The skinny boys whom Alexander tended to favour were quite often heroin addicts. These rent boys were rarely homosexuals: they were straight boys who found that renting their bodies to homosexuals was the easiest way of earning the money for their next fix. Alexander knew that this *demi-monde* he entered when he was between tours was a spiritually corrupted society, and that he was damaging his own soul by entering it. But the lust he felt, usually for one of these young men, but occasionally for a woman, overcame his moral scruples. Had Alexander not frequently been able to escape to the bushveld on tour, where the air was clean and his spirit could shrug off the dirt and degeneracy of his city life, he could not have sustained even a shadow of self regard.

Yet Alexander did retain a certain innocence. In some fashion, his sordid life did not affect his soul. The boy he had once been was buried not very deep beneath the surface. Perhaps this was part of his charm: that his partners were drawn to something they saw in him that had remained pure and unspoiled.

On a night in early March, Alexander brought home a good looking, if somewhat common, young man from Caravans. At the flat they began to undress, and when Alexander saw his partner naked, in a state of arousal, he experienced a sudden and inexplicable access of self disgust and an instant cooling of his own ardor. "I can't do this," he told the youngster. "I just can't do this anymore. But you can stay the night if you want to."

They shared Alexander's narrow bed, lying side by side as chastely as brothers, and in the morning Alexander gave the fellow some breakfast, then drove him to his flat in Bezuidenhout Valley and left him there. Alexander did not yet know it, but he was never to have sex with another man again, nor indeed to have casual sex of any sort ever again. He appeared at last to have achieved satiety: lust – that ravening wolf that had stalked through his life for so many years – was never again to overcome him. He was forty years old. Had his neglected God decided to intervene in Alexander's life?

One Friday night soon after Easter, having returned from a three night Kruger Park tour that late afternoon, Alexander decided to walk to Caravans in Rocky Street. He was tired of driving. He had been driving for three days. The street lighting on Cavendish Street, running down to Rocky Street, was not very bright, but Alexander was thoroughly at home in Yeoville, for all that he was sometimes the only white man in sight, so that night he said to himself "I'll walk." Afterwards, he could not remember how it was that suddenly there were two black men confronting him, and as he backed off, he realised there was at least one other behind him also. One of the two men in front of him had something in his hand. It immediately crossed Alexander's mind to shout loudly, and he opened his mouth to yell, and as he did so, he felt a punch to his abdomen. He staggered and felt his legs give way beneath him, and before he had time to realise what had happened, he was lying on the ground. Quick hands ripped his jacket from him, and felt in his trouser pockets, where they found nothing but the keys to his flat, which they ignored. His wallet – stuffed with South African notes and US dollars (for his guests, who had been Americans, had tipped him generously in dollars at the end of the tour) – was inside an inner pocket in his jacket. Almost before he could work out what had happened, the men were gone, and he became aware after a while of a young black woman bending over him, talking to him.

Alexander took his hand away from his belly, which was in pain, and he could see a heavy stain on his wet palm, almost black in the dim street lighting. Only now did he realise he had been stabbed. "*Sissie*," he said, "they have hurt me. Please call an ambulance."

A dozen or so blacks had gathered by now. Alexander felt his shoes being removed. He experienced no passage of time, though perhaps fifteen minutes passed, before he had a dim awareness of being stretchered into an ambulance. He remembered nothing more after that.

Later the next day, Alexander became aware by slow degrees (his consciousness creeping back as if reluctant to resume residence), through information vouchsafed him by the black nursing staff and after a while, by a young Swiss doctor, that he was in the Johannesburg General Hospital; that he had been stabbed, the knife blade piercing his large intestine, creating an entry and an exit wound. "We have had to create a stoma," the doctor told him, "which we will reverse after eight weeks, to allow the intestine to heal."

Alexander was not only in physical pain, but feeling extremely agitated and anxious. When he left his flat the evening before, he had had his antique silver cigarette case, with ten cigarettes inside it, in his jacket pocket – but the muggers had taken that when they had stolen his jacket. Now he desperately craved a smoke.

"Years ago I was robbed by knifemen in Joubert Park, Doctor," Alexander said. "But I was n't harmed then. Now they've got me at last." The young Swiss doctor had pleasant, mobile features. "Doctor," Alexander continued, "I've been taking ten milligrams of valium daily for some time – on prescription. I'm going to suffer withdrawals if you don't give me some soon."

"I'll see about that," the doctor said. "Right now, I need to know your name, and your home address, and your next of kin."

It took only a few minutes for Alexander to provide this information. Then the doctor looked at his watch. "I must go now. I'll be back later sometime."

But for the rest of that long day, Alexander did not see the young doctor again. The black nursing staff were offhand and Alexander found it difficult to engage their attention. During the afternoon, a bunch of white coated young men – students? – descended on him. By now, Alexander's mind was in a state of considerable agitation, and he felt not only ill and in physical pain, but nauseous and terribly anxious. At times he felt as if his vision was dancing and jittering, then it would regain focus. The nurses administered morphine for the pain of the wound, and Alexander fell into a long but nightmare-filled doze, only to wake in some distress and not know for some moments where he was.

Some days passed, punctuated by nights with even worse nightmares than those which afflicted him during the day, but how many days had passed since his admittance, Alexander no longer knew. It might have been as few as two or three, or it may have been longer than that. At times he knew he was beginning to hallucinate. He thought at one time that he saw a group of blacks bringing a couple of car tyres towards him, and he heard their shouting and laughter as they prepared to place the tyres around him and douse them with petrol and set them alight. He screamed and thrashed in his bed and lashed out, and two nurses held him still until he could be administered a sedative via hypodermic to calm him. Then he passed out again. The next time he came to, he could not breathe.

Alexander could not draw any breath at all. He clutched in terror at his throat, and tried to force some air into his lungs, but his air passage was completely blocked. Panic and terror overwhelmed him. He was asphyxiating. His limbs were jerking in spasms. He fell off the bed onto the hard linoleum tiled floor, and began to bang the back of his head repeatedly on the floor. The terror and anguish he felt were greater than anything he had ever known. He remembered nothing more until he came to, and he was breathing again, and a nurse was sitting by his bedside. She was young and pretty and of mixed race. "You are with us again. Good," she said, smiling. "You must drink this." She proffered a small plastic cup with some thick pink liquid in it.

"What is it?"

"It is valium."

"Thank God," Alexander said. "I almost died."

"You were choking on your own tongue, you were fitting," the pretty nurse told him. "You are alright now. Drink!"

Alexander gulped down the liquid, and within half an hour he began, for the first time since his arrival at the hospital, to feel truly calm.

Thereafter, Alexander drank the valium in a liquid solution three times a day. He began to pay rational attention to his surroundings and to his circumstances. Later that first day of his resurrection, a senior nursing sister sat down alongside his bed and asked him how she could contact his family. "We cannot find a record of your details."

Alexander had to think for a while, then his mother's phone number came to him suddenly. Roy would be at work all day, it was better to ring his mother.

Alexander was dozing when his brother and his mother arrived. He awoke to find them standing looking down at him. "Oh – Mum!" he exclaimed.

"Darling boy! We only learned where you were this afternoon."

"Hullo Sandy," Roy said, smiling. "Looks like you've cheated death again."

"You cannot imagine how happy I am to see you both," Alexander declared. "But oh, I would murder for a cigarette."

Roy reached into his pocket and withdrew a packet of Peter Stuyvesant, the brand Alexander smoked. "I found these in your flat. I thought you would want them."

"You've been to my flat? How did you get in?"

"I have a spare key. Don't you remember?"

Alexander's mother interrupted. "We've got you some things you might need in this bag. Pyjamas, clean underwear, clean clothes, your slippers, a dressing gown – and some *takkies*. The sister who rang me told me you were missing your shoes."

"That's wonderful, Mum. Roy – I'm going to nip into the loo there and have a cigarette. Do you have a light?"

"*Ja* – I found a Bic lighter in your flat, Sandy." He gave Alexander the lighter.

The hospital (he did not know why) had placed Alexander in a private room. There was a lavatory and a shower attached. He hobbled to the little room, bent over like an old man, one hand on his stomach. As he drew on his first cigarette in at least three days, his head spun and he felt dizzy, but overriding all was the bliss he felt. He felt his mind untangling as he smoked, and when he had finished the cigarette and flushed it down the lavatory, he felt human for the first time in days. He rejoined his family. As he sat back against the pillows, he began to tell them what he remembered of the mugging. But he could not finish: he began to cry and tremble.

"That's alright, Darling," his mother said. "Don't think about it. The important thing is that you're safe now."

"I can't go back there," Alexander told Roy. "I can't live there anymore."

"I know. You can move in with me again. They say you'll be here another week at least. I'll begin to pack your stuff at the flat and take it to my place in the meantime. A lot of it can go in the attic. By the way – I rang Standard Bank and cancelled any cards you had in your wallet. It was n't easy, but I explained that you could n't do so yourself, that you were seriously injured in hospital, and they went ahead and cancelled your ATM card and credit card."

"You're a good bro, Roy. I owe you lots," Alexander said, smiling through his tears.

Roy visited again four evenings during the week that followed. Their mother accompanied him on three of those visits. Roy came to collect Alexander seven days after his first visit. They drove back via Alexander's flat: it was a sunny, bright working day, and the residential street was fairly quiet. Alexander was walking, bent and slow, with the aid of a walking stick the hospital had given him. Under his direction, Roy packed the last few things they were taking. He had brought some large cardboard boxes in the car, and two suitcases.

"Do you think you can drive your car, Sandy? Otherwise, I don't know how we'll get it home."

"I think so. Will you walk to my car with me – it's in the garage below – I don't want to be alone here."

When at last they left the block of flats, Alexander did not look back in his rear view mirrors. He did not know it at the time, but he was never to see Yeoville – or Hillbrow – again. That phase of his life – its frantic lusts, its degradation and depravity – was over at last.

Twenty-Six

The Drakensberg

It was mid June, already winter, before Alexander returned to the hospital for the stoma to be reversed. He had been longing for this event for eight weeks. Never before in his life had he had to live with something as disgusting and troublesome as the colostomy. Having to defecate from the front of his belly revolted him. Having to clean the horror at least twice a day appalled him. He became obsessed with the conviction that he stank of feces all the time. He could n't wear trousers: he could only wear his loosely knotted tracksuit pants. For eight weeks he did not leave Roy's house or garden. Smokie the cat was a comfort to him. She was delighted to have someone at home all day, when Roy went out to work. But Alexander had to stop her falling asleep too far up his lap.

Alexander developed a revulsion towards food. He had already lost a great deal of weight, and he was to lose more. From his usual seventy-seven kilos he was, within just a few weeks, down to sixty-eight kilos. Always very lean, he had no reserves of fat to absorb such a loss: he became noticeably emaciated. His skin was pallid, despite the hour or two each day he sat in the winter sunshine in Roy's garden; his hair lost its healthy shine. He took refuge in writing up a lengthy account, using his mother's old Brother portable typewriter which she had given him many years earlier, of his recent years, and in trying to understand how he had reached this point in his life. He read voraciously also, something he had not engaged in properly for a long time. Roy had many of their parents' books in his home. Alexander rediscovered novels by writers such as Graham Green, A.J. Cronin, Ernest Hemingway, Daphne du Maurier, Jack Kerouac, Nevil Shute, John Steinbeck and Evelyn Waugh, most of which he had read at home during his adolescent years, but which he was happy to re-read so many years later. He also paged his way through a vast collection of American National Geographic magazines from the 1960s, which he remembered enjoying as a child, and had not looked at since. There were also a large number of issues of the monthly magazine publication, "Practical Boat Owner," from the United Kingdom.

And Alexander began to pray again. He felt a profound conviction that God had saved him from death, and he felt humbled and contrite. However, he would not go to Sunday mass. It was only with difficulty that he could bring himself to leave Roy's home, even after the stoma had been reversed. His sleep at night was often a thing of violent nightmares. In some of these, he re-lived various versions of the stabbing; he was witnessing shootings in others; in yet others, he was trying desperately to escape from those who wished to do him terrible harm. He was, as a consequence, always tired. Sometimes, during his waking hours, he experienced a sudden, intense recollection of the punch to his belly that had been the knife blow, and he would begin to weep silently. At other times, sensations of horror and fear would overwhelm him: he could not articulate these sensations, but they made him feel nauseous, and he would begin to tremble. He rarely went further from Roy's front door than a few feet into the front garden. He had to be near the front door and safety, even when he sat outside in the sun whilst Roy was away at work. When his mother wished to see him, she had to come and visit him at Roy's home.

Alexander did not touch alcohol in Roy's home. Roy drank a couple of lagers in the evening when he came home from work. Alexander knew however that there was no guarantee he would, or could, remain so abstemious indefinitely.

Alexander spent a week as an in-patient again at the Joburg General in mid-June for the stoma to be reversed. Later, he kept an appointment to return – a short outpatient's visit – for the metal clips holding the lips of the wound together to be removed. Once that had been done, he was shown how to clean the wound, which grew smaller every day, by using a large syringe to wash it with saline water, before applying a clean dressing. With the stoma gone, he began to eat again. But it was to take several months before he regained the weight he had lost.

Alexander made no attempt to return to work for the remainder of 1996. He understood that he needed to heal mentally just as much as physically. But in January 1997, by now dreaming fewer horrible nightmares at night, and less prone to distressing day-time flashbacks, he began reading the employment pages in the *Star*, the Johannesburg daily, and in the *Sunday Times*. This was how he spotted an advertisement for a business writer with a company in Sandton. He attended two interviews, one with the managing director, the founder's son, and one with the founder's wife – who was the business news editor and would be Alexander's immediate boss: the position was offered to him. The pay was not impressive, but it would more than match what he had been earning as a field guide, and it came with a pension and corporate health insurance, as well as injuries and life insurance.

Alexander liked the working environment. The work area was open plan, with a number of offices down one side of the large open space, where Alexander's boss, her son the managing director, the finance director, the IT specialist, and a couple more administrators each had a private office. There were large glazed pottery tubs scattered throughout the office with mature shrubs planted in them. There was plenty of space between individual work stations. Alexander was in time to erect a couple of screens in front of and alongside his desk, to demarcate his creative working area from the general work floor. The office was located in a three-story building set amidst landscaped grounds, not far from the Sandton City complex. There was underground parking for his car. He was not permitted to smoke in the offices, but he could run downstairs every once in a while for a smoke in the gardens.

No one was riding him, or driving him to increase his output. His job was creative and analytical. As long as he covered the business and economic news of the day adequately, culled from reports in the business and financial sections of a dozen newspapers and magazines, and downloaded them onto the infant Internet, he could set his own hours. He soon developed a routine of being at his desk by seven in the morning, taking only a twenty minutes' break for lunch, and leaving for Roy's home at half past three – thus avoiding the rush hours both to and from work. Alexander had no computer at home. He had a semi-word processor his mother had given him at Christmas; an electronic typewriter which allowed you to undertake some of the functions of a word processor, but he was not online. He did not truly understand what the world wide web was. He did understand however that subscribers around the world could read the abstracts he uploaded each day.

Alexander began attending mass on Sunday morning at St. Bonifatius Catholic church in Sundowner, Randburg. But he always felt like something of an outsider there. He still missed the Anglican church, and its friendly, welcoming environment. But in those days he had reservations about belonging to a church that was now beginning to ordain women as priests, and in which active homosexuality was practiced among some of the clergy. Alexander did not in fact enjoy the company of obvious homosexuals. He was in this regard a thorough-paced bigot. He appreciated however that he was also a hypocrite. He was not proud of his sexual history, and he did not much respect himself or like himself. He continued to feel deep down that homosexuality was sinful, and that as long as he practiced it, he stood in divine condemnation. For these reasons Alexander needed to belong to a church that was uncompromising in its rejection of homosexuality. This, the Anglican church was not.

Following the stabbing incident, Alexander felt uncomfortable in crowds. It was not that he felt shy – he was not shy – but crowds now made him feel uneasy and anxious. There were occasions when he was caught in a crowd when he would begin to tremble and perspire, and start taking short, panting breaths. Perhaps this explained why he kept to himself before Sunday mass, sitting in the car smoking a cigarette, until only minutes before the mass was due to begin. When he entered the church he sat at the back near the doors. Something else had begun to trouble him also: he felt like a fraud among born and raised Catholics. He understood that it was unlikely that other Catholics viewed him as a fraud (none now knew anyway that he was a convert); but he did not understand that his persistent feeling of being an imposter among them was a subconscious extension of the lie he felt he was living, for his whole life was an imposture, as he hid his sexual orientation from the world.

Over the Easter weekend, almost a year after he had been stabbed in Yeoville, Alexander and Roy went camping in the Drakensberg. Alexander harried Roy relentlessly in the very early morning of Good Friday, which that year fell on the 28th March, urging him to get a move on so they could make an early start. They had a long journey ahead of them. The two brothers had taken Smokie the cat to the cattery in the late afternoon of the day before. "Come on Roy!" Alexander nagged, "Let's get going!"

"What's the big hurry?" Roy responded.

"I want to arrive before it gets dark."

They finally set off at about nine that morning. They were headed for Injisuti, a Drakensberg wilderness reserve. Driving through the bare Free State corn fields (the corn had been harvested and only the stubble remained on the ground), with the sun shining in a sky that was infinitely vast, Alexander felt himself begin to relax as he had not fully relaxed since long before the stabbing incident. They stopped for fuel and something to eat and drink at the Harrismith service stop, with the rough-hewn bulk of Harrismith mountain overlooking the town. The two brothers used the lavatories, then admired the tiny Shetland ponies and the ostriches, all cohabiting happily together in a large paddock. There were several eateries and fast food takeaways: they ate hamburgers in one of these. Roy drank a coke. Alexander drank a black coffee, well-sweetened (he had avoided milk for many years), and a glass of water.

The two arrived at Injisuti camp at about three in the afternoon. They set up the small two-man tent, then went walking as far as the contour path. Just before the sun went down, they were grilling chicken breasts with chopped tomato, onions and garlic with tomato paste, wrapped in tinfoil, over a bed of coals. They had wrapped some potatoes in tinfoil also and stuck them in the coals. Roy had a bottle of Castle lager, and Alexander drank coffee brewed at the edge of the fire. They would not be able to barbeque the next two evenings, for lack of fuel.

"I don't remember Dad ever *braaing*," Alexander said.

"He did once or twice – not often though. He was n't an outdoors person, was he?"

"No, he was n't," Alexander replied. "He did n't do the things most fathers did with their boys. I wonder if that was because of his fear of the sun?"

Alexander senior had been a red-head, with skin which could n't take the sun.

"I don't think Dad really enjoyed his time in the bush after he left the Army," Alexander continued. "Perhaps he was put off the outdoors for ever."

"Maybe . . . do you miss Dad?"

"Often," Alexander responded. "With Dad gone, there's no one we can turn to for advice and help anymore. We have to grow up now."

"That's the problem. I don't think I can grow up," Roy said.

Alexander thought there was a great deal of truth in what Roy said. Neither brother showed any great gifts for adult life, but Roy was the most childlike of the two, and the most innocent. Sometimes, Alexander wondered whether his brother might be mildly autistic. He was a gifted engineer, and he could tackle any sort of practical problem, but he showed little aptitude for the skills of adult life. There was something extraordinarily unworldly about him. He had not, by the age of forty, had a long term relationship with a woman. It was clear however that women attracted him.

Alexander loved his brother the more as the two grew older, and Alexander came to understand what a good man Roy was. Alexander, by comparison, was not a good man at all. He had to work hard at being a good man – or so he sometimes thought.

"I have n't made a very good job of growing up," Alexander said. "At least you have a well-paid job and a house you own, and a cat, to show for it. I'm still living as if I was in my early twenties."

"You've had some bad luck," Roy replied. "But you handle life much better than me."

The sun had set behind the mountains. It grew suddenly much colder. The summer was over. The first stars were out in a sky the colour of blued gunmetal. The canopy of the heavens seemed inconceivably vast to Alexander, and he became aware of this infinitude's utter disinterest in him, and that very disinterest was a source of hope, for in it there existed neither malice nor favour. Above the eastern horizon, Alexander could see Venus, the evening star. Much of the western sky was hidden behind the mountains. Alexander felt infinitesimally tiny in the face of this uncompromisingly vast universe. He reached for his quilted coat. The two brothers were silent, leaning back in their folding chairs. The following two evenings they would have only the ground, or such natural features as they could find, to sit on, for they could not take the chairs with them as they hiked in the mountains. Alexander smoked. After a while he commented "I guess I should have a shower."

"Is there hot water?"

"There's supposed to be hot water in the ablutions block," Alexander replied. "I'll go see."

He found his sponge bag and a towel, and headed for the ablutions block. He was glad to find, when he got there, that there was ample hot water on tap. He wished a middle aged man who was shaving at one of the basins a good evening. "'*Naand*,'" the man replied. Alexander had a long shower. Tomorrow and the next day there would be only icy cold mountain streams to wash in.

The following three mornings the brothers ate eggs boiled on their tiny gas camping stove for breakfast, with a bowl of muesli each. The milk for the muesli was reconstituted from dried milk powder mixed with water from the mountain streams warmed on the camping stove. On

Saturday and Sunday evenings, far above the contour path, with Monk's Cowl emerging at the head of the high valley in which they were camping, its peak towering clear above the mist and cloud, disembodied, ethereal, and with a stream of cold clear water nearby, they cooked a stew of canned beef chunks into which they added chopped fresh onions, and which they bulked up with canned peeled spring potatoes. They ate the stew on slices of bread with margarine. Alexander had a tremendous appetite. He felt fit and strong and healthy again. He felt safe. He loved the wild places, places where mankind's claim to possession was tenuous. On Saturday morning, as they were walking along the contour path, they had seen a herd of eland; big, golden antelope with a heavy shoulder hump and mid-sized, slightly curved horns, the lower parts of which were corkscrewed. The weather was overcast the entire weekend, and on Easter night it began to rain. There was no tree cover this high up, only low scrub bush, and it was an uncomfortable, rather miserable evening. They had to cook on the little stove in the entrance of the tent, huddled over it to shield it from the rain. Alexander began to long for a warm, dry house with a bathroom and a bed for the night. He said to Roy "I'm not doing this again. My camping days are over now."

"You don't really mean that."

"Oh yes I do. I'm too old for this sort of thing, I've just decided. In future I'm never going away unless there's a proper bed the other end, and a real bathtub."

Indeed, that was to be Alexander's last camping trip.

At Christmas of 1997 the two brothers went on holiday together to Cape Town. They stayed in one of the University of Cape Town student residences on Main Road in Rondebosch. This was far cheaper than staying in a hotel. It was a good central location too, and close to many useful amenities, one of which was the famed Pig 'n Whistle pub. They had supper here several times.

They visited their aunt Margaret at what remained of the old farm: two acres of land, with the original farmhouse, in which their oldest cousin, Jenny, and her husband and two tiny children lived; two wooden framed chalets, in the largest of which lived Mary, Margaret's youngest daughter, together with Mike (who was pleased to see Alexander again); and the new double story house in which their aunt and her husband lived, together with a large collection of dogs and cats. Although not obviously cold towards Alexander, nor was Margaret as warm as she would once have been. She was much more forthcoming with Roy. Alexander added his aunt to the list of people he still loved and who had once loved him, but whom he appeared to have alienated forever. Topping that list of course was Alice, the friend from Hillbrow and Yeoville in the old days.

The visit to their aunt made Alexander sad, not only to find that she had not forgiven him, but to be reminded that his grandfather's farm, a place he had loved so much, was almost all gone. What had he left from childhood and his early manhood? Other than some childhood toys and books, there was nothing left from his childhood now. Nor was there anywhere to call "home." The next morning, while Roy went to visit an ex work colleague who had moved to Cape Town, Alexander walked to a liquor store and bought himself a bottle of whiskey. "I will not get hooked on the stuff," he told himself, though he knew he was lying to himself. He had not touched spirits for three years, not since the end of 1994.

Back at work early the next year, Alexander found himself thinking "I'm over forty years old. I should n't be sharing an open plan office floor in a home-made cubicle with half day female workers and graduates fresh out of university. At my age I should be in one of the offices down the side. Even the twenty-five year old IT manager has an office of his own."

Alexander felt stricken by a profound sense of failure and defeat. He became aware that his ship had sailed long ago, leaving him behind on a barren strand, and he began to hate his job, where he was coming to feel that he was under-valued and under-paid. Soon after his forty-third birthday, the family sold the company to a national publishing concern. A new managing director was helicoptered in. Alexander approached him in July and asked for a raise. He had to explain first what it was that he did. He realised very soon that what he did was of little interest to the new owners: they had wanted to acquire ownership of the title of a well-known business publication the old family-run company had been known for. The new owners viewed the rest of their acquisition's business as of little value.

Alexander's request for a raise in salary was refused. He now began drinking more frequently. He felt a dark foreboding of a fell doom come upon him. His mood began to fluctuate markedly. At times he felt as if he were aboard a runaway train; at others, he felt that the more appropriate metaphor was a train shunted into a siding and forgotten. He requested some leave, which he was granted. He used his leave to find a small garden cottage to rent, not far from the Randburg waterfront, a man-made lake surrounded by a shopping mall, which contained several pubs and restaurants. He hoped he would have stopped drinking before returning to work, but the sense of shame and defeat he felt meant that that was not going to happen: the drink was now a means he employed to avoid looking at his life face-on. It was with something akin to despair that he had left Roy's house and moved into the cottage in Ferndale.

Yet the year marched on, and Alexander continued to bring to his work the same careful, economical prose and insightful analysis that brought him some small sense of personal validation. He usually spent a couple of evenings a week with his brother at Roy's home in Honeydew, for his own garden cottage was a lonely place. Some weekends, during the late afternoons, he would visit one of the pubs at the waterfront development near his cottage, where he found that he was still able to befriend strangers.

Roy remained his only real friend during this unhappy, lonely period of Alexander's life.

Twenty-Seven

Ruin And Disaster

Alexander took a week and a half off from the office over Christmas of 1998, planning to return to work just after New Year. With a Christmas bonus in sight, he felt rich, and he spent his money at pubs in the waterfront development near his cottage, arriving at the pubs in the mid or late afternoons, and often staying until after midnight, when the last of the pubs finally closed.

His frustrations and unhappiness at work had mounted since the new managing director had refused his request for a rise in salary. Now, with no work to prevent him from brooding on his resentments during the day, he began to drink whiskey chasers with his lagers at the pubs he frequented. He was therefore inebriated for most of his time away from work.

When Alexander was drunk, neither his speech nor his mobility were affected. It was very difficult for people who did not know him well to realise that he was intoxicated. Barmen saw no warning signs as they served him the drinks he bought. Until, of a sudden, he would do something outrageous, such as leaping up onto a table and dancing to the beat of the music playing over the bar's sound system, or accosting strangers in such an intrusive and eccentric fashion as to cause the barman to ask him to leave. Very soon, he was banned from two of the three or four bars in the lakeside complex, and from most of the restaurants which also served drinks at a bar. By the time he returned to work on Tuesday 5th January 1999, Alexander was firmly hooked again on spirits. He topped up throughout the working day, taking frequent breaks from his desk (which were not in themselves a cause of suspicion, for he had often taken almost hourly breaks in the past to go downstairs and out into the garden for a quick smoke), and rushing downstairs to the parking basement, where he kept a bottle of scotch in his car.

He began to be something of a nuisance to his colleagues at work, for when Alexander became very drunk, his loneliness welled up, and he sought out company. By now, his behaviour was noticeably erratic, and some of the half day women workers grew nervous of him. He adopted an exaggerated old world manner towards these women, and told them what often seemed to them, with their limited experience of life, rather improbable stories. On the afternoon of Friday 8th January his manager spoke to him in her office. "Sandy, I suggest you take some sick leave due you, and return to work when you are feeling well again."

His manager made no reference to the fact that Alexander was drunk all the time now, but he understood very well what she was saying: if he would not sober up, he would have no job to return to.

Alexander knew that he could not sober up un-aided, not now that spirits had got such a grip on him. He knew therefore that he was going to lose his job, and he would likely lose any further prospects of employment also, for he was forty-three years old, and in South Africa (and in Britain also, as he would learn later), you were unemployable in any meaningful sense if you lost your job after you had turned forty.

Having left the office that Friday afternoon, he did not return to his cottage to change out of his suit, but drove straight to the waterfront development, and began drinking at the one bar left to him, where there was a saturnine, good looking young man with a curl to his lip serving behind the bar counter. The barman permitted Alexander to drink himself into the farther reaches of intoxication. Perhaps he wished to see how far Alexander would go if he drank enough. Alexander no longer realised when he was humiliating himself.

Alexander spent the entire evening in this bar, drinking lagers with whiskey chasers. He had had nothing to eat all day, having had no breakfast before going to work, and he had not bought himself a toasted sandwich or a chicken pie at the little fastfood kiosk near the office complex during his lunch break (as he usually did when sober). He was awash with liquor by the time a group of three or four young men entered the bar at about nine-thirty that evening. Within minutes, Alexander had bought them all drinks, and he began to entertain them with stories of his time in the bushveld. These stories, though mostly true, sounded highly improbable in his present state of advanced intoxication. The more he drank, the more effete his acquired upper class drawl became. Outside of Chelsea and Kensington in London, this exaggerated public school accent, a sign of Alexander's advanced intoxication, did him no favours. In Johannesburg he was often taken to be merely a *moffie* or a fool – or both.

Alexander was later to remember very little of that evening. Indeed, his last memory was of going to find a cash machine in the lakeside complex, three of the young men accompanying him, and of drawing some cash. Thereafter his memory became a blank until the following morning, when he found himself lying on a sofa near a window in his cottage, and he tried to stand up, only to collapse in intense pain from his left foot.

Alexander's left foot and ankle were horribly swollen, and he was missing both sock and shoe. So too was his jacket missing, together with his wallet, cell phone and car keys, and – he was to find – the keys to the cottage. His clothes were very damp. He felt cold. He appeared to have been in the lake. He had a pounding headache, and his face hurt. He desperately needed a pee and a drink. It was with very great difficulty that he dragged himself to the lavatory on his hands and knees, for he could put no weight whatsoever on his left foot. Even to touch it to anything sent sharp shocks of pain up his left leg. He stood up on one leg at the toilet bowl and managed to have a piss. He saw himself in the bathroom mirror: his face was bruised, and he had a black eye, which was half closed. In the sitting room he found a bottle in which about an eighth of scotch remained. He drank some of it, and fought down the urge to vomit it straight up again. He knew he had to keep the liquor inside him, if he was to avoid the shakes. Next, Alexander heaved himself upright at the sink in the kitchenette which adjoined the sitting room, and drank copious amounts of water from the cold tap.

Alexander needed valium also. He was prescribed ten milligrams a day by his compliant young general practitioner. He could find no valium in his cottage. He searched again for the keys to the cottage's only exterior door, which he had established was locked. His left foot kept sending hot fiery bursts of pain up his leg. He could not find the keys to the outer door. He did however find a cigarette packet with about ten cigarettes inside it. He dragged himself back to the sofa on which he had first come to, and lighted a cigarette. It began to grow clear to Alexander that something very bad had happened to him, and that he was in serious difficulties, for he was trapped inside his cottage, with neither alcohol nor valium, nor a phone, to hand. He could not get out via the door, and he could not hope to exit via a window either, for – as was commonplace in South Africa – the windows had sturdy metal burglar bars fixed firmly across them. What was more, the main house, some thirty yards from his cottage, would, he knew, be empty if today was (as he thought it might be) a Saturday – and it would be empty tomorrow also, for the two women who used it as a range of offices and store rooms for their small business would not be there over the weekend. Alexander doubted whether anyone else would hear him if he tried to shout out of an open window. The neighbourhood's residential plots were each an acre in extent; the houses were set far apart behind screens of trees. The full extent of his predicament became suddenly very clear to Alexander, and he grew afraid.

Alexander realised he was very cold indeed, and shivering. He stripped the wet clothes off him, having dragged himself painfully and slowly to the bedroom, and put on a clean pair of underpants, a pair of shorts, a clean vest and a pullover. He found that his left leg appeared to be terribly bruised, and was hugely swollen as far as the knee. He dragged the duvet from his bed back with him to the sitting room, where he wrapped himself in it and lay back on the sofa.

Time passed very slowly. As the day progressed, Alexander began to crave both alcohol and valium with increasing fervour. He was pacing himself with the cigarettes. He felt ill, both hot and cold at the same time, and the shivering grew worse. He began to perspire heavily also. He thought to himself "I'm sick, and I've got withdrawals; I must drink sugar water." So he crawled to the kitchenette and dragged himself up on one leg at the sink, and stirred two teaspoons of sugar into a mug of water, and drank it down. Shortly, he needed a pee again. He could not face crawling to the lavatory, so he relieved himself in his shorts. He was fairly sure by now that he was going to die. He began to pray for help. He prayed to Our Lady; he prayed to Jesus; he prayed to God. It seemed to him that his prayers were bounced straight back to him.

The night passed so slowly it felt eternal. Alexander thought about his parents, and how good they had been to him as a child. He thought about his brother, Roy. He thought about the cats he had loved. He did not think about the young men he had loved and lusted after. It was memories of his family and of his childhood that his tormented mind was conjuring up in the dark. He wept at times. By dawn his withdrawals were very bad. He lost his breath every once in a while and gasped for air, and at random intervals he shook and shuddered convulsively. Despite feeling cold, he continued to sweat. The skin on his swollen leg below the knee had begun to darken ominously.

Dawn broke for a second time, and Alexander smoked his second-last cigarette. He drank more sugar water, and peed again where he stood by the side of the kitchen counter, supporting himself with one hand while directing the jet of urine onto the floor with the other. He lay down again, wrapped in the duvet, and began to pray again. Sometime during the early afternoon, that Sunday of the 10th January 1999, Alexander thought he heard movement outside. He began to shout for help as loudly as he could, which was very loud indeed.

"*Baas?*" he heard from the little courtyard in front of the cottage. The voice was that of a black man, the language Afrikaans. "*Wat's verkeerd baas?*"

Alexander had to think hard. His mind was not working properly. "*Ek's siek!*" he shouted. "*Ek's baaie siek, en ek het die sleutel vir die deur verlos. Dis ontmoontlik vir my om uit to kom. Ek het nie n foon in die huis nie. Asseblief, bel vir my n ambulans!*"

"*Ja baas,*" the man replied. Then there was silence. "God help me," Alexander prayed.

Twenty-Eight

Anguish

The Police – for presumably it was this black gardener from up the road (it was never established what he had been doing outside Alexander's cottage) who had phoned for the Police rather than for an ambulance – broke the lock on the front door, and gained entry, and when they saw Alexander's condition, they radioed for an ambulance. They also rang Roy, whose phone number Alexander gave them, and Roy told them that his brother had medical insurance, and the ambulance was to take Alexander to the Sunning Hill, a private hospital in Johannesburg's northern suburbs. Roy had leapt into his car and driven straight to the hospital, arriving not long after the ambulance did. Alexander had already had a catheter installed, and was being made to drink huge quantities of water to encourage urination. Roy was with his brother when the surgeon, using a needle to prick his skin, found that Alexander had zero skin sensation to his swollen and blackened lower left leg until about four inches below the knee. The surgeon told him that he had gangrene, and that if his life was to be saved, he must have his lower left leg amputated. "Do it," Alexander said. He signed the documents the nurse gave him. Then he was taken to the operating theatre on a gurney, and within a moment, a mask being held to his face, the anesthetic had knocked him out.

Alexander had been having a terrible nightmare: a leopard was chewing his left leg off, and when he came to, he did not know where he was. But his left leg from the knee down was in great pain. He lay there, suffering, his vision clearing, then blurring again, for an indeterminate time, slowly taking in his surroundings. It became clear to him after a while that he was in a hospital, in a noisy, rather crowded area full of beds with metal side guards raised, a room crammed with complex looking machinery, and in the beds lay patients whom he presumed were all sick or injured. Then Alexander discerned that like them, he too was linked to a number of machines via tubes that were attached to him. All the nurses were black women. At last, one of them approached him. "Where am I?" he asked her.

"You are in intensive care," the woman answered. "You have undergone surgery."

"Surgery? For what?"

The nurse's face, the colour of coffee with but a dash of milk in it, went blank. "You wait. I will get a doctor," she replied.

The doctor was a middle aged white man. "Excellent," he said: "You're with us again. How do you feel?"

"Dreadful. And my left leg hurts terribly."

"Let me look at it," the surgeon said. He raised a sheet which appeared to be arranged over a framework of some sort, for it was arched across Alexander's legs. He examined the limb closely for a while, an examination which included sniffing at it.

"Yah . . . mmmm . . . so far so good," the man said.

"What's happened to me, Doctor?" Alexander asked.

"You don't remember?"

Alexander grimaced as a wave of pain stabbed through his lower leg. He shook his head. "We had to amputate your left leg just below the knee, Alexander," the doctor told him. "It was gangrenous; it was killing you."

"It's hurting me."

"I'll give you something for that," the surgeon said. "Nurse – increase the morphine to twelve, but monitor the patient closely."

Alexander shook his head once more, and drifted out of consciousness again.

When next he came to, Roy was sitting by his bedside, with their mother. "Oh my darling, what has happened to you?" she asked Alexander.

"Hullo Mum. I don't know. I feel rotten."

Roy smiled at Alexander. "I'm not surprised," he remarked.

"I need a cigarette," Alexander declared.

"You can't smoke in here, Sandy," Roy answered him. "Maybe later."

One of the black nurses, looking as usual extremely smart in her gleaming, spotless, pressed and starched white uniform and wearing a host of merit badges, awards and decorations (for so they looked to Alexander), appeared at this juncture. "The patient must sleep now," she said. "You can see him again tomorrow morning."

Please take care of my son," Alexander's mother asked the nurse.

"We do that," replied the nurse.

Alexander did not remember his family leaving.

Alexander was never to forget the horror of the next four or five days and nights, though as the years progressed the memory blurred with other nightmare memories. He was by now suffering advanced withdrawals from valium and alcohol deprivation, and he longed for a cigarette. He hallucinated often: nightmarish fancies during one of which he visited Hell, and the Devil told him that if he renounced Christ, his sufferings would end. The despair Alexander felt in that terrible place, where there was an utter absence of God's grace; a profound, eternal, limitless chasm of horror, was beyond bearing, and he said "I renounce Jesus Christ." And then he was back in his private room in the hospital. Roy visited him every evening, almost always bringing their mother with him, but for much of the time, Alexander was trapped in his nightmare world, and they could get nothing but nonsense from him.

Later, Roy told Alexander that it was he who had brought the doctor's attention to Alexander's withdrawals from alcohol and valium, and it was he who had insisted they re-introduce valium to his brother's treatment regime. Within a very short while thereafter, Alexander was lucid once more, his hallucinations gone. From then on Alexander's condition improved rapidly. By the 18th of January he was propelling himself around in a wheelchair, unsupervised, taking the lifts down to the entrance atrium and out through the front doors, where he would move to one side and smoke a cigarette. Then he would use his wheelchair to reach the café in the atrium, where he would drink a properly made coffee. By the 22nd of January, the remedial therapist had taught Alexander how to use a pair of crutches to get about, and he dispensed with the wheelchair.

Alexander's amputation continued however to cause him a lot of pain. He experienced this pain in that part of his leg which was now missing, particularly in the absent foot. He could not reach the pain. He could not alleviate it. It felt as if he was being electrocuted; as if tremendously powerful electric shocks in very rapid succession were being passed through his non-existent foot, or toes, or heel; hour after hour. Sometimes the pain would persist right through the night, leaving Alexander exhausted in the morning, and he would spend most of the morning dozing on his bed. The doctors told him this phantom limb pain was not uncommon, and prescribed carbamazepine by mouth. But this did not seem to Alexander to be of much help.

Towards the end of January Alexander was discharged from the Sunning Hill, and he moved back in with his brother in Honeydew. Alexander had become tremendously skilled with his pair of crutches: there was little he could not manage. He found that he could still drive his Ford Granada, though at present this knowledge was academic. All he needed, after all, to operate the automatic car's foot controls (there was no clutch pedal) was his right foot. Roy had found the spare ignition keys for the Granada in Alexander's cottage a day or two after he had been admitted to hospital. He had, amazingly, found the car still parked where Alexander had left it in the waterfront car park, undamaged. Roy drove the car back to his home in Honeydew, leaving his own car at the waterfront. Then he returned with their mother driving her car, and Roy then drove his own car back home, with their mother following behind. Unsure of the position regarding his insurance, and anyway rather scared of the world out there, Alexander did not use his own car. His mother drove him to his twice weekly remedial therapy sessions at the hospital.

Eating well again, Alexander soon rebuilt his strength, and he was able to get up off the floor on his right leg alone, with an ease which impressed Roy. Alexander continued to undergo twice weekly therapy sessions at the hospital, during which he was made to stretch his left leg repeatedly until it was fully straightened, to counter the tendency of below knee amputees to clench the remains of their lower limb in beneath the knee, and thus contract the big tendons. He was taught how to apply a length of wide elasticated bandaging every day to his stump, to reduce its size and "cone" it, in preparation for a prosthesis to be fitted. He was made to undergo a variety of exercises designed to keep him supple and fit. These exercises he had to keep up at home also. And during this entire period, he used no wheelchair. He got around on his pair of aluminium crutches. He grew very fit, and his shoulders and upper arms became very strong. But Alexander's mind was unquiet. The return of his nightmares, of night-time horrors soaked in blood; of images of blades and gunfire; of plots dripping with malice being directed against him, was evidence of this. And during his waking hours, Alexander lived in a state of constant alertness. For the rest of his life, the sound of running feet behind him, or of voices nearby raised in anger, would send his pulse racing. Loud noises distressed him beyond measure.

Alexander had forgotten that one of the perks of his employment with the company in Sandton had been life and injury insurance. He was astonished when his manager phoned him to tell him that he was due a sixty-seven thousand Rands payout. When within a week his bank had phoned him to inform him that his account had been credited with sixty-seven thousand Rands, he battled to believe he was not dreaming it.

Alexander found his sobriety a blessing. Instead of resorting to liquor, he indulged in a giant bar of Cadbury's dark chocolate every day. His internal economy was so greedy for fuel, he could do so without erupting in the spots on his face such a diet would normally have induced.

And Alexander prayed. He prayed every morning and evening. Despite his amputation, he did so on his knees by the side of his bed. He thanked God for saving his life. He was filled with gratitude for having been granted deliverance from a terrible death. He was certain too that Jesus understood that he had been, literally, out of his mind when he had renounced Him at the Devil's bidding. He knew that Christ had welcomed him back again. Alexander tried hard to maintain a positive outlook, though the loss of his leg – he who had loved the outdoors, and walking and hiking – was a cause of great distress to him. In addition there was also his consciousness of himself, as a whole, good looking (albeit rather thin) man, which was now under severe assault.

In April Alexander was measured for a false limb, and a cast was taken of his stump. When the prosthesis was ready, towards the end of April, it proved to be so painful to wear, he was unable to use it. He could not see himself ever growing accustomed to it. He felt certain that it should not be so painful. Alexander refused to accept the prosthesis and said "Let's start again, and make another one."

The second prosthesis, ready by early June, was only a little better. "I'm struggling to believe this," he said to Roy. "You would think that South African prosthetic technicians, used to dealing with landmine amputees, could make a wearable false leg. I'm going to have to get one made in Britain."

Alexander knew that as a British citizen with right of abode, and a National Insurance number, he would be able to have a prosthesis made for him free of charge on the National Health Service in Britain. The more he thought about this, the more sensible a move to Britain became. He was finished in South Africa. He had blotted his copy book too many times in South Africa. Furthermore, there was the impact of affirmative action employment legislation in South Africa. Where there was both a black and a white applicant for a job, the black candidate would be offered the position rather than the white candidate. The family began to plan for Alexander's return to Britain. But Alexander had never before felt quite so much reluctance to leave South Africa and his family. Both were precious to him now to an extent they had never been in the past. Since the stabbing incident he had grown much closer to his mother and his brother, and with the loss of his leg he grew closer still. He knew

Britain well enough now to have lost the early love he had felt for that cold, damp, unfriendly island. He reveled in South Africa's hot sun; in its life-giving and healing properties. He understood and related to South Africa's people – black and white both – as he could never understand or relate to the British people. Britain had become more than ever a foreign country for him. Yet if he was to hope to walk properly again, he feared he must return to England. Perhaps the sixty-seven thousand Rands – worth about seven thousand Pounds in late June – would make things a bit easier for him over there. He had last seen England almost seven years earlier. So much had happened in his life since then. There had been his stay in Malta, and his time at the Kwando River Lodge. There had been his work as a field guide in South Africa. Since leaving England for Malta in March 1991, Alexander had experienced so much, discovered so many wonderful places, and enjoyed a number of very close relationships.

With Roy doing all the lifting and carrying, Alexander sorted what remained of his household effects. There was very little. Much of the furniture had simply been abandoned in the flat in Yeoville after Alexander had been stabbed. With Alexander's permission, much of what remained at the cottage in Ferndale had been sold by Roy for a few Rands to a house clearance company. But there was a fine desk which had been brought back on top of the roof of Roy's car to the house in Honeydew, and a bookcase, both of which Alexander wished to take with him to England, along with several metal trunks full of books and childhood memorabilia.

Alexander bought an indefinite return air fare to Heathrow, departing Jan Smuts airport the evening of the 5th of July. He withdrew one thousand Pounds cash in sterling of what remained of the sixty-seven thousand Rands; the rest, he converted to Sterling travelers cheques. He was not emigrating formally. He wished to avoid the bureaucratic fuss and paperwork. As far as the South African authorities were concerned, he would be returning to South Africa, a fiction supported by the return air ticket.

Then tragedy struck the Honeydew household. One late afternoon, while it was still daylight, Roy began to worry because Smokie was not to be found for her supper-time. "She's always here, Sandy. You've seen – she's never late for her supper," Roy said.

"I know. I think maybe you ought to look in the *veld* behind the house, Roy."

Behind the house were about thirty acres of scrub and *veld*. Smokie could reach this easily via a hole in the fence behind the house next door. This ground was separated from Roy's garden by a concrete wall six feet high. To reach the *veld*, Roy had to walk down his driveway and continue past three more houses, then he could make his way up into the open ground. The sun was now low in the sky. In Africa, where twilight was brief, there would not be much more daylight left. Roy took a torch with him. He was still away by the time it began to grow properly dark, and Alexander began to feel a growing anxiety. He was by now convinced there was something wrong. Just before it grew fully dark, he heard Roy walking up the driveway. Using his crutches, Alexander went out the front door and into the garden. Roy was carrying Smokie, held in his forearms against his chest. He was sobbing. "Smokie is dead! The dogs – they . . ." his voice choked up and he could not continue.

Alexander felt a horrible sense of shock, then a great compassion for his brother. "Oh, Roy . . ."

Roy walked unsteadily towards the sofa, and half fell onto the cushions, the pathetic body of his darling Smokie-cat on his lap. Alexander sat alongside him, and put his arm round his brother's shoulders. He felt tears begin to gather in his eyes, the harbingers of pain and anguish. He held his brother's shoulders while Roy cried. He touched Smokie's soft fur, and the two brothers wept together.

Twenty-Nine

A Return To London

Dogs had trapped Smokie against the six foot concrete fence behind Roy's house. She had probably died very quickly, her neck broken, but she would have known terror. Neither Alexander nor Roy, in the coming years, could bear to think about her end. As Alexander grew older, the recollection of her death – and the violent deaths of other cats they had loved – would cause him greater and greater distress.

For now, Alexander persuaded Roy to wrap the cat's body in her favourite sleeping blanket, and although both brothers went to bed later that night, neither slept at all well. In the morning, Alexander followed Roy out into the garden, and watched as Roy dug a deep grave for Smokie's body beneath the pin-oak. Afterwards, he said "I think we should go see Mum now. What do you think?"

"Yeah, OK."

Alexander rang South African Airways and had his departure date changed to the 26th July. This gave him an extra three weeks with Roy.

He could not leave him alone right now. They were unhappy weeks. They both grieved for Smokie, but Alexander knew it would be easier for him: he was going to new things. Roy would have to remain behind, alone.

Roy said one evening "I don't want to stay here anymore, not with Smokie gone. And anyway, I don't want to stay in the new South Africa, watching the country being progressively run down. I'm thinking of joining you in England in a few months' time, after I've sold my house."

"I'd like that a lot, Roy, but what about Mum?"

"Once we're settled there, I'll fly back and bring her out too. She's getting old now. This is no place for an old white woman alone."

"Then it makes sense for you to include the stuff you want to take with you along with the things I'm shipping to England. There's your bed, for example: you had that especially made for you, did n't you? An extra-long bed."

"I know. It'll be cheaper if we pay for a half container. We can fill a half container with both our things."

"But it would mean your camping in your house for a while, Roy. Can you do that?"

"I think so."

So Alexander paid Pickfords, the international removers, for a half container, and when the men from Pickfords arrived to box up and seal what remained unpacked of Alexander's possessions, and load them all into the van, Roy's bed and a great many boxes of his own possessions were hauled away with Alexander's things. It would be at least three, probably four months, before these things made their way to Pickfords' warehouse in southern England. Alexander planned by then to have a home for them to be delivered to; a home where Roy could join him.

Alexander of course had absolutely no idea what he was going to do in England. In his heart he was possessed by the conviction that all his options had run out now; that he was probably unemployable – given his age and circumstances – anywhere at all. Although he felt as if the mainspring that powered him had lost its tension, he would trust to Fate to show him his path. His coming move to England had only one certain aim: to obtain a false leg that he could walk with. He did not even have in mind a particular town or district in which he would be looking for somewhere to live.

"If Dad was still alive, he would know what to do."

"Yeah, we're babes in the wood without Dad," Alexander agreed. As always, whenever he remembered his father, Alexander experienced both grief for his absence and remorse at the distance that had grown up between the two of them, a distance much more of his own making than of his father's. He had wasted so much opportunity to love and be loved!

During the following three weeks, feeling more confident in himself now, Alexander often drove his Ford Granada (which was now eleven years old, and which Roy would sell before he departed South Africa) to their mother's home, and spent a morning or afternoon there. At weekends, he and Roy would spend many hours together at their mother's home, or sometimes they would go out, the three of them, to destinations such as Emmarentia dam, where, using his crutches, Alexander could walk a certain distance along the path by the edge of the water, before the three of them would find a bench and sit and watch the water-fowl, and the kayakers and canoeists going round and round the body of water, all in the same anti-clockwise direction, or they would park the car at the botanic gardens above the dam. These gardens were laid out in a series of broad terraces with water features: there were splendid fountains, and life-like stone animal heads spouting water. Alexander had taught himself to get up and down short flights of steps on his crutches, though for appearance sake, he wore the false leg when he was in public, painful though it was. Sometimes they drove to the botanic gardens up against the ridge in Roodepoort municipality, not far from Roy's home, having first collected their mother. Alexander could not manage any of the paths alongside the *kloof*, let alone follow the path which climbed the cliff-face, but he could stand on the little footbridge that crossed the nascent Crocodile River, and watch the bright yellow weaver birds as they flitted from their woven nests that hung from the trees above the stream, or walk across the lawns to the base of the waterfall, and watch for the black-winged eagles which were seen in the district.

As the day of his departure drew nearer, Alexander felt increasingly unhappy. Often he considered canceling his air ticket, then he would remember that almost all his remaining possessions were already (presumably) on the high seas: all that was left to him of his childhood memorabilia was now in transit, along with the last few things that bore witness to his having once lived an independent, competent life of his own. He would remember that his medical insurance had run dry, and he could not now afford to commission a third attempt at a prosthesis. And he would think also "If I stayed, what would I do? There's nothing I could do here anymore. Even field guiding is now closed to me, with only one leg."

So he accepted that he would soon be departing for a country he knew by now could be cold in ways far more fundamental than merely the consequence of the long winters and often miserable summers. He had loved England (and the Scottish West Highlands) once – but back then, he had had a wealth of family relations who loved him, who welcomed his visits, who made him feel valued. His aunt was growing old now, older than his mother, and bound up in the lives of her children and grandchildren; his last remaining great aunts and great uncles were in their extreme dotage; his cousins had rich lives of their own, and some of them had long ago left Britain for Australia, or New Zealand, or even the United States. Alexander was under no illusions that Britain would prove to be a welcoming place for him anymore. But it seemed clear to him that it was his unavoidable destiny to be exiled from Africa. Alexander was already beginning to understand that if you chose to wage war against your destiny, you would suffer needlessly before your inevitable defeat. People have far fewer choices than they like to imagine they have.

At Jan Smuts in the early evening of Monday 26th July, neither Alexander, nor his brother, nor even their mother, gave way to their emotions. Alexander and Roy had not been raised in an emotionally demonstrative family, and their mother only rarely expressed her feelings. Rather than sit for two hours drinking coffee together at the airport and finding there was nothing left to be said anymore, Alexander checked his luggage in immediately, then he took his leave of his family.

He said to the two of them "I don't think it will be very long before we're all together again. Don't be sad." Alexander, brought up in a family that did not hug, hesitated for a moment, then he hugged his mother tightly, and when he took his leave of Roy, he shook his hand and squeezed his shoulder. Then he walked through the barrier and into the international departures hall, all the time possessed by a sense of heavy unreality.

On that Tuesday morning the 27th July 1999, as Alexander landed at Heathrow, he was not entirely sober, for he had begun drinking again during the eleven hour flight, almost overwhelmed by a combination of physical pain (his stump was hurting him; his injured guts, crunched up in the tiny economy class seat, were hurting him) and a profound sense of loss. He knew he would never be able to cease thinking of Africa as "home". He knew he was never to live in Africa again. He had left home for the last and final time.

From Heathrow airport Alexander took an expensive taxi ride to a small hotel in a Regency townhouse in Belgrave Road in Pimlico. With his luggage, and a limb which was causing him much pain, he could not manage the Underground from Heathrow into London. Shortly after clearing immigration, Alexander had made his way to the accommodation bureau at Heathrow, where he had chosen this hotel as being fairly central and relatively inexpensive. It was also close to Pimlico Underground station. He did not want to have to walk any great distances.

It was mid morning by the time he had checked into the hotel. He lay down fully clothed, having removed his prosthesis and his shoe, and pulled the coverlet over himself, and slept for one and a half hours. When he awoke, the sun was streaming into his south facing room, which overlooked Belgrave Road. It took him two or three minutes to remember where he was. He needed to get out in this fine summer weather. He brushed his teeth and washed his face, then put on a light linen jacket and a Panama hat he had bought in London many years earlier. He walked down Belgrave Road, swinging between his crutches, and along Lupus Street and crossed Vauxhall Road, where he found a pub, the White Swan, where he bought a Hansa Pilsener which was brought to him, along with a slice of fish pie, at one of the small iron tables on the pavement in front of the pub. Soon the other three pavement tables were occupied by couples, two of whom were foreign. His table had the only remaining seat available. Despite his current circumstances, something of the old excitement Alexander had always experienced when in London began to energize him. The fine summer weather helped. He could remember again what it had felt like, to be young and optimistic, during his early days in London.

A man who looked to be in his early thirties came out of the pub with a glass and a bottle in his hands. He looked around him, then at Alexander's table. He approached Alexander. "Would you mind if I joined you? I hope to sit outside in this wonderful sunshine."

The man was tall, almost as tall as Alexander. He was bare-headed, with light brown hair which shone in the sun. He had a slight tan. He had pleasant, rather boyish features. He smiled. A dimple formed either side of his mouth. He spoke with a public school accent.

"By all means," Alexander replied, smiling in return, his accent, despite his years in South Africa, not dissimilar to the other's.

"I'm Piers Hawkins," the man remarked, sticking his hand out.

"Sandy Maclean. How do you do." They shook hands. Alexander knew of an absolute certainty that this was one of those meetings that was fated. All of a sudden he felt less of an exile abroad.

Piers poured his beer into his glass. He told Alexander that he had been visiting an elderly cousin who lived in Lupus Street. "Are you a regular here?" he asked Alexander.

Alexander laughed. "Far from it! Yesterday I was still in South Africa. I landed at Heathrow early this morning. I'm spending a few days at a hotel in Belgrave Road."

"You don't sound at all South African," Piers remarked. "I would have taken you for English."

"Well, I am British. I'm certainly not English though, not with names like mine. I have n't lived in Britain for more than eight years. I'm back now. I must find somewhere to live."

"Here in London?"

"I'm not sure. It might be nice to live somewhere in the country," Alexander replied. "I suppose you live in London, Piers?"

"Yes I do. I have a flat in Soho."

The two men chatted while they drank their beers, then Piers said "I must go now. I wonder – would you mind if I gave you my phone number?"

"I'd like that."

"Right!" Piers Hawkins reached inside his blazer and took out a small notebook, from which he tore a piece of paper. He took a pen from another inside pocket. He wrote on the piece of paper.

"Here's my mobile number. And my address."

"That's kind of you, Piers. I'll let you have my number as soon as I get hold of a cell phone."

"Look, I must be going now, Sandy. How about we meet again soon?"

"OK. Can it be during the daytime?"

"My late mornings are fairly flexible," Piers told Alexander.

"Then what about meeting somewhere for a drink one morning?"

"Thursday – eleven-thirty at the Queen's Head in Tryon Street? Do you know it?"

"No –"

"Tryon Street is off the Kings Road. The nearest Tube is Sloane Square. But what about your walking?"

"I can find it," Alexander said. "I can get a taxi from Sloane Square."

"Super. The Queen's Head is an old fashioned, low key gay pub. That's not a problem, Sandy?"

"No, that's not a problem."

"By the way – your crutches: do you have to use them all the time, or what?"

"I do right now. But I foresee a time in the near future when I'll be able to get by without them again."

"Were you in an accident?"

Alexander gave an abrupt laugh. "You could say that."

His new found friend stood, drained his glass, shook Alexander's hand, and saying "See you Thursday at eleven-thirty, then," he strode off in the direction of the River.

Alexander spent Wednesday re-acquainting himself with the West End, re-visiting some of his favourite places. He was limited by how far he could comfortably walk using a pair of crutches, but this was in fact a surprising distance. He was fit and strong now, and his resumption of drinking had not yet made any impact on his health. The weather was superb. It reminded him of his first summer in England in 1976. Alexander had a huge capacity for sitting at pavement tables outside pubs and coffee shops, watching the Human parade. He was a born *flâneur*.

Alexander was early for his rendezvous with Piers at the Queen's Head in Chelsea. He was always early for appointments. In this he differed radically from his brother, Roy, who was never on time for anything. Alexander smiled at the young barman and asked him please to bring his beer to one of the three or four small tables set up on the pavement. When Piers arrived, just a little late, he was wearing a cotton navy blue shirt with the sleeves rolled up over his brown forearms, a pair of brogues, fawn chinos, and a pair of shades. His hair looked very clean in the sun. Alexander too was wearing chinos, a pair of South African Cuthberts brogues to which he had applied so many gleaming coats of polish over time that they looked as if they were bespoke, a cream cotton shirt, and his cream linen jacket. He had his Panama hat with him again. Piers grinned at him, looking younger than his years. "Sandy! I hope I find you well?"

"Indeed you do. I'm enjoying the sun. Hullo Piers. How are you?"

"Not bad at all. I'll go get a drink. Would you like another?"

"I'm OK for now, thanks."

Piers re-appeared after some minutes, a glass and an opened bottle of lager in his hands. "Do tell me, what brings you to London?"

Alexander gave Piers a highly edited and much abbreviated account of the loss of his leg, and of his need for a prosthesis he could wear comfortably. He made it clear however that he had hopped hemispheres many times in the past. Alexander told Piers no lies, but he withheld a great deal of the truth. He did not, after all, yet know Piers very well.

"And you, are you a native Londoner, Piers?"

"No. My people live in Hertfordshire, near a small town called Berkhamsted."

"I knew Berkhamsted. I lived not far from Berkhamsted in the late eighties, up on the hill above Kings Langley. I had a happy time there."

"Who would credit it?" Piers exclaimed. "We'd never met before; you're from the far side of the world – and we're both familiar with that little corner of England. I would be indulging in a cliché if I said that it's a small world." He laughed.

During the next hour or so, each learned more about the other. Alexander learned, for example, that Piers worked at an advertising agency in the Kings Road, not at all far from the pub. Alexander had drunk two bottles of Pilsener by then. His new friend had matched his intake. A genuine *rapport* had developed between the two men.

If, as Piers had told Alexander, the Queen's Head was a gay pub, it barely registered on the gay radar. Alexander had gone inside to use the gents, and he saw no one who struck him as overtly camp. Other than the fact that of the dozen or so customers inside the pub, only two were women, Alexander would not have guessed the pub was a gay rendezvous. Any more than he would have guessed that Piers was gay. If that was what, indeed, he was. Alexander knew that in London it was sometimes not uncommon for straight men to drink at gay venues. Even in Johannesburg, he had sometimes bumped into a couple of self declared heterosexuals drinking at Connections in Hillbrow.

Piers and Alexander met twice more during the next six days. The weather remained idyllic. But Alexander's intake of spirits rose by the day, until he was keeping a bottle of whiskey in his hotel room to supplement his public drinking at pubs. Within just under a week of his landing at Heathrow, Alexander was drinking two thirds of a bottle of scotch a day – in addition to the several beers he drank when he was out and about. He took to keeping a tube of toothpaste in his pocket, with which he would periodically attempt to disguise the smell of spirits on his breath.

Despite the friendship that was developing between himself and Piers, Alexander was deeply unhappy. He had made no sustained efforts yet to find somewhere to live, and as his drinking increased, his will to do so grew less. The despair he had felt after his leg was amputated was as strong as ever. Wearing the false leg put him in mind of the story by

Hans Christian Andersen: the little mermaid who, in exchange for a pair of legs, felt always as if she was walking on knife-blades. Alexander knew that in France he did not need a firearms licence to buy a shotgun and ammunition. He did not think he wanted to live like this. He made up his mind to visit Paris.

Thirty

Cannes And Beyond

On Tuesday 3rd August Alexander checked out of the hotel and took a taxi to Waterloo, where he bought a ticket for Eurostar, the fast train that crosses beneath the Channel from London to Paris. The journey would take something over three hours. Having recently managed to cope with eleven hours in the air without a smoke, he did not have to struggle in going without a cigarette on this comparatively short journey. The last time Alexander had made the Channel crossing had been in October 1988, when he had been visiting his friend in Paris by car. Then he had crossed by ferry. This was the first time he had set off for Paris by train.

Technically, Alexander was never sober anymore, but a stranger would have been hard pressed to recognise the fact. Alexander himself was not good at recognising when he was approaching his capacious limit. One moment he would be functioning quite normally physically, and seemingly with his wits about him: the next, he was embarked upon some wild action – or simply comatose. During periods of extended heavy drinking, Alexander seemed possessed of an almost demonic energy; an inexplicable fund of stamina, for he ate very little, and that only infrequently.

But Alexander had in fact lost his mind. Caught firmly in the grip of an alcoholic manic depressive state, he intended ending his life while he was in Europe. To this end, the day after he arrived at the *Gare du Nord* in Paris (having spent the night at a hotel near the *Parc de Montholon*, a small park situated on *Rue Lafayette* about half way between the *Gare du Nord* and the Opera House, in which mature plane trees provided shade for the colourfully dressed Senegalese nannies as they tended their employers' infant children on the lawns, and gossiped together), he bought a twelve-gauge side-by-side shotgun and a box of boar shot ammunition from an *armurerie* in central Paris. He used his credit card. Perhaps, had he not, the purchase would not have been so easily transacted. He had read that he required no licence to buy a shotgun in France, but he was surprised that he was not even asked for proof of his identity, let alone for proof of domicile. The following morning, having sat in the park for much of the previous afternoon, and having ate a simple but well prepared supper in the small *brasserie* opposite the hotel, he arrived three quarters of an hour early for the TGV to Cannes, and he tipped the taxi-driver fifty francs (about five Pounds) to go find a porter for him.

Alexander drank throughout the long journey to the Mediterranean coastline. He was therefore only partially aware of the increasingly attractive scenery through which he traveled as the train sped south. He had no idea where he would stay in Cannes, but, as he had done upon arrival in Paris, he would ask the taxi driver to take him to a good four or five star hotel. At Cannes he requested a hotel "à la *promenade*." The taxi driver drove him to the Radisson Blu 1835 Hotel, at the start of the *Boulevard du Midi*, and adjacent to the *Vieux Port*, which was crammed with yachts and luxury cruisers. Alexander obtained a sea-front room with a balcony, and commenced to live as if he was a rich man. He was no longer concerned with running out of funds: he did not intend living long enough for this to be a problem.

This luxurious, modern hotel was situated on the *Golfe de la Napoule*, and from his balcony, Alexander could see a heavily wooded island offshore, about one and a half or two miles long; *l'Île Sainte Marguerite*. He could make out what appeared to be medieval fortifications on the island. Alexander ate dinner every night at the hotel's rooftop restaurant, and although drunk, he appreciated that the cuisine was excellent. He drank champagne, which he would order from the wine list in his bedroom, on his balcony in the afternoons, the sleeves of his shirt rolled up in the sun, his tie loosened, and he dozed on the large double bed, sleeping off his alcoholic stupors. Alexander rarely slept a full night anymore. He passed out on the bed for a few hours, most often in the afternoon, and slept a few more hours at night, waking in the early hours and sitting drinking, re-charging his alcohol levels. He continued to have distressing dreams, though far fewer than when he had been sober, and sometimes he dreamed that he was running, fleet of foot and light of body, with Patrick on the mountain slopes below Kirstenbosch, or climbing in the mountains: a whole person again, fit and strong.

Most mornings, wearing his false leg (which did not pain him as long as he had anesthetised himself with sufficient alcohol), and using only a walking stick as an aid, he would go gaze at the yachts and cruisers moored in the harbour, or walk in *le Suquet*, Cannes' original medieval quarter. This was a picturesque district, and Alexander gained much pleasure from the ancient architecture and the narrow, winding lanes and alleys. He sat at *cafés*, always outdoors and in the sun, and drank coffee from tiny cups, with a glass of water to chase the strong coffee down. Alexander, wearing his linen jacket (one of two jackets he had packed), and a white or pink or pale blue cotton shirt laundered and pressed by the hotel laundry, and a tie, together with well-pressed chinos and a pair of highly polished shoes on his feet, his head protected from the sun by a Panama, would gaze from behind his prescription sun glasses at the crowd, many of whose members projected an aura of wealth, good looks and ease which Alexander gave every impression of sharing. He had not lost his South African tan.

The warm days were filled with sunshine. The light, which possessed much the same quality of glowing intensity that the light in Cape Town held, gave the colours a liveliness that Alexander rarely saw in Britain. Alexander luxuriated in the warmth. Walking slowly, topping up his alcohol level frequently, he could manage to get about on the prosthesis which had been so painful when he had still been sober.

Alexander was far from feeling the complete emptiness of spirit and the despair which are preconditions of suicide. During rare moments of honesty with himself, he knew that he would not after all be blowing his head off. Yet he lacked the volition to end his idyll and return to Britain, and – while he still had some money left – make plans to find somewhere to settle. Alexander stayed on at the Radisson Blu 1835 for more than a week, before he screwed his will to the sticking point, and set off on Monday the 16th on his return journey to England.

He spent one more night in the hotel near the *Parc de Montholon*, and at the British Customs desk at the *Gare du Nord* the next morning, he handed over his shotgun and cartridges, providing his Aunt's Wiltshire address as his own residential address. He had three months to obtain a British shotgun licence and reclaim the weapon, but he thought it unlikely he would be doing so. Alexander arrived back in London in the early evening of Tuesday the 17th August 1999. He checked into the hotel in Belgrave Road once again. He had two thousand Pounds left. The following morning, as he was walking with the aid of his crutches to Pimlico Tube station, on his way to meet Piers, he collapsed on the pavement and passed out.

Roy arrived in London on Monday the 4th October. Alexander had remained at the Middlesex hospital in London for about five weeks. As soon as he was able, he had phoned Piers and asked him to fetch him his things from the hotel, along with the hotel's bill for his stay. Piers returned to the hotel a day or two later with a cheque Alexander had written for the hotel. Piers visited Alexander several times during his stay at the hospital. He kept him supplied with cigarettes and he cashed a cheque for Alexander for one hundred Pounds. Alexander wondered what it was that Piers saw in him. "Why do you do so much for me?" he asked during his second visit.

Piers' laugh was somewhat uncertain. "There's something... you have a certain quality about you." Then he laughed more naturally. "I think you're worth the investment, Sandy."

"Thanks. Anyway."

The hospital organised a visit from a social worker, who arranged for Alexander to register for unemployment benefit, and who ensured too that there was somewhere for him to go when the hospital discharged him.

Once he was over the inevitable nightmare of alcoholic withdrawals (this time the doctors had believed Alexander when he had told them about his valium habit, and they had prescribed him an ongoing supply of the drug), Alexander enjoyed his stay at the Middlesex. The ward sister had taken a liking to him. "You look just like a young Peter O'Toole," she told him.

The Middlesex was not a new hospital. Some of the buildings were at least one hundred years old, and Alexander grew to love the walled garden where he could sit and smoke in the sun. There was a very beautiful late nineteenth century chapel also, which was, Alexander thought, reminiscent of the interior of a jewel box: its walls were sheathed in gleaming polychromatic marbles, and its sanctuary and altar piece comprised intricate mosaic work which scintillated in the light from the polished brass-mounted lanterns. Alexander guessed the chapel had been decorated at about the same time as the splendid interior of the Catholic cathedral at Westminster, and probably by the same craftsmen. Alexander spent much time here in prayer, directing his devotions particularly to Our Lady, who brought him much comfort. He wrote almost twenty pages of what amounted to an apologia, outlining the sequence of events that had brought him to this pass. He described his stay at the hospital in some detail. He was thinking that he would edit this material some day, perhaps for his mother to read.

By the time Roy arrived in London in early October, Alexander had been staying at a residential hotel near Kings Cross and St. Pancras for about a week, the bill being picked up by the Camden local authority. He had not been unhappy here. He had a room of his own, which was situated along such a warren of narrow corridors and small flights of stairs going up and then down again, that he was happily isolated, he felt, from the other residents and their noises. His room overlooked an interior court. The hotel provided a proper breakfast. Alexander ate lunch at a pub nearby. He was of course no longer drinking alcohol. He felt a profound sense of deliverance at being sober, and at having landed up in a safe place, where he need make no decisions that he did not wish to have to make. Yet an underlying melancholy that had nothing to do with his recent past or his immediate circumstances shadowed Alexander's days. He was beginning to understand by now that one of the reasons he drank was because only alcohol seemed able to drive out this profound sadness. Sobriety was welcomed with relief, but along with sobriety there returned this underlying unhappiness which Alexander had known in varying degrees since his adolescence.

The hospital had made an appointment for him at the Royal National Orthopaedic Hospital at Stanmore. A taxi had been sent for him within a couple of days of his moving to the residential hotel near Kings Cross, and he had spent a morning having a cast made and measurements taken for a new prosthesis to be built for him.

Landing at Heathrow, Roy hired a car and bravely drove into London, where he managed to locate the residential hotel near Kings Cross where Alexander was staying. This was for Roy, who had no sense of direction at all, an admirable achievement. The two brothers shook hands, then, moved by an access of affection, Alexander embraced his brother, a gesture Roy then returned. "I am so glad to see you, Roy."

"I'm glad I managed to find you."

"You did very well!"

Alexander checked out of the residential hotel immediately, and the two set off in the hired car for the Thames Valley, for they had decided to look for somewhere to live near – but not in – Maidenhead, Reading or Slough, where jobs in engineering were (they hoped) likely to be found. Heading out of London up the A40, the two brothers had lunch at Gerrards Cross, having already decided – from their viewing of properties to rent in estate agents' windows in the High Street – that they could not afford the rents being demanded here. So they proceeded further along the A40, driving past urban ribbon development which alternated with tracts of rural country. What they could see of it was pretty countryside, well-wooded, with fields and pastures bounded by old-established hedgerows. Alexander and his brother repeated their examination of estate agents' windows at Beaconsfield. "I think we're still out of our league, Roy," Alexander remarked, frowning at the rental prices.

"What's the next town called?"

"High Wycombe."

"OK. Let's head there."

It was after four o' clock when they reached High Wycombe, which appeared suddenly amidst countryside which was beginning to consist of gently rolling hills, the foothills of the Chilterns, a range of high hills and chalk ridges which ran in a line from the south-west to the north-east, to the west of London, marching through three counties: Berkshire, Buckinghamshire and Hertfordshire. Sheep grazed in wide pasture land, and there were broad empty fields in which the bare soil looked dark and rich. Of course, Alexander thought, the wheat would long since have been harvested. They took a chance (for they could find no suitable parking) and parked the hire car in a loading zone behind the Octagon shopping centre, for they needed somewhere to spend the night, and Alexander had spotted a tourist information office adjacent to the shopping centre. After some searching, with the help of the woman behind the counter, they two decided on a bed and breakfast in Marlow Bottom, near Marlow, a town that Alexander was to visit many times over the coming years, for it was located on the Thames, and water – rivers, streams, lakes, the sea – always drew him. After buying a coffee each in a café on the first floor of the Octagon centre, looking down on the main shopping thoroughfare below, they walked along the High Street, but soon realised that the estate agencies must be located in some other part of the town. "We'll return tomorrow, and have a proper look," Alexander said. Alexander, sober, could not endure wearing his prosthesis. He had his left trouser leg rolled up to not far below the knee, and he was swinging along one-legged between a pair of aluminium crutches.

With Alexander navigating with the aid of a map provided by the tourist information centre, Roy drove up the steep A404 out of High Wycombe, crossing over the M40 motorway at the crest of the hill, then continuing along the A404 dual carriageway which descended a long, shallow hill through farmland, all the way to the Marlow off-ramp. No sooner were they heading into Marlow than they had to turn right for Marlow Bottom, which was almost entirely surrounded by farmland. The evening was beginning to draw in. Alexander especially was weary, for getting about one-legged on crutches was tiring. Both men were glad to check in at the bed and breakfast. "Let me rest for half an hour, Roy, then we'll head for a pub and supper."

Roy as usual was restless, and found it difficult to stay still, but Alexander fell back in a comfortable armchair and closed his eyes. "Don't let me fall asleep, Roy."

"I wont."

Thirty-One

Life Unravels

The High Wycombe flat that Alexander and Roy signed the standard six months' lease for (six months was all the security of tenure that private tenants usually had in Britain) was located on Priory Road, just beyond the archway carrying the Chiltern Railways track. The town centre was a mere two hundred yards from the converted red brick Edwardian house. Opposite the house was a primary school, and the shrill shrieks from the children at play during break time combined to create a crescendo of sound. The two brothers' furnished flat, on the far side of the house, was however very quiet. It looked across a neighbouring garden, and the property's own rather wild back garden, and consisted of a bedroom (which Alexander took), a long narrow sitting room and dining area (in which Roy slept), a fairly large and well appointed kitchen, a bathroom, and a laundry room doubling as a storage room. The flat was on the first floor, and Alexander had by now become so skilled with his single leg and pair of crutches, that he could get up and down the stairs un-aided.

They had to make the best of it in the flat for three or four days, having left the bed and breakfast in Marlow Bottom on Friday morning the 8th October, before Pickfords delivered their few items of furniture (which included Alexander's desk, Roy's extra-long bed, and a large bookcase) and their boxes of household effects, amongst which were several boxes of books. Both brothers experienced great pleasure in the arrival of these familiar items – they were a breath of home – and they had much fun in arranging them in the flat. However, Roy quickly learned that finding an engineering job nearby (he was searching primarily in and around Maidenhead, Reading and Slough) was proving to be far more difficult than either of them had anticipated. October slipped into a grey, wet November, and the temperature fell, and Roy in particular (for he had never lived in Britain before) yearned for South Africa's benign, sunny climate. He felt terribly homesick, and he fretted far more than Alexander over their mother, left behind alone in Johannesburg.

Their Christmas was a sad affair, just the two of them, though they phoned their mother on Christmas day and tried to put a positive spin on things. "Mum, we'll be together again, you must believe that," Alexander told her over the phone.

Then the cold, drear, dark month of January was upon them. As indeed was the year 2000. The century had turned. It snowed, which Alexander found pleasing (he enjoyed the clean purity and beauty of a snowscape), but his brother did not. Roy's optimism was fading. His mood was turning sour. He was beset by regret at having left South Africa for this cold, unfriendly land, and by concern for their mother. Alexander found his growing negativity difficult to live with, and the two brothers began to bicker and quarrel more and more frequently.

Alexander too was overtaken by misery, but he was already far better equipped than his brother at dealing with unhappiness, having experienced more of it in recent years, and he persisted with his own job searching. However, neither he nor Roy was able to gain even a single job interview, and both of them were beginning to despair of finding employment. Alexander remembered something he had said when his manager from work had visited him in hospital one evening after his leg had been amputated: "I will never work again."

There was one piece of good news for Alexander that month. The Royal National Orthopaedic Hospital at Stanmore in London sent a car for him. It seemed that his prosthesis had been ready since late November, but the hospital had lost track of him. It was only when, in mid January, Alexander had thought to phone the hospital, that he had learned his prosthesis was ready. He spent the whole day away, and he was thrilled with the false leg. The fit was excellent, and best of all, it was almost entirely pain-free, though if Alexander wore the prosthesis for a long time, the toes of his non-existent left foot began to feel painfully pinched, as if he was wearing a tight shoe a size too small on his ghost foot. But Alexander could walk with little pain with just the aid of a walking stick. He had become mobile again, almost exactly a year after his leg had been amputated. Why then did he begin drinking again round this time?

Alexander was articulate and insightful, but when he tried to understand why he was so desperately unhappy, he was struck dumb. He knew only that he was indeed terribly unhappy. He had come close to knowing happiness for a time, but the happiness had soon enough turned to dust and been blown away on the wind. It would be too easy to blame his misery on the loss of his leg. At night, as he slept, Alexander was still sometimes racked by the nightmares of violence and danger he had suffered from for some time now. But the nightmares were offset by his dreaming of times when he was running joyfully, as light-footed and fleet as a deer. In these dreams, he was not crippled. But there was a deeper cause for Alexander's unhappiness than simply the loss of his leg.

When Alexander's eyes happened to fall upon a boy of superlative beauty and grace in town, he felt a complex mix of emotions. There was an access of bright joy, to be sure, but there was also an awareness of acute distress, and at such moments, Alexander could hardly bear living. But he could not yet articulate what he was experiencing at such times. Nor did he understand that his excessive drinking furnished him with the means to live comfortably inside a mind and body some of whose yearnings and longings filled him with shame, self loathing and despair. Roy allowed his own misery, which was compounded of homesickness and frustration at his lack of employment, to express itself more honestly. Alexander found it difficult coping with Roy's unhappiness. Their enforced proximity began to irritate him.

Alexander understood that he was lonely. Piers had phoned him a couple of times towards the end of 1999, but Alexander had n't heard from him since then, and with no good news to impart, and feeling shamed by failure, he had not tried phoning Piers in turn.

As long as Alexander remained more than just mildly intoxicated – which meant that he must constantly top up his alcohol level through the course of the day – his misery was banked down. By the time he was drinking almost a bottle of Scotch a day, Alexander was no longer thinking about the future at all, beyond the unexpressed but sometimes dimly perceived hope that he might succeed in rapidly drinking himself to death.

During the first week of his return to drinking, a total of just two bottles of Scotch for the entire week was sufficient for Alexander to overcome his unhappiness, but thereafter his intake rose rapidly, and within less than a fortnight he was buying a bottle of Scotch every two days. By mid February, Alexander was buying a bottle of Scotch almost every day. He drank in his bedroom, and it was impossible to disguise this fact, for Roy was well versed in recognising the symptoms. Even had he not been, Alexander stank of liquor. Alexander's desperate drinking added to Roy's unhappiness and the brothers' quarrelling became more frequent, and harsh words began to be exchanged between them. In early March, Roy told Alexander that he was going to return to South Africa, for he had found a well-paying engineering job in the Transvaal online. Within just a few days, abandoning most of the things he had brought across from South Africa into Alexander's keeping, Roy had left Alexander alone in High Wycombe.

There was now only just over a month left for the flat's six month lease to run, and as his drinking took him over, Alexander abandoned any pretence of planning for the future. He knew that he could not manage to organise his finances, not as drunk as he always was now, and he was almost certain that with Roy, who was a co-signatory on the lease, gone, he would not have the lease rolled over in early April. On the 7th March, only days after Roy had flown out of Heathrow, Alexander's notice to vacate the flat by the morning of the 9th April, arrived in the post.

Alexander felt utterly defeated by his circumstances. He made his way every night from one town centre pub to the next, drinking prodigious volumes, yet remaining upright, while appearing to be far from heavily intoxicated. He sought out company, relying on his well-bred, educated accent to sustain the image of eccentric toff somewhat down on his luck, rather than one-legged town drunk, and up to a point, his strategy worked. Alexander made several passing acquaintances, some of whom he took back to the flat with him after a long evening's drinking at one of the town's pubs, and at the flat Alexander regaled these casual acquaintances with more liquor, along with stories so tall it was hard to believe that many of them were essentially true, and he played Pink Floyd or the Doors very loudly and very late at night on the tape and CD player that Roy had left behind.

Alexander did not attempt to engage in physical intimacies with any of the generally young men he managed to get to return to the flat with him. Loneliness, not lust, was his primary motivation in seeking out their company. It appeared that in March 1996, living in Yeoville in Johannesburg, he had truly lost his taste for casual homosexual encounters. In addition, his instinct for self-preservation (in what was then still very much a provincial market town with provincial mores, although High Wycombe was situated only thirty miles or so from London), was not completely disabled.

When some time during the morning that would follow Alexander regained consciousness, he was always alone, and he could remember almost nothing from the night before. However, he suspected he would have told many exaggerations, and made many false claims, and he feared being found out or called out for words he could no longer remember. Until he had managed to overcome his terrors once again, as the alcohol he consumed as rapidly as possible during the day took effect, he lived in fear. He was terrified of the possibility of violence in town – or worse:

of violence in the flat, not being sure how many, and what sort of people knew that he lived there, alone and crippled.

Alexander never found out who had alerted the social services – perhaps one of his neighbours; perhaps one of these night-time visitors – but one day a woman social worker, accompanied by a Policeman, knocked on his door. Alexander by now was in a dreadful way. The flat was a tip, for he had given up trying to keep it clean. There were the remains of half-eaten meals in the sitting room, and empty whiskey bottles littered the carpet. Alexander had not shaved for four or five days. He thought he had probably peed in his trousers, and he stank of sweat and drink.

"Alexander, I'm from social services, and I'm here to help you," the youngish woman said.

Alexander felt overwhelmed by intense relief. His eyes filled with tears, and he replied. "I need help. Please help me."

The woman looked at the Policeman and waved a hand at him. The young officer stepped outside. "May I help you pack some things for a stay at a clinic? We could leave immediately."

"Yes," Alexander replied. "Yes. I'ld like that."

Thirty-Two

A Frequent Flyer

The private clinic was a luxurious retreat in Harrow on the Hill, in west London, set in its own large garden near the élite Harrow school, and Alexander wondered how the National Health Service could afford to send him (and the other very ordinary, generally very poor patients with whom he shared a large wing of the establishment), to such a select institution. He knew he was very fortunate, and he determined to get his act cleaned up fast.

"From what social services tells us, Alexander, it appears you have been suffering the occasional psychotic episode," the psychiatrist told him, after he had spent the night mildly medicated in a stark, bare room with just a single bed, a lavatory, a basin, and a large mirror on one wall – which Alexander correctly surmised was a one-way viewing window.

"Once I'm sober, Doctor, you'll find a rational, sane, stable man underneath the mess I'm in right now," Alexander replied. "The difference will amaze you. It's getting sober that's the thing: I could no longer manage that alone, not without help."

After less than one and a half weeks, a new, neatly turned out, very presentable Alexander, his red-blonde hair shining, his skin clear, his eyes sparkling, his manner quiet, rational and restrained, was granted permission (alone among the patients in the lockdown National Health wing, all of whom were suffering from one or another psychotic condition) to eat in the luxurious dining room that served the fee-paying private patients, and to venture unaccompanied into the grounds. It was mid April. The first swallows were returning from Africa, the sun shone, the trees were clothed in vivid, fresh new foliage, and the lawns were bordered by beds of yellow and red tulips. Beneath the trees grew bluebells, wood anemones, hyacinths and primroses. Alexander's spirit absorbed the garden's tranquility thirstily, and he spent several hours every day seated on a bench in the sunshine, with a novel from the clinic's library lying unopened alongside him. He also wrote a very long, loving and remorseful letter to his mother, and another shorter, apologetic one to his brother, which he placed inside his mother's letter, and posted them.

Alexander, whom most of the other National Health patients liked for his quiet manner, which they found reassuring, became even better liked among the other patients, for after two weeks at the clinic he was given permission to leave the grounds unaccompanied, and every morning he would take orders for cigarettes, crisps, sweets, and the occasional newspaper or magazine, and note the sums of money each of his fellows had given him, against their orders. Then he would set off up the High Street with his walking stick, a large gym bag slung from one shoulder, headed for the corner shop which was a few hundred yards down the street.

Alexander had become thoroughly and happily institutionalised when, in mid May, he was discharged. "I must confess I am amazed at how well you are, Alexander," the psychiatrist told him.

"I remember telling you that if the alcohol was removed, you would find a sane man underneath," Alexander replied.

"It seems you were correct."

The social services in High Wycombe had packed up and removed his possessions from the flat, including (they told Alexander) the sound system, the TV, his desk, the paintings that he and Roy had hung on the walls and the books and the bookcase, and were now storing them. The same social worker who had first visited him at the flat had packed Alexander's clothing into two of his large suitcases, and she brought them to him at the clinic. She told him that social services would store the rest of his possessions until they had found him a permanent home in the Wycombe district. She also brought him some additional toiletries.

A National Health Service minibus transferred Alexander to Oxford. He spent the next seven weeks living in solitude in a house set one street back from the Cowley Road. The rent for his room was paid by Wycombe District Council, although Oxford was a long way outside the District Council's authority. There was at the time no one else staying in the house; Alexander was entirely alone. He was glad of his solitude, glad of the peace it brought him. There was a kitchen, in which he boiled eggs and made toast for his breakfast and boiled the kettle for instant coffee, but he ate his main meal of the day at the City Arms pub nearby, where he drank Coca-Cola or coffee with his meal. The weather continued fine. Indeed, it was a warm May. Alexander often went out wearing a pair of bush shorts, his sandals, and a bush shirt, eager to get a tan again if he could. He did not allow his false leg to make him feel self conscious.

The house next door was occupied by a Pakistani family. The little boy asked across the low fence one Saturday morning "What happened to your leg?"

"I had an accident."

"Where are you from?"

"I'm from Africa."

"Have you seen a lion?"

"Oh yes, I saw a whole pride of lions when I was out walking one day."

"Gosh! Did one of them eat your leg?"

Alexander laughed. "No! The lions weren't hungry, and it was midday. They were feeling too sleepy to eat me."

Thereafter, on a Saturday or Sunday morning, when the little boy was not at school but playing in his front garden, he would always greet Alexander when he left the house.

Alexander could still enjoy walking. He could walk a fair distance, perhaps half a mile, with his new prosthesis before it became uncomfortable. But he caught a bus into Oxford (which was n't far at all; he would have walked the distance easily before his amputation), and got off at Magdalen Bridge, then he strolled around the Botanic Gardens, or sat by the banks of the River Cherwell and read a newspaper. Sometimes he walked down Rose Lane and then down the path that ran along the edge of Christ Church Meadow where he followed the course of the River Cherwell. The horse chestnuts were in magnificent bloom, their pink and white blossoms like fanciful candles, and Alexander often walked as far as the Cherwell's confluence with the Thames (which of course was called the Isis in Oxford), where he sat on a bench and watched the cruisers and narrow boats going by. There were youngsters out on the Cherwell along the way, some of them foreign visitors, punting or rowing. Alexander visited the boathouse below Magdalen Bridge one morning and hired a fast rowing skiff. He was a good rower, having learned to row on Zoo Lake in Johannesburg. Being on the water delighted him. He smiled happily at the swans, mallards and coots, many of them with their cute, fluffy young, and once or twice he saw a water vole. He would row as far as the Isis, then turn around and make his way back upstream to Magdalen Bridge. He could row this distance comfortably in an hour, and the hire of the boat for an hour, though fairly costly, was not prohibitively so. Alexander enjoyed the sunshine; he enjoyed watching the attractive, long-legged young people out on the river, and he relished the exercise that rowing gave him, which he could pursue without regard for his false leg. Because he had eaten well for four weeks at the clinic in Harrow on the Hill, he was fit and strong.

One day a late middle aged man asked "Do you mind if I sit here for a while?" and joined Alexander on the bench by the water's edge. The two began chatting after a while. It transpired that the man ran an agency recruiting language teachers for the Far East.

"That could interest me," Alexander said.

"I imagine you have at least an undergraduate degree, yes?"

"I do."

"I'm not sure about your false leg, though. They're funny about physical issues of that nature in the Far East."

"Perhaps now would n't have been the best time . . ." Alexander remarked. But he was to recall that conversation before long.

After a month of this pleasant but aimless life in Oxford, the boredom was making Alexander restless. He had not heard from Wycombe District Council. He had no idea how long this arrangement might continue. He presumed it would last until the Council found him somewhere permanent to live. But when might that be? Alexander wished he could see his mother. He wished he could find a job in South Africa that would pay him a living. Failing that, he wished to talk to his mother and brother about buying a flat or a cottage within the Wycombe district; somewhere registered in his mother's name, but where he could make a permanent home for himself. On Monday morning the 26th June, after brooding about it through the course of the weekend, Alexander found a travel agent in the Clarendon shopping centre in central Oxford. They confirmed that his return air ticket to Johannesburg was still valid.

Alexander should have phoned his mother, and told her he was planning to fly back to Johannesburg. He should have phoned social services, and made a plan for the ongoing storage of his goods. He should above all have ditched completely the idea of returning to South Africa. But he did none of these things. In years to come, during true recovery, he would realise that mere sobriety alone does not of itself rid the alcoholic entirely of the alcoholic's often crazed mindset. For now, he possessed boundless energy, both mental and physical energy; and this energy would not accept the restraints of reason or caution. Instead, Alexander was within three weeks to find himself living and working in the Republic of China, better known as Taiwan.

In the late morning of Friday the 30th June, Alexander took a taxi to the coach station in Oxford. He had with him his pair of aluminium crutches, two large suitcases, a gym bag and a small shoulder bag. He flew from Heathrow that evening, flying through the night, arriving at Jan Smuts airport in Johannesburg early on Saturday morning the 1st July 2000. He had been away just over eleven months. It was winter in South Africa, and the landscape was brown and drear and dry, but even so, Alexander felt a joyful lifting of his spirits at being back in Africa. He rang his mother from the airport, and told her he would be arriving at her home within the next couple of hours. "I must just try to find a taxi I think I can trust not to hijack me."

"Oh, Sandy. You never fail to surprise me," his mother said.

Alexander's mother lived in a walled and gated community with a security guard always stationed at the gate. The Northgate shopping centre was not far away. Roy, who was living and working at Sekunda, a small Highveld town a couple of hours' drive from Johannesburg, happened to be staying at their mother's home that weekend. After a slight hesitation, the two brothers embraced. "I really want to stay," Alexander told Roy. "I miss South Africa so much."

"I can understand that."

Sooty, the tiny black cat Alexander had obtained for his mother from a friend from his Hillbrow days after the old Siamese, Lulu, had died, had herself died of pancreatic cancer not long before Alexander had left for England, but a new cat had turned up very soon after and moved in, in the way that cats do. Alexander's brother had named him Tyson, but his nature was in fact amiable and affectionate. Alexander had not realised how much he had missed having a cat to love, and he made much of Tyson, a big gray neutered tom with white socks and a white bib. Alexander sat on the verandah in the Highveld winter sun during the day, with Tyson nearby, and he checked the situations vacant columns in the big circulation Johannesburg daily, the *Star*, every afternoon, and in the *Sunday Times* at the weekend. It very soon became clear to Alexander that the possibility of finding a decent job in South Africa, at his age (he was forty-five years old now) was slim, unless he returned to field guiding – and with only one leg, he felt ill-equipped to do so. He was also rather scared that he would run into someone who knew how he had blotted his copy book in Namibia. The industry was comparatively small and rather incestuous. Then Alexander saw a small advertisement for a business English teacher in Taiwan. He knew immediately that he could get this job if he applied. Working in Taiwan would, he felt, be a happier option than unemployment in post-Thatcherite Britain. And it would be an adventure.

The man who interviewed him was an English immigrant who introduced himself as Gavin. He lived on a smallholding not very far from Roy's old house in Honeydew. He acted as a recruiter of English language teachers for Taiwan and other Far Eastern countries. Within minutes there were no doubts in either man's mind but that Alexander would be right for the job, particularly when Alexander told Gavin about his experience as a business English language teacher in Malta. "Will my false leg be a problem?" Alexander asked.

"I don't think so."

Alexander agreed to a year's contract in Kaohsiung, Taiwan's second city, a port city of more than two million people on the island's southern tip. He would be provided with a flat and paid the equivalent of two thousand five hundred Rands a month locally in Taiwan Dollars, Gavin told him he would buy Alexander an open-ended return air ticket, valid for a year, with Singapore Airlines, from Johannesburg to Kaohsiung via Changi airport in Singapore.

Later that afternoon, back at his mother's home, Alexander rifled through various documents in his bag. He found a phone number for the social services in High Wycombe. He could remember the social worker's name. Astonishingly, she was in the office, and he was able to talk to her. "Gillian, I'm phoning from Johannesburg. There's a family crisis. I'm going to have to stay here for quite a while. But I'm worried about my stuff you're storing for me. What will become of it until I can return?"

"How long will you be away?"

"I don't know."

"I expect social services can store it for you for a while. But if you're not back within three months, we'll have to levy quite a steep charge. I need your contact address while you're abroad, too."

Alexander gave the woman his mother's address, though he wished he had not had to do so. But he could see no real harm in it. He thanked her for her help, and said he would stay in touch. "Goodbye for now, Gillian."

Roy had taken Wednesday the 19th July, and the next two days, off work, and he was staying with their mother. He drove Alexander and their mother to the airport on the morning of Thursday the 20th July. Alexander had said goodbye to his mother so many times before, and flown so very far from home so often before, that this was just another such goodbye. He had hugged Tyson the cat before leaving. Alexander did not enjoy the flight. Sixteen hours trapped in an aluminium cigar tube, and forbidden to smoke, left his mind increasingly agitated and his nerves jumpy. At Changi airport – the biggest airport terminal Alexander had ever seen – he managed after a considerable search to find a glass enclosed smokers' pod, where he joined an entirely ethnic Chinese and entirely male throng, some of whom were smoking so much so fast that they had turned a curious green in the face. Then, after two cigarettes in succession (oh, the bliss of those first drags, the sublime joy of the hit, the sweet soothing of his jangled nerves), Alexander found his connecting flight for Kaohsiung. He had been traveling now for eighteen and a half hours – not counting the three hours he had spent in the Johannesburg airport terminal before departure – by the time the plane began its descent for Kaohsiung. There was a lot of turbulence; the aircraft bounced and juddered as it descended, and Alexander thought "I don't like this . . ." then suddenly the aircraft banked hard and began to turn sharply, and the noise of the jet engines rose to an angry scream as they began to climb steeply. Kaohsiung was being touched by the fringes of a typhoon, and the runway had become blocked by an aircraft that had crashed in attempting a landing just minutes earlier.

	Alexander spent the night, courtesy of Singapore Airlines, in a very luxuriously appointed hotel in Taipei, Taiwan's capital city, located at the other end of the island, a stay which included a good dinner in one of the hotel's restaurants that evening. Alexander had gone for a walk in the city that late afternoon, and he was impressed at the evidence of a thriving economy and a well-ordered society. After a very early breakfast the next morning, a Saturday, an airport shuttle bus took him and some others to the airport, and he landed at Kaohsiung airport at about nine in the morning, considerably more alert and rested than would have been the case had he arrived at Kaohsiung the day before. A small Chinese man, who introduced himself as Steve Huang (Alexander knew that most Chinese had a European name which they used when they wished to interact with westerners), and who was the owner of the language school Alexander would be working at, arrived at the airport an hour later, after Alexander (who of course spoke no Mandarin, and could read no Chinese ideograms) managed to find someone who would phone him. "I not know when you come," Steve told him. "Airport closed yesterday."

"I'm very glad to see you now, Steve. Thanks for meeting me."

"We go my office now. I take you to flat later. OK?"

"That sounds fine."

Alexander's first impression of Kaohsiung, from the front passenger seat of the Mercedes car Steve was driving, was of an entirely modern city, a highrise city sweltering in humid tropical heat, with an extraordinary amount of traffic on the roads, traffic which included a high proportion of scooters buzzing in and out of the traffic lanes. Nobody wore jackets, nor long sleeved shirts. After some time, they entered a district lined with two, three and four story buildings, pulling up outside one of these. The district appeared to comprise small retail operations, tiny factories and nondescript offices and apartment blocks.

At the back of Steve's office a spirit stove stood on a small table, on which green tea was being perpetually brewed. Alexander was given some tea in a small round cup without a handle. Never much of a tea drinker, he thought it tasted mostly of pulped blotting paper, but he sipped at it because it was hot and wet. Steve's English was very poor, but Alexander had always possessed a flair for understanding, and being understood by, foreigners whose languages he did not speak, and the two men were able to communicate at a very basic level. Alexander showed Steve the contract he had signed with Gavin in Johannesburg, and he took care to communicate that it was for a year's duration; that he was to be paid locally the equivalent of two thousand five hundred Rands monthly, and that a flat was to be provided. Steve agreed that these terms were all in order. "Where will I be teaching?" Alexander asked.

"Ah – here upstairs; some other places – you see. Why you use this?"

Steve pointed at Alexander's walking stick.

Alexander pulled up his left trouser leg. "An accident," he remarked. He could not read Steve's features as the little man stared at the short length of metal alloy shaft that was revealed beneath the turnup of Alexander's trouser leg.

Steve looked up from Alexander's prosthesis. "We go flat now, OK?"

Back in the car, they re-entered the highrise district. They stopped outside a block of flats of about ten stories in height, amidst many other tall blocks of flats, and Steve grabbed both Alexander's large, heavy suitcases. Alexander trailing behind him, with his gym bag and shoulder bag over his shoulders, and his pair of crutches under one arm, they entered a shabby, rather dingy and ill-lit lobby only a couple of steps up from street level, and ascended the lift to the unlucky fourth floor. In China the number four is considered an unlucky number, being nearly homophonous to the word "death," (*si*). In many apartment blocks, the floor numbering passes straight from the third floor to the fifth floor. Here, as they passed down a corridor on the fourth floor, Alexander saw through a number of open doors that the apartments were being used not to live in, but as box rooms and store-rooms.

The flat comprised a large furnished living room, with a kitchenette, in which a kettle was evident, and which also contained some basic crockery along with some cooking implements. There was a bedroom, with a bed made up, and a properly appointed western bathroom with a lavatory with a ceramic bowl and a tip-up plastic seat. The floor throughout the flat was of large white tiles. There were air-conditioning units in the windows of both rooms. A TV set stood against one wall in the living area. "You like?" Steve asked.

"It's very nice."

"I come back Monday morning, at eight o' clock, pick you up." Steve pressed a wad of Taiwan dollars into Alexander's hand. "This from your salary. You rest now."

"I'll see you on Monday morning, then, Steve. Goodbye."

It was coming up for two o' clock. What Alexander really wanted more than anything, was a coffee, but he had noticed not one coffee shop as they had driven through the city. He counted the Taiwan dollars: there seemed a great many of them. He locked the flat behind him, wearing the same cotton shirt (but having removed his tie) and the light linen jacket he had traveled in, and descended to street level in the lift. "This is an adventure," he thought to himself.

The heat and humidity struck Alexander as if he had walked into a sauna. It was worse than Durban in the summer. He was the only man on the street wearing a jacket. Alexander walked down the main street fronting the block of flats, because he could see a 7-Eleven supermarket not far away. Inside the shop he found a jar of instant coffee and a bag of sugar, and at the check-out counter he greeted the man at the till "*Wei ni hao.*"

"*Ni hao.*" The man then continued speaking in Mandarin. Alexander thought his pronunciation must have been fairly good, but he understood not a word the man was saying.

"How much?" Alexander asked.

"Thirty dollar."

Alexander counted out the unfamiliar notes.

After Alexander had left the supermarket, he turned down a narrow side street, and then down another, and found himself in a world somewhat removed from that of the main thoroughfare he had first set out on. The narrow street was lined with tiny retail outlets and very small restaurants, places with just two, three or sometimes four little tables, where customers were hunched over their bowls and shoveling noodles and rice with vegetables into their mouths. Alexander, who was hungry, not having eaten since breakfast in Taipei, went inside one of these. Large numbered photographs of the dishes were mounted above the counter, and when the short-tempered woman behind the counter at last acknowledged him, Alexander pointed at a bowl of noodles with what looked like slivers of beef in it, and at a can of iced coffee behind the glass-fronted counter. (Iced coffee! You live and you learn, he thought). The woman turned to the kitchen behind her, where a man was frying food at a range (Alexander could feel the heat from where he stood), and yelled. Alexander held up a bank note. The woman pointed to the end of the counter, shouting to a girl who sat at a cash till. Alexander paid the girl, once she had managed to communicate, using her fingers, how much he owed her, and she gave him a token numbered with an Arabic numeral. The miniature restaurant was busy with customers, most of whom stood at a counter alongside one wall to eat.

There was some confusion and much shouting when Alexander's number was called, for the Mandarin meant nothing to him, but it was sorted out, and he took his bowl of beef noodles and his can of iced coffee to one of the small tables, where just one other customer sat eating. He greeted the man, "*Ni hao*," pointed at the chair and raised his eyebrows. The man nodded, then returned to his meal. Alexander ate his meal using chopsticks, watching the street life. He was familiar with chopsticks. He used them the way the Chinese used them: to shovel with, the bowl of food brought as close to the mouth as possible. The narrow street was very busy with pedestrians and scooters. The people yelled at each other. Although it sounded as if they were all quarrelling with each other, Alexander doubted this was so. The humidity bore down on him. He quickly removed his jacket and hung it behind him on the back of the chair, first transferring his wallet to his trouser pocket.

After the meal, Alexander set off to explore these back streets, which reminded him of a grittier, rougher, far less sanitised and prettified version of Soho's Chinatown in London. He felt as if he had been transported to some completely alien, off-world society. He lacked any cultural or linguistic reference points, anything he could grasp and find familiar. He had only as much command of the language as he was trying to teach himself from his "How to Speak Mandarin" booklet, and what his quick ear for languages gave him, as he listened to the people around him talking, whilst he lacked even the least comprehension of the ideographic script. Yet he felt for now no particular distress (though he wondered whether exposure for long to the heat and humidity and the constant noise and the crush of humanity might not trigger the worst of his experience of post traumatic stress disorder). Eventually he found his way back to the main thoroughfare his block of flats fronted on.

"I'm going to have to get a tourists' guide to Kaohsiung," he thought, looking down the wide road which seemed to be lined with highrises as far as the eye could see. "There must be more to Kaohsiung than highrises and spatchcocked glazed ducks hanging up in windows."

Alexander felt tired: the cumulative effects of the vast difference in time zones; of the traveling; of the alien impact of the whole experience, were getting to him. He made his way back to his air-conditioned flat through the sweltering afternoon air, put his jar of instant coffee and his bag of sugar on the kitchen counter, and removing his shoes and unbuttoning his shirt, he lay down on top of the bed cover. Before long he was asleep.

When Alexander awoke, the night had fallen. For a minute or two he was extremely disorientated, but his sense of place and time returned in an instant of sudden awareness. It was not much darker: neon lights and street lighting shone bright through the wide bedroom windows with their un-drawn curtains. The street below sounded just as busy as it had been earlier that afternoon. He made some coffee and played with the TV remote while he drank the coffee: he found only Chinese language channels. He felt hungry, so he put on his shoes and grabbed his jacket and went downstairs, headed for one of the tiny eateries he had found in the street behind the apartment block.

Alexander had touched no alcohol for three months.

Thirty-Three

Johnny Chen

The next morning, a Sunday, Alexander realized he had nothing to eat in the flat. Perhaps weariness and the otherworldliness of his surroundings had affected him more than he had realised the day before. He should have stocked up on basic groceries at the 7-Eleven yesterday afternoon. He drank a coffee, smoked a cigarette, then shaved and dressed, and went downstairs without his jacket, his shirt sleeves rolled up to the elbows, his wallet stuffed in one of the back pockets of his trousers. Alexander feared pick-pockets, and he made sure to button the pocket closed. At the 7-Eleven supermarket he bought basic dry foodstuffs and canned goods, along with half a dozen eggs and some powdered milk, and he bought a can opener also. It would be a while before he needed to buy cigarettes, for he had bought two cartons of Peter Stuyvesant duty frees at Jan Smuts airport. He found a map of Kaohsiung which he added to his purchases. He managed to convey to the shop assistant that he wished to be shown on the map where they were currently located. The man pointed with his pen at a spot on Wufu 2nd Road in the Xinxing district. Steve had given Alexander a card with the address of his flat written on it in Chinese script. Alexander showed it to the man, and asked him to indicate this address on the map. The shop assistant did so: as expected, it was not at all far from the point he had indicated for the 7-Eleven. Alexander made sure he made a mental note of the location on the map.

Back at the flat Alexander ate two boiled eggs and some cereal with milk made up from the milk powder. Peering at the map he found the street corner his block of flats was situated on, in relation to the location of the 7-Eleven the man at the supermarket had pointed out on the map. Alexander began to feel a little less disorientated. At least he now knew what direction his flat faced – west for his bedroom, north for the lounge – and where it was in relation to other features of the city. About a third of a mile down Wufu 2nd Road, on the right hand side of the road, was a large park; Central Park. Less than half a mile further on was located the Holy Rosary Cathedral, and the mouth of the Heart of Love River, as it disgorged into Kaohsiung harbour. About two miles to the north – a distance Alexander thought he could walk, even with his false leg, though the extreme heat and humidity might slow him – was the Heart of Love River park, which he read in a small block of bad English on the back of the map contained attractive walkways and paths, and in which were located cafés and restaurants. He decided to head there after another coffee.

With the card on which his address was written safe in his wallet, Alexander felt happier about exploring on his own. He knew he could always take a taxi back to the flat now. It took him forty-five minutes to reach the park along the banks of the Heart of Love River. He was perspiring freely, and he removed his panama hat again to wipe his brow and face. "I need to sit somewhere in the shade and drink something cold," he thought.

The riverside park was rather pretty, with pathways meandering beneath trees of species which appeared very exotic to Alexander's eyes, and very bright green lawns on which families were setting out blankets and folding chairs, their kids running around like puppies. There was a section of paved walkway along the river bank itself which was lined with cafés and restaurants and fast food eateries. Alexander, who felt extremely weary and very hot after the two mile walk to the park, chose a café whose front was open to the river walkway. The clientele seemed younger than usual: young men with their girlfriends. After collecting and paying for an iced coffee together with a glass of cold water, and a sort of pork and pickles hamburger, with the filling closed inside a soft white steamed bun, Alexander looked around for somewhere to sit. He saw a table at which there was just one person seated, a young man, and he greeted him in Mandarin and smiled. "May I sit here?" he asked in English.

"You're welcome," the young man replied in slightly American-accented English. "Are you American?"

"No, British."

"What are you doing here in Kaohsiung?" The young man pronounced the "K" of Kaohsiung with a sharp, near-explosive sound.

"I've only just arrived. I'm here to teach business English."

The young man, who had the fine, somewhat narrow-headed features seen among some of the northern Chinese, and a high arched nose with bright, expressive black eyes, extended his hand. "My name is Johnny Chen. I am pleased to meet you."

"I'm Sandy Maclean. Well, Alexander actually, but Sandy for short. I'm pleased to meet you too," Alexander shook Johnny's hand. "Your English is very good. Were you taught English at school?"

"Yes, we study English at high school. I would like to speak English better. I like your English accent. We mostly hear American English."

Alexander popped the ring tab on his can of iced coffee and poured it into the glass provided. He liked this young Chinaman. "This is only my first full day in Kaohsiung. The city seems vast – it is daunting, in fact. I am hoping I'll learn my way around."

"What is *'fast'*? And that other word, *'dhorting,'* what do they mean, please?"

Alexander drank deeply from his glass of iced coffee – ahh! – the bliss of that ice-cold liquid! He put the glass down. "Vast," he said, emphasizing the 'V' sound; "It means 'big'. And 'daunting' means frightening, scary, too much to handle."

While Alexander drank his iced coffee, along with an occasional sip of water, and began to eat the pork and pickles bun-burger, the two men continued to chat. Johnny told him he was a student at the National Sun Yat-sen University, studying business management. "I would like to be sent by my company to work in America, or England."

"Perhaps you would n't find it as challenging as I find moving to Taiwan. There's so much American TV, is n't there? But we get little on TV about Taiwan or China."

Johnnie laughed. "We *are* in China! The Republic of China!"

Alexander smiled. "Of course, sorry – you are quite correct. I do in fact think of Taiwan as legitimist China, and the mainland as revolutionary China." He offered the young Chinaman a cigarette, which was declined, and lighted one himself. "Tell me, not all Taiwanese are descended from people who were living here already. What percentage of Taiwanese citizens descend from mainland Chinese immigrants?"

"Most of us, I think. My own family were merchants on the mainland, but they fleed – fleed?"

"Fled."

"Thank you. My own grandparents fled mainland China in 1949, in fear of their lives under the communist dictatorship."

"That's interesting. I too descend from immigrants. My grandfather was Scottish, but he settled in Kenya with his family when it was a brand new British colony."

"But you were not born in England?"

"No, I was n't. I was born in Kenya, and I grew up in Kenya and South Africa. But I have a British passport, and I have lived many years in England."

Johnny laughed again. "So your family is what the Communists call imperialists."

Alexander grinned. "Yes, I'm proud of my imperialist roots."

"Would you like to walk with me? We can talk more."

"I would like that, Johnny."

The two got up and set off along the riverside walkway. Johnny was full of questions. Alexander, who was now forty-five years old (though he looked ten years younger), enjoyed his companion's youthful enthusiasm. He missed having young people around him. At about three o' clock in the afternoon, as they sat on a bench and looked across the river, Johnny said "I must go now. I would like to see you again. Can we meet again – not next Saturday; the Saturday after that? I can show you some of the city of Kaohsiung."

"I would enjoy that tremendously."

"Where do you live?"

Alexander found the card on which his address was printed. "Xinxing district. This is the only card I have, but this is my address."

"I have a pen." The young man took his pen from his shirt pocket, along with a cash receipt. "Give me the card, Sandy, and I will copy your address. Do you have a cell?"

"No, not yet. I must get a cell phone."

"No trouble. I will write my cell number on your card." He did so. "It is OK if I come for you at ten a.m?"

"That'll be fine. It's a date."

Johnny smiled. "It's a date! Yes, it's a date. I will like to learn from you."

"And I shall enjoy learning from you."

"Zàijiàn!"

Alexander repeated Johnny's goodbye. "Zàijiàn, Johnny." The two men shook hands, and the young man walked away, a head taller than most of the other people there. Alexander took his little notebook from his shirt pocket and wrote what he had just heard, transcribing the words phonetically, thus: "goodbye – *zhy-jiyan*." Alexander wondered, as he often had in the past, at the way destiny worked. He felt far less lonely now. He hoped very much that Johnny would indeed come fetch him the Saturday after next.

During the week that followed, Alexander did not have to work very hard. Steve fetched him each morning at eight, riding his scooter. Despite his false leg, and the necessity of carrying his walking stick with him, Alexander was able to ride pillion behind his employer, as they wove their way through the traffic and across town to Steve's office and the classroom upstairs. There were in fact two classrooms, but Alexander was at present the only teacher on the premises. There was also a small library of TEFL primers and texts. Alexander took only two two-hour classes a day – one each in the morning and afternoon. His students were adult Chinese, one hundred percent male, ranging in age from their twenties to their forties (though in judging the age of a Chinese person, Alexander was at something of a loss). Alexander presumed the older men had been sent their by their employers, companies which traded with, or hoped to trade with, the west.

There was a small park nearby, and after a modest lunchtime meal at one of the tiny local restaurants of the type with which Alexander had become familiar from his first day in Kaohsiung, he would sit in the park under a shade tree before returning to the office for his afternoon class. During that first week in Kaohsiung, Alexander saw not one other westerner. He was totally immersed within an entirely Chinese environment.

Steve usually returned Alexander to his flat round five in the afternoon, though once, he told Alexander that he would have to get a taxi back to his flat. Early in his second week at work Alexander said to Steve "I would like to buy a scooter. How can I do that, Steve?"

"I get for you, no problem."

Alexander was left uncertain whether Steve meant that he would find a scooter for Alexander to buy – or whether he would buy a scooter for him. He frequently gathered only the broad gist of what Steve was telling him. But on Friday afternoon, after his class had finished, Steve showed him a well-used scooter parked on the pavement in front of the office, alongside the one Steve himself rode. A helmet hung from one handlebar. "This for you," Steve told Alexander. "You use – I keep."

Alexander understood that he was to have not the ownership, but the use, of this scooter. He grinned with pleasure and bent to examine it. It was a pretty little scooter, though far from new; very simple to operate, with an automatic gearbox. There were only three controls: the throttle, the hand-operated front brake on the right handlebar, and a footbrake which operated on the rear wheel.

"What fuel does it use, Steve?"

"Hah?"

Alexander pointed at the cap on the tiny fuel tank. "What gas does it take? Please write it for me in Chinese."

"This for regular gas, this . . ." Steve pointed at a small filler cap on a tiny tank below the petrol tank ". . . this for oil. Come my office please."

In Steve's office which was scented with the tea he poured from the pot steaming above the spirit burner, he searched through a couple of drawers in his desk, then he gave Alexander a user's manual for the scooter – written in Chinese. But paging through it, Alexander saw that the diagrams were clear enough. Steve took it back from him, and wrote something on the inside back page.

"Here is name of gas and oil you use."

Alexander pointed at the first of these two groups of ideograms. "Is this the gas?"

"Yes, that the gas. *Qiyóu.*"

"Ki-yo-ow . . ." Alexander repeated, taking out his notebook and writing the word phonetically. "And the two-stroke oil?"

Steve responded with what sounded to Alexander like "*eh chongcheng-yo-ow.*"

Alexander wrote this word, or words, phonetically also. He could see that Steve was struggling with putting together something else in English. Then Steve said "You come with me," and disappeared through a door at the back of the office. Alexander followed him into a small courtyard, off which a number of doors led. Steve opened one of these. It gave access to a small storeroom. In a corner stood a jerry-can. Steve pointed to it.

"*Qiyóu* . . . gas." Steve indicated a funnel with a built-in filter lying on a shelf. Then he pointed to a small can standing on a shelf, and said "*Er chongchéng-yóu.* You use these for scooter. I not mind."

"*Xièxiè* Steve."

Then Steve said "Friend come fetch you flat at seven, we go restaurant. OK?"

"OK," Alexander replied. Then he said "Steve, I need to see a map of Kaohsiung, so I can find my way back to my flat."

"I show you on map. Come back to office."

The route between the school and the flat was not complicated. The distance was about two or three miles, as best Alexander could judge. He hoped he wouldn't get lost, but if he did, he would have to keep showing people his written address card, until he was back on track again. As Alexander climbed onto the scooter, Steve handed him a mobile phone and a small piece of paper with a row of numerals written on it. "This old cell I not use. And cell number. You need."

"*Xièxiè* Steve. *Zàijiàn!*"

Alexander found the best way of dealing with his walking stick was to rest the stick's rubber-tipped ferrule against the up-curve of the left running-board, the stick then being held between his left thigh and the saddle. He had n't driven on the right hand side of the road since his visit to Paris in 1988. He made it back to the flat without mishap, his nerves jangling. The traffic, especially the myriad other scooters, was a nightmare. Perhaps it would become easier over time. Removing the helmet, Alexander mopped perspiration from his face as he stood next to the scooter outside the block of flats. Now that he was not moving, it felt even hotter, even more humid than usual. Alexander hoped it meant that a storm was brewing. Then he bumped the scooter up the shallow pavement kerb, and up against the wall alongside a number of other scooters, where he fastened the chain-lock Steve had given him round the front wheel and the suspension strut.

Upstairs, Alexander made himself a coffee and lighted a cigarette, and sitting down in one of the cool, comfortable leatherette armchairs in the lounge, he played with the mobile phone until he had found the "English language" option. He wondered whether he should ring or text Johnny. "I'll just send a text," he decided. He felt strung out, taut-stretched. He needed to get out somewhere where there weren't highrises leaning in against him. He texted Johnny: "Hi Johnny. I'm looking forward to our 'date' tomorrow morning. Cheers – Sandy."

After a few minutes had passed Alexander's mobile phone beeped. It was a text from Johnny. "Hi Sandy. Me too. See you at 10 tomorrow. Johnny."

Alexander smiled happily. He turned the TV on and watched a Chinese soap while he waited for his lift to the restaurant to arrive. Shortly after seven o'clock there was a knock at the door. A large Chinese man with pleasant, friendly features stood in the corridor. He looked to Alexander as if he was in his thirties. "Hi," he said, "My name is Phil Zhou. I'm a friend of Steve's. Would you like to join us for a meal out?" His English was fluent American.

"Sandy Maclean. How do you do." They shook hands.

Phil was driving the same Mercedes car in which Steve had collected Alexander from the airport. "How's the teaching going?" Phil asked as he drove.

"It's good, thanks. My students are keen to learn, and quick on the uptake."

"I picked up my English in America as a teenager. My parents were in the diplomatic service in Washington."

The restaurant was located on top of a highrise in the city. Waiting there at the roof terrace bar were Steve and another man, who appeared to have no English at his command. The four men sat at a table under the night sky, high above the city. Two big six hundred and forty milliliter bottles of Tiger beer were brought to the table. Alexander attempted to explain, without making a big deal about it, that for health reasons, he would not be able to have a glass of the pale lager. "I'll get you something else, Sandy," said Phil. "What would you like?"

"A bottle of sparkling mineral water would be nice, thanks Phil."

The meal, served on a huge revolving platter divided into small compartments in which a variety of dishes were arranged, was excellent. For the most part, the three Chinese men chatted among themselves in Mandarin, all three smoking prodigiously, but both Steve and Phil made an effort to include Alexander in the conversation at times, though their attempts consisted mostly of questions directed at him about his education and travels. By ten o'clock the three Chinese men were fairly merry. Alexander presumed they were married, but looking around the roof terrace, he saw very few women at any of the tables, and the few who were present did not look like wives. Alexander felt tired, and he longed for a coffee, but at the end of the meal, only tea was served.

It was just after eleven when Phil, with Steve as a passenger, dropped Alexander off at the flat. Upstairs he made an instant coffee and began to unwind. It had been an interesting and in part, enjoyable, evening, but it had been a strain also.

Thirty-Four

A Kaohsiung Tour

At five minutes past ten the next morning Alexander's mobile phone beeped. He put down the Taiwan News he was reading. He read the text from Johnny. "I'm downstairs. Are you ready? Johnny"

Alexander texted in reply "On my way – Sandy." He grabbed his wallet, his linen jacket, smokes and lighter and walking stick.

Johnny was standing by a scooter downstairs. He looked very young and clean-cut, his jet-black hair, which was cut short, shining with vitality, his freshly ironed white short-sleeved shirt gleaming in the sunshine. He wore tan chinos and slim loafers. His smooth bare arms and face had a dark golden tan. "Hi Sandy," he said, with his slightly American accent, his teeth very white in his broad smile. He shook Alexander's hand. "How are you keeping?"

"Well thanks, Johnny. How are you?"

"I'm good. Are you ready for some sightseeing?"

"Sounds good."

"Let's go then. You can carry this ... this ... what do you say?"

"Day-pack."

"That's right. This day-pack. I have some things we might need inside it."

Alexander shrugged the small pack onto his back.

Johnny said "I will not tell you where we are going. It must be a surprise."

Johnny wore no helmet and he had none to offer Alexander. It was cooler riding bare-headed. Until a short while ago, Alexander had never rode pillion on a motorcycle, but he had taken to it instinctively. He placed his hands either side of Johnny's waist, not so much to hold on, as to steady himself, and he leant into the turns with Johnny. They zipped west down the major thoroughfare which fronted Alexander's block of flats – Wufu 2nd Road – and just beyond what Alexander knew as Central Park, at a large traffic island, Johnny sped round the island and took the exit into another very busy street, heading south. That evening, back in his flat, Alexander retraced the route on his map of Kaohsiung. He knew that they had followed this street – Zhonghua 5th Road – for about a quarter of a mile, and then turned right for a hundred yards or so, and at a narrow harbour-side dock opposite a park alongside the Kaohsiung Exhibition Centre, Johnny had come to a halt. "You OK, Sandy?"

Alexander grinned happily. "I'm fine, thanks!"

"Here we catch a ferry boat. We take the scooter with us. I buy the tickets, please."

"Sure, Johnny."

The two chatted about life in the west. Johnny declined a cigarette, but Alexander lighted one for himself. Johnny was full of questions – how this was done in England, how that was done – and after fifteen minutes Alexander saw a short, fat, tubby three deck ferry boat approaching the dock. Ramps along the side, and a big ramp at one end, were let down once it was tied on, and two or three cars drove down the main ramp. A trickle of people, some with bicycles and scooters, came ashore via the side ramps. A few of the bikes and scooters were remarkably heavily laden, as were many more of those waiting to board. Johnny had bought their tickets at a booth at the dockside. Once they had parked the scooter alongside several cars that had driven up the big ramp at one end of the ferry, the two men mounted a companionway to the deck above, where they leant over the railings. The ferry pulled away and rumbled unhurriedly across the harbour, which seemed to Alexander to enclose a vast expanse of water, and Johnny pointed out the mouth of the Heart of Love River to starboard. Alexander could see many ocean-going vessels and a wide variety of smaller boats tied up alongside the quays they passed to their left. The crossing, which was cooled by the movement of air from their progress across the water, took about ten minutes. Alexander, to whom boats and ships were of infinite fascination, enjoyed it.

"This is Cijin Island," Johnny said as the ferry docked on the far side of the harbour. "The town is old."

Riding pillion once again, Alexander could tell that most of the two, three and four story buildings that lined the narrow street probably dated no further back than the fifties, but there were some buildings among them that clearly dated from the late nineteenth century, to a period when Taiwan, then known as Formosa, was a Japanese colony. The streets were crooked, the buildings crammed in on one another, but suddenly they were through the town and Johnny turned left into a road which ran parallel with a wide stretch of parkland with palm trees growing on it and somewhat sparse lawns beneath them. On the other side of the road which fronted the park the street was lined with apartment blocks, many of which were no taller than four stories, and with shops and restaurants. Beyond the park, separated by an expanse of beach of very dark, almost black volcanic sand, was the ocean. Johnny pulled over. "Let's walk on the beach," he said.

Johnny sat on a bench and rolled up his chinos, then he removed his loafers and socks. He grinned happily as he walked in the water lapping at the shore. The beach was at least half a mile long, perhaps longer. Alexander walked in the dark sand, unwilling to get his false leg wet. But he too was happy. He had known that he missed the open spaces, but he had not realised how much, until Johnny had brought him to this unexpected place with the sparkling sea and big sky and far horizon.

"What do you think?" asked Johnny.

"It's super! In the city I forget Kaohsiung is a sea-port."

"Our university is near the sea. There is a beach below the university. Maybe I'll take you there after lunch."

The two men, the one tall, slim and straight, the other even taller, but with a walking stick and a limp, walked to the far end of the beach. It was a fair distance for Alexander, walking in the sand. Then they found a bench beneath a palm tree, and drank hot green tea from a thermos flask Johnny had packed inside the day-pack. Johnny had brought an extra mug for Alexander. "Unless you want some Coca-Cola, Sandy? I have some cans of Coke in the bag."

"No – the tea will be nice, thanks. You know, all my life I've been a coffee drinker, not a tea drinker. The English love their tea, but I grew up in the colonies, and we like to steep ourselves in strong coffee. But the tea I come across constantly here in Taiwan is beginning to grow on me. It can be quite refreshing"

"The tea 'grows' on you? What does that mean?"

"Oh – it means you become accustomed to it, and after a while you start to enjoy it." Alexander smoked a cigarette as he sipped at the very hot tea. They sat and looked out across the sea, beyond which – though unseen – lay mainland China. After having rested a while, the two men began the walk back along the beach, Johnny still barefoot.

Back at their starting point, Johnny sat down on a bench and wiped his feet with a handkerchief, which he then shook out, before putting his shoes and socks back on again, saying "Time for lunch. But we will not ride – we'll walk. It is not far."

They crossed the wide strip of scraggly green lawn beneath its palm trees, and then crossed the road, and began to walk along the pavement towards the old town. They passed several restaurants. Outside one of these, Johnny stopped. "Here we are." He stood back for Alexander, who pushed the door open and went inside ahead of him.

Alexander had not yet quite got his head around the Chinese approach to mealtimes, which consisted not – as in the west – of a large main course and perhaps an entrée and a dessert course, but of many smaller dishes.

He ordered only two of these: cuttlefish geng (*youyugeng*), a clear, thick soup with cuttlefish covered in fish paste (it had never occurred to him that people could eat any part of the cuttlefish), and at Johnny's insistence, milkfish, whose flaky flesh tasted rather like salmon, but sweeter. Craving a caffeine hit, Alexander drank an iced coffee with the meal.

"When I go out in the evenings to have some supper at one of the tiny restaurants behind my block of flats, what should I be asking for, Johnny?" Alexander extracted his little notebook and a pen. "All I've had so far is beef or pork with noodles. Blessed noodles – and luckily, I like noodles."

Johnny smiled and laughed. "It must be difficult for you – I understand our food is very different to what you are used to in the west. If you have not already been to one of the night markets – there's one nearby where you live, the Liuhe night market – you must try oysters with egg. It is called *ezijian*."

Alexander wrote down the name as it sounded to him. "Genuine oysters, with egg?"

"Oh yes. Egg with oysters. It is chewy. And it is made also with sweet potatoes and . . . and . . . I think you say, chrysanthemum leaves. It is a very popular snack in the city at night." Johnny thought for a moment. "And you must try pork and rice – it is called *lu rou fan*. It is pieces of pork – not stewed or fried, but cooked to . . . to seal the pork, in soy sauce, served with rice."

"*Lu rou fan?*"

"Yes, that's right."

Alexander wrote the name down. "I enjoyed cooking when I lived in Johannesburg. I've been to Chinese restaurants in Johannesburg and London with friends, but I suspect the dishes they serve may not be one hundred percent authentic." He smiled at Johnny. "That's how I learned to use chopsticks."

"*Kuàizi*. That is what we call chopsticks. Our most popular snack is like a hamburger. It is called *guabao*. It is a steamed bun with pork and pickled vegetables inside it. Very filling. In England the most popular food is fish and chips, yes?"

Alexander smiled. "It used to be the most popular. It's certainly the traditional take-away in Britain. Now it competes with many other meals. Curries are probably even more popular in Britain today."

"Curries? I do not think I know this food."

"Britain has a huge immigrant population from the Indian subcontinent. They have brought their cuisine with them – hot, spicy food, usually lamb or chicken and rice, with vegetables – and it has become hugely popular."

Whilst Johnny drank a very dark, almost black tea after the meal, Alexander ordered another iced coffee. "I will show you a very beautiful natural district," said Johnny. "There are monkeys, and much open ground for walking."

"Do you ever go hiking, Johnny?"

"Oh yes – I like to hike. We go hiking in the mountains you can sometimes see from the city. They are unspoiled."

"I was a keen hiker," Alexander responded. "I have n't done much hiking for some years, but even as a teenager at school, I needed to go for long walks in open country. My soul feels smothered if I don't get out in the open sometimes."

"I understand what you are saying. What sort of country do you like to hike in, Sandy?"

"We used to spend two or three days high in the mountains – at almost four thousand metres. Or we would head for some hills an hour's drive from Johannesburg, just for the day. There are monkeys and antelope there – you would know them as 'deer,' I think – and there have been sightings of leopards reported. But my most amazing hikes have been day walks in the bush, in the wilderness, in 'big five' country, where you see elephants, buffalo, many antelope species, giraffes, zebras, and sometimes lions."

Johnny was staring at Alexander. "That is wonderful! I can understand why you must feel trapped in crowded urban areas."

"Sometimes I do. I worry that I wont be able to keep my sanity if I spend a whole year in Kaohsiung."

"Perhaps I can take you hiking in the mountains with some of my friends some day, Sandy."

"I cannot hike at all far anymore, not with a false leg, but I still need to get out into the open. It has done me good, just walking along the beach here, and seeing the ocean."

"You have a false leg? You mean, you have only one leg? I did not know." Johnny frowned momentarily, then his face cleared. "But no one would know. You manage to walk very well." He smiled at Alexander. "I would never know. Was it an accident?"

"Yes, it was. One and a half years ago."

"You are brave, I think. Come! Let's go to Monkey Mountain! There is plenty of open space there, and some nice walking trails, which perhaps you can manage." Johnny laughed. "There are no big dangerous animals, but there are many big greedy monkeys."

At the end of Cijin Old Street, where it abutted against the quayside, after a wait of ten minutes, the two crossed the narrow harbour mouth by ferry. The terrain the far side was hilly and steep. With the day-pack on his back, Alexander held Johnny's waist as they sped north. At the Kaohsiung Martyrs' Shrine at the foot of the hill, Johnny swung onto a narrow road which climbed up the hillside, and then began to zig-zag its way up the increasingly steep slope. At the top, Johnny turned into a parking area, and killed the engine. The view was spectacular. Alexander could see far out across the sea, although the Chinese mainland lay too far away to be glimpsed. The coastline as it ran north up the length of the island appeared to be fairly densely built up. Turning around, he could see the whole of Kaohsiung city laid out beneath him, and to the east, far beyond the city, the mountains loomed clear against the blue sky. From here they seemed so close, but Alexander suspected they were too far away to tackle on his tiny scooter. To the south lay the vast natural harbour, bounded by Cijin Island, where they had come from. Then they were joined by a troop of rather large monkeys, which Alexander guessed correctly were some sort of macaques. "This is fantastic, Johnny! What an incredible view. As for these monkeys, I guess they hope we'll feed them."

"Yes, they're greedy for food. People feed them. I will not. It makes them too tame."

"We have the same problem in Cape Town with our monkeys, baboons. Tourists feed them. They lose their respect for humans, and sometimes become dangerous."

"I have heard that word 'baboon,' but I did not know what it meant. So it means a type of monkey? Like these?"

"Similar, but their muzzles are more dog-like."

"Do you want to walk for a while, Sandy?"

"Yes – I'd like that."

The trail, paved in sturdy wooden planking and incorporating wood planked stairways with railings set between concrete uprights, wound its way along the side of the steep hill. Occasionally other trails would branch off it. The tropical vegetation was dense and lush. Sometimes the two men were walking beneath an interlaced tree canopy. Some of the smooth-barked trees were quite large. It would have been very warm indeed, but up here there was some light wind and the air did not feel as humid as it did down below in the city. Alexander relished walking amidst such riotous greenery. They frequently saw monkeys. The impression of elevation and space made Alexander's spirits rise. They came across other walkers: it was a far cry from the wilderness which Alexander had loved so much in Africa, but it also felt far removed from Kaohsiung city. After half an hour's fairly strenuous walking – for the path was rarely level, but ascended and descended constantly – Johnny said "We turn around now. I will show you a café by the edge of the sea."

They had been walking an hour by the time they got back to Johnny's scooter. Alexander felt as if, for a while, he had been freed of a heavy weight. "I must come here again Johnny," he said. "It's a wonderful place."

"I am pleased you like it. Sometimes I walk here with my girlfriend after class at university. The university is at the bottom of this mountain."

They descended a narrow, very steep road indeed, in a series of tight hairpin bends. The shoreline, far below, grew ever closer. The location of the Ocean Corner Café, squeezed between cliff-side and shoreline, built several metres above the sea, could n't have been bettered. It was an open, unpretentious place, with little attention paid to the décor or furnishings. They sat on the deck outside, on plastic chairs, and whilst Johnny drank more tea, and munched on something that looked to Alexander's eye overly gooey and sweet, Alexander had another iced coffee. He did not think the caffeine strength in the cans of iced coffee was very high. "What do you think of this café, Sandy?" asked Johnny.

"I like it, Johnny. I've enjoyed everything you've shown me today. It has been wonderful to escape from the city. It is hard to believe the city is so close."

"I enjoy showing you. Showing off? Showing off to you." Johnny grinned. "We in Kaohsiung are more than just highrises and factories and traffic."

Thirty-Five

Ortie

Johnny met up with Alexander twice in August, and again twice in September. Their friendship developed a greater ease. Johnny enjoyed listening to the stories Alexander told him, and to descriptions both of Africa and of Britain. "You know," he said to Alexander one Saturday, "We are both exiles. Our families came from somewhere else."

"Johnny, I sometimes feel lost, as if I had nowhere to call home. My heart dwells in Africa, but my culture is broadly British and my ancestry is British. The empire into which I was born does not exist anymore. The Africa I love is fast disappearing. I sometimes feel a profound sadness."

Johnny was staring solemnly at Alexander. "It is the same for those of us whose families escaped from the Communists. Our ancestors' graves are far away. Our history is far away. We dream of returning some day, but we cannot."

"People like your family have built a great country here in Taiwan, though," Alexander responded. "You have made the best of your exile. But I understand how it must be for you."

Johnny smiled. "My generation does not worry about it so much. It is my grandparents who dream of their homeland across the straits."

Alexander's three month temporary work and residence visa would expire on the 21st October. In early October he communicated his concerns to Steve.

"Government doctors at hospital will test you on Monday, nine day October," Steve told him. "I have made appointment for you. You must be in good health to extend your visa."

Alexander had not considered that a health check would be necessary. He worried about his amputation which he feared might be a cause of concern to the health officials. It was with trepidation that he attended the appointment at the Kaohsiung Municipal Da-Tung Hospital. For the examination, he had to strip to his underpants. When it became apparent that he had a false leg, there was considerable conversation between the examining doctor and another doctor who then joined him. Alexander did not like the sense he got of an overly critical interest in his amputation and in the prosthesis.

On Tuesday 17th October, Alexander arrived at Steve's school as usual at eight-thirty on his scooter. After his morning class, Steve said to him "Sandy, you come my office please."

Inside Steve's rather shabby office, Alexander knew that his employer had something unpleasant to tell him. Steve would not meet his eye. "You cannot stay in Taiwan," he said. "Government not extend your visa. You must leave at end of the week." Steve looked up then. "You not pass health examination."

Alexander was not as surprised at his reaction as he might have been: it was in fact one of relief. Only at this moment did he realise that he had been living under an increasing strain, beset by a crush of humanity, constantly made aware of his foreignness, and homesick for another European to talk to. Now he had no choice but to return to a familiar world, a world where he did not always feel as if he had landed on an alien planet. Relief flooded him. But he put on a sad face for Steve.

"You work until Friday 20th. You leave next day."

"That is sad, Steve. I must phone Singapore Airlines," he said, "if you will let me use your phone here."

"You a good teacher. I sorry to see you go."

Alexander returned to his flat during his lunch break and found his air ticket. Later that afternoon he rang Singapore Airlines from Steve's office phone. He would be flying on Saturday morning – but headed for Heathrow, not for Jan Smuts at Johannesburg.

Alexander knew he could not realistically return to South Africa. There was nothing for him there now. He would have to return to England. His mind began racing. Would he have enough money to find somewhere to live in the short term? His mother had agreed in principle, during his brief stay in South Africa, to put up the cash to buy a small house – a bungalow – in England. Did it in fact have to be in England? Why could he not go live in Argyll, where he had been happy way back in 1976? He did not particularly wish to return to High Wycombe, where his history of drunkenness and failure troubled his memory. But were his chances of ever working again in Britain really over? If not, then south-east England made far more sense than western Scotland.

"I will miss Johnny," Alexander thought.

Johnny came by Alexander's flat on Thursday evening, to say goodbye, and he gave Alexander his parents' postal address. Alexander in turn gave Johnny his aunt's address in Wiltshire as a contact point. "I come visit you when I am in England someday," Johnny said.

But Alexander knew that their friendship had been a thing located in a particular place and time: it would not survive beyond them.

"I would like that very much indeed. Perhaps I can repay your kindness here to me, by showing you around London."

"It was not kindness, Sandy. Listening to the way you speak, to your pure English, and hearing your accent, has helped me speak a better English, I think."

"I've always thought you spoke excellent English, Johnny."

They said goodbye outside Alexander's apartment block, shaking hands and wishing each other well. Alexander stood watching as Johnny zipped up the street on his scooter and turned into Wufu 2nd Road. "Oh, gosh . . ." Alexander said out loud; another parting, another goodbye. Then he began thinking of the flights that lay ahead of him, and his uncertain plans once he arrived in Britain. "I wish it was all behind me."

Steve and Phil drove Alexander to Kaohsiung International Airport on Saturday morning. It was not a long drive: the airport lay on the very edge of the city. After changing flights at Singapore's Changi airport (with a smoke break), Alexander flew west through the night. When the flight landed at Heathrow on Sunday 22nd October, it was – because of the time difference – only mid-morning in England. Alexander found a luggage trolley and piled his few pieces of luggage onto it. Then he made for a bank of telephones, and rang his London friend, Piers Hawkins, at his flat in Soho. "Piers? Yes – it's Sandy. How are you? . . . Oh, I'm well. Look, I'm at Heathrow. I've just returned from Taiwan . . . yes, Taiwan. I was teaching business English out there, but my three month work visa could n't be renewed, and I could n't stay, so I was wondering: could you put me up just for a night or two?"

Piers told Alexander he was welcome to stay with him for a while. Unable to manage his luggage on the train from Heathrow to Paddington station, he caught a very expensive taxi from Heathrow to Pier's flat in Frith Street. Piers lived on the top two floors of an eighteenth century Georgian townhouse. His high-ceilinged sitting room was paneled in oak painted a dark bottle green. The fireplace was of carved and embellished white marble. The floor, where it could be seen beneath Persian rugs, was of old, dark, polished oak. It was a huge room, taking up two thirds of the entire width of the street façade. Next to it was a smaller room, used as a dining room, also paneled in oak that had a deep patina. Both rooms had a great many framed original oils and watercolours hanging on the walls, some of which, Alexander knew, had come down to Piers from his family and were very old. Piers, like Alexander, loved old things. There was a collection of antique swords mounted on one wall, and on the opposite wall, between two windows, there was a collection of flintlock and percussion cap pistols, with a Brown Bess Tower musket and an Enfield percussion cap .577 musket-rifle in the centre of the arrangement. The windows had interior folding shutters, those in the sitting room painted the same bottle green as the walls, and those in the dining room painted a soft salmon pink. Either side of the fireplace in the sitting room (there was another fireplace in the dining room), were book cases crammed with books ranging from contemporary non-fiction paperbacks to antique volumes bound in leather. The furniture was classic and timeless: two long well-stuffed sofas covered in chintz were arranged either side of the fireplace, and there were two armchairs in matching chintz. There were several reproduction Sheraton chairs arranged around the room. There was a low coffee table between the two sofas, on which were untidy piles of glossy magazines.

"Sandy! From the far side of the world! Welcome home!"

The two men embraced, Piers warmly, Alexander a trifle awkwardly, as he did not feel entirely easy with such a display of affection. "It's good to be back – I guess. Thank you for putting me up, Piers."

"Think nothing of it. Would you like a sherry – or something stronger?"

"What I would really like is a coffee, if you could. It wasn't easy finding coffee in Kaohsiung." Alexander dug around in his shoulder bag, and found the bottle of scotch he had bought at the duty free at Changi airport. "Here's a small gift for you, Piers – a thank you, you know."

The two friends chatted over their drinks. Piers had poured himself a sherry. Alexander had a good, strong, black coffee, which went down very well.

"What are your plans, then?" Piers asked, after Alexander had told him something about his stay in Taiwan.

"I hate sounding indecisive, but I'm not sure. I think it's finding a bungalow near High Wycombe. My mother will buy it for the family, of which I am the sole representative at present here in England."

"Why High Wycombe in particular?"

"I'm familiar with the district. The countryside in the Chilterns is very lovely. It's hilly and well-wooded. I need hills if I'm to be happy. But it's within easy reach of London."

"Good. So I shall still see something of you, Sandy."

"Yah – I'm not that easy to get rid of!" Both men laughed.

Alexander stayed at Piers' home for four nights, leaving on Thursday morning the 26th October. The weather was not yet cold, though the intense, humid warmth of summer time in London had long passed. It was dry, sometimes overcast, and the two men went out to a pub round the corner the evening of Alexander's arrival, where they had some supper. Alexander refused alcohol. "I'm not drinking at the moment," he told Piers.

"Good for you. You don't mind if I do?"

"Of course not. Go ahead, please."

They went out again on Wednesday night. Alexander enjoyed Soho, which, though no longer the sink of iniquity it had been during his first stay in London, was still full of character. The two friends suited each other. Both were fundamentally chaste – or at least, Piers appeared to be that way to Alexander, whose own chastity, whilst hardly of any great historical standing, was genuine now.

On Thursday morning Alexander took a taxi to Marylebone station, the terminus of the Chiltern Railways line, and caught a train for High Wycombe. On arrival in High Wycombe he moved into a small residential hotel in Priory Avenue, not far from the flat he and Roy had lived in together. Alexander bought himself a cheap, simple, pre-paid mobile phone. He rang his mother, using a service the man at the mobile phone shop had told him about that provided him with very cheap call rates to South Africa. Alexander's mother gave him the go ahead to look for a small house.

Alexander viewed half a dozen properties, using one of High Wycombe's taxi services for his traveling, before, in late November, deciding on a bungalow located in a cul-de-sac leading off the High Street in Chinnor, a village just over the county border into Oxfordshire, a few miles from High Wycombe. The bungalow had two moderate sized bedrooms (one of which was upstairs in a loft conversion), and a third, rather smaller bedroom, a south-facing lounge with a small dining room leading off it through a wide archway, a kitchen, a utility room rather bigger than a large walk in wardrobe, a bathroom and lavatory combination, and an entrance hall. There was an extra-large single garage by the side of the house. The house was located on about a sixth of an acre. There was a trio of decorative fir trees growing in the front garden, and the somewhat bigger back garden had a mature beech tree, leafless and stark at this time of year, growing in it.

Chinnor village crouched below the heavily wooded chalk scarp that marked the edge of the Chiltern hills. In choosing a house to buy, one of Alexander's prime considerations had been how safe it would be to keep a cat there. The cul-de-sac was quiet, with only local traffic. He thought a cat would be safer by far here than in many other locations, for ribbon development was all too common in England's countryside, with houses set not far back from busy trunk roads.

Alexander liked the atmosphere in Chinnor, one of modest restraint and careful white collar propriety, where the houses had well-maintained gardens, and there appeared to be an active sense of community. There was too a steam railway enthusiasts' club in Chinnor, located on the branch line that had once connected Chinnor with the Chiltern Railways main line near Princes Risborough – but which was now stranded in pretty countryside, running from Chinnor to nowhere. There were about seven miles of track, on which the club members could play with the pannier tank locomotive and the several restored carriages.

Alexander's stay at the residential hotel in High Wycombe had to be extended into December, for there were complications with the transfer of funds from his mother's South African bank account, but on Friday 15th December, a miserable, cold, grey, damp day, Alexander, representing his mother, signed the documents of sale at the solicitors' office in High Wycombe's High Street. The bungalow now belonged to the Maclean family. Alexander then phoned Social Services and spoke to Gillian, his contact there. "My family has bought a bungalow in Chinnor," he told her. "I'm moving in there this week – as soon as I can get hold of my things you're storing for me."

"I'm glad to hear it, Sandy," she responded. "I will have to send you an invoice for the last couple of months' storage of your goods, you realise. Would you give me your new postal address?"

Alexander did so. He next phoned a car hire agency with an office in West Wycombe Road, and arranged to hire a small car for a few days. As soon as he had settled into his new home, he would see about buying a second hand car. But right now he had to buy some furniture. He had not even a bed to sleep on – though he had bedding among the things that Social Services had been storing for him. Alexander felt tired when he contemplated how much he had to do, and without anyone to help him. He could not remember what he had in the way of household goods, kitchenware etc., in the boxes that had been stored for him all this time. The day his things were delivered from Social Services was set to be extremely busy and very exhausting.

It was. On Wednesday, five days before Christmas, the goods that Social Services had been storing for Alexander were delivered to the bungalow. The two beds – a double and a single – that Alexander had bought from a discount outlet along the London Road, had been delivered on Monday morning. From a second-hand furniture shop in High Wycombe Alexander bought a very fine 1950s sideboard with a writing bureau and a drinks cabinet inside, and below was a glass-fronted display cabinet to show off his Lady Carlyle tea set, which he had bought second-hand from a shop in Yeoville. There were cupboards and drawers either side. The unit was beautifully veneered and of top quality construction and it cost him only five Pounds. From the same shop he also bought a second-hand lounge suite with a coffee table, along with a dining table with four chairs. For the kitchen he had bought a reconditioned second-hand electric cooker, very much like the one he remembered from his childhood, together with a washing machine and a fridge. These had all been delivered on Tuesday morning, and on Wednesday morning Alexander checked out of the hotel in Priory Avenue at last, and drove in his hire car to Chinnor, to wait at the bungalow for the delivery from Social Services to be made.

By New Year's Eve, with snow lying three inches deep on the ground (for there had been a snowfall across much of Britain on the 29th December), and Christmas having passed almost un-noticed by him, Alexander had arranged things in the house the way he wanted them.

The oil paintings were hanging on the walls in the sitting room and dining room. There were photographs hanging on the walls in his bedroom downstairs. There was a framed print or two on the wall in each of the remaining two bedrooms. He now knew what he possessed in the way of kitchenware, crockery and cutlery. His double bed was made up with bedding which had traveled from South Africa. The single bed in the small bedroom downstairs he left un-made with a dust sheet over it. Roy would use the bedroom upstairs (in which was Roy's custom made extra-long single bed) when he came to visit. Large empty boxes were stored alongside one wall in the garage. Alexander had stocked the kitchen cupboards and the fridge with groceries and foodstuffs. There was much still to buy: although the bungalow was carpeted wall to wall, Alexander wanted to find some large colourful rugs for the sitting room and the two bedrooms that would be in use. He wanted to find colourful plump cushions for the lounge suite. But these could wait.

Early in the new year of 2001, Alexander began hunting for a second hand car. He had returned the hire car shortly before the end of the year and he had resorted to catching the bus into High Wycombe or Thame (which, only four and a half miles away, was the nearest sizable Oxfordshire town to Chinnor), and then to using taxies to extend his search for a car from either of these towns. Alexander would in time obtain a free bus pass due to his physical disability, but that would wait until he had processed the paperwork, along with his application for Disability Living Allowance and his unemployment benefit. In the meanwhile, Alexander, having exhausted his own financial resources, was surviving with help from his mother. By mid-February, Alexander had a small but adequate income of his own coming in, and he calculated that living frugally, he could afford to run a small car.

Alexander found a 1994 Citroën Xantia in Marlow for only six hundred Pounds, the last of the Citroëns made with the classic pneumatic suspension of the marque. The car had just over eighty thousand miles on the clock, but it was in very good condition, with a complete service history from new. The car had an automatic gearbox, a necessity for Alexander, with no fully functioning left leg with which to operate a clutch. Alexander was to drive this car for the next sixteen and a half years. No one in his family, least of all his father, had ever kept a car for anything like that long. There was a Citroën agency in High Wycombe where the car could be serviced, and from which parts could be sourced when needed. This had been an important consideration when Alexander had been searching for a car.

In March, with daffodils blooming throughout the village, including in Alexander's garden (where there were also some early primroses out), Alexander began to think about finding himself a cat to love and care for. He spoke to some of the people he had come to know at Saint Andrew's church in the village. Saint Andrew's was a Church of England parish. There was a Catholic church in Thame, but Alexander had realised he no longer much loved the Catholic church. It was a priest-riddled church, and some of its superstitions repelled him. Perhaps if he had felt a greater sense that the Catholic church loved him, he would not have turned aside from it. Moreover, Alexander enjoyed walking up to the top of the High Street and into Church Road on Sunday mornings. He reverted easily to the Anglican rite. It was, after all (though the language had become more contemporary), the rite of his youth.

One of Alexander's acquaintances in the congregation asked "Do you know of the cat sanctuary in Amersham? I can give you their phone number if you would like."

"Thanks. Yes, please do."

The privately owned cat sanctuary in Amersham in Buckinghamshire was run by a husband and wife team. When Alexander visited it, he wished the cats had larger enclosures, but they were clearly loved, and the enclosures and surroundings were clean. As he walked slowly past them, he wanted to adopt all the pathetic, homeless, unwanted moggies. His heart filled with compassion. "Which cat is most in need of being adopted?" Alexander asked.

Trish, who ran the sanctuary, pointed at an old tabby cat. "She's been with us since early December last year. She's very old, possibly twenty or twenty-one already. She's a darling, but people don't want to adopt very old cats. They're afraid of the expense when they fall ill."

Trish opened the wide mesh-covered door to Ortie's enclosure (for

Ortie was the cat's unusual name). Alexander stepped inside slowly so as not to startle the cat, but she miaowed at him, looking up at him, and he bent down and stroked her. "I'll give her a loving home and take care of her as long as she lives," he said.

Alexander had brought a cat's traveling basket with him. He had found it among the items that had come from South Africa that had never been unpacked, but which had sat in a stack of boxes in a corner of the flat he and Roy had shared. He gave the cat sanctuary a donation of fifteen Pounds, and all the way back to Chinnor, a fairly long drive, Ortie miaowed in her old, husky voice. "It's alright darling," Alexander told her. "We'll soon be home."

Ortie reminded Alexander so much of Lulu during her old age. She was gentle, affectionate, and happy to stay inside the house, preferably in a patch of sunshine. Alexander poured out all the love that had become half-strangled inside him for want of a recipient. He was lonely and often homesick, and still tormented by nightmares filled with violence or the threat of violence, and less frequently, by occasional racking flashbacks during the day, but with Ortie he was able to ground himself again. She needed him, and he needed to be needed. She was lovable, and he needed to love.

During the course of that summer, Alexander, still sober, came to know a couple of the families in Saint Andrew's congregation quite well. Both families invited him into their homes sometimes, to share a meal. Alexander particularly enjoyed visiting the young couple he knew, for they had two little boys and being around children made Alexander happy. Children liked him too.

It was a lovely summer. Alexander took to walking in the Chiltern hills, following paths along the top of the ridge. Usually he would walk slowly for no longer than half an hour at the most each way, but every now and then he surprised himself by staying out longer, once for over two hours. During the week he rarely met other walkers, and if he did, it was usually someone out walking their dog. Alexander began to take an interest in butterflies. He had never given them much conscious attention before, though taking pleasure in their presence, but as he walked now, he became aware of how many butterfly species there were, in such a variety of wonderful designs and colours, so he bought himself a butterfly guide and he began to learn their names and characteristics: he quickly learned to recognise that classic British butterfly, the small tortoiseshell; he was thrilled with his first sighting of the warm orange and dark brown comma, with its ragged-edged wings; the smaller and larger whites, with meadow browns, fritillaries, brimstones and small blues were commonplace but no less enjoyed; a sighting of the rather special (but far from uncommon) red admiral, that splendid large butterfly that had once been a European summer migrant only, but was now beginning to overwinter in southern England, gave him particular pleasure; and he was especially pleased when he spotted the butterfly that brought him more delight than any of the other species for its exotic beauty – the gorgeous peacock butterfly. He kept a butterfly diary, in which he wrote down his "take" that day: the names of the species, their locations, and the dominant plant species nearby each. The happiness he felt when he saw one of his favourite butterflies, so close he could have reached down and touched it had he wished to, was as pure and joyful as his sightings of noteworthy birds – such as a paradise flycatcher, for example, or one of the raptors – had been in the bushveld. This interest in butterflies gave his walks a purpose, if purpose was required.

The ridge (in fact, the entire Chilterns) was well-wooded, covered in a canopy of ancient beech trees amidst which were also found oak, ash and hazel. There was also the occasional plantation of firs, conifers or spruce. Then the land would open up as Alexander passed by a wide meadow, in which he might see a herd of cows dappled black and white, placid and content as they munched the thick juicy green grass, or a couple of horses dreaming beneath the sun, and the vista would suddenly extend for many miles across the wide vale that stretched below the ridge on the southern, or Buckinghamshire side. Then he could see no towns, but only scattered farmsteads and the occasional hint of tiny villages sheltering in the combs. Once he came across a fox – its coat a shining rufous colour – sunning itself on the pathway, and because Alexander (even with a false leg) still walked with a very light tread, the fox did not know that he was there for several minutes, as Alexander gazed at it with happiness in his heart. Sometimes Alexander would hear a blood-curdling shrieking barking in the woods, and the first time he heard this dreadful sound, the hair stood up on the back of his neck. But the next time he heard this terrible noise, he was able to identify its source: it was a tiny muntjac deer, a male with a pair of miniature horns, standing in the trees and yelling at the woods around him. As Alexander walked, the tree canopy above and all around him was alive with birdsong, but it was only rarely that he was able to identify any particular species, for he could not see the birds through the dense leafy cover of summer.

Alexander had obtained a Blue Badge, which allowed him, as a disabled person, to park his car for free in public pay parking grounds, and to park it in the street on white lines. He joined the public library in Thame, and began to read voraciously once again. He discovered Patrick O'Brian, the writer of superb Royal Navy historical fiction set during the Napoleonic wars, and as he read about the adventures of Captain Jack Aubrey, and his "particular friend", Dr. Steven Maturin, he realised he had found the most mature, most wonderfully written and best researched historical fiction he had ever read.

Alexander did not watch much television, although he took to watching "Neighbours" every week day. What was it about this popular Australian soap that he enjoyed so much? It was n't the muscle-bound young male characters in it, who were uniformly dumb as oxen (and whose overblown physiques were anyway not at all to Alexander's taste): it was, he realised, that the setting reminded him so much of suburban South Africa back in the seventies and eighties.

Alexander was watching, by chance, the BBC news channel on the television at 1 p.m. on the 11th September. Thus he witnessed, live as it was happening, the second aircraft crashing into the south tower of the World Trade Centre. He was so horrified by the ghastly scale of the tragedy unfolding on the television before his eyes that he whispered "Oh Jesus. Oh Jesus."

In November, Ortie's health commenced a rapid decline. She was being sick after almost every meal, and she was losing weight fast. Alexander took her to the nearest vet, at Princes Risborough, which was only a few miles away.

"She's begun to die of old age, Mr. Maclean," the vet told him after examining her. "There's not a great deal we could do for her. It might be a kindness to have her put to sleep."

The diagnosis did not shock Alexander. It was as he had feared. But the pain he felt was almost overwhelming. "I'll take her home, and think about what you've told me," he said.

Alexander had tears in his eyes as he drove home with the old cat. He put her on his lap when he got home, and caressed her and spoke to her. Later, after eating very little for supper, and that only because he stroked her tummy, she was sick again. That night he sat up with her until she was fast asleep. The next morning he rang the vet and asked him to make a home visit. "It will be kinder if we put her to sleep at home," he explained.

The morning passed as slowly as a horrible nightmare, but Alexander struggled, for the cat's sake, not to allow his distress to show. He held Ortie on his lap, and then she lay in the sun on the carpet. When the vet arrived in the early afternoon, Alexander insisted that Ortie be put to sleep in his arms, and so she died in Alexander's embrace, his unashamed tears falling on her fur coat.

Now Alexander realised just how truly alone he was. There was no one with whom he felt really close; no one with whom he could share his grief. He buried the old cat's body, wrapped in her favourite sleeping blanket, in the back garden beneath the beech tree, and as he did so he re-lived the pain and anguish he had felt after Lulu's and Smokie's deaths. After a week or so had passed, Alexander found a flat stone on which he painted Ortie's name, and he placed it on top of the grave. For many nights thereafter, he slept even less soundly than was the norm for him. He allowed two weeks to pass, and on the 3rd December he bought a bottle of scotch and poured himself a double when he got back home, and drank it. He followed it immediately with another large measure. Two days later he had to buy another bottle of scotch. To do so, he drove into High Wycombe, where there were many liquor stores. Within just a few days, he was consuming as much liquor again as he had been drinking when he had entered the clinic in Harrow in April 2000. He had managed to remain sober for seventeen months. This time, his bout with alcohol would come very close to killing him, and he was to become re-acquainted with Hell.

Thirty-Six

Deliverance

Whilst Alexander refrained from behaving in the outrageous fashion with which he had pursued his drinking in High Wycombe, he became known as something of an eccentric – and some would say, as a bit of a lush – at the Red Lion, the pub not far from his home at the bottom of the High Street in Chinnor where he did all his public drinking. His eccentricities of character became hugely exaggerated under the influence of prodigious quantities of alcohol, only a fraction of which was taken in public. He would arrive at the Red Lion in the evening having been drinking on and off all through the day, and because he made an enormous effort to keep himself looking presentable, clean and freshly shaved (his experiences in High Wycombe having given him a consciousness, even when very drunk indeed, of the importance of avoiding becoming a byword in Chinnor, which was to be his home for the foreseeable future), no one, not even the landlord who ought to have known better, realised just how drunk he was.

That Alexander, who routinely drove into High Wycombe or Princes Risborough to buy his liquor, managed to avoid having an accident with the car, was nothing less than miraculous. But by the beginning of February the following year, he was struggling even to drive anymore. Alexander was consuming a bottle of scotch a day (together with several pints of beer at the Red Lion), and although his craving for liquor remained unabated, his tolerance was diminishing rapidly. He struggled to reach that point where he felt he had drunk enough not to feel the anxiety associated with an unsatisfied need for alcohol. No matter how much he drank, he felt agitated and distressed. But drinking less was not an option. His body still craved the same large quantities of alcohol as before, or the onset of physical withdrawals would quickly set in.

By midway through February 2002, Alexander seemed to be suffering from near-permanent withdrawals, and no amount of drink would calm them. He was no longer able to keep up the struggle to maintain his personal hygiene, and he could no longer organise himself sufficiently to tackle his laundry. By the 24th February he was trapped in his home, his larder bare, his clothes filthy, and he was soiling himself, losing control of his bowels and bladder. Alexander, with about a quarter of a bottle of scotch left in the house, and aware that he was now incapable of obtaining another bottle, rang Alcoholics Anonymous in the early morning of the 24th. He had in effect already had his final drink shortly before making the phone call, for he could not now keep alcohol down without vomiting – though the craving for more liquor was like a terrible, raging desire that saw Alexander's mind and body united in a descent into Hell.

As Alexander went cold turkey, scared many times that he was dying (as another seizure would grip and shake him like a rat in a terrier-dog's jaws), he took a phone call, expecting that someone from Alcoholics Anonymous was checking up on him, but it was from his mother: it was his forty-seventh birthday. He told his mother he had the flu, that he was being looked after, and that he loved her, and would phone her when he felt better.

Only the twice daily visits by representatives from Alcoholics Anonymous kept him alive. These men, who spoke not one word of judgment against him;

who neither lectured nor browbeat Alexander, kept him supplied with plenty of cigarettes, sugar, tea and coffee, and at his own request, with jars of Bovril (with which Alexander made strong meaty vitamin B-rich hot drinks which helped keep him alive). After three or four days had passed, Alexander began drinking mugs of instant soup with a couple of slices of toast. Alexander lived from one visit by these men from Alcoholics Anonymous to the next, suffering the horrors of medically unsupervised withdrawals with a grim, desperate fortitude. When the demons arrived to torment him at night (for Alexander could see them; they were as visually real to him as the daytime and early evening visits from Alcoholics Anonymous were real), Alexander prayed simply, "Jesus my Lord! Jesus my Lord! Help me!"

After five days, the worst was over. Filthy, stinking, trembling with weakness and fatigue, Alexander found that he was able to think straight again, and that he was suffering no more seizures, and that he could sleep again. After a week had passed, one of the men from Alcoholics Anonymous, having removed enough of Alexander's soiled clothing to make a clean change of clothes for Alexander once he had taken the ghastly bundle back home with him and laundered them, drove Alexander to his first AA meeting. It was a Saturday. The meeting was well attended, and perhaps a quarter of those present were women. Alexander's welcome was genuine. He felt safe. He felt that he could be himself – the wreck of a Human being that he was – and no one would judge him.

Alexander was to attend at least four AA meetings a week for the next four years. He made many friends. His social life blossomed. He was invited to barbeques and garden parties throughout that summer. He experienced a sense of community and belonging that had thus far evaded him throughout his life. He came to know a sense of acceptance that he had never known anywhere, at any stage in his life before. And he remained sober. After just a few short weeks, it was no longer an effort to remain sober, and it would never again be difficult for Alexander to remain sober. The smell of alcohol, the sight and sound of drunkenness, repelled him. Alexander began to learn how to live honestly, and to face up to the worst within his nature – and to recognise and acknowledge what was best in his nature, also.

Alexander ascribed his deliverance from alcoholism (for within six months he had become aware that he had been set free from far more than merely a compulsion to drink: he had been freed from the alcoholic's obsessive, manic-depressive mindset) to his renewed Christian faith. But the God in whom Alexander found himself believing again was a demanding god. In return for gifting Alexander with a greatly renewed faith, and the comforts and strengths that this faith brought him, God desired (so it seemed to Alexander) that he utterly renounce his sexuality. Alexander was eager to do so. His sexuality had been a curse, an affliction, and had brought him nothing but misery and pain since his adolescence. Alexander's God had not, then, let go of him. It seemed there were still some tasks He wished Alexander to fulfill.

One of these tasks appeared to be that Alexander take honest stock of his own fallen nature. Already, during that period of savage, racking addiction withdrawals which had presaged Alexander's deliverance from alcoholism, he had felt as if he was being crucified on a cross made up of every wickedness he had ever committed, and mocked by every failing of his own character. He had suffered agonies of remorse for the many callous, self centred and truly depraved acts of which he now knew he had been guilty. Alexander experienced an acute anguish at the way he had lived much of his life. He feared he had exploited the vulnerability and need and helplessness of every rent boy and drunken woman he had ever taken home, upon whom he had sought temporary satiation of his lust. He was horrified at the advantage he had taken of Guy's youthfulness, and terrified of the long term harm he may have done him. And he was stricken with guilt at the self-imposed distance he had maintained for much of his adult life between his father and himself. Alexander had done with weeping for his sins during the worst of those withdrawals, but the remorse he experienced was heartfelt, and it persisted.

And what a failure he had made at the business of being Human: how little (if at all) the world had been improved by his presence in it; how few people today remembered him with love. He had long ago lost touch with his early friends, those friends he had known in Hillbrow and Yeoville when he had been a young man, who were forever youthful and golden in his memory, eternally proof to aging. He had lost touch with almost every other friend he had ever made since that time. He had not seen Guy – except once or twice from a distance only – since the latter had ended their relationship in November 1990, and he would not now know how to contact him (as he found out, when he tried ringing the last phone number he had for Guy, to beg his forgiveness: Guy was no longer known at that number); nor was he in touch with Max, whom he had liked so much when he had lived in Kings Langley. His friendship with Paul and Monika had already soured before he had left Kings Langley (and perhaps that was not, after all, his fault, for he had being judged and condemned by them, and by the parents of the two little German boys he had been so fond of, for sins he had never committed, and was never to commit). Only his friendships with Piers in London, and with Filippu in Malta, were still alive.

Gratitude, however, persisted in welling up in Alexander's heart. His deliverance from alcoholism was to mark for Alexander throughout the remainder of his life a watershed greater than any other in his life, and when contrition and remorse threatened to overwhelm him, he need only consider this deliverance to know that God had surely forgiven him: he was no longer under condemnation.

Sometimes Alexander attended two communion services at Saint Andrews on a Sunday, and he would attend Communion at least once during the week also. He usually went to Evensong once or twice during the week too, sometimes also on a Sunday. He found that the sense of belonging he experienced in Alcoholics Anonymous was replicated to a lesser extent at Church.

In May, Piers Hawkins came down from London by train one Saturday to spend the day with Alexander. Alexander met him at High Wycombe station, off a fast train non-stop from Marylebone. "Sandy! How good you're looking! Living in the country suits you," Piers greeted Alexander with a smile. "Lucky you – away from the crowds and noise and petrol fumes of London."

The two friends shook hands and Piers clasped Alexander's shoulder. "You're looking good too, Piers," Alexander responded. "Indeed, we're both a sight for sore eyes, eh?"

Piers laughed and grinned.

Once through High Wycombe, the bucolic atmosphere became intensified as Alexander drove Piers past fields of new wheat and pastures in which sheep (with lambs already big and chubby) or cows were grazing, the hedgerows a mass of mayflower in bloom, and they drove past the occasional tiny hamlet, each just a scattering of houses, with (as they climbed towards the spine of the ridge, having turned off the High Wycombe – Princes Risborough road) dense woodland between each hamlet. The traffic was light. The weather was glorious, a bright, clear day, and the blue sky had fluffy white cumulus clouds drifting by high above. There was a slight breeze and the air had a clarity which emphasized the fresh colours in every scene.

Alexander took Piers for lunch to the Pink and Whistle near Princes Risborough, a pub famed for its food. Piers drank wine with his meal, Alexander stuck to sparkling mineral water. They found they were able to chat without the least sense of restraint, and by the time Alexander drove Piers back to the railway station at High Wycombe in the early evening, he judged the day to have been a success.

"I look forward to my next visit, my country friend," said Piers. "Living out here is good for you."

The following month – it was now June 2002 – Alexander began to experience frequent extremely painful bowel cramps, which effectively crippled him for as long as they lasted. He rapidly grew to dread them. He felt intuitively that they were associated with his knife injury. His doctor arranged for a consultant at Wycombe General Hospital to examine him. X-rays and tests persuaded the specialist that Alexander needed bowel surgery to relieve him of the intestinal lesions the clinician said he was suffering from. "They almost certainly arise from the trauma surgery you describe undergoing following the stabbing incident in 1996."

The surgery, performed at the hospital in High Wycombe, was very unpleasant indeed. Alexander suffered a great deal of post-operative pain. He remained in hospital for two weeks; a fortnight that was only made tolerable by the constant stream of visitors from among his AA friends and acquaintances. The most diligent of these visitors was undoubtedly a middle aged woman named Sarah, and Alexander was surprised at her dedication, for up until then, she had been only one of many acquaintances he had made through the Tuesday evening AA meetings in Beaconsfield. "Your visits are something I look forward to tremendously, Sarah," Alexander told her.

"I know how miserable it can be, lying in a hospital bed, Sandy. And perhaps one day you will do the same for someone else."

Alexander was touched by the kindness of these friends and acquaintances, and often his eyes would fill with tears of gratitude and he would have to blow his nose and knuckle his eyes. But the surgery was pronounced a success, and Alexander was not to suffer episodes of extreme bowel pain nearly as often in the future. However, those episodes he did suffer were quite likely to land him in Accident and Emergency at Wycombe General Hospital, when something he had eaten contributed towards the formation of an intestinal blockage, and then the pain was severe, several times causing him to phone for an ambulance. On each such occasion, Alexander would invariably spend a night in hospital, until (with the aid of intra-muscular morphine injections) the bowel restriction had cleared.

Alexander began to learn, by trial and error, that there were certain foods it was better to avoid. Anything with high-volume roughage, such as peas, sweet corn, raisins and sultanas, had to be avoided completely. He learned also that fried foods, in particular, fried eggs, were to be avoided. In this painful experience of trial and error, Alexander was given no guidance by the National Health Service. His visit to a dietician to whom his doctor referred him was worse than useless, he felt: the foolish young woman (who appeared to be of only moderate intelligence) seemed unable to grasp the nutritional challenges Alexander faced, and the issue of which foods to be avoided in his situation was beyond her.

In September 2002 Alexander visited Paris for three nights with a friend from America he had made via Alcoholics Anonymous. Although single, Rick was not a homosexual. He was a few years older than Alexander and he had been raised in Mississippi. Alexander found they shared in common an experience of growing up in a warm climate amidst black segregation and black domestic servants. Rick was passionately interested in antique furniture and he had become fairly knowledgeable in this field. Alexander too was interested in antiques, though he wished he knew more about them. Rick had bought an old farmhouse near Princes Risborough. Although only in his early fifties, he had already retired and seemed to have plenty of money. Alexander never asked him what he had done for a living, for the question seemed irrelevant.

One day in late summer Rick expressed a desire to learn about the French language and culture, and when Alexander suggested they make a visit to Paris together, he was eager to do so. At the public library in Thame, Alexander researched some of the Paris *brasseries* and restaurants. On their first evening in Paris they selected classic *brasserie* dishes at *Le Train Bleu* in the *Gare de Lyon*, with its opulent, *fin de siècle*, heavily gilded interior. The two friends ordered steak tartare for their main course, and for dessert, they both ordered the establishment's famous *Paris-Brest*, made from *choux* pastry and hazelnut cream. On their second night in Paris they ate at *Au Rendezvous des Chauffeurs*, in *Rue des Portes Blanches*. Alexander ate rabbit, Rick ordered *bavettes de boeuf*. And on their third night, Rick and Alexander had supper at *Terminus Nord*, opposite the *Gare du Nord*. Another very well known *brasserie* dating back to the great era of rail travel, it was known for its seafood. For his main course, Alexander ordered wine-poached salmon with black truffle sauce. He believed that as the alcohol evaporated during cooking, he was not breaking his commitment to an alcohol-free life. Rick ordered *Coquilles Saint-Jacques* as an entrée, followed by lobster *thermidor*. During the daytime they visited Montmartre and the basilica of *Sacré Coeur*, together with the cathedral of *Notre Dame*, the *Louvre*, and *L'Église du Dôme*, which housed Napoleon's tomb, carved from a massive block of blood-red porphyry. Alexander was fascinated by Napoleon, whom he saw as the embodiment of utterly amoral, unrestricted ego and masculine genius.

In March 2003, Alexander spent ten days holidaying in Malta. He had stayed loosely in touch with his Maltese friend, Filippu Dingli, since his departure from the islands in September 1992. Filippu, looking somewhat older now, met him at Malta's neat little airport. "Sandy!" he exclaimed, shaking hands with Alexander, "How nice to see you again, it's been ten years, has n't it?"

"I think so Filipppu. *Kif int?*"

"Bearing up – as you used to say. And what about you?"

"*Jien tajjeb grazzi*."

Filippu smiled. "You remember some Maltese. That's pretty good. Do you want to carry on straight to the Preluna Hotel, or shall we look in at the Hole in the Wall?"

"The hotel, I think, Filippu. I no longer drink. A good Maltese coffee is what I would enjoy right now."

At the Preluna, which was located on *Triq It-Torri*, not far from Alexander's old flat, the two men sat in the open air at street level in front of the hotel café. Across the street was the wide promenade that Alexander remembered so well, and beyond that the Mediterranean. Filippu drank a *Kinnie*, while Alexander sipped at his black coffee. They chatted, catching up on each other's lives. Filippu had retired, and spent his days at cafés and bars, or sailing a friend's restored *luzzu*. Listening to Filippu, basking in the warmth and sunshine after the raw March weather of England, Alexander experienced an emotion still infrequent enough to come to his notice: it was happiness. "This is where I belong," he thought. "Not England."

During his remaining eight days clear in Malta, Alexander made no attempt to contact Marija Caruana. He was mature enough to know that some territory was better left un-revisited. He hired a car for some of the while, driving all round the main island, and crossing over to Gozo also. He met up with Filippu three times, once visiting the Hole in the Wall, where he contented himself with a couple of *Kinnies* while Fillipu drank lagers. He had happy memories of the Hole in the Wall, and of Robbie, his Scottish friend. He had long ago lost touch with Robbie, having found over time that they no longer had anything to say to each other, for all the closeness of their friendship in Malta. He sent Piers, his friend in London, a postcard. He also sent postcards to his brother, Roy, and to his mother. "I'm treading in Grandpa's footsteps," he had written on the postcard to his mother. In his memoirs, published in Kenya, Alexander's maternal grandfather had written with much fondness of his time based in Valletta as a young lieutenant in the Royal Navy before the Great War.

By the time of Alexander's return to England, he had decided that if he could, someday he would live permanently in Malta. It was not only that the magnificent Baroque architecture of Valletta and Mdina, and the honey-coloured limestone that you saw everywhere used as a building material in Malta, appealed to his sense of aesthetics: he was drawn to the African feel of the island's somewhat stark, rock-girt landscapes, and the awareness everywhere on the island of the sea being not far away. After England's often vile weather, the steady, benign Maltese climate was of great appeal to him also. But this wish was to go unfulfilled. Alexander was to spend his last few years living somewhere far removed in spirit from Malta.

During the spring of 2003, after Alexander's return from his Maltese break, he had become conscious of a woman he saw at many of the Alcoholics Anonymous meetings he attended. Her name was Victoria, and she looked to Alexander to be about ten years younger than himself. He was to learn later that she was only four years his junior. He listened to her addressing some of the meetings. She was modest and self-possessed, with an appealing, understated sense of humour. Her build was slight but very feminine. She had features he would not normally have been especially drawn to, but in Victoria he found them most attractive. Her pale, flawless complexion; the fair hair gathered and rolled loosely behind her head; the grey eyes; the small, shapely mouth and the touch of colour on each cheek put him in mind of the face of a porcelain doll from the 19th century.

"I like the way you tell the story of your journey towards sobriety, Victoria," Alexander told her after one meeting. "You do so with much humour and humanity."

Victoria smiled at Alexander. "Some of us are going for coffee at the *Café Rouge*," she said. "Would you like to come?"

Thereafter, Alexander often joined Victoria and some of the others for coffee after meetings. Alexander found that not only could Victoria make him laugh at life's comedy, but he was able to make her laugh also. This shared sense of the absurd drew them together after meetings during the course of that summer. One mild August evening, after an Alcoholics Anonymous meeting they had both attended at Thame, Alexander learned that Victoria lived in Princes Risborough, not far from Chinnor. "Stop off at my house in Chinnor for a coffee on your way home, Victoria," he said.

"That would be nice, Sandy."

On Wednesday evenings there was an Alcoholics Anonymous meeting at Princes Risborough, which Victoria always attended. In time, Alexander fell into the habit of having a coffee at Victoria's ground floor flat in Princes Risborough after this meeting. She had a plump, friendly cat which Alexander enjoyed petting. "I must get another cat," he told himself.

Alexander found that where he was fundamentally a conservative on social and cultural issues, Victoria inclined to the liberal-left, but neither of them wished to preach to the other. Instead, they talked for the most part about Britain's social culture: what had been the forces forming contemporary British society? In which direction was it headed? Until then, Alexander had not given much thought to economics. Victoria encouraged him to begin exploring his position *vis-à-vis* capitalism *versus* socialism, and he discovered that he was in fact far more of a socialist than he had realised. Their conversations whilst drinking coffee together after AA meetings began to include discussions not so much of politics, but of political theory. They only rarely talked about their drinking days, and each afforded the other the courtesy of assuming that sobriety was no longer an issue. This was not always the case with members of Alcoholics Anonymous, some of whom feared that unless they attended four, five, or six meetings a week, they would be unable to remain sober, and these people were often compelled to talk about their drinking. Alexander felt not the least temptation to drink and nor did Victoria. In fact, she sometimes referred to herself as a "recovered alcoholic," a term that was anathema with many Alcoholics Anonymous members, but which Alexander understood very well.

By the winter of 2003, Alexander and Victoria had grown very close.

Alexander had not in fact experienced such a close bond with anyone since his friendship with Guy, and this was a friendship altogether more mature: Alexander was not now in the grip of an erotic infatuation. Together with their interests in serious issues – economics and political and social theory – they also talked about their shared interests in classical music, art and architecture, and each played the other sound tracks from their favourite compositions. Quite how they found so much to laugh at together, Alexander was at first unclear, but there was a lot of shared laughter in their friendship. When however he thought about it, Alexander realised they shared an ability not only to laugh at life's comedic absurdities, but at themselves.

But theirs remained a platonic friendship. There were times however when they both came close to overstepping that undeclared boundary. One evening after an Alcoholics Anonymous meeting near the midsummer of 2004, they had continued to Alexander's bungalow, and sitting together on the sofa, Victoria interrupted him as he talked about some happy occasion from his youth and said "You have such a compelling gaze, Sandy. Your eyes seem to shine and dance when you're really caught up in what you're saying." Then she leant across and kissed him on the mouth. Alexander was taken by surprise but he held the back of her head and prolonged the kiss, although it was not arousal he felt as he and Victoria kissed, except on the most instinctive level, but something akin to compassion. When they broke apart, Alexander said "Vicky, I don't know that this is wise. What we've got already is perfect. I don't want to spoil it."

"Yes," Victoria replied, "perhaps you're right."

Thirty-Seven

Tragedy

In September 2004 one of Alexander's friends from Alcoholics Anonymous helped him buy a computer and go online for the first time. Alexander became an online member of a British nationalist political party of some notoriety among liberals and left-wingers during that same month. He had become deeply concerned at high immigration numbers to Britain, and he had also become distrustful of the political aims of the European Union, of which Britain was a member state. Although his political thinking in late 2004 was somewhat naive and simplistic, it was to mature (driven by an ongoing internal discourse he sustained via his writing) over the next fourteen years to such a degree that by late 2018 he had discarded many of his earlier political beliefs, and was now adopting radically opposed positions on many issues to those that he had earlier adhered to.

Alexander very soon began to post regular comments on the party's weekly newspaper online forum, and before long he was submitting articles which were being published in the party's monthly glossy magazine. These essays, while conventional enough in nationalistic terms, were maverick where social issues and economics were concerned: they promoted an extremely conservative social culture, yet espoused socialist, redistributive economics. He argued consistently against what he soon took to calling "corporatism", and against high capitalism and the cult of consumerism, and he favoured a form of national socialism that had nothing at all to do with fascism. He was adamantly opposed to anti-Semitism: he would savagely criticise the anti-Semitic comments that were sometimes posted online by readers of the party's newspaper. He also pursued a growing interest in environmental and conservation issues, and he began to write about the ultimately fatal danger to the environment and to its fauna and flora posed by an exponential growth in Human population numbers. In this, Alexander was in the vanguard of environmental consciousness, and well ahead of the later far more widespread awareness of the dangers of unrestrained human population growth which was beginning to be written about even in the liberal Guardian national daily by early 2019. The editor of the party's magazine invariably published everything Alexander submitted.

Victoria did not understand Alexander's political stance, yet she was convinced that he was no racist, nor was he a cheerleader for capitalism, and in her eyes he was a thoroughly decent and kind man, so she suffered his interest in British nationalist politics in silence.

In October of that year Alexander began to fall prey to a growing physical exhaustion. He lost weight. He found himself falling asleep suddenly, without warning, and several times he dropped burning cigarettes on his bed-clothes while reading in bed, only to wake again as he smelled the acrid smoke from a mattress through which a cigarette was steadily burning its way. Then, in a panic, he would attach his prosthesis and strip the bedclothes from the bed and rush for a bucket of water to douse the slow burn. He frequently fell asleep unawares in his armchair also, a lighted cigarette tumbling from his nerveless fingers onto the carpeted floor, burning a hole in it. His doctor referred him to a consultant in London and in late November, feeling too frail and exhausted to tackle the train and the Tube by himself, he arranged for a South African friend in Alcoholics Anonymous to accompany him to London for the appointment. The consultant, having had Alexander's abdominal region X-rayed and after analyzing the results of a number of tests (some of them painful and unpleasant both at the time and in their after-effects) which were administered at High Wycombe General Hospital, diagnosed him as suffering from a chronic, progressive, and incurable disease named enteric neuropathy.

Alexander's ability to derive adequate nourishment from solids had been severely compromised by a combination of internal damage dating back to his stabbing injuries in Johannesburg in 1996 and (as Alexander was to discover from his own online research) by too much subsequent bowel surgery, along with a regime of powerful codeine-based analgesics prescribed him for more than two years by his doctor to control his bowel pains. Alexander was quite literally slowly starving to death. The London specialist prescribed a clinically formulated liquid food supplement, and within a very short while after commencing this regime, Alexander's weight loss had ceased, and he recovered something of his energy. He only rarely fell asleep now without warning, and he ceased burning holes in his bedding and in the carpet with his cigarettes. Alexander was to rely on this food supplement to keep him alive for the rest of his life.

In early December Alexander flew out to South Africa, where it was summer time, landing at Jan Smuts airport, where Roy met him in the early morning. "Oh gosh, it feels good to be home again!" Alexander exclaimed, as Roy drove him to his home in Sekunda, there to collect Roy's cat (he had adopted a cat which had arrived at his doorstep one winter's evening a year earlier), load her into a traveling basket, and continue their journey through the maize fields of the Orange Free State and then descend the escarpment at Harrismith, entering Natal province, with the northern Drakensberg range visible on the far horizon to their right, a pale grey-blue, jagged line against the darker blue of the sky. Continuing down the N2 they took the off-ramp for the sprawling Natal Midlands village of Hilton, where their mother now lived in a walled and gated retirement complex. She owned a three bedroomed house in a row of other identikit houses, and the complex contained a community centre, with a dining room which served passable meals, a bar and a lounge with a big open fireplace, a frail-care wing, and kitchens (which not only serviced the dining room, but from which residents could order meals to be delivered to their homes). Alexander was to make another four visits to his mother's home in Hilton, with his final visit being made in 2013, for in early 2014 Roy and their mother left South Africa for good, moving to England.

Alexander loved his mother's home, which was full of old familiar things from his childhood, and he walked every day in the complex grounds with their wide lawns and the big, semi-wilded dam which attracted a wealth of water fowl. There were pied kingfishers, grey herons, Egyptian geese and coots to be seen, with masked weaver birds and bright crimson red bishop weavers busy in the dense reedbeds that fringed the dam, and often, as Alexander stood by the banks of the dam, a *hammerkop* would be standing companionably nearby, also gazing at the water.

Being back in South Africa even for only three weeks brought Alexander a tremendous lightening of his spirit. On this his first visit he stayed through Christmas and New Year, hiring a car for some of that time so that he could drive his mother around the pretty, scenic Natal Midlands countryside, stopping for lunch at a number of well known restaurants in the region. Yellowwood restaurant at Howick, with its view of the splendid Howick falls, and the old, beautifully restored house furnished with period antiques, where Alexander and his mother (and Roy also, if he was down from Sekunda at the time), would sit on the *stoep* in the gentle outdoors climate and eat an excellent meal, was one of Alexander's favourite destinations.

Roy, who had returned to Sekunda after their first weekend together, drove down again towards the end of Alexander's stay at his mother's home, and the two brothers (plus Roy's cat), made the three and a half hour journey to Jan Smuts airport on the Monday following, where Alexander boarded the evening departure for Heathrow, eleven and a half hours away.

Alexander and Victoria holidayed together in Malta in March 2005. Alexander had turned fifty the month before. He did not yet look his age. He was still very slim, though he had a small paunch, a consequence of the enteric neuropathy he suffered from, but this he hid beneath his generously cut shirts, and a high, thirty-three inch waistband (he always took his trousers to a tailor in Frogmore in High Wycombe to be taken in from a thirty-four inch waist) and clip-on braces holding his trousers up. His hair, though thinning a little, was still golden (even if some of the shine was beginning to fade). His face was comparatively unlined. He knew that he and Victoria made an attractive couple. It was a tremendously happy holiday. The two of them found that they had no serious disagreements of any sort whilst away together.

"Sandy," Victoria remarked one morning as they were sitting drinking coffee in the spring sunshine in Valletta, having listened to Alexander outline his plans for their afternoon, "you know I don't normally defer to men, but when I'm with you, it's easier just to go along with your plans, because – well, because you're so damned organised, and you always know just what you're doing." This was delivered with a wry smile, and Alexander laughed.

"Thanks for the vote of confidence!"

Alexander remembered having read somewhere that a holiday together was an excellent test of a friendship. Alexander felt that their friendship had passed the test with a high score. Victoria loved Malta as much as Alexander did. It pleased Alexander that at the Preluna Hotel the staff and the other guests they spoke with took them for a married couple. Alexander noted also that people were far friendlier towards a couple than they had generally been when he was holidaying alone. Cynically, he put this down to their feeling less threatened by a couple than by a single man.

"Do you ever think about marrying again?" Alexander asked Victoria one morning in Valletta during this holiday. Victoria had had a brief marriage when she had been much younger. It had ended in divorce.

Victoria thought a while. "Sometimes," she replied. "It would be nice in a way, to make that commitment with someone I loved."

"What if I were to ask you to marry me one day? I think we suit one another amazingly well."

Victoria smiled. "Are you proposing to me, Sandy?"

Alexander grinned. "I suppose I am."

"If I ever marry anyone again," Victoria said, "It would be you."

"So that's a maybe?"

Victoria laughed. "Yes. Maybe I'll marry you – one day!"

Alexander, who had been surprised at the direction his unplanned words had led him, felt both happiness – and relief. It would be right to marry Victoria – but after all, not yet.

Alexander enjoyed introducing Victoria to Filippu. Alexander knew that Victoria was a lovely woman; bright, attractive and personable, and he was proud of her. Victoria took to Filippu, who was very charming towards her.

Soon after Alexander's return from his holiday with Victoria in Malta, he began to attend auctions at a few of the auction houses in the region. He had always been drawn to the delicacy, strength and beauty of English bone china. He came away from his first auction with a Spode tea set, which he sold via Ebay to a buyer in the States. His markup on this first occasion did no more than cover the packing and postage costs, from which Alexander learned that he must take care in future to detail delivery costs to the Americas and further afield alongside his advertised sales price. By August that year Alexander had developed a reliable feel for what he thought the bone china pieces he was after that day would fetch in the wider market, and how much, therefore, he was prepared to bid for them. He began making regular markups, after packing and postage costs, of between twenty-five to fifty percent on the bone china tea sets, dinner services, tea pots and other pieces he was selling. Most of his customers lived abroad: he sold to buyers in the USA, Canada, Australia and South Africa. He had bought a compact digital camera for fifty Pounds with which he photographed the china, arranged on a large piece of black velvet, loading these photographs onto his Ebay site. He packaged the china himself at home, having bought the packaging materials he needed online. Alexander's Ebay vendor's site scored a consistently high customer satisfaction rating.

Alexander was still trading in bone china via Ebay after three years had passed, but by mid-2008 he found his stamina was declining and this hobby-venture was becoming physically exhausting. Alexander ceased going to auctions, and by the end of that year the only evidence that he had ever been a successful trader in a small way in fine English bone china was three Wedgwood *Wonderlust Yellow Tonquin* teacups and saucers he had kept back for himself and which he displayed (together with the Royal Albert *Lady Carlyle* tea set he had acquired years earlier in Yeoville in Johannesburg at a secondhand shop) behind the glass-fronted section of his classic 1950s sideboard.

In July 2005 Roy flew from South Africa to stay with his brother for two weeks. Roy, who had fairly large reserves of energy, none the less sometimes battled to match Alexander's enthusiasm for getting out and about during his stay. Despite his lowered energy levels, Alexander was possessed of a great hunger for living, and he could drive himself to a point just short of collapse. He was almost always up by seven at the latest every morning. Together, the two brothers took the train into London twice, and Alexander enjoyed showing Roy some of his favourite sights. It was the Catholic cathedral in Westminster, with its magnificent towering campanile and its splendid mosaic-work side chapels, which seemed to impress Roy most. A Bach fugue was being played on the cathedral's huge organ when they visited, the sound filling the vast building, making the air vibrate, and Roy was astonished and impressed at the profundity of the organ's bass notes, which, as he commented, you felt through the soles of your shoes, rather than heard. Roy was also captivated by the Japanese Garden at Holland Park. They took a pleasure cruise down the River to Greenwich where they stood astride the prime meridian at the Royal Observatory, a foot in either hemisphere, and they admired the displays in the National Maritime Museum.

They drove to Oxford also, and Alexander hired one of the skiffs from the boathouse below Magdalen Bridge, and he and Roy rowed down the Cherwell as far as the Thames and back again. The footpath alongside the river teemed with tourists and idlers dressed for summer; the waterfowl on the river quacked contentedly in the sunshine; the Cherwell itself was busy with young visitors from abroad, most trying, very ineptly, to punt. Alexander had learned how to punt, but he did not wish to tackle punting anymore, not with a false leg. They visited a couple of the colleges and walked in Magdalen college's deer park. They visited the Botanic Gardens alongside the Cherwell and spent some time exploring the hothouses. At Alexander's insistence, they also visited the world famous Ashmolean Museum, which, with its magnificent collections of English silver and Minoan and Egyptian artefacts and art, was admittedly of greater interest to Alexander than to Roy. "I guess these are the sort of things an educated person ought to be interested in, Sandy," Roy remarked.

"I think a cultured man needs to know of the existence of such things, yes – but we cannot all be passionately interested in this sort of stuff. The Minoan and Egyptian art fascinates me. I remember studying Egyptian and Minoan art at university, and it is wonderful to see many of the actual items I had only known of through photographs back then."

In September, Alexander and Victoria spent two nights in Paris. Victoria hadn't visited Paris since her final year at school. They took the Eurostar cross-Channel train together. During their meal together on their first evening, a meal Alexander had negotiated in comprehensible – if not passable – French, at a tiny restaurant they had chosen pretty much at random on *l'île de la Cité*, Victoria told him "Since I met you my life has become far more adventurous, Sandy. Nothing scares you. And I feel safe with you."

Alexander was touched by these words. "And since I met you, Vicky my life has acquired a fullness it lacked before. I'm happier than I ever thought I would be."

They smiled at each other. "Tenderness," Alexander thought, "is probably a better basis for a close and loving relationship than many other emotions." For tenderness, *agape*, rather than erotic love, was what he truly felt towards Victoria. He was honest enough to confess to himself that he enjoyed that she was, to his eyes, beautiful also, and that many other men probably envied him when they saw the two of them together, but what he felt for her was a tender, protective love.

Alexander had been honest with Victoria. She knew that he had had homosexual relationships with young men in the past, and that certain young men could still make him turn and stare. He wished that whatever direction their relationship took, it did so from a basis of honesty on his part.

The summer drew suddenly to a close, with the coming of grey skies and days of relentless rain from late September. Alexander's outdoor excursions ceased. He spent long cosy evenings with Victoria, either at her comfortable ground floor garden flat in Princes Risborough, or at his home, sitting in front of a wood fire. He spent Christmas day with Sarah, the friend he had made through Alcoholics Anonymous, whose visits to him in hospital had done so much to raise his spirits. But he spent Christmas Eve with Victoria at her home, and they had exchanged small but thoughtful gifts. "You have become such a very important part of my life, Vicky," Alexander said to her that evening.

"What I feel for you I have n't felt for anyone else for a very long time," Victoria replied. "I think that means you've become important to me too."

Alexander leant across and kissed her on the cheek. "Is this then how love should really feel?" Alexander wondered. "Something warm and comforting, rather than that mad unhappy passion I felt for Guy?"

In March the following year, 2006, Alexander and Victoria once again holidayed in Malta. As before, it was a holiday without a single moment of conflict or disagreement between the two of them. Alexander had hired a car, and crossing to Gozo by ferry, they had spent a magical day exploring the island, with lunch on a hotel terrace at the water's edge in Xlendi Bay.

Roy had booked his annual three weeks' vacation and was planning a trip to England in July to stay with his brother again. But this visit was not to take place. In mid-June, Victoria and a girlfriend flew to Turkey for a holiday on the Black Sea shore for ten days. Whilst there, Victoria fell ill. During the afternoon of Saturday 24th June, Alexander received a phone call from Victoria's holiday companion in Turkey. "Vicky has been taken ill, Sandy. No – it's not serious, but it's rather unpleasant for her. Yes – food poisoning. She asked me to ask you to pray for her."

"Tell Vicky I'll be praying for her, and give her my love."

Alexander got to his knees and prayed for his friend. That evening Alexander rang Victoria's parents in High Wycombe. Victoria was "comfortable," they had been told, and he was n't to be alarmed: the Turkish doctors with her had told them that her condition was "stabilized."

The story was much the same when Alexander rang Victoria's parents again the next evening, Sunday. And again, on Monday evening. Her condition was unchanged, it appeared, by Tuesday evening. But when Alexander rang Victoria's family on Wednesday evening, it was her brother, Hugh, who answered the phone. "Vicky's condition is fairly serious," he told Alexander. "It's E.coli. That very dangerous strain – I forget its name. My Dad flew to Turkey this morning."

"Oh my gosh! Perhaps I should join them."

"Maybe... I don't know. Perhaps it's better if it's just my Dad for now, Sandy."

After the phone call, Alexander found that his eyes were moist. He got to his knees and prayed very earnestly indeed.

When Alexander rang Victoria's family on Thursday evening, Hugh picked up the phone again. "Dad rang me," he told Alexander. "He said that tonight is likely to be the crisis."

Alexander was struggling to believe that Victoria's illness appeared to be life-threatening. "May I ring you again in the morning? Yeah – after ten."

Alexander rang Victoria's family number at ten-fifteen the following morning. "Vicky has come through the crisis," her brother declared. "They think the worst is over now."

"Thank God. Tell me, is your mother holding up well, Hugh?"

Victoria's mother was a nervous, anxious, birdlike creature. "'She'll feel a lot better now."

When Alexander rang Hugh on Saturday morning the 1st July, he was told that Victoria's condition had deteriorated suddenly, and was now said to be "critical". After the phone call, Alexander went for a walk along the ridge, and far above him he could hear the red winged kites calling in the summer sky, their whistling cries high, thin, and lonely. The wild roses were in bloom all along the hedgerows, and the verges of the path were heavy with tall foxgloves and Queen Anne's lace and cow parsley, and rank with nettles. There were many butterflies. The heads of golden wheat in the big field he was passing would soon be ready for harvesting. The beech woods to one side of the field of wheat were heavy and dark with leaf. Everywhere Alexander saw lush, verdant growth. He came to a gate giving access to the field of wheat. He leant his arms on the top bar of the gate and looked across woodland in the distance as the gentle slope fell away into the far valley, and he closed his eyes and began to pray.

Alexander phoned Victoria's family number again that Saturday evening. Victoria's condition was unchanged, Hugh told him. It was still said to be very serious. Alexander did not sleep very well that night. He woke even more frequently than usual. (He woke two or three times most nights, to go to the lavatory). He was up very early on Sunday morning. He rang Hugh at half past nine. There was no news of any improvement, Hugh told him, but Vickie was battling through. Alexander went to the communion service at Saint Andrews in the village. His prayers were for Victoria.

Alexander rang Victoria's family again early that evening. He knew in an instant, before Hugh had done more than say "Hullo," what he was about to hear. He felt a sudden contraction of the muscles of his face and neck, and his breath caught in his throat.

"Alexander – I'm afraid Vicky died this afternoon."

Thirty-Eight

The Family Re-United

Alexander remained seated and he let out a sound somewhere between a moan and a keening cry, rising in intensity, and this terrible cry of pain and grief subsided into a series of racking, dry sobs. But not even at the funeral service was he to weep properly. Weeping would come much later. On Monday morning he rang his mother in South Africa, and told her what had happened. Then he walked to the village shop and bought a greeting card which featured a photograph of Saint Andrew's church. There was almost nothing truly suitable available in the tiny store. The card was blank inside and he wrote a short note of condolence, addressing it to Vicky's father, mother and brother. He went out again, to post it. He hoped it would catch that morning's post.

Alexander did not know what to do next. He was in a great deal of distress. He did not pray. He remembered his heartfelt prayers for Victoria's recovery. "Prayer is useless," he thought.

Alexander rang his brother in the Transvaal. Roy was due to spent two weeks with him later that month. Alexander cancelled that visit. "I may go away for a few days. I may take the train to Oban, and a ferry across to the Islands. It's where I go when I'm hurting more than I can bear. But don't worry about me. I'll be OK. I'll ring when I get back."

With no one at home to worry about, no cat to be concerned for, Alexander drove to Boots the chemist in Princes Risborough and bought a box of sachets of food supplement powders which he thought would keep him going: the nutritional drinks in bottles he was prescribed were a weighty, massy nuisance on journeys. Late the next morning, the 4th July, he took the train to Marylebone, and a taxi along the A501 past Madame Tussaud's to Euston. It was by now early afternoon. There was a sleeper leaving for Glasgow Central that early evening. He bought himself a ticket for a *coupé*. Alexander passed the next few hours first by drinking a coffee in the railway station, then walking down Eversholt Street to Tavistock Square Gardens, where he sat and smoked in the sunshine. His mind was almost entirely blank. The actions he was performing were being done at one remove from himself.

It was early the next morning when the train pulled in at Glasgow Central. It was not far to walk to Glasgow Queen Street station, and here he caught a train for Oban. Arriving in Oban at about midday, Alexander hired a car from a car-hire agency which he had located by asking at the desk of the Royal Hotel where he had worked in 1976. Then he paid for a passage on the next MacBrayne ferry to Lochboisdale on the Hebridean island of South Uist.

As Alexander made his way up the island chain, this beautiful, stark, wild, world's edge was the right place for him to be right then. He spoke with almost no one during the day, but in the evenings, and at breakfast also (at which he ate smoked kippers if they offered them, otherwise only toast and marmalade, relying on the powdered food supplement he had with him, mixed with water, for sustenance), he was obliged to interact with other people, for he stayed at bed and breakfast establishments the three nights he spent working his way up the archipelago. He had to take the ferry once more during this journey, this time on the eighty minute crossing from Berneray to Leverburgh, on Harris. He spent his last night in the Hebrides on the main island, Lewis, at a bed and breakfast establishment in the small capital port town of Stornoway, and crossed over to Ullapool on the north-west Highland coast by ferry the next morning. From here he drove to Fort William, some distance to the south, then he continued along the beautiful coastal route south to Oban, where he handed the hire car in and booked into the Royal Hotel for two nights. It was a Saturday: the next London-bound train would be leaving on Monday morning. His grief had become banked down, like a fire which might flare up again if permitted to do so. For the most part, his mind was empty. It was in this condition of mental vacuity that it occurred to him, as he sat in the hotel's lounge after supper in the dining room that first evening, that he had never imagined, in 1976, when he had been working at the Royal Hotel, that he would be spending a couple of nights here as a paying guest thirty years later.

On Sunday morning he walked along the promenade at Oban, sitting down for a while on a bench near the Episcopalian and Catholic cathedrals and staring at distant Mull across the water. He tried to maintain his mental emptiness, to spare himself pain. He spent another night at the Royal Hotel, and he spoke to no one that evening, but sat drinking coffee in the hotel lounge, reading a Patrick O' Brian novel he had bought early that afternoon at W.H. Smith. He caught the train for London on Monday morning the 10th July, arriving at Euston in the late afternoon. Later that evening, back home again, physically exhausted but emotionally calm, he rang his brother in South Africa. The next morning he rang the cat sanctuary in Amersham and spoke to Trish, who had founded the sanctuary and who ran it with her husband.

"I have a cat, perhaps thirteen years old, whom no one wants to adopt, because she's deaf," Trish told him. "She's a darling though, a pure white cat called Bridie."

"May I come by later today?"

You're more than welcome, Sandy."

Bridie proved to be an affectionate, playful cat with a pure white coat and green eyes. Alexander loved her from the start. In her need for loving attention, and via the daily routine of caring for her, Alexander was able to manage his grief for Victoria. Bridie was with Alexander for the next four years, before, in late 2010, he had to have her put to sleep, for by then she had become very frail and emaciated, and was obviously suffering. Alexander had spent a lot of money on veterinary costs for her. In 2008 he had paid for surgery to remove one of her thyroid glands, in a successful attempt to control the hyperthyroidism with which she had been diagnosed. The following year she had undergone dental surgery, having two of her teeth extracted under general anesthetic. Alexander loved the tiny animal, and he did not begrudge the money he spent on her.

One winter morning in December 2006, as Alexander stood at the basin in the bathroom shaving, he noticed with some surprise that his hair was more white than gold. He had observed, ever since late summer, that more and more white hairs were creeping in between his blonde hairs – but somehow it had escaped his awareness, until now, that he was more white than blonde. Alexander thought that if he were to grow a moustache, it would come out white also. He decided to let his moustache grow anyway.

Alexander did not go abroad for almost five years. He did not want to place Bridie in a cattery, and he was afraid that if he asked one of his neighbors to feed her, she would manage to escape from the house. For a totally deaf cat, getting lost would be very dangerous. So Alexander remained in England over this period, his friendship with Sarah becoming firmly established.

Sarah, attractive and vivacious, was a few years older than Alexander, but having been widowed in her thirties and left very comfortably provided for, she was not searching for a romantic attachment. Their easy-going friendship suited both of them. Sarah went abroad several times a year, and then Alexander would drive her to Heathrow, and meet her again on her return. In the summer they often went out together for lunch at country pubs, and several times Alexander drove the two of them to Oxford, where, using his disabled badge, he was able to park his car just off the High Street not far from Magdalen Bridge, and they would take a small picnic hamper with them and hire a rowing boat on the Cherwell for two hours. One summer they visited Waddesdon Manor, the splendid 19th century Rothschild mansion near Aylesbury, built in the style of a grand French chateau. This fabulous country house, with its opulent interiors and magnificent landscaped grounds, was already known to Alexander from a visit he had made with his mother in May 1976. He had been living in London then, and when his mother had visited England from South Africa to see family, Alexander had hired a car for the day to drive her to the Rothschild house in the lovely Buckinghamshire countryside.

Alexander had made two visits of his own to Oxford, to buy four pairs of trousers tailored for proper, button-on braces. He had ordered two pairs of sturdy corduroy trousers and two pairs of summer chinos – to be altered to his exact measurements – from Walters, the old fashioned gentlemen's outfitters in Turl Street. These trousers were cut in a pattern very close to that which had prevailed in England during the war: they had high waists which incorporated a particularly high "fish-tail" waist at the back, and pleats, and the trouser legs had broad turnups . They had buttoned flies, which Alexander had not had to contend with since he was a boy at primary school. Walters also sold Alexander a pair of strong button-on braces and three cravats. Alexander was to wear these trousers, the corduroys more often than the chinos, for the remainder of his life. Nor was he to shave off his white moustache for the rest of his life, but he kept it carefully trimmed.

For several years, hardly a day went by that Alexander did not think of Victoria. How different his life would have been had she lived! Alexander feared that Vicky had been his last chance at a truly close and intimate friendship, and as the years went by, he began to think that his fears were well grounded in fact. In the years following Victoria's death, Alexander began to experience a profound loneliness: he was marked by a singularity of spirit which repelled any attempts made by others to break through his reserve. With increasingly limited physical stamina, and fragile, quickly exhausted energy, he could no longer engage in protracted physical pursuits. With uncertain bowels and bladder, he had to bear in mind speedy and timely access, often with only minimal warning, to a lavatory whenever he went out. Alexander no longer went to Alcoholics

Anonymous meetings. Friends he knew from Alcoholics Anonymous ceased over time to phone him, for he was not very forthcoming when they did, and he always declined invitations for social gatherings.

Alexander gave up smoking and turned to vaping. He switched from what he thought of as "hot" tobacco cigarettes to electronic or e-cigarettes without any difficulty. Within a week or two his wind was returning, along with his sense of smell and his sense of taste. Alexander never smoked another cigarette again for the rest of his life. He put away his Zippo lighters – old friends they were! – for he would have no more need of their service.

During this period, a time when Alexander's closest remaining friendship was that with Sarah, a time when he was becoming otherwise increasingly solitary in his habits, Alexander began to buy and sell the occasional collectible antique sword or antique percussion cap firearm, sourcing the items from a variety of online sites, but always selling them via a specialist online website that dealt primarily in antique and obsolete caliber firearms, although swords were also bought and sold on this site. The value of such swords as second world war Japanese Army and Imperial Japanese Navy officers' katanas was rising steadily, as was the value of sought after percussion cap revolvers such as the Colt Army .44 and the Remington .44. Alexander rarely made a profit on these deals however, as he did not hang onto the items long enough for their values to appreciate. He bought and sold for the pleasure of their possession, learning more and more about old swords and antique percussion cap firearms as time went by. These deals involved what were huge sums of money for Alexander, running into almost two thousand Pounds for the first Colt percussion cap revolver he bought, a Colt Army .44. Over time, dozens of antique weapons passed through Alexander's hands, until in about 2013 he ceased this activity, stricken suddenly by a sense of guilt at the money he had spent and was still spending on these beautiful blades and on the once deadly (and in all cases, still potentially deadly) superbly crafted percussion cap firearms.

When he gave up this expensive hobby, Alexander kept back just a few of the weapons he then owned, selling the rest, and he was never to buy another sword or firearm. In buying and selling and owning percussion cap firearms that were more than one hundred and fifty years old, Alexander was acting entirely within the law: gun licences were not required in Britain for antique and obsolete caliber firearms owned for purposes of collection and/or display.

Alexander read extensively during this time, almost entirely works of non-fiction, and his own library of non-fiction grew year by year. He sublimated his unhappiness through writing articles for the publications of the political party of which he was still a member, pieces in which he strongly criticized high capitalism, or as he often called it, corporatism, and he savaged the rootless, de-nationalised plutocrats who in his view were enemies of the British people. Sometimes he wrote almost metaphysical analyses on the issues of nationhood, race and blood, themes which were anathema to the British liberal-left, and around 2010, if the meetings were not too far away, he began speaking at some of the party's public meetings in the region, where the focus was on re-enthusing existing members and expanding the party's membership. Alexander found to his surprise that he was an inspired public speaker, and he was often asked to address public meetings.

As a consequence Alexander became known to some of the party's leaders, including the chairman, and he made several acquaintances among party members possessed of a more than usual degree of intellectual curiosity. But Sarah remained his only true friend, although it was a friendship curiously lacking in emotional depth. Alexander did not understand that he was now afraid of emotional investment in any human relationship. For two years following Victoria's death, Alexander ceased attending church services. It was only during the Easter of 2008 that he began to attend communion services once again at Saint Andrews in the village.

Roy visited for ten days in October 2006, and again every year for several years thereafter, usually in July or August. It was only once Bridie had died that Alexander made three more visits to South Africa, one each in 2011, 2012 and 2013, to be met by Roy at the airport, and to drive down together to Hilton, to their mother's home. Alexander cherished these visits. He found that he was now much closer to his mother than he had been during his thirties and forties. But he never imagined his living in South Africa again. He did not like the direction the South African social culture had taken since 1994, and the manner in which the most corrupt and toxic version possible of corporatist high capitalism now flourished in that country, appalled and disgusted him.

By 2011 then, although far from a recluse, Alexander seemed marked by a loneliness of spirit that contact with others could not alleviate. The only deep love he felt for another human being, he reserved now for his mother. Nor did he acquire another cat immediately after Bridie's death in November 2010. He knew he needed to have a cat to love and care for, but he wished to be able to go abroad a couple of times a year, and he realised that once he had another cat, he would be unable to bring himself to do so.

Yet the years passed, the seasons came and went, and in March 2014 Roy's cat died of a kidney disease, and Roy lost heart, as he had after Smokie's death. Despite his previous experience of living in England, Roy and their mother quit South Africa for good, traveling to England together. Alexander met them at Heathrow airport in the morning. His mother was in a wheelchair. "Hullo Mum," he said, bending to kiss her.

"Do you know why I'm here?" she asked him.

Alexander was nonplussed. What did his mother mean? Roy, looking thoroughly stressed, rolled his eyes. "We're going home to our house in Chinnor, Mum – where I live," Alexander responded.

As Roy was helping Alexander load the car's boot, he said in a low voice "I don't know what's happened to her. She's lost her mind."

"Perhaps she'll improve once she's settled."

Their mother did not, however, improve once Alexander had shown her her room downstairs, and then made her a coffee. She was both confused and agitated, and for the rest of the day she was forever unpacking and re-packing the contents of her airline bag. During the next few days it became very clear to Alexander that their mother was suffering from what he thought must be a form of dementia. She appeared to be incapable of comprehending that she was now in Alexander's home, in

England. "When are we going home?" she kept on asking Roy.

"How long has Mum been like this?" Alexander asked Roy. "Why didn't I pick it up from my phone calls?"

"I think it was the move that did this," Roy replied. "That, and the flights."

"But Mum must have been working up to this for a long time," Alexander responded. "Didn't you notice?"

"She wasn't anything like as bad as this back home – you didn't pick up anything from your phone calls to her – and anyway, I put it down to the stress of packing and getting rid of the furniture and stuff."

"Perhaps Mum will settle down."

In some respects their mother did improve during the next few weeks. Alexander however found it exhausting looking after her. There were times when she no longer appeared to know what her colostomy bag was, and both brothers were called on frequently to undertake changing it for their mother. This was a vile task, something at once very intimate and also extremely repellent: demeaning and humiliating for all parties. But far worse in some respects was their mother's failing memory, both short term and long term. Alexander found that when narratives could no longer be sustained, conversation at any meaningful level became very difficult to achieve. And worse than both the horror of dealing with the stoma, and the increasing infantilisation of the conversations with their mother, was the sometimes very pronounced sense of absence for Alexander of the mother he remembered loving so much. He began feeling that her death would have been easier to manage than this hopeless collapse of personality, of memory.

"Mum can't stay here indefinitely," Alexander told Roy. "She needs constant attention. I'll become ill trying to look after her like this. And she's going to get worse, you do realise?"

Alexander, with two guests staying with him, one of whom was almost out of her mind, was indeed worn to exhaustion after a couple of weeks. Worse than the physical strain was the mental strain. He began looking at care homes in the district, and of the three or four he visited in person (Roy could not accompany him, as it would clearly be unsafe to leave their mother alone), it was a home in Princes Risborough which impressed him the most. This establishment occupied what had once been the vicarage, a solid, sizable Victorian house built of brick. The location, opposite the old parish church, which was built of flints strengthened with bands of pink brick, in whose churchyard grew large, well established trees, charmed Alexander. The home's residents appeared to be middle class, well spoken: he could imagine their mother being able to relate to them. The staff seemed to him to be both friendly and professional. And there were two rooms coming vacant within days. One of these was at the back of the house, overlooking the walled garden, in which grew an apple tree which was about to come into new leaf, and which would soon be covered in blossom. Roy was very reluctant to move their mother into the care home, but Alexander prevailed upon him by sheer force of will. On Friday 21st March, the two brothers moved their mother into the home.

"How could we have done this to her?" Roy asked, as they drove back to the bungalow in Chinnor in the early evening, having stayed with their mother all afternoon, during which time they walked with her in the churchyard, and sat on a bench in the garden. "I must get a car soon, so I can visit Mum often," Roy said.

"We'll both visit her often, and if you want to make independent visits too, you can borrow my car for now, Roy. We're very lucky, finding a very good care home so close by. It's the right thing we're doing. If Mum was living with us, you'd never find the time to look for a job, and I would soon become ill and have a complete physical – and I think, mental – breakdown."

But Alexander was grieving for the mother he had loved so much: the creative, capable, intelligent, loving mother he had known. He knew he was never going to get her back. This, from what he had been reading online of dementia, was the beginning of a long road leading only through ever darker, ever more unhappy terrain.

Thirty-Nine

The West Highlands

The two brothers observed their mother's mental state worsening rapidly, the one determined not to believe what he was witnessing; but Alexander, having quickly recognised her affliction, had foreseen this rapid decline. Illness, pain and loss had taught Alexander that you faced up to uncomfortable truths and dealt with them. Alexander convinced his brother of the need to obtain power of attorney for their mother's health and wellbeing, and for her financial affairs. The two brothers took their mother to a solicitors' office in High Wycombe. A new will was drawn up. In due course, power of attorney was granted to each of the brothers, independently of, or together with, the other.

Within a short while Roy was able to escape the ravaging of their mother's mind, for soon after buying a car of his own, he began working for an engineering company in Portsmouth, coming home only on the weekends. Alexander however felt obliged to visit his mother at least three times a week, and he found that she still enjoyed being taken for drives through the lovely Buckinghamshire countryside. His mother took pleasure in the rolling, wooded hills, the fertile combs and picturesque old farm houses, with sudden distant vistas of scenes so pretty they might have been found on the cover of a glossy guide for tourists to England. She had by now accepted that she was living in England, for her memories of South Africa were fast fading.

When in late October Roy's six month contract ended, and he returned to Alexander's home in Chinnor, Alexander soon found that he yearned to have his home to himself. He longed for the opportunities to rest his mind and soothe his spirit that only solitude could bring him. He missed very much no longer being able to sit and read, undisturbed. He regretted that he could no longer take a nap in his armchair whenever he pleased. He found a flat advertised in the property section of the local weekly newspaper, and after he and Roy had looked at it together, Alexander persuaded Roy to sign the lease. "You need a place of your own. It's unnatural to live together permanently at our age," he told Roy. "I need time to be alone."

The flat was in a short *cul-de-sac* leading off the West Wycombe road, shortly before the road reached the village of West Wycombe. The countryside was on Roy's doorstep; he could hear sheep bleating from his flat and he could go running up a narrow farm road round the corner from the block of flats and so into the countryside and the hills above the town.

With Roy at a loose end until he managed to find another engineering contract, Alexander could reduce the frequency of his visits to their mother. Roy was only too happy to take up the slack. Indeed, he visited their mother almost every day. Alexander did not understand how he could bear to spend so much time with this less than accurately rendered facsimile of the mother he had once loved so much. But even so, Alexander brought their mother home every Sunday after he had been to the ten o'clock communion service in the village, and he prepared a meal for the three of them. Alexander enjoyed cooking for other people. He became more adventurous after a while, and he served up dishes that were increasingly ambitious.

During the week Alexander sometimes drove to High Wycombe, only a few miles away, and sat drinking coffee at the Costa coffee shop on Church Square, looking onto the rear of the 18th century octagonal Cornmarket building, rebuilt to a design by Robert Adam in 1761. He had often met Victoria at Costas coffee shop, and he had come to know two or three of the regulars after her death. With the arrival of his family, Alexander had become less reclusive: he enjoyed – up to a point – social interaction once again. His church friends in Chinnor continued to invite him into their homes for a meal sometimes. Alexander reciprocated on two or three occasions. He understood that he had been becoming something of a recluse: human beings were, he told himself, social animals, after all. At heart, however, Alexander remained a solitary creature. His life had, it seemed, come full circle: he had rediscovered his enjoyment of solitude.

It seemed to Alexander that the changes made in High Wycombe within the last few years were changes for the worse. He did not like the new Eden shopping mall, a stark, ugly, bare concrete wind-tunnel of a place, and he considered almost none of the shops it contained to be useful. The mall was a celebration of the materialism and conspicuous consumption which was such a feature of the Blair years – and of the Tory governments that followed. The road traffic in High Wycombe (with developments like the Eden shopping centre drawing people in from further afield) was far heavier now than it had been in 1999, when Alexander and Roy had first lived there. The streets were dirtier; there were more homeless people and beggars in evidence. There were many more empty shop-fronts, the retailers gone out of business. The town's demographic contained a huge proportion of immigrants, and, while of the Europeans the Poles were the dominant group, the majority of foreigners in the town and its satellite villages seemed to Alexander to be Africans and Asians. Few appeared to have made much of an attempt at integrating within the English social culture.

In the south of England the summers were growing much warmer; the humid, sultry summer heat-waves that Alexander loathed so much and which made him feel ill were becoming more commonplace. The winters were growing shorter; the snowfalls scarcer and less deep. The country lanes carried so much more traffic than Alexander remembered from his earlier years in the district. Driving through the Chiltern hills and woods and combs was no longer as pleasant as it had once been. There were more people out walking when Alexander took one of his favourite ridgeway walks in the countryside. The south of England, Alexander felt, was buckling under excessive and growing human population numbers.

Alexander began to feel overwhelmed by these things: by the growing volume of road traffic; by the increasing atmospheric pollution from vehicle exhausts; by the weight of numbers of concentrated humanity. When he visited High Wycombe he could see and hear that at least half of this great crush of humanity was not even of British origin. Yet Alexander had allowed his membership of the nationalist, anti-immigration political party he had belonged to, to lapse. Why was this? Alexander had a horror of anti-semitism. And he had begun to discern a growing anti-semitism within the party. At first he had sought to counter it through two or three articles he had written for the party magazine, and via the comments he had posted on the party newspaper's online readers' forum. Nor did he like the growing malice expressed against homosexuals by party members. This too he strove to counter, without at any point coming out in favour of militant gay rights. He began to feel, however, that the strident bigotry that was becoming more and more prevalent within the party was making it difficult for his voice to be heard, and at the start of 2013 he made a decision not to pay his annual membership subscription, but to allow his party membership to lapse. At the same time he ceased submitting articles for the party magazine; nor did he continue to post on the party newspaper's online forum. He completely disassociated himself then and for all time from a political party that had always been notorious in liberal and left-wing circles in England, and with whose cultural environment he felt he had less and less in common.

Instead, driven still by a compulsion to write, and by the need to express his views on current affairs and on topical issues, he took to posting comments almost every day on the online readers' forums of a number of newspapers. He began to develop and refine his political, social and economic theories in the process of doing so. He grew increasingly left-wing, though in terms of the social culture – of the ordering of society – he remained (and was always to remain) a conservative by instinct. By the start of 2015 Alexander was posting comments exclusively in the liberal-left Guardian, for he found the smug self regard and callous disinterest in the poor and the marginalised which were characteristics of the Times and of the Telegraph, increasingly repulsive.

During the summer of 2016, when Alexander was sixty-one years old, he experienced several rather frightening episodes of extreme chest pain and breathlessness, almost always when he was sitting up late at night, reading in bed, though once or twice these episodes awoke him from sleep. The first time this happened to him he thought he should probably ring for an ambulance, but he dreaded the idea of a hospital stay, and he made the decision to sit it out. "If I die, so be it," he thought. "Life is n't so grand anymore, after all."

During these episodes he would lean back against his pillows, close his eyes, say a prayer, and concentrate on mastering his breathing, and after what seemed a long while, the pain would diminish, and his breathing would return to normal. But afterwards, Alexander would feel ill and very frail for many hours. When Alexander mentioned these episodes to his doctor, he was referred to the cardiology unit at Stokenchurch Hospital near Amersham for tests, and these tests, which were conducted over a period of two months, were exhaustive. Alexander was diagnosed with angina. He was prescribed a glyceryl trinitrate spray, to spray beneath his tongue when the pains began, and it proved to be effective. However, following a particularly savage and unexpected attack one night in September 2017, and further tests (this time on the far side of Scotland, at Raigmore Hospital in Inverness, for Alexander was by then living in Scotland), Alexander had begun taking statins and beta-blockers every day. This medication was extremely effective, although Alexander found that he had to be careful not to over exert himself, for if he did so, he would feel his upper left chest begin to ache, and he would become short of breath.

Alexander accepted this latest affliction as he had accepted the ones that had gone before: calmly, without rancour. Over the years he had arrived at a stoic's acceptance of pain and debilitation, for it seemed to him that his sufferings were deserved. The burden of guilt and remorse that he bore required that he suffer his afflictions in silence, without complaint. Alexander hoped that this illness might spare him from growing too old; that he might thus evade the slow, pain-filled anguish of gradually starving to death that lay in wait for him because of the progressive nature of the enteric neuropathy he suffered from.

On a deeper level of consciousness, Alexander believed that his suffering was cleansing his corrupt spirit: he hoped that when he died, he might go straight to Heaven, avoiding the necessity of being reborn on the wheel of life. A sincere Christian though he was, Alexander was a believer in reincarnation: such a doctrine made sense of otherwise inexplicable and seemingly random sufferings and injustices in life. However, he also believed that a sincere acknowledgement that Jesus Christ was Saviour and Redeemer would, as it were, short circuit this process of rebirths, and bring it to an end. Alexander did not truly believe in a Heaven anymore: if it existed at all, it was not, he thought, a cosy cuddly place where you lived happily ever after with all your loved ones, but a spiritual state, in which it was quite possible that your consciousness of your unique earthly identity would have faded away altogether. Alexander's beliefs owed much to his reading over the years on eastern mysticism, an interest that had first been ignited as long ago as late 1976 via his friendship with Patrick. Heaven, Alexander believed, was a condition of spiritual perfection; it was not the comforting, domesticated place that most Christians (particularly the fundamentalists) believed in.

Alexander's idea of Heaven had become as rarified and stripped down as his hopes in the here and now.

Alexander drew up a will, which was translated into legal form by a firm of solicitors. He always had some money in his current account, and some savings, which grew month by month, and he owned several good oil paintings that had been in the family for some generations, each valued at several hundred Pounds. He had a few Kruger Rands hidden away. He owned a valuable collection of half a dozen old swords, along with a couple of black powder percussion cap antique firearms which were each about one hundred and sixty years old. Aside from a bequest to the charity Cats Protection, he made his brother, Roy, his only beneficiary. Roy was also named as his primary executor, with his friend from Alcoholics Anonymous, Sarah, as an additional executor.

By late 2016 Roy had not yet found another engineering contract. Alexander believed that if Roy continued to devote so much of his time to their mother – he made almost daily, lengthy visits to see her – he would never find another job. "I want to move to Scotland's West Highland coast," Alexander told Roy in late 2016. "You know how much I've grown to dislike the overcrowded south-east of England."

"But how will you manage a move like that?"

"By making it happen! If you want something in life, you have to make it happen."

"What about me?"

"I think you should stay down here. There's the bungalow – it would be yours to move into if you found an engineering job locally. You wont find the work you're after in the West Highlands. And I think Mum should join me up there after I'm settled, to leave you free to conduct a thorough job search – or to take up employment when you find it. If your job meant moving elsewhere in England, as it might well do, you would be free to do so, if Mum was living near me."

Roy was looking stricken. Alexander continued "You wont find another job at this rate, not with so much of your time spent visiting Mum. You must know that."

The two brothers talked the idea through for the next two months. It was only in December that year that Roy finally agreed it made sense to leave him behind in southern England. "Molly should go with you, I think."

"Yes, she needs a garden; after all, she was a bold street cat when you found her, used to her freedom." Molly was a young female tabby cat whom Roy in particular had got to know on his visits to the care home in Princes Risborough. She was almost always to be found near the care home, and the cat had made it clear that she was looking for a home. Roy had a very tender heart indeed. As a little boy he had frequently come home with a strange cat in his arms, and their mother had had to find out where he had found it, and take the cat back there. It had become clear over time to both Roy and Alexander, during their visits to their mother, that this friendly, pretty tabby was homeless, living on the streets, and in March 2016 Roy had adopted her and taken her back to his flat to live with him. But both brothers knew that she missed the outdoor life, and that she needed a home with a garden.

Roy looked thoughtful. "I would be able to come stay with you and see Molly as often as I wished, would n't I?"

"Of course. You would be welcome."

"What's five hundred miles, after all?"

In January 2017 Alexander began searching online for a house to rent in Lochaber in the West Highlands. He longed to escape the overcrowded and polyglot south-east of England. Scotland's West Highland coast beckoned him in his memory. There was something akin to wilderness there in the dramatic mountainous landscapes; there were great stretches of dark forest; there were lonely, uninhabited glens; and Alexander remembered the long sea lochs, like Norwegian fjords, thrusting many miles inland between the high hills and mountains.

Alexander saw an advertisement in the *Gumtree* online site "To rent – long stay tenant preferred" for a house situated in a high, sparsely inhabited glen above Fort William. In March 2017 Roy drove Alexander to Luton airport, where he caught a flight for Glasgow. He had a hire-car waiting for him at Glasgow airport, with which he followed the M8 motorway across Glasgow, and after crossing the high Erskine Bridge which spanned the Clyde, he drove north up the A82, very soon finding himself north of the Highland Line (a boundary both geographical and conceptual) and following the western shore of Loch Lomond, that island-studded and immensely picturesque inland loch more than twenty-four miles long. He stopped for a coffee and a visit to the lavatory at the village of Crianlarich, then continued across the bleak, austere uplands of Rannoch Moor, where there was not a trace of human habitation, not a tree to be seen for many miles. It was a watery landscape of lochans, bogs and marshes, broken by rocky outcrops, with low groundcover growing: bog myrtle and rushes, grasses and mosses. It was a land of no practical use to Man at all. The far mountains which bounded the moor were capped in snow. Alexander had left the rain behind somewhere north of Glasgow, and the sky was now a perfect, cloudless, cerulean blue. As he began his descent into Glencoe on the far side of the moor, the outside temperature reading on the car's dashboard rose to an unusually high 11 Centigrade. Alexander was to drive up Glencoe pass many times during the next two years, never tiring of the dramatic, sublime beauty of the landscape, but that first time he gazed down Glencoe as he descended from Rannoch Moor, he thought he had never seen any landscape quite so awe inspiring, nor so beautiful. On the far horizon range after range of snow-capped mountains disappeared into infinity. On either side, steep-sided crags tumbled to the road's edge. At the Glencoe Visitors' Centre at the bottom of the pass Alexander parked the car and used the lavatory, then drank a coffee in the cafeteria. It was a Friday afternoon, the 10th March.

Alexander checked in at the Alexandra Hotel in Fort William, a commercially important but aesthetically neglected town squeezed between the lower slopes of Ben Nevis and the shores of Loch Linnhe, a town he had last seen in July 2006, shortly after Victoria's death. He had an appointment to view the house and to meet the owner at eleven the next morning. On Saturday morning he ascended the hill behind Fort William; driving slowly up Lundavra road, and crossing a cattle grid he left the town behind, following the single track Old Military Road – part of the road system built by General Wade in the 18th century to keep the Highlands down – through very beautiful, sparsely inhabited upland countryside. Away to the east, over his left shoulder, Alexander could see Ben Nevis' vast bulk rising high above the rest of the skyline. Britain's highest mountain was crowned with snow which showed a brilliant white against the blue sky. There were sheep everywhere, some wandering along the verges of the track. The road wound and dipped and climbed for several miles, passing the occasional isolated house or steading. After some time Alexander crossed another cattle grid, and he realised he had driven too far. With some care he managed to turn the car around on the narrow road, and after a couple of miles of retracing his route he saw the house he had at first passed without noticing it, for a belt of pines had hidden it from his view coming the other way. The house sat in just over an acre of land, demarcated by a triple-strand hip-high wire fence strung on wooden posts, except on the northern boundary, where a small burn flowed over rounded and worn rocks and pebbles. The house was surrounded by open, treeless country in which sheep grazed and in which heather and broom grew, the latter now in bright acid-yellow bloom. Its nearest neighbor was about half a mile distant. Alexander turned into the driveway.

The house, built of grey cut stone with a dark slate roof, was a small double story facing west, located a hundred yards back from the road, situated on a gently rising slope. It had a pair of dormer windows in the roof, and there was a separate brick-built garage, along with some much older outbuildings built of stone. The driveway was of packed gravel and stones. There was no established garden as such, but there was a rough, bumpy lawn in front of the house, with a large, wintry oak tree standing in the middle of the lawn, with cheerful yellow daffodils and a very few clumps of late, tiny white snowdrops in bloom beneath it. Alexander was to learn that daffodils are one of the few flowers that deer will never eat. There was a Land Rover Defender parked in front of the garage. "Molly would love it here," Alexander thought.

The house had two bedrooms upstairs, with a big lounge-dining room downstairs, a bathroom and lavatory, a kitchen of average size, and a back door opening off a pantry with a lean-to roof, in which was a washing machine and a tumble dryer. There was a solid fuel iron stove in the lounge hearth-place, whose flue disappeared up the chimney. Alexander took to the owner of the house, an attractive thirty-something woman, and she seemed just as taken by him. Before he left, Alexander and she signed a memorandum of understanding, with the lease to be signed in front of a witness in a month's time. It was agreed that Alexander would begin paying rent to the owner in a month's time, on the 11th April. It would be springtime in the Highlands by then. It was the very best time of year to make a new start.

Alexander spent a second night at the hotel in Fort William, and on Sunday, after a breakfast of kippers and toast, he drove back to Glasgow airport, returned the hire car, and caught a flight for Luton. Roy was waiting for him at the airport. Alexander spent a month packing up slowly, arranging for the hire of a small removals van owned by a young man who, with his mate, would drive it, and searching online for a pet-friendly hotel in Carlisle, where the two brothers would break their journey on their way up to the West Highlands by road. With Molly the cat in Roy's car behind, they set off from Chinnor on Monday morning 10th April. Over-nighting at Carlisle, at what proved to be a very pleasant, family-run hotel, where Molly (reassured by the presence of her two humans with her in the bedroom all night) was quite content, they reached Fort William at 3.30 p.m. the next day. Alexander had had to indicate to Roy in the car behind him that he was turning off the road many times during the journey from Chinnor, obeying the sudden and insistent demands of his bladder. He had always found somewhere with a lavatory: sometimes a motorway rest stop, at other times a hotel or a pub not far from the road, with his final stop being made once again at the Glencoe Visitors' Centre below Rannoch Moor. The sky was low and leaden and there was persistent rain. It was much colder than it had been during Alexander's visit in mid-March.

Twenty minutes after reaching Fort William the two brothers turned into the driveway of the little double story house in its high lonely glen. The removals van was only half an hour behind them, with the BT phone technician whom Alexander had arranged beforehand, arriving only five minutes after that, to re-connect the phone line. Before they went to sleep that night, Alexander, in the grip of an astonishing, sustained bout of energy, had found their bedding, and unpacked the coffee, milk and sugar, along with Molly's supper and the makings of their own microwave suppers. He had also set up his PC and was back online.

Roy stayed a week. Alexander spent every day that week unpacking and setting the house in order, and Roy supervised acclimatizing Molly to her new home, a home the cat took to within three days, and gave every sign of finding much to her taste. Alexander was amazed and gratified at the energy he was able to draw on: where was he finding it? Would it last? He was careful however not to push himself: he did not wish to trigger an episode of chest pains and breathlessness. Much to Roy's disgust it rained much of the time, although when the drizzle slackened, Molly would go outside. When the rain cleared momentarily, snow-capped hilltops were visible. Alexander kept the wood stove burning in the lounge's fireplace. Most of the time Molly the cat lay stretched out in front of the stove on the hearth-rug, and in the evening, both brothers gazed into the flames, chatting quietly. Alexander thanked God at night, before he went to bed, for His blessings: for the strength and energy he was enjoying, and for Roy's help and company; and he prayed for their mother, whom he would be seeing within a few more months, if all went as planned, for there was an Abbeyfield care home about an hour's drive from the house in Ballachulish, on the far side of the narrows of Loch Leven (which, like Loch Linnhe, was a long sea-loch reaching far into the mountains).

In July Roy hitched a trailer to his car and piled the few things their mother had with her in the care home at Princes Risborough onto the trailer, and drove up to Fort William with their mother. She stayed with Alexander and Roy in the little house for two nights (two days and nights which Alexander found stressful and distressing, for their mother was on vacation from what remained of her mind), then the two brothers drove her and her modest possessions to the care home at Ballachulish, and settled her there. Alexander would visit her two or three times a week, and sometimes take her out for drives during the remainder of that summer (for his mother still enjoyed drives in the countryside), and he would treat her to an occasional light lunch at the golf club's cafetaria in Ballachulish, with its fine view across Loch Linnhe. Unfortunately the rotten spring weather continued right through the summer of 2017. The sun was rarely seen, and there was not an evening all summer that Alexander did not have the stove in the sitting room burning.

Alexander had met his nearest neighbours, who lived on a croft half a mile further up the Old Military Road, by the end of May. He heard a car coming up his driveway one mid-morning, and looking out the window he saw a Land Rover Discovery come to a halt. The middle aged couple who got out of the car introduced themselves to him as his nearest neighbours, the Mackenzies. "Come in," Alexander invited the couple. "Would you like some coffee?"

Alexander found a packet of chocolate biscuits in his larder and made coffee in his cafetière. "It's very kind of you to call on me," he said as he served them their coffee.

"Ye'll find we're a community up the glen," said Colin Mackenzie, who looked to be in his late fifties and had short grey hair and open, high-coloured features. "Which is not to say we stick our noses in others' affairs neither."

"But we wanted you to feel you could call on us for anything you needed," Colin's wife, Kirstie, continued. She was perhaps in her early fifties and her hair was still raven-black. Her skin was pale, seemingly unaffected by the elements, with that quality of denseness and glowing depth and purity Alexander had noticed in people locally whose dark haired genes clearly stemmed from the pure Celtic line pre-dating the many later invasions that had settled the west coast of the Highlands. As the couple drank their coffees they told Alexander a little about some of the families living in the high glen, and there were not many of them, perhaps little more than half a dozen, including the owners of Lundavra, the steading at the end of the road, very much further up the glen. Alexander was grateful to Colin and Kirstie. He had no great wish to socialize anymore, but he felt less isolated after their visit.

Despite the frequent wet weather, the springtime and summer of 2017 was an extended honeymoon period of magical discovery and exploration. It was a time of near-happiness for Alexander. He was very conscious of his good fortune in being able to live in this magnificent West Highlands region of Scotland. He had yet to face his first winter . . .

Forty

Finis

As the winter of 2017-2018 set in, Alexander's health began to decline again. By the beginning of Advent he had ceased attending Sunday morning communion services in Fort William. He abandoned the struggle to try to ready himself early on the miserable winter mornings, in a daytime hardly begun, and often in the face of appalling weather and bitter cold. The narrow single track Old Military Road, his only access to the town, would become impassable for his saloon car after a heavy snowfall, until the gritting lorry, with its bulldozer blade mounted in front, had cleared the drifts from the road later in the day. Alexander maintained a huge woodpile of sawn logs in one of the outbuildings, for the stove in the lounge. He kept up stocks of light bulbs, of candles, of torch batteries, and he had a small gas camping stove with spare gas cylinders, to boil water in the event of power cuts. He kept his larder well stocked with tea, coffee, sugar, milk for Molly, marmalade, margarine, packets of crisps and tins of fruit salad, with a couple of loaves of bread always to be found in the freezer. He always ensured that he had a reserve stock of his nutritional food supplement drinks in store, along with several bags of Molly's dry and wet cat foods and a couple of spare bags of Molly's cat litter. He made sure that he never ran out of medicines. He kept a first aid kit in the house. He tried to ensure that in the event of being snowed in, or of feeling unwell, he would cope comfortably for quite a while alone in the house but for Molly.

Molly loved the house, with its upstairs-downstairs, and its large garden barely distinguishable from the surrounding heather, broom and bracken of the rough sheep pasture. She spent a great deal of time outside during the long summer days (though Alexander always brought her inside for the night). She enjoyed climbing the big oak tree in front of the house. With the onset of very cold weather in November 2017 however, she hardly ever went outdoors for more than a few minutes at a time. Alexander had provided her with a litter tray in the pantry where the washing machine was kept.

Molly spent the winter evenings on his lap, or stretched out in front of the wood-burner. Alexander was concerned that Molly be taken care of should he become long-term hospitalized, or – at the worst – die suddenly. With his heart condition, these was always possibilities. Quite a number of the boys he had been to school with, men his own age, had now died. So Alexander made arrangements with the Cats Protection charity for Molly to be cared for under their Cat Guardians scheme, in the event of his brother Roy, for whatever reason, being unable to care for Molly himself. The two brothers agreed that if Roy did not hear from Alexander for more than twenty-four hours, either by text, phone call or email, and if he could then elicit no response from him when he tried to contact him, Roy was to phone the MacKays, an elderly couple Alexander knew from church who lived not far away, who would come to check on him and Molly. The MacKays knew where Alexander kept a spare front door key hidden in one of the outhouses.

Alexander watched some TV, but for the most part he relaxed by reading and writing, or by listening to music CDs on the excellent CD player that Roy had left behind in their shared High Wycombe flat in 2000. Alexander's musical tastes were catholic: they ranged from traditional Greek country music, through a selection of traditional Scots Gaelic and Scottish Highlands and Islands recordings, and across the entire body of classical music, including grand opera, and his interests included some more arcane musical *genres*, such as that represented by the two recordings he had of instrumental duets performed by a pair of musicians from Mali, Ali Farka Touré (who played guitar) and Toumani Diabaté (who played the *kora*).

Sometimes Alexander simply sat in silence and let his thoughts wander. He often found himself remembering incidents, places and people dating from his childhood, or from his early manhood. He was often moved to spontaneous penitential prayer, much of it on his knees, for he also remembered with increasing frequency and distress the shameful acts of which he was guilty in the past. That he struggled to get down on his knees, and up again, and that kneeling was very uncomfortable for him, made his prayers (he felt) the more sincere and the more likely to be heard by God.

Despite his afflictions, Alexander felt blessed. He was often filled with gratitude to God. He gave thanks that he had survived long enough to have attained a penitent's heart and that he had come to some degree of spiritual maturity. He was grateful, after all the anxiety he had caused his parents during his years of drinking, that he now had the opportunity to help care for his mother. Alexander's Christian faith, although sometimes the flame flickered for a short while (particularly when he had to suffer prolonged pain and ill health), burned without cease. Alexander saw his physical sufferings as a penance he must welcome paying. Through his suffering, he reasoned, he was being made spiritually whole again. God had indeed won him at the last.

During the day Alexander would sometimes hear the faint sound of a vehicle down on the road. Forestry Commission vehicles passed by sometimes, and from 2018 onwards there were also some vehicles on the road which were associated with the construction of a couple of small hydro-electric catchment dams in the hills at the head of the glen, which fed pipes leading down to a small hydro-turbine house being built on the north shore of Loch Leven, on the far side of the hills. Most of the heavier construction traffic however used the un-metaled road on the far side of the glen which the construction company had built. Once the hydro-electric turbine installation on the shore and the new electricity cables being led from it on pylons across the hills and down the length of the glen were completed, even the light construction traffic using the Old Military Road would cease. Then the narrow road would once again carry almost entirely only sparse local traffic. When Alexander sat in his garden, he could hear no neighbours. There was only the sound of birdsong in the ancient oak tree and in the belt of Scots pines that fronted the property alongside the road, or the background bleating of sheep, or the wind blowing. At night the peace was profound, although from October through to March the Atlantic gales would sometimes roar across the hills from the west with such an intensity that the air was filled with howling and shrieking. Alexander, who was not in general very fond of his own species, felt deeply grateful that he had no neighbor living nearer than half a mile.

The specialist in London had told Alexander in 2004 that his condition was chronic, progressive, and incurable. He found during that winter of 2017-2018 that he had less stamina than before: he could not imagine holidaying abroad anymore. He often felt extremely frail. He was frequently in some degree of bowel pain, sometimes fairly severe pain sustained over many hours. His doctor had earlier prescribed opiates: tramadol hydrochloride 50mg capsules. Within a short while Alexander was taking the maximum dose he was permitted – six tablets over a period of twenty-four hours – on a regular basis. His appetite began to diminish at the same time as his physical capacity for food continued to decline. During the winter of 2017-2018 Alexander gave up eating meat, fish and fowl, as he was finding these foods increasingly difficult to digest without their causing him pain. He was glad to have to do so: he had been experiencing growing moral qualms with eating meat for many years. By the time the first snowdrops of late winter appeared in early 2018, the nutritional liquid supplements prescribed him were his main source of nourishment. "I'm glad I no longer eat meat," he told Roy, during one of the visits Roy made every three to four months, when Roy (who had still not found another engineering contract), would stay with Alexander for between ten days to two weeks. "I've wanted to become a vegetarian for a long time, and now I'm able to do so."

Alexander ate no eggs either, nor did he drink milk. But despite his long-standing allergy to dairy products, he found that he could still occasionally manage goats' or sheep's cheese without ill effect. He was also fond of tinned fruit salad, and plain cakes which he bought pre-packaged in the Co-Op supermarket. He cat-napped often during the day, as he ran out of energy very quickly. But on some rare mornings during the spring or summertime, particularly when the sun was shining, he awoke feeling much stronger than usual, and he would take a proper walk along the Old Military Road, or he would set out along the West Highland Way, beginning his walk at the point where, for a short distance, the trail met with the Old Military Road, and he would follow the trail south through the forest. Once or twice he walked far enough to see Loch Leven far below, and across the loch he could see the mountains through which the A82 to Glasgow ascended Glencoe pass, with the distinctive Pap of Glencoe indicating the location of Glencoe village. There were however many days when exhaustion or bowel pains kept Alexander at home in his armchair. Alexander found that the seasons of the year had a far more profound effect on his health and wellbeing than he had experienced in the south.

Alexander experienced winter as a physical and mental assault. There were periods when gale force winds howled, sometimes rising to a banshee crescendo, for day after day, with driving rain and sleet borne in from the Atlantic. A good snowfall was a blessing, because after the snowfall the air was still and the weak winter sun would invariably shine for two or even three days, and Alexander would take his camera and (if the Old Military Road had been cleared of snow drifts) he would go for long drives, capturing the fairy-tale beauty of the region in the snow. He posted the best of his photographs on Flickr, where, after he had requested Face Book to delete and close his account in April 2018, the few online friends abroad who had kept in touch with him, could continue to view them.

Since moving to the West Highlands Alexander had developed an interest in Scots Gaelic, buying a primer in the language, and paying attention to place names in Gaelic on street signs and to the Gaelic written on notice boards, striving to make sense of the structure of the Gaelic in light of the English translations on the signs. In this way for example he realised early on that the name of the village where his mother's care home was located, Ballachulish, was an Anglicised contraction of the Gaelic *"Baile a' Chaolais"*, or "village on the narrows" (for Ballachulish was located at the very narrow mouth of Loch Leven).

In February 2018, as birthday present from himself, Alexander threw away his cheap, poor recordings on CD of Verdi's La Traviata and Puccini's La Bohème, replacing them with two excellent and expensive Decca recordings. He bought Decca's La Traviata conducted by Richard Bonynge, with Joan Sutherland singing Violetta and Luciano Pavarotti as Alfredo, and he bought a Decca recording of Puccini's La Bohème conducted by Herbert Von Karajan, with Pavarotti as Rodolfo and Mirella Freni as Mimi. Often Alexander would play just the final scene from Act Four of La Bohème, of the duet between Rodolfo and the dying Mimi, and at the conclusion of the opera, with Rodolfo's anguished cry "Mimi! Mimi!" when he realises Mimi has died, Alexander would usually have to sniff and wipe away tears from his eyes.

A production of La Bohème had been the first live opera performance Alexander had ever attended, in 1974, for he had bought a season ticket for the opera that year. The Nico Malan theatre in Cape Town was a splendid, dramatic venue, and Alexander was just nineteen years old. He bought a season ticket for the following year also, and by the end of the 1975 season he had heard most of the well known grand operas performed live.

With the coming of spring in April 2018, Alexander's spirits lifted and there came a general improvement in his health. He began to feel glad to be alive again. In late April Alexander discovered a wonderful forest walk at Glen Righ, which he reached via a turn-off on the A82 between the Corran Ferry and Onich. The trail led him through a forest of Scots pine and spruce trees, the latter in bright green new leaf. The ground between the tall trees was covered in a lush, deep growth of verdant moss more luxurious than the most expensive deep pile carpeting. The well-made track climbed by degrees, the slope gradual and easy except towards the top, where it grew steeper for a while. But even here, the path was well-constructed, and Alexander could tackle the gradient with the aid of his walking stick. As he walked, he came across not one other member of his own fallen species, and he heard no sound of Man's blighting presence. He heard bird song high in the tree canopy above him, and he made out the call of a very early cuckoo from somewhere nearby. He could hear the wind soughing in the tree-tops, and when he stopped to ease his breathing, he could hear the beating of his own heart.

Rising from a deep gorge to his left Alexander could hear an aquatic symphony of profound echoing bass notes which underscored the music of fast-flowing water in a range of far higher octaves, a symphony performed by a mountain burn flowing urgently across the boulders and stones of a deeply-cut water-course. Alexander's gradual ascent through the forest took him about one hour and twenty minutes to complete, and gained him sufficient elevation to reach an open, sun-lit table-land above the forest, where the dead brown bracken of the past winter had just begun to send up new green shoots, and heather and broom grew, the dense blossom of the broom a bright mustard yellow, and Alexander saw dozens of early peacock butterflies – though smaller than the variety he saw in summer in his own garden – brought to life by the sunshine, and the warm sun on the dusty trail of broken schist and sandstone and gleaming white quartzite rock put Alexander in mind of countless hikes in the mountains around Cape Town when he was a young man, and his spirit felt glad. Beyond the open table-land, the trees continued again, dark forest seemingly reaching as far as the distant Mamores and the Nevis range, which just broke the farthest horizons, pale and indistinct under their mantles of snow.

"I love this land," he thought.

Alexander sat for a while on a large flat-topped boulder in the sunshine, taking a drink of cool water from the water bottle he had in his satchel, and sipping at a bottle of his nutritional supplement to recharge his energy levels. On his way down again, a robin hopped onto a branch only just above Alexander's sight-line and regarded him from a cheery, curious, shining eye, as if to say "I see you!" Alexander felt as if, via these hours spent in the open air, a blessing had been vouchsafed him.

That spring of 2018, Alexander began work on his autobiography. It quickly became an act of spiritual catharsis; a penitential exercise. He had just completed the first draft by mid April 2019.

Alexander had resumed his church-going in early April. His outlook on life became more positive, but how he craved the sunshine: he could not get enough sun. The West Highlands were notoriously damp. But the first half of the summer of 2018 was glorious, with almost daily sunshine for ten weeks, from early May through to late July, and Alexander sat out in the garden with Molly almost every day, and his face and the backs of his hands and his forearms became tanned. But with the coming of August, the rains set in again, and thereafter they alternated only with sleet or snow until mid-April in 2019.

"You don't come here for love of the weather," an acquaintance at church joked. But of course Alexander, with his loathing for the breathless, sweaty, humid heat-waves of a southern English summer, could be said to have done just that.

With the long distance technical help of a classmate from school he was in communication with via email, Alexander had set up a blog page of his own in July 2017, within three months of moving to the West Highlands. In it he wrote short essays in which he expressed his views on Britain's social culture; he wrote about theoretical and practical economics and about political theory. He commented on current affairs around the world. He sometimes wrote poetry, or reminiscences, or short pieces on historical themes. He explored spiritual and moral themes. He developed a growing hatred of high capitalism. In a series of articles for his blog, Alexander explored his ideas for replacing capitalism with some less rapacious, less environmentally damaging economic system. When the Democrat's "Green new deal" began to gain traction and supporters around the world, Alexander seized eagerly upon its ideas. During the latter half of 2018 Alexander underwent an almost Damascene conversion. He had previously denied the part played by Man in global warming; now he came to believe unreservedly in anthropogenic (man-made) global warming. From that time on he began to research and write increasingly frequently about environmental and conservation issues.

Alexander's blog pieces became more polished: he spent much more time in researching them online (although in certain fields he referred to books in his own library of non-fiction), including in them facts and statistics in support of his viewpoints and arguments, or as background material. Alexander took to drawing up a list of largely online citations after each blog piece, referenced and numbered within the text. The reader, if interested, could follow up the online references Alexander made. Alexander did not make a statement of fact or quote a statistic without such a numbered citation to verify it. Alexander publicized his blog in the early days via mention in occasional comments he posted in the Guardian's online readers' forum. The Guardian was a British national daily with a liberal-left editorial slant, whose online readership far exceeded its hard copy readership. By the latter half of 2018, Alexander had perhaps three score fairly regular readers from around the world, including Russia, China, South Korea, Canada, the USA, Ireland, a number of European countries, and the United Kingdom itself, with less frequent visitors from South Africa, Saudi Arabia, Israel, Japan, India and Pakistan. Alexander found his blog was most read in the Far East. He did not understand why this was so. Over time, a few readers from English-speaking countries began to post in the comments sections below the individual articles. Some of these comments were highly critical; a very few were downright nasty; but the majority were honest and generally supportive responses to the articles.

Researching and writing articles for his blog brought Alexander much satisfaction. He was no longer physically fit enough to consider environmental activism in the field, but via his blog, he felt that he was doing all he could on behalf of a world which he hoped might one day be liberated from the socially and environmentally destructive embrace of high capitalism.

"I am surprised at how radical your writing is," the minister of Saint Andrew's, the beautiful stone-built Scottish Episcopal church near the

Parade in Fort William, said to him one day, having read some of the entries in his blog.

"This is an age when a radical response to global issues is called for," Alexander replied.

The autumn of 2018 was a season of great splendor, the hardwoods decked in chrome yellow, ochre, scarlet and gold, and the sun shone frequently, but Alexander felt acutely the sadness of the drawing in of the days and the winding down of the cycle of life. After another dreadful winter, during which Alexander sometimes saw no sunshine for more than three weeks at a time, he felt hugely grateful for the coming of the spring of 2019. Alexander had suffered frequent bouts of low spirits during the long dark winter-time. Lacking the renewal and spiritual rejuvenation he experienced through attending holy communion, (for Alexander had not gone to church during the months of January, February and March, unable to overcome his pronounced disinclination to get ready early enough on such horrible dark, cold mornings), his view of God's works had become somewhat embittered: it appeared to him at times that it was suffering and anguish that underlay all Creation. With Donald Trump's Twitter-Presidency much in the news, and the election of the anti-environmentalist and climate change denier, Jair Bolsonaro, as President of Brazil, Alexander's views of his own species became noticeably jaundiced. He recognised the dangers of succumbing to such a wholly negative outlook, and he sought to counter this near-despairing view of the world and of Man's part in it, through assiduous prayer. But the days were dark and wet and they were often caught in the grip of shrieking gale force westerlies racing in from across the Atlantic and the Outer Isles, and Alexander found it a struggle to keep his spirits up. In general that winter Alexander left the house as little as possible. However, he kept up his duty visits to his mother at Ballachulish, although her memory no longer functioned at all; neither for the distant past – for once cherished memories of childhood in Kenya and South Africa – nor for the words he had spoken to her only a minute earlier. She lived an eternal and uncomprehending present tense.

Alexander's work on his autobiography, during the course of that winter, continued to serve him as a vehicle for catharsis. By means of it, he shed much of the legacy of pain and hurt and misery which still afflicted him, and by late February of 2019, with the snowdrops appearing beneath the oak tree in his garden (although the tiny flowers were often covered by fresh snowfalls), Alexander's spirits were beginning to look up again, although he was obsessed by the dearth of sunshine. Always after a snowfall, however, there would arrive a rare crisp, cold, clear, still day or two and the sun, low above the horizon, would shine bravely, the snow lying heavy on the ground, its surface alternating between blue shadows and dazzling sun-lit white, and the cloudless sky, shading from powder blue at the horizon through azure, to near cobalt blue directly overhead, was pristine and pure. Then Alexander would experience an intense joyfulness, accompanied by a sense of deep gratitude, and he would know a brief rejuvenation of the love he felt for this wild region.

From mid-April Alexander was able to sit out in the garden without having to wear a woolen beanie, a scarf, or an overcoat. Molly always joined him then. She was a companionable, affectionate cat, always happy in his company. Alexander resumed his church-going on Palm Sunday. Easter of 2019 was celebrated on a late date. It was the 14th April before Alexander began going to church again that year. During the past two years he had come to know many of the members of the congregation of Saint Andrew's in Fort William, along with three or four people he came to know a little more closely, such as a widower his own age, Robert Dewar, who was a journalist, with whom he often chatted after the Sunday morning communion service. But Alexander was closest to a couple in their early seventies, the MacKays (with whom, at sixty-four years old, Alexander now felt as if he was a contemporary). Thomas MacKay was a church warden. The MacKays lived in a bungalow on Lundavra Road, the street climbing the hill above Fort William, from which the Old Military Road continued. Thomas was almost as tall and lean as Alexander, with a shock of thick white hair and dark bushy eyebrows. He and Mairi MacKay, who was short and plump, with grey hair cut fairly short and a face of exceptional sweetness, had called on Alexander two or three times during the long winter months. With the coming of spring the MacKays twice invited Alexander over for coffee during the late morning, and he was expected to stay for lunch, but because his diet was so restricted, he would accept only a bowl of soup and a bread roll. Alexander recognised these two Highlanders to be truly good and decent people. He felt privileged to call them friends.

After holy communion at Saint Andrew's on Easter Sunday morning in late April 2019, a woman who was perhaps in her late thirties or early forties approached Alexander in the church hall, a lovely smile on her face. Alexander had observed her earlier, not having seen her before at Saint Andrew's. She wore a very full black frock which reached well below her knees and was richly embroidered in heavy gold, green and scarlet thread in a stylized floral design, along with a very full cut white blouse with thick gold embroidery at the neck and cuffs. She wore a necklace of several strands of chunky black beads of what Alexander thought must be amber and jet, each bead separated by beads of gold filigree. Her dark hair was bound in a green silk headscarf, and she wore calf-length black leather boots. She had an olive complexion, with hair and eyes of such a dark brown they appeared to be black. She was small and slightly built, and altogether very attractive indeed. Alexander thought there must surely be Mediterranean or Middle Eastern ancestry in her background. She introduced herself as Miriam. Her English was accented but idiomatic.

"I'm Sandy Maclean," Alexander responded. He put down his mug of coffee and shook her hand, which seemed tiny in his own hand.

"Are you a visitor?" she asked him.

Alexander was smiling back at her. "No, I live here," he replied.

"Why have n't I seen you before?" Miriam asked.

"I don't come to church during the winter," Alexander replied. "How long have you been coming here?"

"I live in North Ballachulish. There's only one minister for half a dozen local parishes, including St. Bride's. So I've been visiting here quite often recently."

Alexander felt an immediate connection with Miriam. The connection was so powerful that he was reminded of those occasions so common during his young manhood, but rare now, when a meeting with an erstwhile stranger had quickly developed into a close friendship.

Alexander felt excitement and happy anticipation well up inside him. Miriam sat down alongside him, and within minutes they were so caught up in a conversation of mutual discovery that Alexander almost forgot that there were people nearby all around him. "Do you mind if I ask you where you come from?" he said to her.

"I don't mind." Again that wonderful smile. "I'm a refugee from Mosul. My husband and I left just before ISIL occupied Mosul in 2014. As Christians, our prospects were not good."

"You speak such excellent English!"

"I studied English at home with an English language tutor. My family was quite well off. We're Assyrian Christians."

Alexander felt as if someone from an era dating back one and a half thousand years had just materialized in front of him. Yet Miriam was no relic. She was full of vitality. "You're married, then?"

"I was. My husband has passed away."

"I'm sorry," he said. He was silent for a moment, then he continued "I know it's not the same, but I lost someone to illness whom I loved very much, in 2006, and I felt as if I would never know any happiness again."

Miriam rested her hand on Alexander's for a moment. "Our faith sees us through."

Alexander felt an enormous empathy emanating from this woman. He was talking easily with her about things he rarely discussed with others. Alexander wrote in his diary for that day "I met a lovely woman, Miriam, an Assyrian Christian (!) at church today. I felt a strong empathetic connection with her. I think and hope we shall become friends."

The two met again the following Sunday, the 28th April, and after the communion service, with the sun shining, they went for a stroll together in the Parade. Before they parted, Miriam tore a page from a small notebook she took from an embroidered cloth bag she was carrying on a strap over her shoulder, and produced a pen, and they exchanged phone numbers. When Alexander drove home to the high glen and his peaceful home, he felt an extraordinary happiness.

This mood of wellbeing persisted into the evening, and it was still with Alexander when he went up to bed shortly before eleven-thirty.

Molly was already fast asleep: she was curled up in her cosy little covered cat-bed on a table near the radiator. Alexander said good night to her and stroked the top of her head, then he got into bed and leant back against the pillows. Alexander had a book with him. He had finally gotten round to reading Harper Lee's "To Kill a Mockingbird." He was enjoying it tremendously. It was one of the few novels that his parents had bought in Kenya during the late fifties and early sixties that he had not already read. He wondered why he had spurned it as a teenager, when he had read so much else during those years?

The pain in his left chest and in his jaw began as a very dull ache, and Alexander was not particularly concerned. These pains came and went. But it grew slowly worse, until he began to feel anxious, and looking at the time on his wrist watch he took his glyceryl trinitrate spray from the bedside unit and sprayed a single spurt beneath his tongue. He waited for the spray to take effect. It did not. After five minutes had passed, with the pain still increasing, and his breath now growing short, Alexander sprayed another short spurt beneath his tongue. He was allowed no more than two sprays, five minutes apart, so his doctor had told him.

Scared now, Alexander closed his eyes and leant back and tried to calm his breathing. His forehead was wet with perspiration. He did not, he really did not wish to have to phone for an ambulance. Then in a moment, stricken by a shockingly savage pain that seized his entire chest and spread instantly beneath his clavicles and into his left arm and left him utterly breathless – a pain which, incredibly, grew rapidly even worse – Alexander realised it was too late to try using his mobile phone. His face drenched in sweat, he could not catch his breath, and he knew he was dying. The long hard struggle was over at last.

Alexander Maclean died around midnight of the 28th April 2019, alone but for his sleeping cat. He was sixty-four years old, the same age his father had been when he had died. His last day on this sweet Earth had been a happy one. God is good.

EPILOGUE

A day and a half later, Thomas and Mairi MacKay let themselves into Alexander's home using the spare key they had located in an outhouse. They found Alexander's body, still sitting back against the pillows in his bed. The couple stood and said a prayer for Alexander, then Thomas, a soft-hearted old gentleman, comforted Molly, while Mairi went to find the cat's food and water dishes, which she cleaned and re-filled, before cleaning her litter tray. When the MacKays got home again, they began phoning whom they must, including Roy, who had first alerted them that there must be something wrong.

Roy drove all night, arriving at the lonely house in mid-morning of the 1st May. Alexander's body had been collected by the undertakers in town. Thomas and Mairi MacKay, along with the minister of Saint Andrew's, came by to see Roy the next morning. Roy stayed a week, until, in accordance with Alexander's will, his brother's remains were cremated. The minister of Saint Andrew's drove to the crematorium outside Inverness, the MacKays and Miriam as passengers in his car. I drove Roy there and back in my own car. I liked Roy, who had to struggle hard to keep his grief in check.

After the funeral and the long drive back through the Great Glen, the MacKays and I sat with Roy for two hours. Miriam also stayed. "May I visit you again?" Miriam asked Roy, when we were finally leaving.

"*Yes – yes,*" Roy replied.

Roy had not yet got in touch with any of the people who had known Alexander in England. Their mother had been told – the tears running from Roy's eyes – and she too had begun weeping, but within less than five minutes, Roy told me later, she was no longer aware that her eldest son had died, though she was to ask "*Where's Sandy?*" over and over, for many months to come, each time Roy visited her.

As the two brothers had discussed, in the event of Alexander's death, and with the agreement of Alexander's landlady, Roy had taken up Alexander's lease on the house in the high glen, and after spending a fortnight down south setting his affairs in order (which included letting out the house in Chinnor), Roy had returned with Molly (whom he had taken down south with him) and moved into the house in the glen. Roy told me that he had not found another engineering job after his most recent contract had ended in early 2017. He was but three years or so away from drawing his state pension. The rent from the bungalow in Chinnor, together with social security benefits, would permit him to live in the house his brother had been renting. Roy had Molly for companionship, and his mother, to whom he was still devoted, was living not far away.

But Roy missed his older brother terribly and he grieved for him, and both the MacKays and I dropped in to see him from time to time. My visits in fact were soon to become very frequent. Miriam, who had a car of her own, also called on Roy. The wild cherries were in blossom and the bluebells in the woods spread like a soft blue mist beneath the beech and oak trees, which were covered in bright new leaf of a green as innocent and fresh as the green of the first tree, when Roy told me that his brother had kept a diary throughout most of his adult life, and had been working on an autobiography towards its end. Roy knew that I had been a writer and a journalist on the local weekly newspaper until my comparatively recent retirement – I still wrote occasional pieces for the paper – and he suggested that I tell the story of Alexander's life, which though it had made little impact on the world at large, had been (he thought) a remarkable one, and deserved to be celebrated and remembered. And so I began to dip into Alexander's diaries, which he had begun keeping during his first visit to the British Isles in 1976, and to read what was a completed first draft of his autobiography. "I'll write Alexander's biography," I said after a week or so of reading. "It's not the sort of thing I usually write, but Alexander's story does deserve telling."

I was to observe that as the year unfolded, Roy's pain was not so much diminished as become more manageable. Roy confided to me that he dreaded the day his mother, who was eighty-nine when Alexander died, would no longer be with him. Roy, an agnostic, had not the comfort of Alexander's Christian faith. Nor had he Alexander's easy manner with people, and making new friends was not as easy for Roy as it had always been for his brother. He sometimes found himself regretting (so he told me once) that he had not died before his brother. But then he would remember that he was to see Miriam again soon, and he was not unhappy to be alive.

And I? I believe that recounting the story of Alexander's life has made me a less dogmatic and a kindlier man than I had once been. How few of us truly know the burdens our fellows may be labouring under! Rest in peace, Alexander – no, I shall call you Sandy at last, for I feel that you and I are close friends now – and know that you will not be forgotten. Thank you for your story.

R.D.Dewar, Lochaber, February 2020.